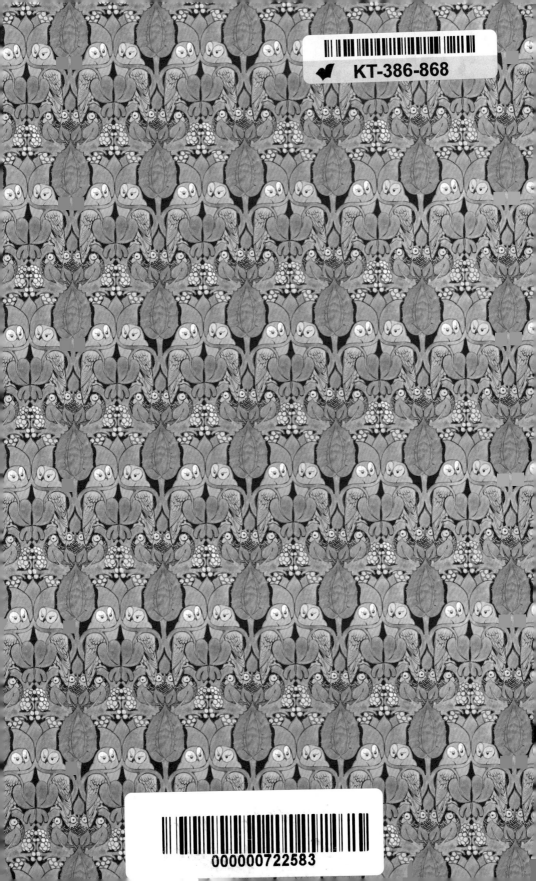

The Quick

For my parents

Published by Jonathan Cape 2014

2 4 6 8 10 9 7 5 3 1

Copyright © Lauren Owen 2014
Lauren Owen has asserted her right under the Copyright, Designs
and Patents Act 1988 to be identified as the author of this work

First published in the United States in 2014 by Random House,
an imprint of The Random House Publishing Group,
a division of Random House, Inc., New York.

First published in Great Britain in 2014 by
Jonathan Cape
Random House, 20 Vauxhall Bridge Road,
London SW1V 2SA

www.vintage-books.co.uk

Addresses for companies within The Random House Group Limited can be found at:
www.randomhouse.co.uk/offices.htm

The Random House Group Limited Reg. No. 954009

A CIP catalogue record for this book is available from the British Library

ISBN 9780224096386
TPB ISBN 9780224096393

The Random House Group Limited supports the Forest Stewardship Council® (FSC®),
the leading international forest-certification organisation. Our books carrying the FSC label are
printed on FSC®-certified paper. FSC is the only forest-certification scheme supported by the
leading environmental organisations, including Greenpeace. Our paper procurement policy can be
found at www.randomhouse.co.uk/environment

Typeset in Dante MT Std by Palimpsest Book Production Ltd,
Falkirk, Stirlingshire

Printed and bound in Great Britain by Clays Ltd, St Ives PLC

The Quick

LAUREN OWEN

JONATHAN CAPE
LONDON

The Quick

From *Clubs of London,* by Major Samuel Hobbs
(1890)

A brief word here on the Aegolius, which bears the dubious distinction of being the most mysterious club in London. The Aegolius's character and affairs are kept a profound secret, known only to its initiates. The club's windows are forever darkened, one rarely sees members enter or leave the premises, and – strangest of all – there appear to be no club servants to speak of.

Records of the Aegolius date back as far as 1705, though it is likely that the club had existed for many years earlier. The club has never been known for any distinguishing artistic, literary or political bent. Nor did it ever attain the fashionable heights of White's or Boodle's. Instead, despite its secrecy, the Aegolius has always borne a great reputation for respectability. It is well known that neither gaming nor the consumption of intoxicants has ever been permitted within its doors, and its early members were quite innocent of the deplorable excesses of the 'Hawkabites', the 'Mohocks' and their ilk.

Membership is reputed to require a yearly subscription of thirty guineas, a ruinous sum paid with perfect equanimity by the

Aegolius men (who were, until about halfway through the present century, drawn exclusively from the oldest and most illustrious families in the country).

From around 1830, the club's premises have been situated on Ormond Yard, off St James's Square. The process of being elected for membership is extraordinarily difficult, and the number of club men is limited to fifty-two (at this time it is significantly lower). The club has never waived this restriction – not even for the most august candidates.

It is said that in 1785, the Prince of Wales insisted upon joining the Aegolius's ranks, though there was at that time no vacancy. After conversation with the club chairman, the Prince (to the astonishment of those who knew him) graciously condescended to accept a mere honorary membership. There are some who claim the discovery that the club possesses no wine cellar was the secret to the Prince's capitulation. Others hold that it was a sight of the club's bill of fare which persuaded him. Whatever the truth of the matter, it is certain that the disappointing cuisine provided at the Aegolius is proverbial. 'I'd rather dine at the Aegolius' is, to this day, among the most vituperative criticisms it is possible to levy against any club, café or restaurant.

The Aegolius rarely, if ever, permits visitors, and it is chiefly due to the strict enforcement of this rule that so little information can be gleaned about the club's doings – whatever these may be. One wag has suggested that there is no mystery to the organisation at all, and that its members are simply men who delight in needless obfuscation and concealment. Perhaps this is the true answer to the riddle.

Part One

Chapter One

There were owls in the nursery when James was a boy. The room was papered in a pattern of winding branches, amongst which great green parent owls perched in identical courting couples. Beneath each pair, a trio of green owlets huddled, their sharp beaks slightly ajar. They sat between big, thistling green flowers with tiny white blossoms which made James think of mother-of-pearl buttons, the kind on Charlotte's Sunday dress. When he was alone in the nursery, James thought he could hear the owls chatter together softly, like monkeys, scratching and scratching their claws against the endless green branches. But when Charlotte was there, they were quiet, because she had told them that if they did not behave, she would get her box of watercolours and paint out their eyes.

At night James would hear the real owls screech outside and imagine them gliding through the dark. Sometimes there was the high sudden cry of a fox. And sometimes there was a noise from the house itself, a whispering creaking sound, as if the walls were sighing.

Often he would slip out of bed and down the corridor to

Charlotte's room. Charlotte would always be sound asleep: face down on the pillow, though Mrs Rowley, the housekeeper, said it was unnatural and would lead to Charlotte being smothered to death one of these days. James would slip under the blankets and lie down topsy-turvy, with his head at the bottom of the bed, his feet near the top. Charlotte would sometimes murmur and kick half-heartedly against him, then fall asleep again, and James would do the same, his feet pressed against her back until they grew warm. They would lie all night like that, snug as the pair of pistols that lived in the blue-lined case in Father's study.

When morning came James liked to wake early, open Charlotte's bedroom window and look down onto the grounds of Aiskew Hall, which went on for as far as he could see. There were wide lawns and gardens edged by paths and stately, lovely old trees – oaks and horse chestnuts and copper beeches and silver birches. Between the trees there were two grassy mounds. These were the icehouses, which now held gardening tools and other odd things.

At a distance, the gardens still had the illusion of being neat and well tended, as they had been before James and Charlotte were born. Long ago, in the prosperous days, there had been people to look after things: gardeners and undergardeners, two gamekeepers and a carpenter. A fire engine, too, drawn by horses. Now there was only Griswold, strange and grim-faced and sixty-three. There had been a young Griswold once – the gardener's son, who had been expected to take over from his father and who instead went off to foreign parts and then died (fighting the Shantee, said Ann, the housemaid. James thought perhaps this was a sort of banshee.)

After his son went away, Griswold had been left alone to wage a vain and bitter war against the gardens. He shot the rabbits but they came back, grazing the lawns at their leisure. The mighty rhododendron bushes flourished unchecked, and in the orchard the trees turned wild and the apples were eaten by blackbirds.

• • •

At the end of the hall gardens, the ground gave way to a sudden drop that felt like the edge of the world. Below was a ditch full of nettles, which was called a ha-ha. Beyond that there were wide flat fields for miles, green and gold in the spring, red-brown earth in the winter. There were oak trees and black sheep grazing and the ruins of a small Grecian temple, where long ago the ladies of the hall would sit to enjoy their books and needlework. Part of the roof had given way, and the pillars looked slightly crooked. It was not safe to sit there any more.

Charlotte had heard Mrs Rowley say that people in Aiskew village thought it was a scandal to leave the hall so neglected. Before now the hall people had always done their part in the village: there had been treats for the Sunday-school children; sometimes the hall ladies would take baskets to the villagers who were poor or ill. More than that, there was any amount of work at the hall: mouths to be fed, washing to be done, windows to be cleaned, horses to be stabled. It had been a fine place, back in the old days. Now it was mostly shut up. Everyone wondered why Charlotte and James's father troubled himself to keep the house at all, since he did nothing with it.

Charlotte thought that if Mother were still alive, then Father would have lived with them, at least some of the time, when he could be spared from his business, and the people in the village would have been friendlier. As things were, nobody much cared for James and her. Even Mrs Rowley seemed to prefer them to be elsewhere: outside in the gardens or at their lessons or in the nursery, anywhere as long as they were out of the way.

When Father had left Charlotte and James at Aiskew after Mother's death, he had said that he would make all the proper arrangements. Then they did not hear from him for a long while. Eventually he wrote to tell Mrs Rowley that he had engaged a governess. The letter went on to say that he would approach Mrs Chickering, his aunt, who might be able to make a long visit to Aiskew, to help Mrs Rowley set things in order and make the place comfortable again. Once all this was done, perhaps he could be spared from business long enough to come back to Yorkshire himself and see them.

At first they were all of them – Charlotte and James, Mrs Rowley and Ann, and Mrs Scholes, the cook – in the habit of speaking as if Mrs Chickering might arrive any day. But months went by, and she did not appear. It was her health, Mrs Rowley said, sounding rather scornful. Mrs Chickering never seemed strong enough to travel. A year passed, then another.

Ann and Mrs Scholes were the only servants at Aiskew – apart from Griswold, who scarcely counted. They were both up from York and spent a great deal of time huddled in the kitchen for warmth, complaining over the remoteness of the house, the dreariness of the mists, and the loneliness of their situation. Sometimes there was a governess for Charlotte and James – but these ladies never stayed for very long.

So Charlotte did her best: they would have to be brave, she told James, and she devised ordeals for them to perform – walking down one of the long corridors alone after dark, or keeping one's head under the bathwater for a minute at a time. Or – this was worst of all – shutting oneself in the priest hole in the library.

The library was full of treasures. The cousin – the very distant cousin who had owned the hall before them – had bought books at a fearful rate, adding to an already extensive collection. There was no one to stop Charlotte and James from taking what they wanted, poring over whichever old, delicious-smelling volumes they chose.

It was a beautiful room, too: there was a red carpet and red-and-gold paper on the walls and a beautiful marble fireplace with a pattern of grapes carved all the way round.

The priest hole had been added to the house by the cousin. He had many romantic ideas and had lavished money on trifles. Much of the grounds and the farmland had been sold to pay the resulting debts, and the estate had been much reduced, and the cousin had died in Italy of grief or something else.

The cousin had thought that the priest hole might make the house seem older than it really was, though why he should have wanted this neither Charlotte nor James could have said. It was frightening inside – stuffy and smelling of wood and polish. Ann sometimes left dusters and brooms in there, and if you weren't careful you could knock them over in the dark. The door to the priest hole was hidden, fitted cunningly behind one of the book-shelves. It opened with a secret spring concealed behind a dummy book – *Fungi of the British Isles, Vol II*. The false spine was scruffy claret-coloured leather, faded from the touch of many hands. If you didn't know which one it was, you might never find it. From inside the priest hole, there was no way of getting out again.

You passed the ordeal if you didn't scream for help. When the door was shut, it was so close to your face that it felt difficult to breathe. There was no light. It felt as if everyone outside had gone away and there would be no one ever coming to let you out.

They did not do this ordeal often – only when the door's fascin-ation grew too much. It was the best ordeal of all and would make you the bravest, Charlotte said. And this was good, because if you did enough ordeals, you would be grown up.

• • •

One June morning, when Charlotte was nine-and-a-half and James was five, she took a box of coloured chalks out to the terrace and set about teaching him his letters. This was neces-sary because Miss Prince, their latest governess, had gone home to Shropshire two weeks earlier without being able to make James properly acquainted with any letter other than *S* (with which, for reasons he was unable to explain, he had an odd fascination).

The terrace had large flagstones which would grow warm in the sun, so that in the hottest days of summer it was pleasant to walk over them barefoot. Charlotte took a piece of white chalk and drew a large *A* onto one of the stones. Then she moved a little way along, stooped again, and drew *B*.

'What're you doing?' James asked.

Charlotte glanced up, brushing her hair out of her eyes with a chalky hand. It left a dusting of white at the top of her head, making her look as if she were wearing a powdered wig, like a lady of a hundred years ago.

'You have to know the alphabet,' she said.

'Why?' James asked, staring at *A* with vague mistrustful remembrance.

Charlotte looked up from *F* with a frown. 'Because you have to. What would you do if you grew up and you couldn't read? People would think you were ignorant.'

She said *ignorant* in a disagreeable way she had learned from Miss Prince – leaning on the *ig*, making it sound like a finger jab to the ribs.

James scowled. 'I don't care.'

'Well, Father probably thinks you can read already,' Charlotte said, and drew *N* – it came out bigger than she had intended, all pointed angles, making James think of a gate locked shut.

He watched her in silence and made no further argument. After a moment, he went over to where she was kneeling, the twenty-sixth flagstone, and inspected what she had drawn. It was an angry angular slash, a diagonal stroke, its elbows pointing both directions in a standoffish sort of way.

'What's that?' James asked, pointing at it with his foot.

'It's *Z*,' said Charlotte.

'It looks like half an hourglass.'

'Well, it isn't.' Charlotte stood up and brushed the dust from her hands. 'Now go and stand by the fountain.'

James did as he was told. The fountain was a bone-dry stone

bowl at the middle of the terrace, supported by three naked cherubs with mossy legs and expressions of baffled malignity. One of them was missing his nose, and this misfortune, which ought to have made James feel sorry for him, only made him the most hateful of the three.

Charlotte had climbed onto the low wall of the terrace and was pacing up and down. 'When I call the letter, you have to go and stand on it.'

'I can't. I don't know what they are.'

'You have to work them out. When you know them all, then you win.'

'Win what?'

'A prize.'

'What prize?'

'You'll find out when you win,' Charlotte replied, and then she took a breath and bellowed, '*R!*'

It was a magnificent cry – *ARRRR!* – like a pirate with rum on his breath and matches smoking in his beard. (They had a book about pirates, which Charlotte would sometimes read aloud, though not on Sundays.)

James hesitated. The chalk lines seemed to run into one another, squirming away from him when he looked at them.

'Go on,' Charlotte said – and James moved reluctantly in search of the right letter.

They stayed out until it was time for lunch, and then again until it was sunset and the shadows from the great trees in the grounds were stretching across the lawn towards the house. It took a long time for James to learn, but, though Charlotte was often cross, she never lost her temper.

She never lied, either; that was one of the nice things about her. She had said that James would manage to do it, and after a time she was proved right and the letters were safe in his head, like the days of the week or the sound of his own name. And there was a prize, just as she had said: a sugar mouse, pure white, with a piece of string for a tail. James decided that he was called Aljijohn.

'Algernon, you mean.' Charlotte said.

But James shook his head. 'Aljijohn,' he said, and took Aljijohn upstairs and made a bed for him on the chest of drawers out of an empty matchbox and a handkerchief.

'You should eat him,' Charlotte suggested, when she saw Aljijohn's bed. 'Otherwise he'll go bad.'

James frowned. 'He's my friend,' he said. But that evening it was liver for dinner, and James went to bed hungrier than usual, and in the morning there was nothing left of Aljijohn but a mournful-looking piece of string and an empty matchbox.

'He would have wanted you to eat him,' Charlotte said later. 'It was what he was for.'

'Are you sure?' James asked.

She nodded.

'But I feel all horrible inside, like hurting. I wish I hadn't thought of him being Aljijohn.'

'It wasn't real, though,' Charlotte said.

Last year, she had been reading to him from a very old book called *The Surprising Adventures of Baron Munchausen,* and the pictures had frightened him so much that Mrs Rowley had taken it away. He had bad dreams afterwards for three nights running. Already she knew that an idea could pain him like a bruise. He had grey eyes that showed every thought, and Charlotte sometimes worried that he might be hurt in some way that she would not be able to prevent.

• • •

This was the way things used to be, and afterwards it seemed to have lasted for many years. This was the way things used to be, and at the time it did not feel as if anything would ever change. As far as they could see, all that happened was they got older. James was six now and could climb higher than before;

he could follow Charlotte over walls and fences. Mrs Rowley began to say that he ought to be sent away to school, but nothing came of it.

Some evenings they would sit in front of the nursery fire, whilst Charlotte taught James to read words the same way she remembered being taught: with short sentences, sounding each letter as she went, as if she were testing a rotten floorboard that might give way beneath her. James liked a rhyme, and so they had *the cat sat on the mat,* and *the fox sat on the box.* After a while they progressed to *the robin sat on the bobbin,* and *the weasel sat on the easel,* and from then onwards James began to write for himself – small stories and rhymes, which were not usually very good. But he was still young, and Charlotte tried to be encouraging.

'You could write a whole book,' she told him. 'When you're grown up. And have a house in London.'

James said, 'I want to live here when we're grown up. But just us.'

The hall was going to belong to James when they were older. They had always known this.

'Read,' she ordered, pointing to the slate that lay on the floor between them.

Aiskew was still everything, of course. Later she would not recall feeling discontented at that age, but she had known, even then, that there would be a time when she would want to be elsewhere. Sometimes she dreamed of a view she had seen once, fleetingly, from a train window – the moors, dark purple beneath a grey sky.

A little while afterwards, something unexpected happened. Father wrote to say that instead of sending a new governess to replace Miss Prince's successor – as everyone had expected – he would shortly be coming back to Yorkshire himself.

'Why's he coming back?' James said, when Mrs Rowley told them the news over breakfast.

'Why shouldn't he?' Mrs Rowley replied. 'Eat your porridge.'

'Does he want to see us?' Charlotte asked.

'Of course,' said Mrs Rowley, frowning, as if Charlotte's question were somehow impertinent. 'And he writes that he requires some rest. His physician says that his health is not all it should be.'

'What's wrong with him?' Charlotte said. 'Is he ill?'

'The porridge has got hedgehog in it,' James announced suddenly, dropping his spoon onto the table. 'Look!' He pointed to a dark husk of oat.

'Don't slop your breakfast about like that, James,' Mrs Rowley said, ignoring this accusation, which James had made many times before. She put Father's letter away, and the chance to ask further questions was lost.

On the afternoon that Father was expected, James and Charlotte were sent into the garden to be out of the way. There was enough to do in preparing the house without having them to worry about as well, Mrs Rowley said. They were to be back by four o'clock sharp, to be washed and dressed in time to greet their father.

Shooed outside – like chickens – they wandered rather aimlessly into the grounds. Somehow it was always less fun to be told to go out and play.

They went past the rose garden (where Griswold looked up from his work and stared at them), past the lake and the orchard, out to the rhododendrons, which crowded thickly around the secret statues: a beautiful lady in a scarf and nothing else, a fawn, a centurion (he was getting a bit mossy in places), and a blue-metal gentleman wearing a hat like an upturned mixing bowl, sitting astride a cow. The statues were further additions of the cousin's. There had been wonderful summer parties in the gardens in his day; they would string coloured lanterns up in the trees and dance outside as darkness fell. Sometimes Charlotte and James found odd relics of that time – half a shattered champagne glass, a playing card wiped blank with rain.

They played amongst the statues for a while, and when they

were tired they sat down to rest on the steps outside the arbour at the end of the yew walk. Inside, the arbour was overgrown with honeysuckle and home to a large family of spiders, which liked to drop from the ceiling without warning. On the top step, Charlotte had tried to carve her name but had only got as far as *Cha* before giving up, exhausted by the effort.

It would be half past four by now, Charlotte thought, perhaps even later. Father must have arrived.

'Perhaps he'll come and find us,' she said. She remembered a Christmas a long time ago, a game of hide-and-seek. Father had been laughing, searching for her in the silliest places, like Mother's bureau or inside a thimble.

'There's someone coming.' James pointed straight ahead, to the end of the yew walk. 'There.'

It was Mrs Rowley. She was walking briskly, holding her skirts out of the damp grass. 'There you are,' she said, when she was within speaking distance. 'I told you to be back at four o'clock.'

'Sorry,' Charlotte replied. 'We forgot. Is Father here?'

'Yes. He's been— He's gone upstairs.'

'Can we see him?'

'Tomorrow, perhaps,' Mrs Rowley said. 'The doctor's with him now.'

She looked worried, Charlotte thought. Frowning but not angry.

'Is he all right?' she asked.

'He needs rest,' Mrs Rowley answered. 'You children must be very quiet when you're inside, so as not to disturb him.' She glanced around her, eyeing the arbour with evident disapproval. 'You'd best play outside for a little while longer,' she added. 'Come in before dark.'

She gave them one last, sterner look, then turned away and started back towards the house.

They did not see Father the next day, because he was too ill to have visitors. From Mrs Rowley they heard that he was no better.

There was a different doctor with him now – not from Aiskew or even brought in from York but all the way from London. It must be interesting to be so important, Charlotte thought – like being the king in a play. She heard Mrs Rowley telling Ann that really, Mrs Chickering ought to be there, that someone from the family should.

The doctor did not leave, nor did Father come downstairs. Mrs Rowley was crosser than usual, and Ann began to look at Charlotte and James strangely. The weather grew worse. On some days it was too cold and wet to venture out of doors. In the house there were only a few rooms which were not forbidden – their bedrooms and the nursery, where they also took most of their meals now. They were not to run and they were not to raise their voices.

At first they did their best to carry on being good. But as the house stayed hushed and Father remained upstairs, they began to make small trespasses: downstairs to the ballroom (all shut up now), or out to the stables. Nobody seemed to notice what they did. Charlotte thought perhaps it would be good to store up some more bravery – the way you could save up hunger, when you knew there was going to be cake later. So they did more ordeals.

In the orchard they climbed to higher branches, balanced their way across the narrow red-brick garden wall. Then in the wider grounds they turned over rocks and forced themselves to pick up spiders – and later a toad, which had strayed onto the terrace.

Afterwards it would be one of the things Charlotte remembered clearly: the cool, warty brown skin of the creature, the rough sensation of its webbed feet against her palm. It was smaller than she had imagined, with wide yellow eyes. She was afraid it might bite (*could* toads bite?) but it did not. It sat quiet, still and frightened in her clasped hands as she carried it down to the lake. When she set it down, it took a few seconds for it to understand its freedom and hop away.

It had been raining for three days when they went back to the library. They were not seen on their way down – the servants were elsewhere, the doctor was with Father, Mrs Rowley was in her own room. She had told them that morning that Mrs Chickering would be arriving today at long last, and though neither of the children could quite believe her, the news made Charlotte feel restless, uneasy.

'Let's do an ordeal,' she said to James.

Though there was hardly any need for stealth, they crept into the library as if they were housebreakers, enjoying the furtiveness of it. The clock above the mantel ticked to itself, a low, friendly sound that one hardly noticed after a little while. Apart from this there was silence.

Charlotte thought about saying to James that just coming downstairs without being seen was a good enough ordeal, and perhaps they had better go back. But he had already gone to the priest hole and, with his hand on *Fungi of the British Isles, Vol II*, was struggling to open the door. He could manage it for himself, usually, though sometimes he would stand on a pile of books, to make it easier to reach.

Charlotte pushed him aside – not too roughly. 'Let me do it.'

They never grew tired of watching part of the bookcase suddenly jolt forwards and swing open. Once, Charlotte had pushed at the spring with too much force, and two shelves of books had crashed to the floor. Today she was very careful.

'Do you want to go first,' she asked, 'or shall I?'

'Can I?' James said. It was best to go first – it meant the ordeal would be over sooner.

She nodded. 'I'll shut it and count to a hundred.'

The door was heavy, and though Charlotte was tall and strong for her age – Mrs Rowley had taken to calling her a *great girl*, in a tone not at all complimentary – it was a struggle to push it closed.

When it was done, she leaned against the door and called to James, 'Are you all right?'

'Yes,' James said, and sneezed. 'Go on, count.'

She always counted loudly, so that he would know how long there was to wait.

She had reached twenty when she heard the footsteps. It was Mrs Rowley – Charlotte knew her tread well enough. She was outside, hurrying closer. And as she approached she called, 'Charlotte? James? Are you here?' Charlotte looked about for somewhere to hide, but there was no time – Mrs Rowley had already opened the library door.

Charlotte thought she would be angry, but instead she only said brusquely, 'Where's your brother?'

'I don't know.'

She sighed, then took Charlotte by the wrist and said, 'Well, come along.'

'Where—'

'Your father wants to see you.' She hurried Charlotte out of the library before Charlotte could say another word.

Father's room was dark, and smelled wrong somehow. There was the doctor from London standing by the bed – he was quite young, with yellow hair and a bony face.

Father was lying still. Charlotte remembered him tall and broad-shouldered, infinitely strong. Now he was thin and wrecked, and his eyes – dark like Charlotte's – were bloodshot and stared nowhere. He gasped as he breathed.

He could not speak, Mrs Rowley said, but Charlotte might take his hand and speak to him, if she did not raise her voice.

She couldn't think what to say. In the end she muttered that she hoped he would be better soon and that James hoped so, too. She thought he turned his head slightly at James's name.

'That's enough,' Mrs Rowley said. 'Your father will be tired. You may kiss him.'

She would rather have not, but there seemed nothing else to be done. He was very hot and smelled of sweat and fever and sourness. She wanted to rub her mouth afterwards, to wipe the sickness off.

'There, now,' Mrs Rowley said. She looked at the doctor, who shrugged. 'Perhaps you may see him again tomorrow—'

Then the doctor said, sharp and sudden, 'Take the child away.'

Father's face had changed. Something bad had happened, perhaps as Charlotte kissed him.

The doctor leaned over Father with a frown, and Mrs Rowley took Charlotte's hand and pulled her outside. She shut the door.

Charlotte turned and ran – down the corridor, down the stairs, back to the library. But she halted at the door: there were voices coming from inside. It was Ann, talking to someone.

'. . . see if she can be spared,' she was saying, and the other person murmured something in reply. The stranger sounded like an old lady – it must be Mrs Chickering, arrived at last.

Charlotte barely had time to duck out of sight before Ann came out of the library, heading in the direction of Father's room. Charlotte hoped that Mrs Chickering might follow Ann upstairs to see Father, but she did not. Instead, Mrs Rowley entered the library – followed, a short time afterwards, by the doctor. He was wiping his hands. She thought later that she might have imagined this detail, but there it was in her memory – a tall, thin-faced man, fastidiously wiping his fingers on a handkerchief. He went into the library and shut the door.

The three of them stayed in the library for the better part of an hour. Charlotte could hear voices but not words. She waited, growing cold in the draughty, wood-panelled corridor.

At last they emerged, and all went upstairs again. Charlotte ran at once into the library, hardly caring if they were out of earshot or not. The room was as it had been before. She rushed to the priest hole and opened the door. James was sitting there – leaning against the wall, his eyes closed.

'Are you all right?' she asked.

James opened his eyes. 'Did you see him?'

'Yes,' she said. She saw what a bad thing she had done. She tried to think of something comforting. 'He said your name.'

He looked at her and didn't speak.

'I'm sorry.' She knelt, tried to help him up, but he wouldn't let her.

His fingers were bleeding – he must have been scrabbling at the door, the rough, splintery wood.

'We'd have been in trouble if they found you here,' Charlotte said.

He stared up at her and drew his knees up to his chest so he was curled up on one side, reminding her of the woodlice that lived in the shady places of the garden, which would roll into a ball if you shook them from their rotten log.

'I'm sorry,' Charlotte repeated.

'I hate you.'

She didn't know what to do.

'Well,' she said at last, 'there's no need to be a baby about it, anyway.' She hated herself for saying that, and hated him for flinching and saying nothing, and she stalked out and went to her own room and lay down on the bed, trembling.

It was later that she discovered what the grown-ups had been talking about in the library. Hidden behind the bookshelf, James would have heard the doctor telling the others that Father was dead.

A mouse died somewhere under the floorboards, a few days before the funeral. There was no smell like that of a dead mouse, nothing so insistently rotten. Griswold was brought in to try to find the body, but without any success. Mrs Rowley had said that they would just have to wait for the odour to depart on its own. It was worst in the room where Father was laid out, but they did not like to move him.

Mrs Chickering had been the one to give Charlotte and James the news of Father's death. Some hours after her arrival, they were brought into the library and introduced to her. She was thin and white-haired and kept her mouth held tight in a way which must have been very uncomfortable. Perhaps she had forgotten she was doing it. She inspected them both in silence for a little bit, and then told them that Father had gone away, and they would both have to be very good from now on.

Mrs Chickering was afraid of things, Charlotte soon discovered – afraid of fire and rats, afraid that the servants were dishonest, afraid that the dinner had not been properly cooked. She was afraid that the children had been spoiled, she was afraid that they were both very ignorant and that Charlotte was grown into a hoyden. She never ate very much at mealtimes but consumed lavender lozenges almost incessantly; the scent went with her everywhere.

Mrs Chickering said that of course Charlotte and James might not attend the funeral. Instead, they sat in the nursery on the day Father was buried – James in front of the fire, Charlotte curled in a chair, watching him. She wanted to go over and sit beside him but was afraid he would tell her to go away. And so she sat quietly, as if it were still all right between them.

In the days after the funeral, things began to change quickly. James was to be sent to school. Money would be more difficult now, Charlotte learned. They would have to economise. The hall would be shut up entirely. Charlotte would live with Mrs Chickering (and James, when he was not at school) in East Lodge, the cottage close to the ha-ha, near the edge of the estate. This was bad enough; worse was the fact that James remained changed. One wet afternoon, the day before he was to be sent away to school, Charlotte discovered him in the library, writing. The library was the only place that was much the same – everywhere else was already packed away. They had made so little impression on the dust and quiet of the house, Charlotte thought. In a few days, when they and the servants and Mrs Rowley were all gone, there would be scarcely any sign they had lived there at all.

'What's that?' she asked, looking at James's writing.

'Story.'

His handwriting was still terrible. She peered over his shoulder and could not make out a word. He kept his head bent over his work.

There was something wrong, something hurt somewhere in him. It was her fault, of course. He must be anxious about being sent away to school, but he refused to talk about it.

She wanted to say again that she was sorry, but she had told him this many times already, and the time for it was long past.

Instead, she said, 'I wish you weren't going.'

Still he said nothing, which was becoming his way. After a pause she went back upstairs, to finish her packing.

James's school term seemed to last a long while. For reasons of economy and also tradition, he was sent to Father's old school – a small institution of no great academic reputation. He wrote regularly to Mrs Chickering and Charlotte – dutiful letters, addressed to them both. When he was at last released for the holidays, the dogcart was despatched to bring him from York station, and Charlotte went out of the house to meet him. She walked slowly through East Lodge's small garden, down the path that led into the hall grounds. There was no distant sign of light from the hall. Every room was shut up now. Some of the more expensive pieces of furniture had been sold. It was as if their lives were a pencil line drawn on a piece of paper and someone had followed behind with an India rubber, erasing the line as they went. Charlotte still had the key to the French windows that led from the terrace into the library. Sometimes she would visit, but only in daylight and only this room. Gradually her footsteps began to show in the dust. Mrs Chickering said that she would not be able to return for much longer; sooner or later the place would have to be let.

It began to rain as Charlotte went through the trees, skirting the yew walk and the statues – which would soon disappear entirely into the bushes. She was grateful for the cool air and the silence. She was not sure what James would say to her, and if he could not forgive her now, then she did not know how she was to stand the months and years ahead of her, with only Mrs Chickering for company.

At the edge of the trees she saw him – a little way distant, wearing a scarf against the damp evening. With his face hidden by fog, he looked like someone else, and for an instant she was afraid. But it was him, and they embraced without speaking under the dark, rain-heavy trees.

She had feared that he might be a stranger now, but he was still himself – older and more serious in just those few months, and with a new, watchful expression, but still James. As they embraced, she realised that he had grown. She would not always be taller.

She decided that things would be all right. She would keep him happy, and the memory of what she had done to him would help her, would make her more vigilant and loving, so that no harm would ever come to him again.

He was looking back at the hall – the unlit, uncurtained windows. She did not like the place in dusk any more. It was too melancholy.

'We'd better go in,' she said. She turned away, and together they made their way through the trees towards East Lodge, down the old paths they both knew well.

Chapter Two

Was it Shakespeare or not Shakespeare? James paused, pen in hand, and considered. He had been writing for some time without interruption, and yet the distant memory of someone else's words would not leave him alone. Probably it was Shakespeare. Things which sounded like him usually were. From *Julius Caesar* – no, it had happened in England, hadn't it? There had been a fool, and someone had been betrayed or murdered or perhaps both. Or was it *Timon of Athens,* after all?

It was the last week of James's final term at Oxford, and almost summer. His room in college was high up, high enough to look down on the Isis at dusk and see the ducks, black shapes drifting on the dark glimmer of the water. In spite of Mrs Chickering's warnings about moths, he had taken to sleeping with his window open. The nights were delicious in those last few weeks, the skies clear indigo blue, the air cool and sweet.

The days were less pleasant, James thought. Too hot to concentrate, muggy enough to make one in love with autumn. The upper gallery of the Radcliffe Camera was uncomfortably warm today.

He looked down, resumed his inspection of the words he had just written. He was filled with a sudden disgust – a specific sort of self-loathing he only ever experienced when confronting his own prose. It was feeble, all of it. At this rate the article would never be finished. He drew a line through the last paragraph and stood up. He might feel better for a change of air.

Downstairs, at the library door, he hesitated. The place seemed unaccountably quiet today, with neither librarian nor janitor in evidence. He might take the exit or follow the staircase down to the Lower Camera. He had spent the better part of three years in Oxford feeling out of place in the great libraries, always afraid of being too loud, disturbing the other readers, or of wandering out of bounds and provoking the ire of one of the librarians. He had never dared make an unselfconscious exploration. Now, recklessly – it was the end of term, after all, the end of everything – he thought he might venture.

The Lower Camera was deserted – not a sound, not a human voice, it was only James and the books. There was enough light from the arched windows for James to wander amongst the shelves, enjoying the smell, the quiet and the tidy procession of names, some known, others strange, all ordered into sensible patterns.

Then he stopped – that didn't belong here, surely? A book had been left carelessly on top of a row of shelved volumes, entirely out of place: *The Martyrdom of Man*. It was not even a library book but a brand-new copy, the gilt title still bright against the green cloth binding. It was then that he heard, through the silence of the library and the chatter of his own thoughts, the sound of a woman laughing.

Of course, James had seen women at lectures from time to time. He had been to Somerville once for tea with someone's sister – an earnest New Woman in Nile green, whose Greek was better than his own. There was really no reason to be taken aback at the sound of a woman's voice. It was, besides, a rather nice laugh. But there was a softness to it that was quite private, and which James had never heard before. It seemed to him that a woman would laugh like that only when she was alone – almost alone.

More whispering – another voice now, a man's – and more stifled laughter. They would have to be standing very close to hear each other talking so low. Then he heard the sound of a swift kiss. They were on the other side of the bookcase. There was a noise like ruffling feathers.

'My hat,' James heard the woman warn her companion, the laugh still there in her voice, and he saw her quite clearly in his head: blonde, very young, too innocent to care for the appearance of things.

'It would be a pity to spoil it,' the man agreed – and now there was a rustle, as if ribbons were being undone. 'There,' he said.

'You did that quite well,' she said, sounding amused. 'Perhaps you should give up the law idea and become a lady's maid instead.'

'Well, if I could be yours . . .' Another kiss. He would be fair also, James thought – barely older than she, innocents both, Daphnis and Chloe in a grave green forest of books. The lovers, as he had seen them in many different names and guises, in many stories and songs. So it was like this, then, James thought—

Then the girl sneezed, and James started, as the time and the place came back to him. To remain where he was would be out of the question. But he would probably make a noise if he tried to move. He took an experimental step backwards and immediately heard the floor creak. He stopped abruptly, hearing them do the same on the other side of the bookcase.

James imagined them, laughter suddenly cold on their faces, listening intently. This was no engaged couple, then, no signed and sanctified pair of lovers.

'Who's there?' the man said. His voice had turned louder – one could hear the self-assurance now in the way he spoke. Whoever he was, he was used to having his questions answered.

James hesitated but remained silent. Perhaps they would go away.

'You may as well come out,' the man said. 'We can hear you breathing.'

There was no helping it. James found himself walking, very slowly, round to their side of the bookcase.

They were not at all as they had sounded – both were slightly older than James had imagined. The girl was delightful: dark and buxom, with a heart-shaped face and a mouth which was very slightly too full. James realised that he had seen her before. She was someone's fiancée – she had been pointed out to him because she had money, or an uncle who was a baronet, or some other claim to distinction. Her name, if he remembered rightly, was Miss Emily Richter. In one hand she held a hat of delicate artifice, which looked like a white dove snared in silk.

Her companion was not her intended, James was certain. He was about James's height and stood like a prince in disguise, with the kind of good looks which challenged one to glance away. His hair was soft brown; his gaze made James immediately uncomfortable.

'I'm terribly sorry,' James said.

He saw them exchange a look. There was worry there – the situation was an awkward one, though not untenable. But there was a private knowledge in their eyes, too, and it made him feel lonely.

James said desperately, 'I'm really very sorry. I had no idea that you were here. . . .'

Perhaps the girl said something – James had a vague impression that she might have spoken and held out her hand – but he was already turning away, confused and embarrassed, eager to leave them. His footsteps sounded far too loud on the wooden floor. He went back up the spiral staircase and returned to his desk and his books and his papers. He imagined the pair of them still behind the bookcase: serious over such a near miss, or perhaps laughing at James's clumsiness.

His last paragraph, determinedly crossed out, seemed suddenly like a taunt:

The idea that immoral action may add depth to art surely conceives of art as something supremely selfish, and art ought not to be selfish – any more than is it truly selfless. Indeed the exquisite balance of it ought to convince anyone of the divine ordering of our universe: the artist delights in creation, his audience in beholding the creation – their interests are united, there is a harmony, a mutuality of benefit which is much like love.

He had been wrong earlier: the whole thing was feeble, not merely that last paragraph. What did he know about art, or about anything else? He folded the papers away, attempted another beginning.

• • •

That evening, he took a walk past Christ Church meadow. He stopped by the river to tear his article into fragments and scatter it into the water – attracting a flurry of ducks, which mistook the paper for bread crumbs. He thought, with a touch of melancholy: what now, what next?

He had enjoyed himself in Oxford, in his fashion. He had an idea that he would retain little of what he had learned, and yet his studies had made him happy. He was respectfully fond of Latin, which seemed to him a language of sentences ready to be dismantled and reassembled elsewhere, eminently practical for a conquering people.

He had his secret yearning, however, an illicit passion: there was talk that the university was soon to offer tuition in English literature. On hearing the news, he had experienced a baffled sense of a missed step, for this ought to have been his fate, and he was only a few years ahead of himself, most likely – if only his birth had been better timed.

He walked further, thought further, thought of the strangers in the library:

There had been so much life to them. They existed in that place where things happened, a vivid, vital centre of things. He saw now that he had always existed at a quiet distance from reality.

There came to him then an urge to do something, to live before it was too late. Beneath this was a childish wish to show them.

And, of course, there was something he could do – if he had the nerve for it.

It had occurred to him when he was quite young that it would be the very best of things to spend his life writing. The idea had not gone away, and neither had the words, which sang in his ears at night, in the space between his prayers and the deliberately vague thoughts of soft embraces with which he would send himself to sleep. Thanks to a small legacy received some years ago, James had enough to live in relative comfort, without the need of pursuing a profession. Charlotte was sufficiently provided for. So he might still write, if he wanted. And he could live in London, where a writer ought to live and where things would happen. He would be a flâneur, wandering the streets, seeing everything, observed by none. That evening he wrote in his memo-randum book, *Life with a capital must be lived in the Capital,* and was pleased with the sentiment.

A few days later, he settled down to write his final Oxford letter to Charlotte. For now she remained with Mrs Chickering, whose health was steadily declining. He thought she might have expected him to return home, at least to begin with. But – and James reasoned this out very carefully in his letter – it was important that he live by himself at the onset of his career. He hoped she would not think he was selfish. He must have this time – a year, at least – to see if there was any real talent in him. He sent her a parcel of books, and his love, and hoped that Mrs Chickering was doing better. Charlotte replied by return of post:

Of course I understand, and I want you to have the best start possible in London. (Naturally our aunt still says that she cannot see why it <u>must</u> be London and not somewhere closer, but I am sure she <u>will</u> get used to the idea.) You'll have so much to occupy you, doing whatever it is that young men do in the city, and even if our aunt could spare me, I should be in your way, especially at first. Besides, that rose of mine is still in a critical state; I couldn't think of leaving it at present. But what will you do about the hall?

Here he stopped reading, because he preferred not to consider Aiskew Hall at present. It was his, now that he was of age, and he had a responsibility to it. As a child it had seemed a marvellous thing, to be master of the place. Now it was only a source of unceasing demands and tedious papers and figures and beneath that a memory of wood panels, darkness and cold. The building must be restored and then sold or let (the debate between these two alternatives furnished the chief topic of conversation between Mrs Chickering and himself whenever he returned to Yorkshire). The longer he left matters undecided, the more pressing the situation became, so that now the mere mention of the place, from Charlotte or his aunt, was enough to depress his spirits.

At length, he wrote back that he would certainly attend to the hall in due course, and in the meantime he was sure that they both would manage well enough without the extra income.

As he had expected, Charlotte was understanding:

I don't suppose the delay in deciding about the hall will much matter, though the house will need some care quite soon. I walked through the gardens today – our usual walk, you know – and pressed my face against the library window. I felt a bit like a ghost or a thief, peering in like that. I went inside to get some books, and the volumes are all safe and sound, you will be glad to know, though they really ought to be stored elsewhere. The dust is dreadful – thick as velvet.

I am sending you a present to help you on your way to literary giantdom – <u>Froude's Life of Carlyle</u>. I hope you have not read it already. Also sending <u>The Art of Authorship</u>, which I understand is a very useful guide to pursuing a literary career. Aunt says that you should not stoop over when you read or write, or the blood will gorge your eyes. And you must be very careful in choosing your lodgings and always pay particular attention to the drains. She knows a promising young man who did not and later died as a consequence.

He reread her letter on the train to London and smiled over it in spite of his nerves. He was anxious now about this unprecedented step, and somewhat taken aback at how quickly everything had changed. He had not expected to make a decision about his life and see it come so immediately into effect. He had boxed and bundled his papers and books, taken set of rooms – it had all been rather easier than he expected. Now he could not help wishing that he had decided to delay things, to return to Yorkshire first.

His new residence was not far from Paddington – on Wyndham Street, decent and prosaic. The daunting business of giving the address to the cabman and having him strap James's luggage to the roof of a four-wheeler was accomplished without any difficulty. Quicker than he had expected, he was installed in his rooms, provided by his landlady with a key and a long catechism of rules for his tenancy, and left in peace.

His lodgings were small but comfortable – innocent of damp, soot and black beetles. They were let by a distant acquaintance of Mrs Chickering's. James had at first rather regretted this connection; he had wanted to make his own place in London without being indebted to anyone. But the association was now welcome – it was a link to home, that old world where everything was easy to understand.

When he was left to himself, he went to the window. He leaned against the sill, stared through the glass. Outside was London – modern and commonplace and very busy. The city did not appear to have marked his arrival.

He did not venture far from his rooms for several days, during which time it rained unceasingly – even the rain was not clean, he discovered. Everything here felt smoky, slightly rotten. He felt jostled and ill at ease. His first impulse on returning to his rooms was always to wash his hands. Later, as summer failed, the fogs descended and stayed for days. James would look out of his window and see nothing but the dirty light of the streetlamps, and it was as if the city were hiding itself, playing with him like a cat. So he drew the curtains and stayed indoors.

He tried to work. His latest literary effort, *Demeter,* was not progressing well. It was an attempt at merging a description of Hades with a depiction of London (this idea drawn, or even stolen, he admitted to himself, from Doré's illustrations of the city and from Baudelaire's *capitale infâme*). Having brooded over the thing for several weeks, he succumbed to a moment of weakness and submitted an extract to *The Spirit Lamp.* Afterwards he went through agonies of regret, and when the piece was promptly rejected he put the entire poem in a drawer and could not look at it for some time.

He had not shown his work to anyone for so long that his reaction to this failure took him by surprise – a wincing feeling of self-exposure, self-disgust. He had expected a few initial rejections and had imagined dismissing such minor stings with a wry smile and a shrug. He was disappointed in himself.

Not long afterwards, there was another unwelcome discovery: his landlady announced that she would shortly be selling the house and moving to Canada to live with her married daughter.

Tasked with finding new lodgings at short notice, James immediately ran into difficulties. Suitable lodgings were not affordable,
affordable lodgings were not suitable – on one or two occasions,
barely sanitary.

One evening, after a visit to look at one such dubious property
– a place in Islington with mould growing on the walls, more
dismal than he had supposed a human habitation possibly could
be – James returned home to find a letter from Charlotte waiting
for him:

> *I hope the search for lodgings is not too arduous and that you
> have found the city as you anticipated. I imagine it must be
> quite brilliant, especially at night – so different to the absolute
> country blackness we get here. I think I should find it a difficult
> change, after Oxford, though of course an exciting one. You said
> that the crowds were a little oppressive at first, but I think that
> is natural – and you are very sensitive to your surroundings.
> You'll get accustomed to it all after a few weeks. Perhaps if you
> go about and look at people, it might be easier? See some of the
> attractions, too – if it is not beneath your dignity to wander the
> Tower of London behind a gaggle of country schoolgirls up for a
> day of sightseeing.*

The letter was well timed (as Charlotte's letters usually were).
James read it and read it again, at first cheered and irritated in
equal measure, and finally resolved to take her advice. He had
been anxious amongst the crowds and traffic, tramping about
until his feet were sore, choking uncontrollably from the smoke
of the Underground, but had taken no time to stop and observe.
As Charlotte had probably guessed, he had been thinking of other
things. Poetry made him clumsy – absorbed in his own thoughts,
he had run into people by mistake, taken wrong turnings, missed
a great deal. Now he would try to do things differently.

He was living close enough to Oxford Street to make a walk

there feasible. He would take a stroll, perhaps wander into Hyde Park. He had not yet seen the Serpentine, and would enjoy a sight of the water.

It was six o'clock and Oxford Street was busy; there was much to observe. Stopping to glance at a display of watercolour prints in a shop window, James was suddenly pushed forwards as a man elbowed past him, a hatstand wrapped in brown paper slung over his shoulder like a rifle. The fleeting contact, rough and impersonal, upset him in spite of himself. It was as if the city itself had reached out and pushed him aside. This vast place, with its shifting, trampling crowds, would never make sense to him. His blithe expectations were now an embarrassment. He understood nothing here. The human soul might perhaps be laid open, its devices and desires brought to the light – but to comprehend London? Surely it was impossible.

He turned his footsteps back the way he had come, deciding that the experiment had not been a success.

He was at the corner of Portman Street when he realised that someone was calling his name – someone waving from the other side of the road. It was Geoffrey Margoyle, whom James remembered from Oxford. Margoyle was older than James, loud and ambitious, with a decided fondness for giving good advice. He had left Oxford a year ago, and James had almost forgotten about him.

He was waving now; James could hardly pretend not to see him. Instead, he waited as Margoyle darted across the street, nimbly dodging the traffic (and how many months in London would it take for James to be able to manage that?).

'Norbury!' he said, as soon as he was within speaking distance. 'How are you?'

To James's great surprise, Margoyle proved a blessing, in his way: after telling James in some detail about his flourishing career at the Foreign Office, he added that he had just the solution to James's problems. He knew an excellent fellow who needed someone to go halves with him on a very nice set of rooms. He was in abruptly straitened circumstances due to an unlucky conjunction of pressing debts, cancelled allowance and a family quarrel (Margoyle knew James would keep this to himself), and in fact James had probably met him at Oxford – Christopher Paige. Surely he remembered . . . ?

'Paige?' James repeated. 'Ah.'

'You don't remember him?'

'Was he at Corpus?'

'Magdalen. Did you do *anything* useful at Oxford?'

'I fed the ducks, sometimes.'

Margoyle ignored this remark. 'Anyway, I'll introduce you. He's a decent chap, you'll see.'

'I'm grateful, Margoyle, but I'm not really sure if—'

'Don't be an ass,' Margoyle said, as if this settled the matter. 'You can meet him at my club tomorrow afternoon. Three o'clock. Be on time, if you can manage it.' He took out his watch. 'Now I must go.'

He disregarded James's continuing protests and departed with aplomb, leaving James feeling rather more rueful and bewildered than he had been before.

Margoyle's club was a grand old place in Pall Mall, ponderously, expensively silent. Inside, it was difficult to imagine the noise of the streets only a yard or so distant. Margoyle, who liked directing things, was in a cheerful mood. James was uneasy. He was sitting opposite Margoyle, listening to a very long story (about how Margoyle's father had once met General Gordon on a train, and what Margoyle's father had said to General Gordon, and what General Gordon had said to him), when the door was opened and a man paused, breathless, on the threshold. James recognised him immediately – the same dark eyes and careless good looks. He had an air of enjoying himself tremendously – which, James would later learn, was habitual.

'Paige,' Margoyle said, genial and reproachful. 'We'd nearly given up hope.'

'Well, there's a story there,' Paige said. He looked from Margoyle to James and then blinked. 'Ah.'

James stared back at him, quite at a loss. He remembered *The Martyrdom of Man,* and the gentle shade of the library, and the smell of dust and sweat.

It might, in that moment, have fallen out in a number of ways. James ought to have pretended not to recognise Paige at all.

Instead, he said incredulously, 'It's you.'

'Yes,' Paige agreed.

'You've met before?' said Margoyle.

Paige glanced at James. 'We were never introduced, were we, Mr . . . ?'

'Norbury.'

James saw Paige's mouth twitch and thought that he was struggling with suppressed fury. Then he realised it was not rage at all but laughter, and this unsettled him more than outright hostility would have done.

'Actually,' James added desperately, 'I think perhaps I ought to reconsider – about the rooms, I mean. I'm sorry to inconvenience you, but—'

'Reconsider?' Margoyle repeated coldly.

'Yes, I – I've just thought, I know I ought to have mentioned this before, but I should probably think about going back to the country soon, and I wouldn't want to . . .'

Margoyle was still looking at him in unconcealed disapproval, but Paige smiled again and sat down in the chair nearest to James.

'Nonsense,' he said.

James said nothing. It had dawned on him how well Paige was dressed, the way he could say *nonsense* as if fate could not possibly have the audacity to disregard his wishes.

'Come and see the rooms, at least,' he said. 'You'll think

differently when you see them. Besides, I'll be an ideal person to share with. Won't I, Margoyle?'

Margoyle smiled sardonically – it seemed he had become expert in sardonic smiles since leaving Oxford; perhaps it was something they taught one at the Foreign Office. 'You'd be a fool not to see the rooms,' he told James. 'You were so down in the mouth before, about having nowhere to live.'

This was indisputable. And so Margoyle left for another appointment, and together James and Paige departed to look at the rooms.

The house was 75 Egerton Gardens, not far from the Natural History Museum, opposite the Brompton Oratory, on a street of high red houses. It was all exceedingly genteel. James thought of Aiskew, of the times when Charlotte and he would open a window at the top of the house and scream out of it, for the delight of hearing their whoops and yells echo across the grounds. There would be no yelling here. Even the horses' hooves sounded different, as if the animals were on their best behaviour. From the pavement, the sky above looked oddly removed.

The rooms belonged to a Mrs Morris, Paige explained – a distant relation, who, being confronted by unexpected pecuniary difficulties (rather like himself), was obliged to let rooms after her husband's death. Paige and James's advent would be a considerable relief, for letting ordinary lodgers into the house would probably have been the death of her. James would be doing her a great favour if he kept his discussion of delicate financial matters – like the rent – as brief as possible.

Inside, the house was evidently still in mourning and seemed far too grand to be broken up by tenants. But it was also a little emptier than might have been expected. There were blank spaces on walls and shelves, indentations on the carpet where articles of furniture must once have stood. James suspected that Mrs

Morris had been forced to part with certain household treasures to settle her husband's debts.

Mrs Morris met them in the drawing-room. Like her house, she was very respectable and rather sad. She was white-haired but younger than James had expected, a gentle lady still in mourning, half swallowed in bombazine and crêpe.

'I prepared the second floor,' she said. 'I hope that will suit you both.'

'It will, indeed,' James said, feeling almost unbearably sorry for her, her desolate house, her nervous, fluttering manner. It would be impossible not to take the rooms now.

She led them up to the second floor, which they would have entirely to themselves. They would have a bedroom each and a sitting-room to share between them. Mrs Morris's rooms were on the next floor, the servant's room above those.

Their rooms were let furnished, but this did not stop Paige from altering their appearance as far as was possible. He replaced all of the pictures with art of his own choosing, including one painting he had done himself: a large, livid sunflower which glared down on the sitting-room like a furious eye. There were also two blue-and-white vases, which were too large for the mantelpiece where they stood, and a Japanese folding screen that was forever getting in the way.

Better than these were the flowers – always exquisite, though never very tidily arranged. Paige liked tulips especially and would keep them for days, letting the petals come loose and the stems wind across the table like slender green snakes.

He never explained why he had elected to share with James. At first, James half-thought it might be to keep him in sight, in case he was the sort to spread tales and cause trouble. More likely it was simply a matter of convenience: there were the rooms, and there was James. For his part, James thought it was well to observe people like Paige. From a literary point of view, he was good raw material.

Though, to begin with, James saw little of him. Paige was usually out or asleep during the day, and what conversations they did have generally took place after dark. Paige would return home at some unwholesome hour of the morning to find James still awake, writing in the sitting-room, busy with *Gondoline,* his latest poetical work.

Sometimes Paige's friends accompanied him home. The two who visited most often were called Soames and Bleasdale – loud and tiresome young men, very modern, much given to puerile humour. If either of them had a profession, James saw no evidence of it. They would return with Paige after an all-night debauch and spend hours in the sitting-room, drinking and trying to smoke up the chimney (in a half-hearted attempt to avoid upsetting Mrs Morris, who abhorred the smell of tobacco). Often they did not leave until the morning – once, they had terrified the housemaid by disturbing her as she came upstairs to clean the grates. They called James 'Jimmy' and made ridiculous puns on his surname and pretended to believe that, as a poet, he must lead a life of intrigue and depravity. After a few tiresome encounters, James began to avoid them. Whenever he heard their steps on the stairs, he would gather his work together and retreat to his bedroom. But when Paige came home alone, James would remain where he was, because the desk in the sitting-room was far bigger than the one in his own room, and he had as much right to be there as Paige did.

Paige never stumbled, even when sponge-heavy with drink. Not even on the night in late September, not long after James first moved to Egerton Gardens, when he came home absolutely squiffed, soaked to the skin, and dressed in a much-abused doublet and hose and a long, mud-spattered cloak. James – deep in an irritating metrical negotiation – had started and looked up to see what the noise was. He blinked, taking in Paige's disarray, his peculiar costume.

'Don't laugh,' Paige said.

'I wasn't going to.'

'Of course you were. You're an awfully bad liar, you know. Cabby had a few things to say, I can tell you. And that was before we ran out of money.' He pushed the door shut slowly, with concentration that was almost comical, and then turned to look at James with an expression of infinite weariness.

'Is there any tea?' he asked.

'Beg your pardon?'

'Tea,' Paige said – enunciating very, very precisely. 'Is there any?'

The housemaid had probably been asleep for several hours, as Paige surely knew quite well. James looked around the room briefly and then said, 'No.'

Paige sighed and looked so tired and put out that James was sorry he had been brusque.

'I could make you some, if you like,' he offered.

'Really?'

James had been accustomed to making his own tea at Oxford, and he had brought the things with him. 'There's no sugar, though,' he said. 'No milk, either.'

'That's all right.' Paige sat down and closed his eyes. 'Party at Mrs – party at Mrs someone's. Dancing, feast, mock tournament, all medieval. Picturesque age, everyone said. We all had to go in costume . . . My God, what an evening.' He needed an audience, perhaps, because when James made no reply he added, 'Really, you wouldn't credit what happened.'

'Oh?' said James. 'What happened?'

And Paige leaned further back on the settee and began to tell him all about it.

• • •

This slowly became a habit between them. At night, sometimes one or two o'clock, or later, James would look up from his work to find that Paige had returned. He might have been to the theatre, or to dinner at the Café Royal, or to a ball at the home of a society hostess. Or in the company of less exalted ladies, somewhere around Charing Cross. Once he had visited a skating rink; another time he went to see the remains of Bentham, embalmed and preserved at University College. ('Bored,' he said, when James asked him how the corpse had looked.) Living his life, James thought, must be like wandering in a hothouse, every fruit and flower at one's fingertips. He sometimes spoke of pursuing the law – it seemed to be a standing agreement with his family – but surely there was no time for anything of that sort, living as he did.

'Good evening?' James would always ask when Paige got back, and would raise his eyebrows at Paige's dishevelled appearance. 'You look done in,' he might add, if Paige seemed particularly worn.

'Oh, be quiet,' Paige would counter – or words to that effect, perhaps more colourful or less distinctly articulated, depending on how much he had had to drink. 'And for the love of God, make me some tea.' Then he would decline gently into a chair and close his eyes, as if, like the philosopher of Ecclesiastes, he had exhausted all the pleasures of the world and found them wanting.

And James would sigh and make some tea on the fire. By the time the tea was made, Paige would have recovered sufficiently to talk. His stories were generally about himself, his friends or his family. They were rather interesting. Paige had an older brother, Eustace, who was a bore and sanctimonious to boot, and a sister, Lydia – who was, Paige said gravely, no gentleman. She could freeze out a suitor so thoroughly that the poor fellow was never the same afterwards. Several of Paige's friends had fallen victim. Worse still, she kept an ungenerously accurate tally of Paige's debts. When she wasn't doing that, she was treasurer to dozens of charitable concerns – so industrious, in fact, that he wondered how there came to be any ill-used match girls or crippled crossing sweepers or friendless young women of good character left for anyone else to patronise.

Then there was Paige's mother, who had quarrelled with him without any fair cause, and who, through various slights and pointed remarks, had made it impossible for him to remain on speaking terms with her without losing all self-respect.

'Which would have been out of the question,' said Paige.

'Well, of course,' James replied.

The family money was all from his mother's side, Paige said. She'd been widowed at eighteen, and her first husband had left her everything, tied up so tightly that no one could touch it – not his family, not even her second husband. That was love for you. Paige's father had been poor but very aristocratic and with an excellent profile, and Queen Cophetua had just snapped him up. He might have done something for Paige, if only to annoy his wife, but he had died some years ago.

'Drink and a Welsh mistress,' Paige said. 'That's what did for him, in the end.'

'Ah,' James said. 'I'm sorry.'

Paige shook his head. 'We weren't friendly. We disapproved of each other.'

(What an odd idea, James thought later, when Paige had gone to bed. To disapprove of one's father, as if he were simply another person about whom one might be allowed to have an opinion.)

There was one evening, in mid-October, when it had begun to rain as it grew dark. It was pleasant to sit with the curtains drawn and the fire built up, and to hear the storm growing outside. James wondered if Paige enjoyed being out in such weather, and in the cosy sitting-room, with only the noise of the fire and the gentle scratch of his pen to break the silence, he had felt content. Slowly he had grown tired and descended gradually into a comfortable doze.

He woke abruptly to the feel of icy water trickling down his neck. He jumped, cursed, and looked up to see Paige holding a dripping umbrella over him.

'You were asleep,' he said cheerfully. His eyes were slightly unfocused, and his breath smelled of stale wine and tobacco and something else – an odd, acrid smell James couldn't place. Wherever he had been, it appeared that the storm had in no way spoiled his evening's entertainment.

James glanced down at the page of *Gondoline* on which he had been working – it was spotted with water, as if he had been weeping over the manuscript. 'Look what you've done,' he said. 'You utter—'

'Sorry, sorry,' Paige said. Then, unexpectedly, he laughed.

'What? What is it?'

'Have you been drinking ink?'

'What? Of course not.' But James looked at his hands. There were the usual black smudges, the writer's marks of which he was rather proud. He must have rubbed his mouth or begun to bite his nails. He could taste it now, a bitterness of black ink. He took out his handkerchief and rubbed at his mouth.

'No,' Paige said impatiently. 'Other side.' He glanced at the pages of *Gondoline*, still drying on the desk. 'What are you writing, anyway?'

'A poem.'

'Can I read it?'

'No.' James shuffled the pages out of sight, wary of the sudden gleam in Paige's eyes and afraid he might seize *Gondoline* by main force.

'Is it so bad?'

'I won't know until it's finished.'

'Well, what's it about? Something serious – decline of the race, o tempora o mores, whither England, death of some great man, that sort of thing?'

James smiled in spite of himself. 'Not really, no.' (He had, in fact, once attempted a verse eulogy of Browning but had given it up in despair.) 'There's . . . well, there's an old man. He appears at a christening, scarred and withered of visage, and insists on telling his tale before the child is baptised.'

'Then what happens?'

'He tells his tale. It's about a virtuous maid stranded in a remote mansion. There's something horrible after her, I think.'

He had seen Gondoline often in his mind; sometimes a girl in the street reminded him of her – the pale oval of her face, the masses of dark hair, the sharp black line of the velvet ribbon around her throat. She had wide brown eyes and would endure any number of trials, poor thing, before the poem was ended.

'It's not a ghost after her, is it?' Paige asked.

'What's wrong with ghosts?'

'Too flimsy. You can walk right through them – what's the fun in that?'

'Well, it isn't a ghost. At least I don't think it is. I haven't got to that part yet. It's taken me these last six stanzas just to describe the old man.'

Paige smiled at him – really smiled at him, without mockery. James couldn't remember him ever doing such a thing before.

He said, 'I suppose that makes sense. The old men are impor-tant, aren't they? In this type of poem. People will want to know what he looks like, whether he has a beard, that sort of thing. You did give him a beard, didn't you?'

'I don't think so.'

'Well you'll put one in, if you take my advice.'

'I'll make a note,' James said. He turned back to his work.

When he next glanced up, Paige had fallen asleep, sprawled out in his chair as if determined to take up as much space as possible. Even drunk and unconscious, he still contrived to look agreeable. After a moment, James returned to his poem, to the lines he had just added. Not entirely bad, he decided, but certainly not good. There was time enough for improvement, though. There was tomorrow. He sat back in his chair, abruptly pleased with the world and himself – and with Paige, who smiled in his sleep.

James thought, proud and wondering: this is my friend. Only now did he realise how solitary his life had been before.

But as he sat and watched the fire, he was also uneasy. This was not what he was used to. Perhaps it was like being in a poorly lit room: you saw well enough, because your eyes were accustomed to it. But if someone brought in a lamp, everything was suddenly very bright – unpleasantly so at first. You might well hate the person with the light, for arriving so rudely and unannounced.

And how odd, how interestingly perverse, to be frightened by happiness. It was the dread of getting things wrong, fear of losing this friend he had (by sheer luck) managed to find.

He would not dwell on these things. It was growing cold and the fire would soon be out, and he was getting morbid. He should wake Paige up – it would be an unkindness to leave him there all night. And he would go to bed soon, though not just yet. He sat up a while longer and watched the fire burn low.

Chapter Three

It was a London Christmas, quite by accident. James had intended to go back to Yorkshire, but an attack of influenza had left him too weak to travel. Charlotte and Mrs Chickering were disappointed not to see him, of course, and worried to think of him ill and alone. He wrote back that it was not half as bad as they imagined, for Mrs Morris was there – sending up homeopathic medicines and nourishing dishes, insisting that the fires be built up, forever enquiring if he did not need another blanket.

Paige did not leave London either. He hated the country and he hated shooting, he told James, and he liked the city once half the people he knew had gone; it was enjoyably lonely. The park was absolutely deserted.

At the beginning of December he spoke of spending Christmas at his family's house in the country – it was tradition, apparently, that they all make their way back to the old place, no matter how badly they might have quarrelled during the year – but the days passed and he did not leave. James had refrained from mentioning the subject.

Paige was more restless than usual but not otherwise out of sorts. Mrs Morris liked him about the place. He would occasionally claim the privilege of blood relation to bring her flowers or other small tokens, bright touches of colour in the house of mourning.

The months after Christmas passed quickly, comfortably. One bright morning in February, James returned from a long walk to find Paige in his room: smoking, and turning over the photograph of Charlotte which stood on the dressing table. He was wearing evening dress and had probably been out all night – a ball until dawn, and then back to Soames's or Bleasdale's for breakfast. He was pale and his eyes glittered; the flower in his buttonhole had lost half its petals; his sleeves were pushed up to the elbow.

'Hello,' he said, not looking at all abashed at being discovered. 'Is this your sister?'

James nodded. It was not, he knew, an especially good photograph: to a stranger it would show only a sturdy female in her middle twenties, wearing a stern expression. She had chestnut hair and a country-girl's complexion, with a freshness born of long walks and early nights – but this was all lost in sepia. She was standing awkwardly – a tall woman with a bad habit of stooping. The photographer (a visiting clergyman, an enthusiastic amateur) had caught her as she raised a hand to adjust her hat, a pose that made her look as if she were waving farewell.

James took the picture from Paige and set it back on the table, where it belonged.

'Did you want something?' he asked.

'No,' Paige said. He turned, his cigarette drifting smoke, to survey the rest of the bedroom. It was as if the place fascinated him, James thought, though in truth there was nothing very remarkable about it, save the clutter. There were a few pictures James liked – a couple had been rescued from the sitting-room after Paige's improvements. Over the bed hung a preposterous engraving of which James was rather fond, entitled *Theseus's Farewell to Pirithous*.

There were also many books, kept in no particular order and giving the whole room a comforting smell of damp paper.

He sat down on the bed and watched Paige continue his investigations, unconcerned by James's scrutiny. The very outrageousness of his behaviour disarmed James's indignation. And, then, there was a lazy enjoyment in watching Paige turning over his books, reading the spines with care, leafing through his discarded papers as if searching for something.

Perhaps he would make fun of James's taste in literature – so hopelessly old-fashioned and provincial. Upon moving to London, James had done his best to educate himself, had gone scrabbling after new theories – naturalism, symbolism – but had never quite been able to catch up. Anyway, he thought, if one preferred *Armadale* to *La Bête Humaine*, then what was so dreadful about that? Dickens, Thackeray, George Eliot – there was no shame in having such friends amongst the dead.

Paige held up a volume. 'What's this? *Etiquette: What to Do, and How to Do It?*'

With dismay, James recalled the guides which he had bought weeks ago in an attempt to acquire a little social polish. Like a fool he had left them out on the table in plain sight.

Before James could stop him, Paige had already opened the book and read aloud, '*Any lady who walks much in London, whether alone or with a friend or relation, should be careful to select a very quiet costume—*' He broke off, smiling. 'Why do you have this?'

'Give it back.'

But Paige was still flicking through the book: '*. . . in the present day, the deepest mourning, and the strictest seclusion are often observed, for friends only, while a period of mourning and the extent of it is materially curtailed when—*'

'Stop it.' And James reached out and snatched the book away from him.

Paige stared at him, looking slightly surprised. 'All right. Sorry.' After a pause, he added, 'You've got a temper, you know.'

'I didn't,' James said, 'until I moved here.'

Paige put out his cigarette in an empty saucer. 'I really am sorry. I was just curious. I don't think I've met anyone like you before.' It did not sound complimentary, the way he said it. In all likelihood he simply meant that James was rather peculiar. James remembered that Mrs Chickering had always said that eccentricity was first cousin to madness.

There was a silence, whilst Paige pressed his cigarette into the saucer with some force, though surely it must be out by now.

'Well,' James said at last, attempting a smile, 'I am a poet, some of the time—'

Paige cut him off with a laugh, the one he generally used for his fashionable friends. 'Oh, yes, of course, that's it,' he said. 'You're a poet.' And he began to sing mockingly under his breath:

> A most intense young man,
> A soulful-eyed young man,
> An ultra-poetical, super-æsthetical,
> Out-of-the-way young man!

'I'll see you later,' he added at the door, and then he was gone, leaving the smell of smoke in his wake.

James took a breath. The room seemed different, which was ridiculous. Perhaps he should open the window.

Then there was a knock at the door – sharp, hurried. It was Paige again. 'Are you busy next Saturday?' he asked without preamble.

'No,' James said. When Paige said nothing else, he added, 'Why?'

'I've got seats at the theatre. It's opening night. And it's at the St James's, so you should certainly come.'

'What about Soames?' James asked. 'And Bleasdale?'

Paige shrugged, as if Soames and Bleasdale were nothing to

him, rather than his close friends and boon companions since Oxford.

'Well, all right,' James said. 'Sorry. I mean thank you, of course.'

'Lady something-or-other, it's called. Something like that. There's a lady involved, anyway, which is promising.'

And before James could say anything else, Paige had let the door snap closed for a second time.

• • •

On the evening of the play, they decided to walk to the theatre. It was a pleasant evening, for the time of year, and the city seemed new-made. To James – delightfully conscious of having had precisely the right amount of champagne at dinner – its mysteries seemed far more benign than they ever had before. They stopped in Trafalgar Square for Paige to light a cigar, and as they paused London went on its way around them – all noise and motion and smoky air. There were lights burning in the windows of shops and hotels, reflected in the water of the fountains.

'Of course, we don't have to go to the theatre,' Paige said. 'We could go somewhere else.'

Somewhere else – oh. That sort of elsewhere. James thought of red velvet curtains and bedrooms full of orchids, and even shaking hands with a new acquaintance was still awkward for him, and did Paige seriously expect them to tramp around London in the cold in search of the sort of female who would allow or indeed require—

But Paige had already smiled, blown a feathery breath of smoke into the night. 'No?' he said, as if James had spoken. 'All right. Seats are already paid for, anyway.' They resumed walking. 'You're a good influence, I think. Mother would be pleased to hear.'

The theatre was crowded when they arrived. They were at the door when a voice from behind them called out: 'Christopher!'

It was Emily Richter, hastening towards them with a smile.

She had changed, James thought, since the last time he saw her, crumpled and laughing amongst the bookshelves. She had grown a little – up and outwards like a tree – and it suited her. She wore a long evening coat of olive-green silk, patterned with flowers and vines and trimmed with tawny fur. Her hair was done in careful curls on her forehead.

Paige moved over to meet her. 'Emmy! What on earth are you doing here? Surely you're not alone?'

'It's Mrs Hyssops now, if you please.'

'Hyssops?'

'Yes. Don't look at me like that. I—' Then her eyes met James's and she broke off in surprise. 'Oh.' She might have faltered last year. Now she simply looked rather more serious for a moment, before her smile returned. 'It is you, isn't it?'

She and Paige both looked at James, their expressions oddly similar, so that for an instant James felt as if he were back in the Camera.

'Yes,' James admitted. 'Hello,' he added, as an afterthought. 'How do you do.'

'I'm so pleased to see you again, Mr . . .'

'Norbury,' Paige said, amusement glimmering beneath the surface of his politeness.

'How strange to meet like this, don't you think?' They both looked about to laugh. 'Almost like predestination, really – although of course you don't believe in that, do you?' She turned to James. 'Do you know, the first time Christopher ever visited us at home, he spent half an hour telling me about all the things he didn't believe in. He was particularly scathing about vegetarians, if I remember rightly.'

'Well, I was a wild young man back then,' Paige said. 'Do you remember Mr Benson?'

They began to discuss a number of people whose names were meaningless to James – before, finally, Mrs Hyssops turned to James with a charming apologetic look.

'I'm so sorry,' she said, 'you must be awfully bored.'

'Oh, no,' James answered vaguely.

'It's all your doing,' Mrs Hyssops said to Paige. 'I said I'd be only a minute, and Adam hates to wait.' She looked rather pleased by this reflection. James had the idea of a long, private game of hide-and-seek. 'You'll come and see me, won't you?' She looked again at James. 'And of course I haven't seen you for even longer, Mr Norbury, though I remember the occasion well.'

She paused kindly, to allow James to say something witty.

'So do I,' James said finally.

'Let him alone,' Paige said. 'He's from the country; they don't have your sort there.'

She smiled, bowed, and disappeared into the theatre, leaving them with only a few minutes to find their seats before the play began.

• • •

To James's satisfaction, the story ended happily.

'Well?' Paige asked, as the applause clattered around them like a sudden downpour. 'Did you like it?'

'Good, I thought.' He was not ready to talk yet: his ideas had not settled, and he was still half dazed by the end of the performance, the return to his own life.

'You see what it does, of course?' said Paige.

'You mean . . .'

'Yes, exactly. All the hypocrisy, that façade that needs ripping away from society, the masks that have to be – what? Come on, then, what do you think?'

'Well, I could be wrong,' James began, 'but surely if it was only about . . .' He lost confidence in his ideas halfway through and gave up with a shrug. 'Anyway, I'm glad Mrs . . . Mrs . . . I've forgotten her name already – you know, the mother.'

'Oh, yes, the mother—'

'I'm glad it ended well for her.'

Paige grinned. 'Uncomplicated verdict, but from the heart.'

He could really be insufferable at times. James was about to point this out to him when – 'Oh, look,' Paige said suddenly, leaning forwards. 'Isn't that Wilde?'

James squinted. (Their seats were at the very back of the dress circle.) 'The author? You mean that man who's just come on?'

'Yes.'

Wilde was dark and pale, a tall man, a giant – who seemed, for an instant, to be breathing fire.

James looked at Paige, taken aback. 'Is he smoking?'

'I think so. . . . What's the matter?'

'Well, you know. Onstage like that. There are ladies here.'

'Shh,' Paige said. 'Listen.'

From the stage, Wilde regarded the audience briefly, smoke still floating from his lips. His gloves were mauve; the flower in his buttonhole was green: he looked like someone from a story. Finally, he began to speak.

'Ladies and gentlemen: I have enjoyed this evening immensely . . .'

They were sitting much too far away. The speech drifted back to them in bright fragments, like scraps of coloured paper on a breeze. It was as though the man were part of the play, James thought, as if he had written his lines out in advance.

'. . . and your great appreciation has been most intelligent. I congratulate you on the great success of your performance.'

James turned to Paige. 'What did he say? About the audience?'

'I didn't hear,' Paige answered, sounding irritated.

They both leaned further forwards – but a moment later the figure was bowing, smiling, and the audience was applauding once more.

Paige turned back to James. 'That was interesting. Unusual man . . . A genius, I suppose.'

James was beginning to say that he had always thought it

seemed wrong somehow to call someone a genius before he was dead, but Paige interrupted him:

'Perhaps you ought to write a play.'

'A play?' James had never considered such a thing before. 'I don't think I could.'

Paige shrugged. 'You could try, couldn't you?' He retrieved his hat from under his seat and stood up. 'Shall we go?'

On the stairs, James felt Paige nudge him.

'What is it?'

'There.' Paige nodded towards a man ahead of them, who had offered his arm to a lady in dark blue.

'Who is it?'

'My brother. And mother. I didn't think they'd be here.' And Paige called out: 'Eustace! Over here!'

The man turned, and James had a brief sight of his face – an impression of pallor, a disapproving stare. Then Eustace Paige turned back to his mother. James saw him murmur something to her – and in another moment they were gone.

James had never seen anyone cut before, certainly not by his own family. He took a gamble: 'I think perhaps they didn't see you. And it's so loud in here, you know.'

Paige finally looked at him. 'I don't really care what you think,' he said flatly. 'And would it be beyond you to find a clean shirt?'

James followed Paige's gaze to his own cuffs, realising that they were spotted with black ink. There had been a phrase to alter before he left; he had been rather in a hurry.

He looked back at his friend. Of course Paige was angry and longing to strike out at someone. If James had thought that Paige cared only shallowly for his family – or for anyone or anything – then here was the proof of how unjust he had been.

'Do you want to get a cab?' James asked.

'You get one. I'm going out.'

'No,' James said. 'I don't think you should.'

'What?'

'For one thing, you're in no mood for it, and for another you borrowed five pounds from Soames yesterday, so you certainly can't afford it.'

Paige stared at him, his expression rather startled. James began walking again, and after a pause Paige followed him.

At the door they lingered, looking out into the darkness as people pushed past them. James turned to Paige. 'I could write a play, you know,' he said awkwardly. 'Perhaps I'll give it a try.'

Paige smiled faintly. 'What about Gondoline?' he asked, his voice ordinary again. 'Are you deserting her?'

James shrugged and felt only a little guilty towards his heroine when he replied, 'I think so. She can shift for herself from now on.' He squinted into the night, trying to determine whether or not it was raining. 'Come on,' he said, turning back to Paige. 'Let's go.'

• • •

April came and the season began in earnest, and Paige seemed to abandon any thought of pursuing a profession. His stories, when he returned after the absence of a night or a few days, became more extravagant. Sometimes he would invite James to accompany him to some picnic or party or luncheon or dinner, and James – always uncertain of how seriously to take such offers – would invariably refuse.

He thought of beginning his play but could not yet bring himself to start. Instead, he turned over old odds and ends, wrote the beginnings to five different stories which would never be finished.

One morning in June, Paige was awake rather earlier than usual. As James sat at the desk in the sitting-room, writing a letter to Charlotte (it being too early for literature), Paige sat down at the breakfast table and began on the toast and coffee.

He seemed in an excellent mood and was humming under his breath. 'Have you eaten?'

'Not really,' James said. 'That's my toast you've got there, actually. It's probably cold by now. Why don't you have some more sent up?'

'I like cold toast, as it happens.'

'Well, so do I.'

'Do you want some?'

'Not now,' James said, but Paige had already wandered over to his desk, carrying a plate of buttered toast.

'Here,' he said.

'I'm writing,' James said.

'I'm not stopping you.' Paige held a piece of toast under James's nose. 'Go on.'

James continued to write, but opened his mouth and took a bite. *I hope your cold is better* came out rather untidily and smudged.

'There,' Paige said, wiping butter off his fingers. 'Bit like feeding a horse.' He went back to the table and sat down. 'Have you started your play?'

'No.'

'But you are going to write it, aren't you?'

'Probably I will.' James began to write a new sentence and then laid down his pen again. 'I do have a title,' he said hurriedly. '*A Want of Charity*. What do you think?'

Paige took a sip of coffee, considered a moment. 'Yes. I think I'd buy tickets to that. Or I'd go if someone else bought me a ticket.'

'Thank you.'

'I suppose it will involve a female named Charity?'

'Yes,' James said, a little put out that Paige had guessed this so easily.

'Well, that's all right, then. By the way, I saw Emmy Richter – or Hyssops, I suppose. She's inviting us both to her ball next month. You ought to go, you're starting to turn into a hermit.'

'I'm not.'

'You are. You don't go anywhere, you never see anyone.'

'I see you,' James said absently, having returned to his letter. 'We went to the theatre.'

'That was ages ago. Come with me next month.'

'No. But thanks for getting me an invitation.'

'Come with me,' Paige persisted. 'It'll be interesting, I promise you. Eustace is going to be there, and I'm going to have words with him. I think he's been carrying tales of me to Mother.'

'True ones?'

Paige smiled, shrugged. 'That's not the point,' he said. 'Look, I really think you should go. You'll enjoy yourself. And if you say yes, I'll leave you in peace now. How's that for a bargain?'

It felt churlish to argue further. James agreed, and Paige kept his promise and left him alone with his letter, already regretting his capitulation.

The appointed hour of the appointed evening found them at the Hyssops' house, a tall and gracious building on Eaton Square, already hectic with guests. A long line of carriages trailed slowly by the door, passengers alighting in turn.

Inside, the house was large and grand – awfully modern, James thought – with a stylish and probably very expensive sort of simplicity. The hall looked as if everything had been chosen to go together, to form a whole – so different to Aiskew, where the furniture cohabited as best it could, shuffled in a haphazard fashion from room to room with the vicissitudes of the years.

There were flowers everywhere, lamps burning bright, music coming from upstairs. Everyone, James thought, seemed to know precisely what to do.

Paige steered him towards the cloakroom; he was deprived of his hat and coat, directed – before he quite knew how it was happening – towards the stairs. Here they were obliged to wait for some minutes behind a line of other guests, all engaged in the same slow ascent. Paige said little; he appeared almost nervous. From time to time he looked about him, searching the crowd – for his brother, perhaps.

At last they reached the top of the stairs, and their names were announced one after another, with dreadful distinctness, by a superior butler.

Mrs Hyssops greeted them, held out her hand to Paige with her brightest look.

'I'm so glad to see you, Christopher,' she said. She was dressed in silk taffeta the colour of butter. 'And Mr Norbury.' She smiled at James. 'How nice to see you again.'

The music and conversation were already growing louder, James noticed. The doors had been taken off their hinges; there was no chance of a moment's solitude, no possible escape from the noise, the endless people.

'Has Eustace arrived yet?' Paige asked.

Mrs Hyssops shook her head. 'He's not well, poor thing. He sent a nice note this morning, very apologetic.'

'Ah, well, I can't say I'm surprised,' Paige said – cheated of a difficult conversation, pleased and disappointed at once. 'I didn't really expect to see him here. He only ever goes to Mother's house and to his club now, from what I hear.'

After Mrs Hyssops had turned to the next guests, Paige introduced James to several people in quick succession: a very old man with medals pinned onto him, two women in artistic dresses (who seemed to know Paige very well already, judging by their gentle shrieks of delight at seeing him), and many others whose names and faces vanished from James's mind almost immediately.

He became separated from Paige fairly early in the evening. He thought it was for the best – to trail about after him would only be ridiculous. It was not unpleasant, anyway, to simply sit and observe.

He had been afraid that Mrs Hyssops might offer to introduce him to someone, and oblige him to dance. Instead, to his relief, he was left alone to admire the dancing, the music, the glittering chandelier above the staircase, the rustling, many-coloured progression of women's dresses – cream and rose pink and heliotrope, taffeta and satin and crêpe de Chine, patterned with flowers and butterflies. There were so many people that he was not conspicuous. The only awkward thing was deciding what to do with his hands.

As he sat at the edge of a large group of guests, listening to them talk, he was accosted by Soames and Bleasdale, both exquisitely turned out and claiming to be very pleased indeed to see him again.

'But where have you been?' Soames demanded – sitting down, uninvited, on the arm of James's chair. 'We never see you any more. Why won't you ever come out with us?'

'Yes, why don't you?' Bleasdale added. 'I know a place you'd love, Jimmy. There's this one girl there . . .'

He began to describe the lady's charms, Soames contributing the occasional detail. She was a celebrated skirt-dancer; all the chaps were crazy about her. One friend of Bleasdale's was so terribly gone on her that he'd almost ruined himself buying her jewellery. Really, he'd probably be marrying the tart if things went on like this. . . .

James found it best not to listen to any more of the conversation, instead gazing around the room, wondering if it would be utterly unpardonable to simply get up and leave. Strange, he thought, that he could easily stay awake all night at home – here, he was already tired; his eyes had turned dry. The crowd had thinned a little. Could it at last be time for supper?

'. . . and then she tipped a strawberry ice down his neck, and that was the end of that—'

Soames broke off suddenly, and James looked up to see that Paige had wandered over, accompanied by a blonde young lady whose pink dress frothed over the carpet like spilled champagne.

'Hello,' Paige said. 'Enjoying yourselves?' He nodded towards his companion. 'Miss Smythe, these two are Soames and Bleasdale. Don't ask me which one is which, because it doesn't matter – they're both as bad as each other. And this is Mr Norbury. He writes poetry.' He licked his lips, meeting James's gaze, and James saw that the red wine had turned his tongue black.

'They share rooms,' Soames remarked to Miss Smythe. 'Dreadful place, they've got. Isn't it, Paige?'

'It's not too bad,' said Paige.

'I don't know why you stay,' Bleasdale put in. 'You got your allowance back ages ago. Surely you could find somewhere better?'

Paige shrugged. 'I've hung all the pictures now.'

'You must have got used to the place,' Soames said, 'if it was better than spending Christmas at the Noakeses'. They did ask you, didn't they?'

'Yes,' Paige said. He did not look at James – and James, after a startled moment, stared down at his hands and made an effort to appear caught up in his own thoughts.

Miss Smythe, seeming rather bored, turned to Paige. 'Is that a waltz they're playing?'

It was not a waltz. The tempo, even from the next room, could hardly be mistaken: one-two, one-two, a double iamb, a heartbeat (I am, I am).

All at once he found the room, the atmosphere, intolerable. James stood up so hastily that they all stared at him.

'I'm – not feeling well, I'm afraid,' he said. 'I think it might be better if I make my excuses.'

'Do you need someone to get you a cab?' Paige asked.

'No, thanks. I'll be all right.' He made his retreat as best he could – bowing to Miss Smythe without looking at her, ignoring the others, anxious only to be away.

As he moved through the crowd, he realised that he was being watched by Emily Richter. She was at the door to the drawing-room, ostrich-feather fan unfurled, studying him with interest – which, after so many blank, bored stares, he found rather disquieting. He was almost afraid to approach her to make his apologies.

'Mr Norbury,' she said, 'is it possible that you're leaving? Before supper?'

'I'm afraid so. I'm much obliged to you for inviting me, but I'm afraid I've begun to feel rather ill.'

'Oh dear, I am sorry.' She glanced over his shoulder. 'Where's your friend gone?'

James gestured vaguely towards the room he had just left. 'Waltzing, maybe.'

'He seems to be enjoying himself.'

'Yes. He's good at that.'

She took his hand then, as calmly as if he were a child. 'Be careful.'

'I beg your pardon?'

She frowned, as if puzzled at herself. 'I don't know. I'm sorry. I don't know why I said that. Well, do be careful anyway, Mr Norbury. It's good general advice, I suppose. And come and see me again, soon. Goodbye.'

And she was gone. James wanted desperately to go after her and beg her to tell him what was wrong, to tell him that it was something else she had to warn him about, not what he feared – anything else at all.

He did not hail a cab but walked home, hurrying as if it were possible to outpace himself, heedless of the traffic and the people he passed. His thoughts followed close at his heels – silly-giddy elation and dread and self-contempt. He had been a fool as usual; he had spoiled things. It was terrible and he would be miserably awkward with Paige forever now – and yet strangely he wanted to laugh, he was suddenly wide awake, he wanted to run.

For the space of two streets, he let himself consider what would happen if it were possible for this to end happily. Well, why not – to pretend would hurt no one but himself. For two streets he thought about it, as he had not had the courage or clarity to do before. Imagine, he told himself. Just for now imagine, don't hide or hold back. Think the words that will never pass your lips.

At last he brought his mind to order, reminded himself how things really stood. His energy left him. He felt chilled, wished he had not made the mistake of walking.

Back at home, he found the sitting-room cold and cheerless. The house was quiet. Mrs Morris would certainly be asleep by this time. He took the white rose out of his buttonhole and threw it away, dropped his new kid gloves carelessly onto the table.

He thought of making tea and instead went to the shelf where Paige's brandy lived. There was not a great deal left. James tipped all of it into a glass. He sat by the fire, and sipped his drink, and tried hard to think of nothing at all.

Instead, despising himself, he fell to thinking of his advice manuals. There would be nothing there, of course, to advise one's conduct in a case like this.

He would have liked to go to bed but had not the energy to stand and go to his room and undress. He sat for the better part of an hour without moving.

Then he heard footsteps. The door swung open, and Paige staggered carefully in. James moved – perhaps to stand up, he wasn't quite sure – and knocked his brandy over. It spilled over the hearthrug.

Paige grinned. 'You've done it now. Is that my brandy?'

'Yes,' James said. 'I've finished it,' he added, in case Paige might not have noticed.

He turned his face towards the fire and wished that Paige would go away.

Paige moved closer. 'Well, since you finished my brandy, the least you can do is make me a cup of tea. I'm very thirsty and slightly drunk. Or slightly thirsty and very drunk – anyway, I want some tea.'

'Make it yourself. I'm tired.'

'You do look tired,' Paige said. 'I thought—' He broke off, distracted by something in James's appearance. Before James could quite realise what he was doing, Paige had reached towards him. 'Look.' He plucked something from James's hair. A pale feather. He held it up, like a magician ending a trick. 'How on earth did you—'

'I don't know,' James said. The sudden closeness, the quickness and deftness of his touch, had been almost intolerable. He looked up at Paige, and this was a mistake – because there was clearly something in James's face which should not have been there, and Paige saw everything.

Quietly, Paige said, 'James.'

He could not remember, just then, if Paige had ever said his first name before. He wondered whether Paige would grow cold and distant, or simply flee, disgusted – it would be a relief if he would at least do *something,* for he had not moved, he was still staring, silently, into James's face.

At last Paige leaned over James's chair, so that their eyes were level.

'Look,' James began pointlessly.

'I'm right, aren't I?'

'I—'

'Look at me.' There was a stain at the corner of Paige's mouth, a dark-purple smear of wine. 'James,' he said again, as if it were some kind of charm, and they were nose-to-nose now; he had his hands on both arms of the chair and was leaning precariously forwards, staring into James's eyes.

This will be the end of me, James thought quite distinctly.

Paige's face showed misgiving like a mirror. His hands were very hot, and he was afraid, too, perhaps, though that would make no difference in the end. He moved closer, the uncertainty in his eyes about to overbalance into something else, and James shuddered, as if a bullet or a gold-tipped arrow had finally found its mark. But he did not move away.

Chapter Four

A little while till dawn, and the rain was falling. It did not seem long since they had stumbled – tangled up in each other, the drink snaring their feet like a briar – into James's bedroom, toppled onto the narrow bed. It did not seem long since that one awkward moment when they both hesitated. Outside, a cab went by with a brutally ordinary rattle, and James had hated it.

But Paige had smiled at him, and that was enough at least for a kiss. James had heard himself murmur *Christopher*, a confession in it, a hissed breath and a sigh.

And the look on his face at that. James would never again be able to think of him by any other name.

Christopher, who was never patient, had knelt before James slowly, moved slowly, a smile in his eyes. And James, who never hurried, had hissed *now, now*, clutching with a force which would bruise and mark. He drew back, shocked at himself, and whispered an apology, and Christopher had muttered *no-fine-good—*

It did not seem long ago, any of this, and yet now it was past, and the world was different. James lay without moving, the sheet thrown off, the memories still warm on him, as Christopher's hands and mouth had been. Surely it would be best to lie for ever in the quiet, listening to the rain.

Christopher was stirring. In his sleep he mumbled something unintelligible.

The light was returning, grey and commonplace and out of sympathy with his mood. London mornings were never up to much – not like at Aiskew, where in summer the dawns would come cool and fresh, green and dandelion-gold, the sky untainted blue. It should have been a morning like that.

Already the city outside was stirring itself, preparing for work. Christopher gazed at James with dreamy incomprehension. Then he blinked and looked past him to the window.

'What's the time?' he asked.

'I don't know,' James said.

'No, you never do.'

'It's early, anyway.'

Christopher sat up, shook off the bedclothes, eased out of bed with a sigh. 'We shouldn't have fallen asleep.'

'What do you mean?'

'Look at it. Look at the bed.'

James looked. 'Oh,' he said. They had tried to be careful; they had not been careful enough. The housemaid might assume that James alone was responsible, or she might not. It seemed to him – sensitive, guilty – that he could not bear to chance the risk. 'What shall we do?'

'Take the sheet off,' Christopher said. 'We'll have to put a new one on.'

'I don't know where they keep them.'

'I do. Listen, you take these off, I'll get some more from the linen closet. No one will be up yet.'

'All right.' They were talking in hushed voices. It was as if they had killed someone and now had to dispose of the body.

'Right,' Christopher said. 'Where's your dressing gown?'

'What?'

'Well, I can hardly go out like this.' He gestured towards himself, as if it might have escaped James's notice that he wore nothing but his skin.

'You can't wear my dressing gown,' James said.

'Why not?'

'Why would you be wearing my dressing gown? You'll have to get dressed.'

Christopher, grumbling, complied, dressing with haste. When he was ready he opened the door, went out onto the corridor with exaggerated stealth that made James want to laugh.

Whilst he was gone, James gathered up the clothes he had worn the night before – it seemed too much, too tiring, to find any clean things. His shirt felt clammy and unfriendly against his skin. By the time he was dressed, Christopher had returned, carrying a sheet with him.

'Awful time of it,' he said. 'Nearly came away with a tablecloth by mistake.'

'How did you get the lock open?'

Christopher smiled. He must have been a wicked child, James thought, a thief of sugar lumps and spoonfuls of jam.

'I don't know how to make a bed,' Christopher said.

'Neither do I.'

'In that case, this ought to be amusing.'

James had not lit the gas, in case the light should show under the door, and so they worked in semi-darkness. The final result was not as tidy as might be desired, but it would pass muster.

'Well, I'd better go back,' Christopher said, when they were finished.

'Yes.'

They were standing a little way apart. Christopher said, 'Imagine. If someone found me here.'

They both smiled at that – and then James realised what it would really mean if they were found out. The very walls began to seem thin, the curtains translucent. The daylight world was full of eyes. The morning tasted bitter – his mouth was dry and foul from the wine of last night.

Outside, the rain had stopped. James wanted to ask him what they ought to do but could not bring himself to speak.

'Mrs Morris visits her sister sometimes, you know,' Christopher said after a pause. 'She stays overnight. So . . . we could manage again. If you wanted.'

'Yes.'

'Good.' He looked towards the door – was someone climbing the stairs? – then back at James. 'That's settled, then.'

'Yes,' he said again. 'Good. Thank you.'

'Thank you?' Christopher imitated, eyebrows raised.

'I didn't – I don't know why I said that. Stop laughing.'

The fear was receding a little way. Things might be all right. If one was careful, there was no need for anything unfortunate to occur.

Christopher went to the door. 'Good night,' he said.

'Good night. Morning.'

James thought Christopher might say something else, but instead he simply nodded and went out, as quietly as if he had been born to subterfuge.

It seemed best to open the window. The noise of the street outside was unpleasantly loud. James sat down on the new-made bed, quite abruptly tired. He ought not to fall asleep. Things must be thought over; the future would be complicated and perhaps frightening, and this present moment should be preserved for as long as possible – he should stay here, now, for as long as he could.

It was no use. His head felt thick and at the same time empty; his eyes were blurring with fatigue.

Downstairs, there were heavy footsteps and a grumble of voices – someone was having a dispute with the milkman. The day had begun.

• • •

It was strange, James would think afterwards, how much of the happy time was spent enjoying past unhappiness. It was his delight to discover his old troubles, his hidden misgivings, the thoughts he had forbidden himself before.

In those first weeks, the secrecy seemed almost comic, making them players in a private farce. When Margoyle called (to tell them of his engagement and how well he was doing at the Foreign Office), Christopher had nearly reduced James to laughter with one look and one seemingly innocent remark. But then Margoyle left and they were alone in the sitting-room, the maid dusting James's bedroom next door, and at once it had not been at all amusing. If one was hungry or tired, one could eat or sleep unchallenged. To be close to Christopher, in the same room, and not to touch – this was privation.

Sometimes they would walk together. James was fond of Kensington Gardens, and the green expanse was a relief from being indoors, from sitting and staring at each other across an impassable yard of carpet. They had tried to go on as normal, but it was difficult at times. Conversation would fade into silence, and James would have to get up and pace about, tormented by a waiting that might never end.

On one of these walks, James asked, in spite of himself, 'Do you think we could manage again – soon?'

'No.' It was strange to see Christopher cautious. 'But she's going to see her sister next month. I suppose you can wait that long?'

James said nothing. His attention had been caught by a lady and gentleman walking ahead on the path – not a well-dressed or handsome pair, there was nothing to distinguish them from any other pedestrians but the way they looked at each other. They had an everyday tenderness that anyone might see.

James and Christopher went home shortly afterwards: back to the small sitting-room and the fire. Later, as evening became night and the house grew quiet, Christopher edged his chair closer to

James's and muttered his idea of how they should spend the nights of Mrs Morris's impending absence.

When Christopher had exhausted his imagination, James said, 'Look, everyone's asleep, we could—'

'No,' Christopher cut him off, immediately serious again.

'Well, it's not really fair, then, to talk like that,' James said. 'You make it worse.'

Christopher sighed out smoke, a grey colour like regret. He said nothing more.

This was how they managed: infinite care and patience, secrecy which ceased to be a comic novelty, which began to feel unnatural. James thought Christopher might tire of it all, but he did not. In September Mrs Morris went to see her sister for a week, and the days passed quickly.

• • •

They were to Christmas apart. Christopher had received a letter from his mother – he could hardly ignore the invitation. James, meanwhile, knew that he ought to be in Yorkshire. It had been more than a year since he had last been back. He had put off the visit for far too long.

His stay proved pleasant enough. He enjoyed spending quiet afternoons with Charlotte in front of the fire, reading or writing. When the weather was tolerable, they went for walks through the grounds, out into the fields, stepping gingerly through grass that threatened to turn to marsh. Once they went looking for the stone statues hidden amongst the rhododendrons, but the trees had grown up and the grass was even wilder than it had been when they were children, and they could not find them again.

Christopher wrote to him twice – wonderful profane letters too dangerous to be kept. Christopher had printed EAT THIS LETTER at the bottom of each missive, but instead James burned them secretly, guiltily.

During his stay he discovered that Mrs Chickering's health was growing worse. Charlotte's duties as nurse were absorbing more time than he had realised. The professional nurse had left, and another had not yet been found. Charlotte did not complain, though she looked more tired than he remembered her. They had less opportunity to talk than he had hoped, and when they did have a chance to speak away from Mrs Chickering, he found that a restraint had grown up between them.

He left with regret and relief in early January. Returning to London felt like a homecoming. But Christopher was away for longer than expected. After Christmas he had been obliged to visit several other people, he wrote – friends who couldn't be neglected any longer. It was almost the end of the month before he was back in London again, arriving with a great slam of the front door that startled everyone in the house.

He was full of amusing tales of his family, in whom Christmas apparently brought out the worst. When he had finished his account of his time away, he asked James, 'Did you enjoy yourself?'

'Oh, yes. It's nice to be back, though.'

They were in the sitting-room. Mrs Morris was on the stairs outside, discussing with the housemaid a stain which had appeared on the top step – was it coffee or not? The women's voices came clearly through the half-open door.

There was any number of things James wanted to say to him, few of which could be uttered with other people close by. He tried to think of something commonplace: 'What's a good name for a wicked but likeable lord? I have Lord Grimshaw, but perhaps that's more sinister than degenerate.'

'It is, rather. How's the play doing?'

'Not so badly.'

Christopher looked towards the door. 'Dinner later?'

But at that moment they were interrupted by Soames and Bleasdale – voices audible even two floors down. They had come to bear Christopher off for an evening's spree in celebration of his return.

'I could put them off,' Christopher muttered, as the approaching footsteps grew louder.

'No, it's all right.' They had agreed long before that it was best not to change their habits in any way likely to excite remark. 'Dinner tomorrow instead. Curry, maybe? At the Criterion?'

'Tomorrow, yes – curry, no,' Christopher said, and James stood up and kissed the top of his head very briefly – what a marvellous thing, to be able to do that – and took himself away before Bleasdale and Soames made their appearance. In his bedroom, he opened a book, and became so absorbed that he did not hear the others leave. Christopher had still not returned at two in the morning, when James decided that he had read enough for one night and went to bed.

He must have been overtired, because he dreamed of eerie, unpleasant things: Christopher and himself embracing closely in a place where they need never be interrupted – a narrow box in the ground. He brushed earth out of Christopher's eyes and mouth, and Christopher smiled at him. In the morning he dismissed these meaningless grotesques for what they were, and did not think of them again.

• • •

Things went on smoothly, pleasantly, peacefully – until a morning in March when James woke feeling unusually out of sorts. He found that he could not write. Act Two failed to cooperate; characters turned mulish and would not speak to him or to each other. At last he retreated to the sofa with the newspaper, which did little to cheer him: the funeral of a man killed in an anarchist explosion, a distasteful divorce case, a ghastly murder.

At about eleven, Christopher finally emerged from his room, in a pristine shirt and a filthy temper. He took up the newspaper without speaking, turning over pages rapidly before stopping to peruse an article in full. 'Have you read this?' he said. 'About the 'Temple Church Horror'?'

'Oh. Yes, I read it.'

James had tried to set aside his old fear of the city. But how often it was proved conclusively that this was not a safe place, that one had to be on one's guard. The man's throat had been ripped out, according to the newspaper. James would rather not think about such things.

But Christopher (who always did enjoy hearing himself speak) began to read the article aloud: '*Either "Jack the Ripper" of Whitechapel has transferred his gruesome attentions to another part of London, or he has found an imitator. Yesterday evening, one of the most atrocious murders ever to be committed within the limits of this city was discovered—*'

'Yes,' James interrupted, 'thank you. I did read it.'

Christopher shrugged, laid down the paper and began to read. After a while, he asked abruptly, 'Are you damned?'

James stared, perplexed. 'Damned what?'

'No. I meant flames and sulphur and the like.'

'Oh.'

It occurred to James to wonder at his own egotism, the way he had accepted – had not even questioned, in fact – the rightness of his own actions. What guilt he had suffered had been from a sense of distance, from the fact that he could not share the secret with Charlotte, who had celebrated every other good thing in his life. Now he had to be careful what he wrote to her, and he found that if one was careful about one thing, one gradually became careful about everything. He had stopped writing as frequently.

'Come on,' Christopher persisted, lighting a cigarette, 'you're not a heathen like me. Surely you know all about souls. Are you damned, or aren't you?'

'I don't think so,' James said slowly.

'And do you believe that because your ideas are very modern and heterodox, or because you think that the rules needn't apply to you, or because you can't bear to think otherwise?'

'All three, I suppose.'

'Don't you feel a hypocrite on Sundays, amongst all the faithful?'

He had never seen Christopher in this mood before; it alarmed him. He did not know how to answer. 'Why are you—'

'You know what they'd think, don't you – what they'd call us. How it'd be. Respectable people are the worst.'

James sat up and turned to look at him properly. 'What is it? Has something happened?'

Christopher held up the letter he had been reading. 'Sorry,' he said. 'Sorry. It's nothing. It's Mother. She's back in London, wants me to go to one of her awful dinners.'

'Well, that's good, isn't it?'

'You should see the letter. She sounds as if she's angry with me for something or other. Always gets extra formal when she's cross.' He shrugged. 'Will you come with me?'

'If you want. If your mother doesn't mind.'

'No – she asked you, too, in fact. Your invitation's probably in the basket. If you don't go, the numbers will be wrong, and then she really will never forgive me. Emmy will be there. I think Mother wanted to cultivate her husband for some charity or other. The rest of them will all be awful, of course. Don't let Eustace talk to you about shooting, whatever you do. He's boring on every subject, but that's his speciality.'

• • •

Mrs Paige's house was in Upper Brook Street, Grosvenor Square. It was very tall and very white, with very sharp-looking black railings. A child walking past would want to run a stick along them – and would probably never dare.

They had been mostly silent on the way over. Christopher had watched the street through the cab window with a tense look, getting his watch out of his pocket every few minutes to glare at it.

'Sorry,' James said at last. They were late, which was his fault. At the door he had had a stroke of inspiration about the play, in the form of a few lines of absolutely necessary badinage – he had wasted several minutes scribbling them down and admiring them.

'It isn't that I mind,' Christopher said, 'but Mother will.'

'You can tell her it was my fault. Surely she won't hold that against you.'

'Well. Look very contrite when she speaks to you. I don't suppose it'll much matter.' He turned to stare through the window again. 'We ought to go away,' he added suddenly.

'Where?'

'I don't know. Somewhere warm. This rain gets on my nerves.' It had been a wet spring so far, a bad beginning to the season.

At the door they were admitted by a tall footman of magnificent gravity, relieved of their coats and hats, and directed upstairs to the drawing-room.

The house was done up in almost unbearable good taste. The place had been utterly purged of vulgarity, papered in soft olive green and burned sienna and subtle gold, Louis Seize chairs arranged carefully against the wall. The well-chosen, well-ordered furnishings were rather overpowering, James thought. One must be on one's mettle, prove oneself sufficiently refined to stand amidst such excellent taste. What would Christopher say to Mrs Chickering's old-fashioned mahogany, the smoky oil paintings in East Lodge? Or the shabby grandeur of the hall?

On the landing, Christopher stopped abruptly – to the evident disapproval of the footman preceding them. Someone was watching them from the stair leading to the upper part of the house – a lady, resting one hand on the bannister, about to descend.

'Lyddy,' Christopher called, a fraction too loud for politeness. 'How are you?'

'You're late, Christopher.'

'So are you.'

As she approached, James saw that she was like Christopher

and yet not like him – darker hair, less handsome, but with the same graceful bearing. She came downstairs rather slowly, one cautious hand on the indigo silk of her dress. She wore neither jewellery nor flowers, and it suited her. Any addition would have detracted from her air of distinction – her paleness, her slender throat, the gleam of her hair. Even the shadows under her eyes made her more interesting. She looked as if she had been sitting up late, thinking on curious things.

Christopher sighed – James had the idea of a disagreeable duty, reluctantly undertaken. The social formula sounded unnatural when he spoke it:

'Mr Norbury, Miss Paige, my sister.'

James bowed, and she regarded him with some interest. 'Good evening, Mr Norbury,' she said.

'I'm very pleased to meet you, Miss Paige.'

'Yes, an equal pleasure. I had wondered about you.'

'Really?'

'To have lived so long with Christopher, you must be an unusually patient man, Mr Norbury.'

She smiled at Christopher – a look of killing sweetness, a look James could not imagine Charlotte ever wearing.

'You haven't missed me, Lyddy?' Christopher said. 'I thought you might have done, a little.'

'I've managed well enough,' Miss Paige replied. 'In fact, I'm rather surprised to see you.'

'Didn't you get Mother to invite me?'

'No, that was Eustace. He insisted, in fact. I think he wants to bring you back into the fold of respectability.' She looked at James again. 'I'm sorry, Mr Norbury. We must seem dreadful. Do you have sisters or brothers yourself?'

'Just one sister,' James said.

'Perhaps you tease her, as Christopher does me.'

'Not really . . . She's older, you see. I'm still slightly in awe of her – I'd be too afraid to tease her.'

'You must be a delightful brother to have.' She glanced at Christopher. 'Sadly, Christopher hasn't been afraid of me for years. Shall we go in?'

Christopher let his sister walk ahead of him, fell into step behind.

'Lydia's a reformer,' he told James. 'I told you about that, didn't I? She sends money to missionaries and educates orphans and donates to the National Vigilance Association and organises charitable bazaars, and when she's not doing that, she's working on me. I think I'm your only failure, aren't I, Lyddy?'

'Perhaps Mr Norbury will have better luck. You've been behaving much better since you began to live together.'

'Well, James is a great succour.'

'Really,' Miss Paige said. She turned to look at James over her shoulder. 'A civilising influence?'

It seemed better, under such circumstances, to say nothing. James attempted a modest smile and hoped this would suffice.

The drawing-room was full when they entered. The first person James saw was Miss Richter (Mrs Hyssops – he was still struggling to get that right). She was sitting near the door, and looked up at James as he came in. Her smile was as open as it had ever been, but her eyes were thoughtful as she looked at him.

'I'm sorry we haven't met before this,' she said. 'I've been so busy. Being married takes up such a great deal of one's time.'

'Where is your husband, anyway?' Christopher asked.

'Oh, he's here. Talking to people, poor thing. I'll have to rescue him in a minute. These social occasions are hard on him.'

'On all of us,' said Christopher.

'Not on me, thank you. I'm very pleased to be here. Lydia, you look especially beautiful. Come and sit with me.' And she drew Miss Paige away to sit beside her – managing it so graciously that there was no possibility of giving offence. Watching them, James saw their faces change – Miss Paige shed her smile like a cloak. Perhaps, away from Christopher and him, the women were relieved of the responsibility of being charming. James sometimes wondered if it was not rather exhausting being a woman. At least Charlotte was spared that sort of thing, living as she did.

It appeared to be a pattern dinner party, and might have come straight out of one of James's etiquette books. At the heart of one knot of guests was a woman whom he recognised from his fleeting sight of her at the theatre last year – Christopher's mother. Her hair was the same dark shade as her daughter's, but it had begun to turn silver. Like Christopher and Miss Paige, she possessed an unstudied elegance – one would have to, living in such a house. Beside her stood a man in his late twenties, whose face gave James a slight shock of recognition: of course, he was Eustace Paige. He was slightly taller than Christopher, a little broader in the shoulders, rather less handsome. His face had a peculiarly blank quality – perhaps, like Mr Hyssops, he found dinner parties a bore. He was as wan as he had been the night that James had seen him at the theatre; his lips were so colourless they barely showed at all. On first sight, his face gave one the disagreeable impression of a cardboard mask.

'Christopher,' Mrs Paige said as they approached her. She did not look especially pleased to see her younger son.

'Mother, this is my friend, James Norbury.'

'Ah, yes.' Mrs Paige held out her hand to James as if she regretted the necessity.

'How do you do,' James said. He felt as if he were speaking a part written with someone else in mind, and speaking it rather badly.

Christopher turned to his brother. 'I hope you're well, Eustace?'

'Quite.'

'He's been working very hard, of late,' Mrs Paige said.

There was a flat note somewhere. James was not sure if he was the cause of the awkwardness or not. It seemed to him that there was something not quite right about the way Christopher was looking at Mrs Paige, the way Mrs Paige watched her elder son.

'Eustace was made MP for Chelmsford last year,' Mrs Paige remarked. 'I suppose Christopher has already told you, Mr Norbury?'

'Ah. Of course,' James replied, though Christopher had never mentioned the fact. 'It must be a great responsibility,' he added – obliged now to continue talking. 'I suppose politics must be tiring at times.'

'I don't find it so,' Eustace Paige said.

'You do look tired, you know,' observed Christopher. 'Rather ill, actually.'

'I am not ill.'

Christopher was frowning. 'Mother, don't you think he looks ill? Eustace, you're shivering. You should go upstairs at once.'

'Don't be ridiculous, Christopher,' Mrs Paige replied. 'If it's cold, we shall have a larger fire. Now, you might make yourself useful and introduce Mr Norbury to Mrs Hyssops – he will be taking her in to dinner in a moment.'

Away from them, James muttered, 'I think they regret inviting me.'

'That wasn't on your account,' Christopher said. They were standing by the fire. Christopher was watching the room behind them in the mirror above the mantelpiece. 'Though what is wrong with Eustace, I can't imagine. He's never so quiet. I think he is ill. Why she won't let him go to bed, I don't know.'

'You're worried?'

'Well, I don't especially want him carried off by some fever or other. Or inflicting it upon the rest of us, come to that.'

'It probably isn't serious. Surely your mother wouldn't let him stay if it were.'

'I suppose so. Look.' He showed James a card edged with green, printed with a tiny green owl. It had been left propped up on the mantelpiece. 'Pretty, isn't it? I ought to get some like this.'

At this moment, the butler announced dinner, and the first guests began to make their way downstairs.

Christopher sighed and put the card back, turned to face the room again. 'Come on, you'd better find Emmy.'

'Who're you taking in?'

'Damn, I forgot to ask. Mother didn't tell me, did she? I'll have to go and find out. Look, Emmy's over there. I'll see you downstairs.'

Emily Richter was waiting for him by the piano. She smiled at James as he approached, which made the whole thing a little easier.

'Dinner?' James asked. This struck him as disagreeably interrogative and abrupt, and he added hastily, 'I mean, may I—'

'Thanks.' She took his arm. 'I'm glad it's you. Are you enjoying yourself?'

'Yes. I've never been here before, you know. It's all very . . . everything's very elegant. And the people, too, of course.'

'Do you like Lydia?'

'Yes, very much.'

'You didn't find her distracted at all?'

'I didn't really observe.'

'Well. I suppose she may be tired. Society's a beast: it sucks the life out of us all until we're nothing but wrecks. And I say this as one who enjoys it.'

James opened his mouth to speak – it seemed a good opportunity to say that he had never met anyone who looked less like a wreck – but by the time he had framed the compliment, she had already spoken again:

'You seem happier since I saw you last,' she said in a low voice, as they entered the dining room.

'Well, I'm writing. . . .'

'Oh, that must be it.'

There was no opportunity to say anything further, for everyone was taking their places at the dining table, and she had turned her attention to removing her gloves.

It was a very smart gathering indeed, and most of the guests seemed to know one another well. Mrs Hyssops was quickly monopolised by the gentleman to her other side – a man with no hair but prodigious eyebrows, whose jokes James considered quite unsuitable for mixed company but who was evidently too important to be ignored. (James was unreasonably disappointed to see her tolerating a boor like anyone else.) Christopher had been placed far from him. The lady on James's left (blonde and befrizzled, dressed in mauve silk trimmed with sealskin) was engrossed in conversation with the man – a Mr Harris – who had brought her down to dinner. He had tucked his napkin into his waistcoat with an expectant air and was now regaling her with horrors from the *Illustrated Police News*.

'. . . found him dead, and the thing was, everything was left in his pockets. Not a thing taken, so it couldn't have been robbery.'

'Oh, that's horrible,' said the lady in the mauve silk. 'Was his throat really—'

'Yes. Quite ripped out.'

She swallowed a mouthful of soup, reached for her sherry glass. 'How shocking. Was there a great quantity of blood, do you think?'

'What blood?' said Mrs Hyssops, from James's other side, the gentleman with the eyebrows having turned his attention to his food. 'Why are you talking about blood?'

'Didn't you hear?' said Harris. 'That murder – the "Temple Church Horror"?'

'Who's been murdered?'

'Chap was a lawyer, I think. Disappeared on Tuesday. They found him outside Temple Church, close by Charing Cross – God knows what he was doing there. Fellow's got connections, which is why they're making such a fuss about it. I should think the police will have their work cut out.'

'I read about the disappearance,' said the mauve silk – rather piqued that her companion was talking across her to Mrs Hyssops, three places down. 'I didn't realise he'd been found. But, then, one reads about so many people disappearing.' Her tone seemed to imply that to vanish was a vulgar act of whimsy, a display of poor taste.

'People do disappear quite frequently in a city this size,' Harris said. 'Mostly of their own volition, I think.'

'Husbands, I shouldn't wonder,' said the gentleman of the eyebrows (who had exhausted his cutlet). 'Can't stand the domestic life any more. Not that I blame them.'

'Well, if Adam ever disappears, I'll know exactly what to think,' Mrs Hyssops said.

'I don't think any man in his senses would run away from *you*, my dear,' said the eyebrows, with horrible gallantry.

They began to talk about something else – someone whose son had recently declared his intention of becoming a missionary, and from there to the influence of the followers of Islam in Africa, the evils of which the gentleman of the eyebrows explained to them all at considerable length.

James sat, unable to eat much more, and made a pretence of reading his menu, as dish succeeded dish. He had an odd sensation, watching the other guests eat – so civilised, and at the same time so barbarous, when one really thought of it. How much they consumed, and so politely, teeth and hands so busy, knives slicing.

It seemed a long time before Mrs Paige nodded very slightly towards the woman sitting on Eustace Paige's right – a woman with vague eyes and a dress which reminded James of fern leaves. She was, it appeared, the most distinguished female present. As she stood up, the other ladies followed suit.

'Gentlemen, we will leave you now,' Mrs Paige said.

General pushing back of chairs and standing up. As James got to his feet, Mrs Hyssops muttered his name softly, nodded towards the door. Of course, he was sitting closest to the exit. Her kindly hint prompted him to open the door to allow the ladies to depart.

As Miss Paige passed him, she looked up and tried to smile. He realised then what he ought to have realised earlier, what he would have noticed if he had not been absorbed in his own nervousness – she was struggling against something. Her face suggested a stern exercise of self-control.

With the departure of the ladies, the conversation speedily became less restrained. The gentleman of the eyebrows was holding forth unchecked, his glass of claret almost empty, whilst further down the table Eustace Paige was watching his brother with a look James could not decipher. After a little while the coffee was brought in, and Christopher stood up – coffee cup in one hand – and moved down the table to James, taking the vacant seat on his right. At the other end of the table, the conversation had turned to politics, and no one was paying them much attention.

'How's your brother?' James asked quietly.

'There's something up with him. And Mother looks awful. But if they aren't going to say anything, there's nothing I can do. I thought they'd dragged me here for a lecture, not to treat me like a bloody stranger all evening.'

'What do you think the matter is?'

'I don't know. Perhaps they've all fallen out with one another, as well as with me.'

Christopher was fond of them all, James realised, fond even of Eustace. He was baffled and irritated – and, beneath this, worried – by the signs of discord. Watching Eustace Paige, the curious immobility in his countenance, James thought that Christopher was right to be concerned; there was indeed something wrong with him. Or wrong about him.

As if to prove the point, at this moment Eustace Paige got to his feet, went to the door, opened it, and stalked upstairs without a word. The men left behind – scarcely done with their coffee and cigarettes – looked at one another in astonishment.

'Shall we go up?' Christopher stood quickly, spoke with polished blandness. 'The ladies must be missing us by this time.'

Upstairs in the drawing-room, tea was being served. Talk was rather subdued. A few of the guests were quite evidently meditating when it would be polite to depart. Only Harris, the man who had recounted the Temple Church story, was talking with any animation – standing at the centre of a group, gesturing theatrically with an empty cup.

Mrs Paige sat in a chair in the corner. Before dinner she had been busy, attending to her guests. Now she seemed to have given up the attempt. Miss Paige had taken over her duties – as James watched, he saw her go from one group to another, smiling determinedly.

'Shall we sit somewhere?' Christopher said. 'I don't want to talk to anyone at the moment.'

'We could go,' James suggested.

'No. I'd better stay and talk to Mother, if I can.'

Emily Richter and her husband were going on to the theatre and had already sent for their carriage. Now they stood to take their leave. With their departure, the conversation began to fail.

It was at this point that Miss Paige suggested some music. When no one objected, she opened the piano, made a graceful apology for her modest talent as a musician, and began to play.

Her eyes were very bright, and James was reminded of the times he had seen Christopher drunk. She played something he recognised – a grave nocturne of Chopin's, clear as a gem, lovely and precise and delicately touched with romance.

Eustace Paige stood by the fireplace. No one had approached him. As Miss Paige played, James saw an expression finally break through her brother's blank look – an expression of intense pain and heartfelt disgust. Miss Paige glanced up from the piano and saw what James had seen. Her closing notes did not sound quite as sure as the rest of the piece.

When Miss Paige was finished, the fern-dress lady took her place at the piano. But no one else seemed willing to follow her, and the guests began to make their farewells. Carriages were ordered, coats and hats were fetched by Mrs Paige's excellent domestics, and the drawing-room started to empty.

Christopher stood up, put his hand in his pocket. 'Damn. I think I've left my cigarette case.'

'You were smoking cigars,' James reminded him.

'Not to begin with.'

'Well, I'll get it, shall I? Then you can talk to your mother.'

In the dining room, he found that the white cloth had been removed, revealing a green felt cover. Christopher's cigarette case was lying on the sideboard. As James reached across and picked it up, he heard the door open.

He turned round to discover Eustace Paige watching him from the doorway.

'That's Christopher's, isn't it?' Absolute politeness combined with absolute want of good humour; his tone was not accusatory, and yet James felt as if he was being suspected of theft.

'He asked me to fetch it,' he said. He tried to appear careless, but could not force his smile in time.

The gas had been turned down after the end of the meal, and the candles had been extinguished. In the dim light, it struck James afresh how empty the man's expression was and how noticeably he shivered, though the room was warm to the point of stuffiness. And his collar—

'You're wounded,' James said, looking at a dark-red mark on the starched white linen.

'Shaving accident,' said Eustace Paige. He did not lie well. Or he did not care whether James believed him or not.

'I think I ought to—'

'Don't come here again.'

'I beg your pardon?'

'You're not to come here again. I don't want my mother and sister associating with men like you.'

'What do you mean?'

'You must think yourselves rather clever, deceiving us all. But I know, Mr Norbury, and I'm telling you now to give it up.'

'I don't understand—'

'It will go very badly for you, otherwise. Must I say it more plainly?'

James stared back at him, too horrified to make any denial.

'I'm surprised that you can look me in the face,' Paige said. 'I'm not sure if that means you're entirely shameless or just utterly stupid. Have you seen a doctor?'

'A doctor?'

'Obviously not. Well, that would be my recommendation. Or they can do clever things with hypnotism these days, I understand. I do know the blame is not entirely yours. Christopher was bound to go to the devil in one way or another. But I won't have creatures like you underfoot, and I won't have Christopher ruining this family's reputation for the sake of his own depraved inclinations.'

'We are *not* depraved.'

'What?' Eustace Paige seemed taken aback. James was no less surprised in himself – he had spoken with the passionate fury of a child, without considering what he said. Now he felt only humiliation to think that he had stooped to defend himself to this man.

Then Paige smiled. This alarmed James more than anything that had gone before.

'You're sick,' he said, 'and you make me sick to look at you. Take yourself off, Mr Norbury. I will give you a week to part company with my brother. That's more than generous, under the circumstances.'

He did not wait for a reply; in another moment James was alone in the dining room again.

On the way home, neither Christopher nor he spoke much – James wasn't sure what Christopher's mother had said to him, but it had done nothing to improve his temper. James sat back in his seat and listened to the rain, which had not stopped all evening.

It was only when they were back in the privacy of their sitting-room that James finally said, 'I spoke with your brother.'

'Tales of the hunt? I'm so sorry.'

James had gone to the desk and was turning over scraps of his manuscript. It was impossible to look at Christopher squarely and tell him what had happened. 'He says that we have a week to separate.'

'James.' All the lightness in Christopher's voice had vanished. 'What did he say?'

James turned around. 'He said if I don't leave you alone, something will happen to me.'

'We'll tell him to go to hell, then.'

James smiled faintly, a little comforted. 'We can hardly do that.'

'He can't prove anything, and if he could, he wouldn't. He wouldn't want the scandal. So unless he's going to have an assassin put strychnine in your tea—'

'What if he told your mother?'

Christopher was still for a moment. 'What do you suggest, then?'

'Perhaps we have to give this up,' James said slowly. As he spoke, the bleakness of the prospect came home to him. He had not considered how things would happen in the months to come; he had not made plans of any sort. Or he had made only one plan, which was to keep things as they were for as long as was possible.

'Do you want to?' Christopher asked.

Suddenly irritated – with Eustace Paige's bullying, with the pure injustice of the situation – James snapped, 'Of course not. Don't be a fool.'

'Well, that's something,' Christopher said. He smiled faintly. 'Shall we have a drink?'

'Didn't you have enough at dinner?'

'No,' Christopher said. 'I've been teetotal all evening. Eustace wanted me to make a fool of myself, I had to disappoint him. And you haven't had enough, either, I suppose. Let's make up for it now.'

But Soames and Bleasdale had visited a few days earlier. They were thorough in their dissipation, one could say that for them, at least: they had consumed everything worth drinking.

Christopher went through the bookcase from Aristophanes to Zola, in case something should have been spared, concealed behind one of the volumes – a regular trick of his. At last he conceded defeat. 'Sorry. There's nothing left.'

'It doesn't matter.'

'I suppose we should go to bed,' Christopher said after a pause. James had never heard him sound so defeated.

'But what are we going to do?'

'We can decide something in the morning.'

He went out, and James heard him go down the hall to his own room. James sat a few minutes longer, listening to the rain, before following suit.

In his bedroom, he undressed as far as his shirt, and when this was done, despite the cold, he sat down on the bed and stared at the carpet, following the dreary red-swirling pattern round and round. He was too tired to move or to prepare himself further for sleep.

Eustace Paige's scorn seemed to have permeated everything, like the smell of smoke. It was as if he had spoken aloud the very worst things that James had feared about himself. There were words for what Christopher and he were, for what they had done. He flinched from it – the coarse yell in the street, the doctor's diagnosis, the judge's edict.

Then the bedroom door was opened softly. It was Christopher, still wearing his overcoat. He did not speak but closed the door behind him and crossed the floor to James's bed, soft as a shadow.

'Can't stay long,' he muttered.

'No,' James said, and stood up to help him off with his coat, all heavy and gleaming with rain.

Chapter Five

The next day was fine enough to go out but too cold and damp for the park. Rather than remain indoors, where they might be overheard, James suggested that they walk to the Natural History Museum.

Inside, they found the museum almost silent; it was too early for the crowds. There was a relief in the size of the place, the cool and the quiet. Within the pretty blue-and-yellow terra-cotta walls, one could breathe more easily.

James paused before a great dark skeleton – a dragonish reptile, strung up with slender wires, arms stretched forwards, mouth ajar. The card at its feet labelled it *Allosaurus fragilis*. Odd and apt, to name such teeth and such brutal fierceness in precise Latin. It was difficult to imagine it ever having had eyes and flesh, muscle and skin.

Christopher had walked on. He was frowning, evidently thinking something through, and James was reluctant to interrupt him. Now that they were free to talk, he did not want to begin.

He lingered near the exhibit which dominated the central hall: the skeleton of a whale, its jaws long and narrow, like a beak set with teeth. Its fins were like clawed and spindly hands.

Christopher turned, came closer, stopping on the other side of the whale. He looked at James through the lattice of bones and said, 'Well, then. What shall we do?'

James glanced around; there was nobody close enough to hear. 'Supposing Eustace did tell your mother something – would she understand? Would she believe him?'

'I don't know. She might not want to believe it. She is fond of me, you know, in her way.' He said this with a note of challenge in his voice, as if he expected James to doubt him. Then he grimaced. 'This is exactly how it was when we were children, you know. Eustace had a knack of finding things out, and then he'd hold whatever I'd done over my head for days.'

'It might be worse this time.' James had not told Christopher the degree to which Eustace had alarmed him. Christopher would think he was being ridiculous.

'Then we keep it quiet,' Christopher said. 'And I'll tell them you wrote a story satirising me and we had a big falling-out and we're never going to speak again.'

'He'll be watching.'

'He's not God Almighty, James. He's always complaining about how he's too busy to hunt any more, he certainly doesn't have enough time to go chasing you all over London. I think we'll manage.'

'Which of us should move?' He tried to speak lightly, to make it sound simple – little more than an inconvenience.

'Since it was my brother who started all the trouble, I suppose it ought to be me.'

It was going to be unpleasant, difficult. James could see it in Christopher's face. They could never be the same again. They would become fearful and furtive, snatching hours here and there. Eventually it might be too much; they might end up parting entirely.

But then Christopher smiled. 'I know what we could do. We could run away.'

'What?'

'We could take a holiday.'

'For how long?'

Christopher shrugged. 'Years, if you want. Somewhere warm, for a very long time. What do you think?'

But there was Christopher's family to think of, there was his social position in London, there was everything. It was out of the question for James to ask him to risk these.

'Are you sure?' he said. 'All of this . . . sneaking around, lying to people. Leaving the country—'

'Doesn't matter,' Christopher replied. 'It really doesn't.' He had turned away from James to examine a massive skull: dark like the other skeletons, a monster with a plated head and tusks and a great jaw like a parrot's beak. 'I want a holiday, anyway.'

'But—'

'You think it's worth it, don't you?'

'Yes.'

'Well, so do I. Let's leave it at that.'

James was unable to keep from smiling. 'All right, then.'

The place was exquisite, really, when one looked about; they might be inside a palace. Though of course this palace of learning belonged not to a king or an emperor but to anyone who sought it out. James stepped closer to look at the parrotlike skull – not sinister, this one, so much as sad. *Triceratops horridus*.

'What about Italy?' he suggested, after a pause, turning back to Christopher.

'Good,' Christopher said. 'Which part?'

'Rome?'

'No, Florence would be better. You'll like the bridges at sunset – you're maudlin like that.'

'Do you speak Italian?'

'I can say all the important things. We'll manage.'

'Well, then,' James said.

He was going to be happy. He would feel things properly later, he thought, when the reality of the situation came home to him. For now he could only manage a timid, tentative sort of gladness, coupled with an irrational feeling they were being watched – though the dry bones had no eyes, the shadows in them seemed to see, and wonder.

Impatient with himself, he began walking again, round to Christopher's side of the skeleton.

'They have some rocks here from Vesuvius,' Christopher said. 'Let's go and find them.'

• • •

Christopher organised the journey with an efficiency that rather surprised James. There was a kind of urgency to the way he arranged hotels and their sea passage and devised lists of things that they would need. Despite James's objections to the extravagance, they would keep the rooms in London. After all, they were not quite certain when they would return.

He knew that he ought to let Charlotte know what they had planned. It was wrong, unkind to delay. Each night he would think of her guiltily, resolve to send the letter the next morning. But the days towards their departure began to run out quickly, and still he put off the duty. At last he decided he would write to her once they had left – he would invite her and Mrs Chickering to visit; surely that would be all right. She would miss him, naturally, but one could write just as easily from Italy as from London, and she would adjust to the change in time and be happy in his happiness.

Meanwhile, he worked on the play. He seemed to gather speed as their time in London ran out, and if he kept going at this pace he would soon be finished. Secretly, when he sat up alone over his work, he had even begun to imagine seeing it staged – no sense thinking of that so early, of course, and yet he could not help envisioning it. (What if it *were* staged one day? It was not absolutely impossible. What if – here his imagination ran away with itself – what if Mr Irving were to stage it at the Lyceum?)

Christopher went out a good deal, most often with Soames and Bleasdale. Hearing them depart at some late hour, James found it difficult to believe that anything could really have changed. How could they possibly be leaving?

When Christopher was at home, they would sometimes spend an evening reading the play through, dividing the roles between them. There was a kind of suppressed hilarity to these performances. They would start laughing at the smallest thing, Christopher would put on silly voices, they would drink wine and brandy indiscriminately, until neither of them could hold the pages steady. It was difficult to keep their voices down. More than once Mrs Morris had knocked at the door, enquiring timorously if everything was all right, was someone unwell?

'It's not bad, though, you know,' Christopher said one evening. They had almost reached the last page of the current manuscript before collapsing into laughter.

'Really?' James had sunk into an armchair, dizzy with drink and quick words. 'You're sure that's not just the wine?'

'No.' Christopher stooped over the armchair, kissed James fleetingly on the side of the mouth. 'Carry on. Get it finished.'

He kept writing. Often he would look up from his work to discover that hours had passed, he had grown hungry and cold, and his right hand was stained with ink and dented where the pen had dug into his finger. The skin roughened there and was like a badge of honour. The play was a quiet happiness to think of idly as he walked or combed his hair or ate breakfast. Perhaps this was the best thing Christopher had done for him, giving him this blissful sense of possibility. He had become the sort of person who could leave the country – leave the country indefinitely – he could write plays, he was the sort of person to whom things happened.

And then, one day, the day before they were to leave London, James wrote:

LORD ABERCROMBIE (Embracing LADY ABERCROMBIE):
And never, from this day forwards, my dear, never again can
you accuse me of a proper want of Charity!

He paused before writing more slowly, in capitals:

THE END

There. This was the good copy done. (He had written it up from his rough version, which was stained with picturesque – and not always accidental – spills of coffee and wine, scrawled all over with corrections.) He shuffled the manuscript pages, hardly able to believe it. Though there was one line he already knew would need removing – a silly witticism he regretted. There were probably others, too, waiting to be brought to light.

Still, it was finished, more or less. He stood, almost knocking over his chair, and went, pages in hand, to find Christopher. He had gone out earlier in the day, but James had heard him return an hour ago.

In his room, Christopher was sitting on his bed, a suitcase open before him. Inside were shirts, folded in tidy squares. Christopher was staring at them, his expression unreadable.

'Christopher,' James said gently.

Christopher started. 'What?'

'The play. I've finished it.'

'Oh. Well done.'

'Are you all right? You look—'

'I'm fine, thank you.'

He looked like his mother. James had forgotten the resemblance. What would they say, in that white house with the black railings, when they found that Christopher had fled?

'Did you go home?' James asked.

'Yes.'

'Was your brother there?'

'No. Just Mother and Lydia. But they were strange.'

'Angry?'

'Not exactly. They won't talk about anything important. I don't know if it's me or something else.'

Eustace Paige would not have told them anything, James thought. But he might have spoken against James; he might have made dark hints about his bad influence – enough to cause a degree of discord.

'Have you told them you're going?' James asked.

'What do you think?'

James took a breath. 'If you'd rather stay, then . . .'

His words failed. Christopher, staring into space, did not seem to hear him. James went out. Back in the sitting-room, he realised he was still holding the play. He set it down carefully on the table and looked at the first page:

To Christopher Paige, my friend.

True and inadequate; simple, as if written by a child. Perhaps it was childish, all of this, this dream of Italy, this hope that he might have everything he wished for.

James decided to go out. He would say goodbye to London, take his old walk down Cromwell Road. Outside in the street, everything seemed very real and very dismal. Passers-by were rude and sharp-elbowed; the sky had clouded over. The city was a contrary creature, never loveable on demand. He turned back before he reached the park.

When he returned it was evening, and inside the house was

pleasantly snug. Mrs Morris nodded to him on the stairs, her expression reproachful, as it had been ever since he had told her that they would be going away. She would miss them both, she had said. The house would be quiet. He thought of making some reference to his departure, saying again how much he regretted leaving – but she was already gone, down the stairs in a soft rustle of black silk.

In the sitting-room, Christopher was sprawled in front of the fire. He looked up when James came in. Something simmered in his expression. His earlier gloom had disappeared.

'Have a drink.' There were two glasses and an opened bottle of wine on the table.

James went to the table. 'Do you want some more?' he asked.

'Yes.' Christopher sat up and watched him pour. 'Bit more,' he said, when James stopped. 'No need to be mean about it.'

'It's my wine,' James said, filling the glass higher. 'I was saving it.'

'Well, this is a good occasion. Our last night in England.'

It was a surprise, James thought, now that they had come to it. All the final tasks were done, and yet he had not really expected the plan to come to anything.

He sat beside Christopher on the rug, passed him a glass. 'Here.'

'So. You finished, then.' He toasted James. 'Congratulations. What did you do with the daughter, in the end?'

'She made a good match,' James replied. 'Youngest son of an earl. Nice fellow, called Winchley. Exactly the sort of person one wants one's sister to marry.'

'You can't have him called Winchley,' Christopher said.

'What would you suggest, then?' James asked, slightly peevish.

'Oh, I don't know. But not Winchley.'

'Fitzroy, then?'

'No.'

'Mason?'

'No.'

'Quincy?'

'No. You're terrible at this sort of thing. I'll have to rechristen all your characters before you send it off anywhere.'

'Send it off?' James repeated. He had never voiced this possibility to anyone.

'Well, now that it's done, you probably ought to. Surely there's someone you can persuade to read it?'

'I don't know anyone in the theatre.'

Christopher appeared to have an idea: 'Oscar Wilde.'

James waited for him to continue, but he remained silent, evidently expecting a response.

'What are you suggesting, exactly?' James asked.

'Send it to Oscar Wilde. It was his play that set you off. Ask him to read it.'

'I don't know Oscar Wilde. Neither do you.'

'I know where he lives.'

'You can't just send plays to people without warning,' James said. 'There are rules about that sort of thing.'

Christopher shrugged. 'Literary types aren't great sticklers for convention. At least, none of the ones I knew at Oxford were. He'll be impressed by your ingenuity.'

'Hardly ingenious, putting a parcel in the post,' James replied. 'Anyway, we're leaving in the morning. And you want me to change all the names.'

He had one last bag to fill. This was his Gladstone, bought new for the trip. He had been superstitious about packing it, for once this was done, everything would be ready.

Christopher ignored his protests, refused to abandon his ridiculous idea: 'It isn't very far from here. We could take a cab—'

James shook his head. 'Leave it. I'm not doing it.'

'Well, have another drink, anyway,' Christopher said. 'And I'll have one, too.'

• • •

Later – two hours, another bottle – they arrived at the decision that the good copy of James's manuscript should be left on Mr Wilde's doorstep like a foundling child.

As they went downstairs, James sent a fleeting apology to his tomorrow self, who would have to face the consequences of the late night and this rash action – and then he followed Christopher into the night.

Outside, to his surprise, it was rather warm. The clouds had disappeared, the night sky was clear, the air was the freshest he had ever experienced in London. He had forgotten that it was spring. He had a scarf around his neck – a hideous yellow-and-green tartan-patterned thing Mrs Chickering had given him. Now, uncomfortable in the mild evening, he took it off and put it in his pocket. He had parcelled the manuscript up in paper and string, and it was a satisfying weight under his arm.

A cab took them some of the way, until both realised that they had forgotten to bring sufficient money to last the entire journey, short though it was. They were deposited unceremoniously on Fulham Road, close by a smart crescent of high white houses, the cabman driving away with a grunt of disapproval.

On the pavement, the world seemed to sway slightly, as if they were walking a ship's deck. James's scarf dropped out of his pocket and Christopher picked it up, refused to return it, draped it round his own neck.

He had a way of making the night city seem like a fairground, a brick-and-stone garden of delights. In his company it made perfect sense to wander London until dawn. They watched the people passing, lingered to hear music drifting out of the windows from a nearby house – a grand ball in progress, a lady disappearing into a carriage, wrapped in a fur-trimmed cloak. Three gentleman went past, packed into a private hansom – friends of Christopher's, it seemed, for they called out to him as they passed. James saw a hand clutching a champagne bottle wave to them as the carriage drove away.

But as they walked further, the streets became quieter. A lady passed them, wearing a grey cloak. James nodded in the woman's direction, 'Is she . . .'

'Bit off her beat if she is,' Christopher muttered.

The frail sisterhood, Mrs Chickering termed such females. When he was much younger, James, confused by the expression, had thought of gingerbread women, currant-eyed and crumbling at the edges.

If the woman thought there was anything untoward about James and Christopher, she made no sign of it – indeed, she looked too tired to think of anything but her own body. Her face, as they passed her, was grim with weariness. James reached into his pocket. With half a crown, she might be able to go somewhere and sleep.

He held out the coin to Christopher, nodded after the retreating woman. 'Will you?'

Christopher, to James's surprise, looked rather awkward. 'Do it yourself.'

'I can't. You'd be much better at that sort of thing.'

'Oh, thank you. But if you're going to be a philanthropist, you should at least do your own spadework.'

'But—' James began, then broke off. The woman had already disappeared, lost to the dark.

They resumed their journey. Neither talked for a time. Somehow the woman had spoiled James's mood.

After a little while, Christopher spoke:

'You realise, of course, that you could have used that half crown for the hansom?'

'Yes,' James said. 'I'd forgotten I had it with me.'

'Too mean to pay your share, that's what it really is.'

They began to argue peaceably about the matter, and after a few more streets, James's good humour was restored.

At last Christopher stopped at the end of a quiet street, looking about him with an air of recognition.

'Here,' he said, with a touch of triumph. 'This is it.'

'What?'

'We're here. Are you still drunk?'

'Aren't you?'

This struck them both as rather funny, and it was difficult not to laugh aloud.

The house itself was red brick, smaller than James had expected. For a moment he stared at the parcelled manuscript, the fragile world he had made out of paper and ink, wrapped in brown paper and tied with string.

'Do you think he'll like it?' he asked.

'Of course,' Christopher said. 'He'll want to stage it and take you on as his literary protégé. And you'll say' – here he raised his voice slightly, took on a tone of polite arrogance – '"Well, Mr Wilde, I suppose you may as well take on the play as not. I think quite well of your work, after all."' He gave a rather unsteady mock bow.

James smiled – then hesitated. That one horrible line. It was still in there. Hurriedly, at the foot of the steps, he began to untie the parcel with clumsy hands.

'What are you doing?' asked Christopher.

'I just want to see—'

'It's fine. Come on.'

James ignored him, extricated the manuscript from its brown paper, and began to leaf through anxiously.

'James, Christopher said. 'It's late. Please hurry up.'

'Yes,' James answered without looking up. He scanned faster. 'It's only—'

Christopher lost patience, grabbed the play away from him. 'It's fine. Now can we—' His hold was not sure enough. The play slipped through his fingers and fell, stray pages flurrying into the street.

Christopher swore loudly. And James called him an idiot, and together they began to chase after the pages. Fortunately, the breeze was not strong; the pages had not blown far.

'I don't suppose you numbered them, did you?' Christopher said, bundling handfuls of paper together.

'No.'

'Ah. Sorry.'

James stooped to collect a single errant page, and then started: he found himself unexpectedly staring at a pair of black shoes. Forgetting the paper, he stood up with an effort. It was still difficult to keep his balance.

He was face-to-face with a young man of about his own age. The man's hair, picked out by the glare of a distant streetlamp, was dark blond, an abrupt contrast to the black of his silk hat. What struck James was how very handsome he was – not in Christopher's easy, graceful style, but with a beauty so self-evident, so concrete, that it was almost heavy. Looking at him, James thought, was like being hit in the face with a gold bar.

The stray page drifted beyond James's reach. The stranger caught it.

'This is yours, I presume?' He studied the page briefly, then held it out to James. 'Excellent work, if I may say so.'

He couldn't possibly have read it, James thought; there wasn't nearly enough light.

'Thank you. Very much,' he said, trying to be gracious and to speak distinctly.

'I'm sure it's quite up to your usual standard,' the stranger added.

'Thank you,' James repeated. It took him a moment to realise there was something wrong with what the man had just said. 'I beg your pardon?'

The stranger did not reply – his gaze fell on Christopher, who had gathered up the remaining pages of the play, and was now watching the stranger curiously.

'Good evening,' Christopher said.

The stranger sighed. 'Sorry,' he said to James, 'I thought you were alone.'

'No,' said Christopher shortly. He turned to James. 'Come on, we ought to be getting back.'

The stranger was smiling wide now. He did not seem to have heard Christopher. To James's astonishment, he took off his hat and gloves, carefully hung the hat on the nearby railings, put the gloves in his pocket.

'What are you—' James began.

Then Christopher yelled something – a warning, he had seen the danger – but it was too late. The stranger had already lunged for James.

James tripped and fell, hit the pavement, smashing his head against stone.

He heard Christopher shout his name. His face, in the uncertain light of the streetlamp, was full of rage. He rushed at the stranger, and James thought dazedly: he's going to kill him.

'No,' the stranger said, sounding bored. 'None of that, thank you.' He gripped Christopher's arm, which was raised to strike, and twisted it back – and he pushed Christopher against the railings, faster than James could have imagined possible.

The stranger forced Christopher's head to one side with as little difficulty as if he were subduing a child. Then his teeth were at his throat. They remained there for a long, awful moment, the two bodies merged in the half-light, and then Christopher's hands, desperately scrabbling about to throw off his attacker, stopped moving. The stranger stepped back, blood on his mouth. Christopher swayed, his eyes wide and surprised, his hands pressed over the wound as if ashamed, as if to hide it from James's gaze. There was blood seeping through his fingers.

He fell like one who had no care left for his body. His eyes were fixed on James, and he might have been about to speak, or might not have really seen him at all.

James tried to scream out – to Christopher, to anyone nearby, for help – but he had no voice left.

For a few seconds none of them moved – not James, still half stunned, not Christopher, lying crumpled up on the pavement, and not the stranger, standing over them both, watching James composedly.

'Sorry,' he said. 'Had to be done.'

James saw in the man's face that he was about to die. There was an odd, edged pleasure to the knowledge, like pressing against the blade of a knife. He turned for the last time to Christopher, sprawled out on the pavement as he had been, a few hours ago, before the fire.

The pages had slipped out of Christopher's grasp. They were caught by the breeze, began to drift away down the street. The stranger shrugged, let the last page of James's play fall, joining the others.

'Sorry,' he said. 'I really am an admirer. But you won't need those now.' He stooped and raised James to his feet, as easily as if James were made of paper. 'Don't worry. This won't take a minute.'

Part Two

He could not wake. Far down in his obscurity, far away from himself, he felt vaguely that it was very cold, and that he was alone.

Chapter Six

The Notebook of Augustus Mould[1]

10th December 1868

I wrote to him. There is no one else whom I can ask, and the case is desperate. No prospect of a new situation at present; my savings will not sustain me for much longer. Sitting awake now, cannot sleep – bad thoughts. I don't know why I write this.

21st December

Still nothing from him. Perhaps he is angry after all – though really he was more to blame than I.

I have been reading over the letter he sent me in September,

---

[1] The notebook has suffered rough treatment. A number of loose sheets of paper are folded between its pages. Marks on the leather binding suggest that it was at one time held shut by a piece of ribbon or an elastic band. This has since been removed, and now stray leaves spill out whenever the covers are opened. Some pages have already been lost.

inviting me to visit them both in Cambridge – to discuss a matter too important to entrust to writing.

It was a beautiful day. I remember it still seemed like summer, the morning felt like a gift. When I imagined Cambridge as a boy, it was always with such a sky.

I had brought Father's ivory-handled umbrella in a silly attempt to impress them. It is handsome but heavy, and I regretted having to carry it about in the warmth.

They showed me over Trinity College – Michael talking a great deal, Edmund listening tolerantly, affectionately, pointing out some curious or lovely detail from time to time. The splendour of the noble buildings almost hurt me.

Then we walked by the river. The water was so still that it made a perfect reflection, each arch of the bridge mirrored into a lovely oval. The breeze just stirred the willows, and from far off one could hear birdsong. I should have been happy there.

Michael broke the silence with some coarse remark about the filthiness of the water – I had succeeded in ignoring the odour until this point. He insisted upon recounting a long, puerile anecdote on the subject, though Edmund tried several times to stop him.

As I always expected, Michael's character has been entirely ruined by dissipation and self-indulgence. He had been threatened with rustication, had exchanged high words with his tutor – told me all this with a touch of pride. Well, his parents always did spoil him dreadfully. He is handsome now and lets his hair grow in gold curls. Of course, he has become quite the lady-killer. During our walk that day, he was forever breaking off conversation to ogle passing females of every degree, bowing and smiling with the most elaborate show of gallantry I ever beheld.

There is a faint likeness between him and Edmund, a similarity of colouring, but only in the eyes do they really resemble each other. Edmund is taller – his face is more angular, more sensitive and intelligent in expression. When I saw him in

Cambridge he was rather tanned; he said that he had been out of doors for much of the summer. He gives one the impression of strength – both of character and of body, a fitness for some worthy endeavour. What his brother is fit for I cannot guess. Certainly nothing requiring silence or steady application – he is never still, never quiet. Forever drumming his fingers, humming under his breath. One never really feels that he hears what one says.

Their mother always favoured Michael, but it was for Edmund that she predicted the great future. I had agreed with her. I had expected him to devote himself to politics – and I thought him destined for an illustrious career.

What rankles even now is how calm he was, how absolutely serious. We had strolled out onto the bridge; the sun was setting over the water, the river turned orange and pink. Michael had wandered a little way down the bank, idly throwing sticks into the water. Then, at last, Edmund said he would tell me why he had summoned me to Cambridge.

'I need you to listen, first of all,' he said, 'and don't judge until you've heard it all. I'll warn you now, it's a strange tale.'

I said that I would listen. And this is what he told me:

A few months earlier, he had become acquainted with a man named Kingstead. He is a little older than Edmund and reputed to be exceedingly rich. Also intelligent, Edmund says – knowledgeable about many things, particularly history. He has been in India, which of course is a sure passport to Edmund's regard. A friendship had quickly grown up between the two of them; Edmund dined at Kingstead's house in London a number of times. On one of these evenings, Kingstead mentioned his club. He was the chairman, he said, and he was eager for Edmund to join. He told Edmund that he showed considerable promise and ability. I suppose his good family and extensive fortune were hardly points against him, either. Edmund was honoured to be nominated, since the organisation is very old and exclusive.

When he had told me all of this, he stopped, apparently unsure of how to continue.

'And which club is it?' I asked, thinking this might throw some light upon the matter.

'The Aegolius,' he replied.

The organisation was not familiar to me. But I do not move in illustrious circles.

'That's a genus of owl, isn't it?' I said.

'Is it?' he answered, rather carelessly. 'I'm sure you're right.'

'You aren't ornithologists, then.'

'No.'

I saw that he was nervous, steeling himself to tell me something important. And so I waited patiently for him to continue.

When I was his tutor, I always believed him capable of greatness. He was so desperate to do good, even as a child. He was in love with earlier times, ages of chivalry, ancient and glorious empires. And he was so famished for stories when we first met. I pillaged Livy and Thucydides and Suetonius to bring him the tales that delighted him – Greeks and Romans, senators and centurions. He wanted to be a hero in those days, as most small boys do. Whenever I have thought – wearily, contemptuously – of the endless dismal mass of humanity, he alone has given me some slight feeling of hope. I had always thought he would grow into a better man than most – a better man than I.

Then that day he began to talk of monsters.

He told me that Kingstead had shown him a remarkable truth: that a man may die, only to revive blessed with marvellous powers, practically immortal. ~~They are~~ ███████ ~~neither dead nor alive.~~

It was the stuff of melodrama and silly poetry and bloated penny dreadfuls – and he was reciting it all as incontrovertible fact. He said it was a gift, which might be used for good. He said that their nature had been misrepresented. He said that the Aegolius was a club for such creatures.

I can't bring myself to set down everything he told me. I

suppose the humour lay in treating the preposterous story with absolute seriousness and observing my incredulous response.

When he finished at last, I did not know what to say. I have never felt such disappointment. I could not square my recollection of him as a lad of thirteen with the fact that he had brought me all that distance for a mere practical joke.

I had considered us friends – foolish though that may be, given the difference in our circumstances. I thought that I had earned some measure of his respect. When I was in his father's employ, he seemed to enjoy our conversations – Lord knows there was little other companionship for him in that house. There is less than ten years' difference in our ages, and he was always so thoughtful and intelligent for one so young. I still remember the kindness he showed me when I was dismissed. He was the only one who took my part; he never believed that the letter was mine. As if I could have devised such coarse slanders. As if I would have written so indiscreetly of my employers.

Far off I thought I heard a bird shriek – a swan, perhaps. The sound was almost human. Apart from this there was silence.

'I thought better of you than this,' I said at last.

'Can't you believe me? You've known me so long, won't you trust me now?'

I did not understand why he would not admit the joke. There was not the trace of a smile on his face, only regret – I could almost say he looked lonely.

'I suppose this was Michael's idea,' I said. 'You used to know better than to go along with his schemes.'

He sighed. 'This was too soon,' he said. 'I'm sorry. I ought to have waited.'

I turned away without speaking, and he caught my arm.

'Look,' he persisted, 'it's all true. You'll see.'

I tried to free myself. But he is stronger than I am now – taller, as well. Time is an odd, cruel thing.

'I shall need your help,' he said. 'I have plans, you see, and you're the only man I know with the brains to assist me. That's why I asked you here today, to prepare you. I wanted to see you once more before—'

'Before what?'

'They call it the Exchange. They say it's not painful.'

I had not thought him such a good actor – he had actually turned pale.

I said, 'Let me go.'

He released my arm. 'You won't help me?'

'Write when you're ready to apologise. Until then I don't want to hear from you.'

With that I turned and left, made my way back to the railway station alone. The considerable expense of my train fare, the loss of time, the inconvenience he had caused me – this was nothing to him. But I was not halfway there before I was sorry for speaking so harshly. I have not heard from him since then.

And yet, reading this over now, I almost regret writing to him at all. I should have waited for an apology.

Besides, the more I consider his behaviour that day, the stranger it seems – it was all most unlike him. He is not like Michael; he was never a cruel child. He was willing to imagine another's experiences, sympathise with his sorrows and joys. He took an interest in my life as no one else had ever done.

Perhaps a plausible trickster has made him the victim of some outrageous fraud. He is wealthy – and his own master, for both his parents are now dead. He would be a likely victim for such an imposition. But then, how could he ever believe such a story? How could anyone?

24th December

Tonight there was a knock downstairs very late. Everyone else – my fellow lodgers and the landlady – was already in bed. Seized by some presentiment, I went to see who it was. He was waiting on the doorstep, snow on his coat and hat. At first he did not speak, and for an instant I did not recognise him.

'Augustus,' he said. He was shivering violently. 'May I come in?'

I was so astonished to see him that I did not consider just then what he would think of my current abode. I have dwelled in worse places in the past, and may do so again – but to Edmund I am sure it would have all looked very dreary.

I led him upstairs in the darkness and did not see him clearly until we were both inside my meagre sitting-room–bedroom, seated before the fire. He crouched close to the blaze, and for minutes he did not speak.

I was ill at ease and did not wish to be the first to break the silence. At length he sat back, letting the glow from the fire fall on his face. He said, 'Well?'

I saw the change then. I did not understand, and yet I saw it.

I said, 'What have you done?'

He laughed – and his laughter was dreadful to me. 'You know what I've done. I told you all about it.'

'Impossible.'

I cannot I am not quite sure how to describe what he did then. He did not move or speak and yet he was there, suddenly, in my thoughts. It was a sensation like a hand placed behind the brow, a cold feeling, an utter trespass – a sickening invasion.

It was only for an instant. Then he let me go. 'It's called the mazement,' he said.

I could no longer doubt him. What he had done was undeniable. My next, horrified thought was that he had come to kill me.

He spoke very gently: 'Don't be afraid. I haven't come here for that. I want your help.'

I said nothing, and my confusion must have been evident in my face.

'Let me show you,' he offered. 'Look what I've seen.'

Then he returned to my mind – and this time he lingered.

I think I cried out in surprise and pain, but he ignored me, and in my own mind he showed me what he had seen: the very worst of this rotten old city. Filth and degradation, vice and misery – as if I had not seen these before. But I saw them now through his thoughts, with his indignation and outrage. He showed me two harlots brawling on the Haymarket, their male companions shouting coarse encouragements. He showed me shivering wanderers sleeping under Waterloo Bridge. He showed a grim brick alley beyond Leadenhall Street, a drunken husband driving his wife out of doors. He showed me thieves, beggars, ugly little street Arabs, starving men sifting refuse for any edible scrap – he had dragged me as far as the Angel at Islington before I quite understood what he was doing.

I tried to drive him out, but I was helpless. When he at last released me, he sat back in his chair, apparently tired by the effort.

'You see?' he demanded.

'That was cruel.' I was shaking, but he seemed not to hear me. 'Edmund,' I said. 'Are you listening? You mustn't – don't do that again.'

'I'm sorry. I didn't mean to hurt you. I just wanted you to understand. You do see, don't you?'

I did not make any reply to this. I was still hurt and bewildered by his sudden assault. He did not say anything, either, but stared into the fire for a little while.

At last he spoke: 'I'm cold. Can you put some more coal on?'

I added nearly all of the coal I had hoarded for the week ahead. The blaze grew so fierce that I could hardly bear to sit close by. Still he shivered.

'Takes a while to get used to – they told me one feels unwell at first. I think I've had the worst of it. Just tired now. Dizzy . . .'

He looked almost <u>faded</u>. The very blue of his eyes was washed out. I could not bear to gaze at him for long.

I have little interest in fiction or folklore, but I am not

absolutely ignorant of these superstitions. I knew what sustenance he required.

'Have you . . .' I began.

He understood me. 'A few hours ago. You needn't look like that, I left him alive.'

'Ah.'

'It's more than he deserved. He was about to do worse. I saved a life.' He wasn't looking at me. 'I could have killed him. The power of it was wonderful. But there are rules. Have to put it in the club book before you do anything else. And it has to be someone who won't be missed.' I confess I thought of myself when he said that. But he continued: 'A criminal, a drunkard, a beggar, a brute – anyone who presents a drain on society. One has to get the club's approval.'

'But are you hungry now?'

'Yes. It nags at me. I'll have to go soon.'

'You mustn't,' I said.

'I'll have to,' he replied. 'It'll get too much, otherwise.'

I might have let him leave, I suppose. But I could not send him out into the snow, to bring harm to himself or to others.

I said, 'If you need it, take it.'

'Are you certain?' He turned quickly to look at me.

'If you can stop when I ask you,' I said hurriedly, to prevent losing my nerve, 'then I see no reason why not. <u>Can</u> you stop?'

'I think so. Yes.'

'And it won't – change me, at all?'

It was gracelessly put, but he saw what I meant. 'No. The Exchange – the transformation – is more complex than that.'

'Then I'll trust you.' (Was I drunk on his presence, on an ecstasy of fear? I might have died, I believe, and yet I have not lived so intensely in all my life as I did in those few minutes.) 'Is the wrist all right?'

'Yes,' he said.

His touch was cold. As he bit down, I think I must have gasped and tried to draw back, but he held me steady – weak as he looked, he was extraordinarily strong. I tried not to pull away, and let him drink his fill.

I do not know how long it took – not long, I think. I remember giddiness and some pain. My blood was on his lips – this sight, more than anything else, made me feel weak and dizzied.

He was oddly expressionless, as if he did not comprehend what he had done. I got out my handkerchief and passed it to him. My wound did not smart, but I did not think of that until later. (Already there is scarcely any mark to show for what happened.) He dried his mouth and thanked me.

I brought him blankets – all the blankets I could find – and built up the fire again and told him to sleep.

I sit in my chair opposite, still dressed and wrapped in my overcoat (it is a <u>bitter</u> night), keeping the fire alight and writing this. It's good to have set it down; I feel steadier.

Clock struck midnight a while ago – Christmas Day now.

26th December

I could not write before. Yesterday morning after he left, I was overtaken by a nervous reaction of some kind, fit of uncontrollable weeping, a strange grief.

On Christmas morning, I woke up shivering, having fallen asleep in spite of myself. I found Edmund awake. He was crouched before the fire – his hands were not warming in front of the blaze but <u>in</u> the blaze, thrust into the hottest part of the fire.

I cried out in alarm, and he turned and held up his hands. 'I don't burn,' he said. 'At least, if I do, it must be very slowly.'

'You're still cold?' I asked.

'All the time. They say one grows used to it.'

For a few minutes I watched him warm his hands – after my

first alarm, I found myself fascinated by the sight. (I wish I had taken notes at the time – must ask him to demonstrate again.)

At last hunger claimed my attention, and I turned my thoughts to breakfast. I did not offer Edmund any food but went to the shelf where the rest of the bread was kept. As I sat down with my meal, he glanced at it with disgust. 'If you're going to have breakfast, I'll leave you,' he said. 'I don't think I'd like to watch you eat just now.' He did not say it to insult me, I know – it was merely an observation, a new discovery about his altered state.

Before he left, he wrote a cheque and gave it to me. The amount made me stare at him in astonishment.

'This is for rent and other expenses,' he said. 'Get all the books you need; find somewhere better to live. When you run out, let me know.'

'Are you proposing to employ me?' I asked.

'Why not? I must know all there is to know, if I am to put this gift to the best use. You would be an enormous help to me.'

'What about the men at the club? Surely they know—'

'They don't go in for scholarship, as a rule. They're not curious. Most of them are content with their situation; they don't care to know the limits of their own strength. And I want to know every-thing.' He was trying to smile. 'Of course, perhaps if you wait long enough, another clerk's position may turn up, but I think you're fitted for something better, don't you?'

I was very weak and tired. I still felt the effects of the bloodletting.

'I don't want to overwhelm you,' he said. 'I do hope you'll accept my offer, though. I am in great need of someone to make a thorough investigation of my new condition.'

'What do you propose to use this knowledge for, when you have it?' I asked. 'Wealth? Position? Influence?'

'No.' He looked disapproving. More than this – I believe he was actually shocked at the suggestion. It went to my heart in a strange way, that quaint idealism. It was so like him; he has always been thus. In the corner of the schoolroom (once the nursery) of his parents' house, I remember a splintering wooden sword, which he would never allow his mother to give away. 'For the good of humanity,' he said. 'Imagine, dozens of men – <u>good</u> men – with abilities like mine. Imagine a society regulated by men with the wisdom of centuries. Think how just and well ordered things could be.' He was still shivering. 'Do you understand?'

I said I would help him, as far as I am able. I think he knew that I would. Certainly he needs assistance. I suppose I still imagine myself responsible for him. Besides, I am curious now. He has not told me half of what there is to know about these creatures. Curious that they know so little about themselves – that it may take an outsider to subject this phenomenon to rigorous scientific enquiry. We shook hands at parting. I feel I have signed a contract of sorts.

Well, it is done. It would be difficult to draw back now, even if I wished to.

11th April 1869

Got back an hour ago but I am still shaking. Overwhelming feeling of nausea and exhaustion – relief, I suppose.

I had been waiting so long for Kingstead to agree to me making an initial visit to the club. Then Edmund called yesterday, announced that permission had at last been granted. This concession is a testament to Kingstead's high opinion of him. In the ordinary way of things, he would not be permitted even to speak to me of the Aegolius's affairs, let alone take me to see the place for myself. Bodes well, I think – suggests that he may be amenable to me making further researches, using the club library.

Naturally I was pleased at Edmund's news – anxious, also. I had been brought to this decisive moment so unexpectedly, there was little time to prepare.

The club's address is Ormond Yard – a peculiarity, since the front door is situated on Jermyn Street. The club building is so large that it spans the distance between these two streets. I had walked past the club in these last months, of course – very quickly, curious and fearful at the same time. Afterwards I could remember little of the building, only an impression of grey stone, pillars and curtained windows.

The street is very quiet. I could scarcely believe that I was so close to the noise of Piccadilly Circus. (I understand that the club bought the surrounding buildings a while ago, in order to ensure additional peace and privacy.) The building is marked out by a simple sign: a brass plaque with a small engraving of an owl.

At the door, I thought I would not have the courage to proceed any further. I thought that I could not bear to be shut in with so many of them. What might happen to me, helpless and alone with them in that place? It was all I could do not to ask Edmund if I would be safe.

Edmund admitted us. He has a key – a privilege, he told me, afforded to all club members.

'You're not too frightened?' he asked as he opened the door.

'Of course not.' Naturally I <u>was</u> afraid – only a madman would not have quailed at the door to that place – but I could not fail him by turning back. It had taken him so long to obtain permission for the visit. Besides, I think it best not to show weakness – fear or pain – with him, if I can help it.

'That's good,' he said. 'It would be understandable if you were.'

All I could do then was nod, muster my courage, follow him.

He led me into semi-darkness. At first I was blind, turning rapidly this way and that, expecting an attack at any second. But little by little, I could see more clearly:

The windows were screened by heavy drapes, and the only light came from a few candles burning behind peculiar green glass shades – the impression was rather ghastly. The other thing that struck me was the quiet. It is absolute, oppressive. (The club men dislike loud noises.) It makes it easy to imagine hidden listeners.

I could see no trace of uncleanness, and yet there was a faint smell of dust and aged fabric. Somehow it does not feel wholesome in there. I suppose they do not air the place. I do not know if the windows can even be opened.

It is a vast building in the Italian Renaissance style. (Mem. ask Edmund for account of building's history.) One is admitted first of all to the atrium, paved in black and white, a great space which rises almost to the top floor. The effect is like standing in a roofed courtyard. There is no furniture save a round mahogany table, polished to an uncanny sheen, bearing a green glass bowl of cards.

'Here,' Edmund said, and he took two cards and gave them to me. 'Keep one with you, and leave one out on the mantelpiece at home. In a place where visitors will see it.'

'What do the cards signify?'

'Protection. Or a prior claim.'

'I see.' I think that was my worst point. The reality of my situation came home to me in the most unpleasant fashion. Edmund must have heard the tremble in my voice, the shudder of my breath.

'Ah,' he said. 'Here's Treadwell.'

I started – a man had approached without my noticing, emerging from some dim corridor beyond the atrium, moving very softly.

He addressed Edmund with an air of gracious deference: 'Good evening, Mr Bier.'

'Good evening, Treadwell. You were expecting my visitor, I think?'

'Yes, sir.'

Treadwell is the club servant. Edmund had mentioned him before – he is not one of the club men proper, but he shares their unusual nature. He is far older than he appears, and no one could tell how long he had been in the club's employ. He is deemed indispensable, and they all hold him in the very highest esteem.

In his appearance he is neat, pristine, everything suitable. He might be any age between forty and sixty. His face is singularly lacking in colour and expression – puts one in mind of an empty plate.

'This is Mr Mould,' Edmund said. 'He'll be coming to the club regularly in the future.'

'Indeed, sir. And will he have full run of the premises?'

'He'll chiefly be in the attic. I'll accompany him if he goes anywhere else. And he's to be left alone. I've already told everybody, but you'll remind anyone you see, won't you? Maylie and some of the others can be a little forgetful on these points.'

'Certainly, sir.' As Treadwell spoke, he watched me. Such unnaturally fixed scrutiny. One could be driven frantic under such a stare.

'Thank you,' I said.

I ought to have remained silent. Edmund had warned me not to talk at first, to give them the opportunity to grow accustomed to my presence. I knew I was making a grievous error before I even finished speaking.

Treadwell – he did not frown or look angry or anything like that. It was worse. There was nothing in his face, but I felt that he was . . . gathering himself somehow. I had offended him; I had transgressed.

He came closer, and in spite of myself I stepped backwards. I had a craven thought of running for the door. (As if this would have profited me anything, had he decided to attack.)

'Thank you, Treadwell,' Edmund said very firmly.

Treadwell made no reply but, to my fervent relief, merely bowed and went away. I was too relieved even to apologise to Edmund for my blunder. He made no comment on what had occurred but instead took me to look at the library.

Here I lost my fears. I have never seen a place like it – books upon books, many centuries' wealth of knowledge. Like the rest of the building, it is lavishly decorated – walls faced with marble, scagliola. The ceiling is gilded. Above the fireplace is an exquisitely detailed map of the world, with 'the Empire upon which the Sun never Sets' coloured in red. Edmund said that a fire is always kept burning – the club men cannot abide the cold. The books are diverse in subject matter and include a number of rare and precious volumes. But they are not kept in good order – I shall find it difficult to locate particular titles, I fear. There is no catalogue; most club members take little interest in reading on the whole – this is in part why Edmund requires my help. I cannot understand their attitude: they have such a luxury of time. If I had their advantages, I would spend my days mastering every science known to man. I should read <u>everything</u>.

After I had seen the library, Edmund led me upstairs (he went ahead of me with a lamp – in spite of the candles, it was difficult for me to see my way).

My room is to be at the very top of the building, in the attic. Always quiet there, Edmund says, no one to disturb me. There are three other rooms not in use; I may take possession of any of these if I should need to later on. I should like to see to the door at the end of the corridor – some modifications of the lock. (Silver?)

I found that everything had been prepared just as I requested – the shelves, space for instruments &c, tray of sawdust, two desks. Most impressive is the operating table (special order – a deal construction would be useless here). The natural light is good – I do regret that there is no gas, however. There is no sink, either – and the club is not likely to make such an alteration for my convenience. Treadwell will bring up all the water I require, Edmund says. I suppose this will have to do.

Unfortunately, there has been a stipulation about my using the room: I shall have a companion. The club men are a little suspicious of my sort, and so one of their number is to observe my researches and assist me. His name is Verner, and he was a scientist, before his Exchange.

He is short, lean, redheaded, dull-eyed. There is an ugly sore in the corner of his mouth. I suppose it must have been there at the time of his Exchange and never healed afterwards. He picked at it incessantly as we talked. He has a thin, high voice, speaks as if someone were pinching his nose – most unpleasant to listen to for very long.

To begin with, he and Edmund spoke together and I listened in silence. After my mistake with Treadwell, I was determined to make no further blunders.

Verner had not Treadwell's disconcerting steady gaze. But I had the uncanny feeling that when he looked in my direction he saw only . . . mere sustenance, a matter of pints. Nothing more.

We have made a bad beginning. Verner is angry that I insisted we work in daylight. He is less alert then, though indoors he suffers no serious discomfort.

Edmund will be present at our sessions, at least at first. I am grateful he agreed to this. I do not think I could bear to be alone with Verner just yet.

But he understands our work, at least, and the path we must follow. We are to start with a thorough exploration of their physical limits – these have never been adequately defined, and the sources contradict one another. First we complete the reading. Then practical experiments.

[Several pages have been torn out of the notebook here]

I have been drawing maps of the place (at least the rooms I saw), in an effort to make sense of the building. Cannot quite manage a clear plan.

On the first and second floors there are wide landings – they call them the lower and upper galleries – running all four sides of the atrium. One can look down over the stone bannister and just make out the black and white tiles of the atrium below. From the galleries there are doors leading off into various rooms – library, smoking room, coffee room, cardroom, many others – and corridors leading off the open square of the atrium. I think it is here that I became lost. I will have to pay closer attention next time.

Still shaking. Chilled and weak, also – I feel capable of nothing else tonight. It has been a struggle writing this legibly.

I will get nowhere if I cannot throw off this fear of them. Must proceed with researches as speedily as possible – knowledge is best antidote. For my own sake and for Edmund's, I must know all about them.

Important object – vivisection (if term is strictly accurate here). Must arrange with Edmund as soon as possible.

Lock for door?
Candles
Lamps
Photographic equipment
Books (give list to E.)
Silver
Smelling salts
Garlic
Knives

———

Somewhere far off, someone was running. James could hear footsteps pelting desperately against wood – then a cry, a fall. A voice called something James could not make out. Then someone was dragged upstairs – a door was opened close by, slammed shut. A man said, '—but you can do as you please, of course.' Then nothing more.

———

Chapter Seven

The Notebook of Augustus Mould

1st August 1869

To the club again. I have seen more of the club men. Edmund introduced two whose names are already familiar to me from my study of the club book – Mr Spurgeon Corvish and Mr Harry Maylie. Corvish is middle-aged, thin, with a sallow complexion; he hails from the north, I believe. He dresses chiefly in black – nothing shines about him. Does that make sense? Difficult to convey the flat drabness he presents – light leaves him respectfully alone. But he seems a sensible man. Maylie I liked less. He is younger, redheaded, underwent the Exchange only two years ago. He is fashionable but showy – the sort of man who wears too many rings. He was loud-spoken, facetiously polite to me.

It is getting easier to be amongst them. I have not seen Kingstead yet. From what Edmund says, I suspect he would consider an interview with me to be beneath his dignity.

I have noticed that the men most frequently at the club are of an older generation. One can see a certain oddity in their attire

– high-ended collars, gaudy waistcoats, and old-fashioned dress coats, the occasional show of breeches and boots. One fellow – who never leaves the club at all, as far as I can tell, but spends most of his days in the smoking room – is never seen without his 'Cossack' trousers. Taken together, these gentlemen give one the impression of stepping back in time a few decades, or further still.

Edmund tells me that club men of this ilk find the modern city increasingly strange and irksome and prefer to remain in the club for days on end, leaving only to feed. Though they have the initial appearance of men in the prime of life, on closer inspection there is a peculiar, dusty look to them. They are very quiet; their skin looks faded, like old cloth. One of them is a great landowner in Ireland, a man once notorious for his severity towards his tenants – now he scarcely speaks, and his heirs (and their heirs) administer the estate. Another was pointed out to me as a clergyman whose parish vanished under the sea fifty years ago. He still receives his stipend and has nothing to do now but sit in the library and stare at the fire. Even more than the other club men, this group is preoccupied by money. I suppose if one is to live for ever, one's income is of the utmost importance. They regard Edmund's attempts at improvement with little interest. Some of the younger members call them the 'owlmen' – a mockery originating in that old owl myth, I presume.

Re. Sabbatarians

'The Σαββατιανοὶ, or Sabbatarians, are the creatures' human enemies. The name originates from the belief that those born on a Saturday were gifted with the ability to detect and destroy the un-dead. Also perhaps from the myth that the creature was restricted to his coffin on a Saturday, making this day auspicious for hunting him.'

G. Uske – <u>Truths of Superstition</u>

Research further – any such people currently in operation in England?

9th September 1869

I am learning photography. Edmund has purchased the necessary equipment for me; he agrees that it will be useful to have photographic records. I have requested a darkroom be prepared in the club (the room next door to my 'studio' would be ideal). I am enjoying the study, I find – there is a careful deliberation to the process which I appreciate. One needs steady hands, particularly when dealing with chemicals. I have already acquired an ugly black stain on one hand, through incautious use of the nitrate of silver.

Elsewhere, my researches continue well enough. I am not a scientist by training, of course, but I am learning quickly. It is curious – my knowledge is inferior to Verner's, and yet he achieves far less than I do. His presence grows more and more tiresome. Whilst we work, he drinks tea incessantly to stave off his hunger for blood. (The warmth of this beverage makes it popular amongst his kind.)

We work alone; Edmund is rarely in attendance now. I am less fearful than before, but it is still not comfortable. I can never apply myself entirely to a task – always I am listening, anxious that Verner may make some attack.

Sometimes he will have rats brought upstairs (Treadwell obligingly traps these for him) and then amuses himself by playing with and eating the vermin, though he and I both know that they will disagree with him. I think it fair to say he is no gentleman and, I hope, atypical of the general run of club men.

Even when he is not engaged in such unsavoury pursuits, there is little intellectual curiosity in him, and he has an exasperating habit of seizing upon some theory or other and then refusing to alter it in the face of any new facts we may unearth. He is especially strict on the matter of the observances. These are those special weaknesses to which the creatures are supposedly subject (I do not have a complete list as yet). The real virtue of such defences as garlic, holy symbols, &c must be one of the mysteries I address. Shall get little help from Verner, who will not hear of investigating how far such restrictions may be overcome. (When I proposed an experiment – he should visit a stranger's home and attempt to go inside without an invitation, an alleged impossibility for his kind – he was very angry.)

[Several pages torn out here]

loyalty is all very well, but I am sure this will be a mistake. What earthly use will Michael be to the club? He has just become engaged, too, which will make things awkward for him.

In earlier times, there were cases of club men who transformed their wives, but this practice is now forbidden (perhaps 'till death us do part' becomes too heavy a stipulation, when extended past a century). Naturally female club members have never been admitted.

Michael's fiancée is named Miss Lee. She was at one time engaged to Edmund, I understand. But this is all I know of the matter. I suppose as long as Michael does not damage Edmund's prospects, he can do as he pleases.

Working as fast as I can. Will proceed to practical experiment as soon as ready. There is so much to learn. I do not think any of them are quite sure of the limits of their own strength and recuperative capacity. The thing that worries me the most is obtaining the subject for our experiments. There is one possibility only.

The club men are not the only ones of their kind in London. There also exists a residuum: a disreputable set upon whom the club exert a restraining influence. Edmund tells me that these dubious characters are usually known as the 'Alia'. They have their own particular haunt, a vile street somewhere east of Aldgate. In accordance with an ancient agreement, the club men rarely venture there. Every so often the 'Alia' will become troublesome – will hunt in the club men's streets, or grow too numerous, or be careless in concealing the bodies of their prey – and then the club will take steps to check their excesses.

Removing one or two of them to serve as subjects would be a boon to society, as well as advance Edmund's cause. Study of physical limitations &c will be most enlightening. The only trouble is bringing one back alive.

• • •

[Letter, in Mould's hand, undated, unfinished, and apparently unsent, folded between two pages]

Edmund,
Thank you for your assistance – Treadwell is always far more amenable if the request comes from you. Please could you have him find the following:

Philip Rehrius, De Masticatione Mortuorum
Abbe Alberto Fortis, Viaggio in Dalmazia
Michael Psellus, De Operatione Daemonum
Michael Ranfft, Dissertatio prior historico-critica de masticatione mortuorum in tumulis
Thomas Suttlee, Epistulae (Godwin translation unless copy of original can be found)
Samuel Cooke, The Hidden World
The Life of St Veep
Dom Augustin Calmet, Dissertations sur les apparitions des anges, des démons &c
William of Newburgh, Historia rerum Anglicarum

Flückinger, <u>Visum et repertum</u>
M Toeppen, <u>Aberglauben aus Masuren</u>

[Further lines obscured by blot of ink]

• • •

Owls

But why? Mem. get record of myth, different accounts of story.

20th December 1869

I am not at all surprised. He is foolish enough to do something of this sort. Naturally the girl agreed to the Exchange without a thought. Michael was positively proud of himself, Edmund says – he thought he had found a clever way out of his difficulty. The fact that it was forbidden had apparently escaped his attention.

According to the rules of the club, Michael had to be the one to perform the execution. Edmund came today to tell me all about it. Michael did not quite have the heart for the task, ended in drawing out the girl's death far longer than necessary. In the end Edmund had to intervene, and of course Kingstead did not approve of <u>that</u> (he is strict about the rules). I suppose it is too much to hope that this affair will have taught Michael prudence. Edmund thinks it may have quite the opposite effect. He is resentful and difficult to manage at present.

[Date illegible]

Edmund was here tonight; this is the second time in a month. He seems to have no care for himself at all when he goes on these nighttime adventures; he comes to me blood-stained and white-faced, clothes torn and dirty. Last night he appeared hatless, collar torn off, shirt stained red, a cut across his head.

He insisted on telling me all about it – his measured pursuit, the man's breathless horror, the heat of his blood. I do not know why he thinks I need to know these things.

'Did you kill him?' I asked, when he had finished.

'No,' he said. 'But I stopped him before he could do what he planned. It was worth it all, just to know that.'

'What did he have in mind?'

Edmund told me. He is always <u>surprised</u>, even after all this time. Every revelation of vice and iniquity astonishes and disappoints him.

He says that he cannot help it – the mazement has shown him too much. Once his eyes were opened, he could not stand by and watch men plot violence in their secret hearts and do nothing to prevent it. He has saved more than one life in the past few months.

I think that these night walks bring him relief because it is simple – punish the guilty one, protect the innocent. He finds it a comfort, when other matters become difficult and complex.

One such matter is the problem of Michael. He has been causing further trouble. The club's rules on the disposal of human remains are stringent, and he is careless. He gossips, too – barely holds his tongue about the club &c. Edmund worries that Kingstead will regret his Exchange.

When Edmund was clean and dressed, I made him sit in front of the fire and brought him tea, one cup after another. He always lets himself get chilled when he goes out on these wanderings.

I was almost impatient with him. Every attack he makes carries a risk of discovery. It is not the approved manner of feeding. When a name is written in the club book, the man or woman selected is brought to the club, despatched there safely, discreetly. The system is beautifully managed. There are fifty-two club men (the rules prohibit a larger number), each with his own part of London from which to draw his prey. But Edmund's illicit attacks have necessarily taken place in the streets – where he might be seen at any time, seized upon by the police or even by another Aegolius man.

I asked Edmund if he could not operate through the club's official channels. (For, as I often remind myself, the club feeds only upon the worst of the society. Those selected are invariably deserving of their fate.)

'It's too slow,' he replied. 'And requests may be refused.'

'Then find another way,' I said. 'What about your great plans?'

He shrugged – it was one of those times when I could see the boy he used to be.

'I don't know what to do,' he told me. 'I thought it would happen so easily, you know. Now I have marvellous abilities and no notion of what to do with them.'

I thought it best not to press him any further. Instead, I asked whether Kingstead had responded to his latest proposal.

'In a fashion,' he said. 'He put me off.'

'You know he's not like you. He sees no reason to intervene in the fate of the living. I rather think he despises us.' I hesitated before I added, 'Of course, you may feel the same way eventually.'

'No,' he said – but almost absently, as if the suggestion weighed very little on him. 'He said that they might consider my ideas later, but they're busy just now. The Alia have been indiscreet.'

Some violent transgression, no doubt – an incautious hunt, a body ill concealed. I forbore enquiring into the distasteful particulars.

'If I were in Kingstead's position, I should clear the Alia out of London entirely,' he went on. 'They're a blot on the city. But that's not how he manages things.'

If Edmund were chairman, he could do as he wished, with none of this waiting and pleading. Cannot say as much to him, however – I think he would be shocked. For now we shall have to continue as we are.

16th February 1870

New addition to the club – of a sort. He is a new servant, though reporting chiefly to Edmund. Unusually, he had already undergone the Exchange prior to his admission. His name is Makeweight. He called with Edmund today, though I have always asked Edmund not to bring any other club men to the house.

I think Makeweight might be the worst of any that I have met. Even before the Exchange he must have been an objectionable presence. He is tall, broad – remarkably strong, Edmund says, even amongst his own kind. He looks like a prize-fighter who has contrived to find a gentleman's suit to fit him. When he is in the room, one feels as if there is no free space left, no air.

If he were a mere strong brute, he would be bad enough. But I suspect that he is also cunning, with a sharp eye for weakness.

He said little to me during his visit. But I could see that he did not take my position as Edmund's assistant seriously. I did not like the way he inspected the room, and me—

I am used to contempt from them, of course. They will accept my help, but they will always despise me. I have this from Verner, too. They will not admit that a living man may have intellect equal to their own.

Should not be bitter on this point. Sooner or later, I shall join them. Edmund has promised me this, when the time is right. For now I must remember that I am amongst them on sufferance.

I asked Edmund not to bring Makeweight here again. He said that he would not if his presence upset me. I could see that he thought I was being ridiculous. I am astonished that he would associate himself with such a man.

He said, however, that Kingstead does not care for Makeweight at all. This is no surprise. I wonder if Edmund has something in mind, some use for Makeweight already planned? Surely he would discuss it with me, if so.

Importance of names–

Most appellations appear to displease them; they would prefer not to be discussed at all, I believe. The expression 'un-dead' is often considered distasteful. (I use it privately here, but would never utter it aloud in the club.) 'Revenant' will do at a pinch, though the connotations of burial and return are a little indelicate. I asked Verner what name he preferred. He said that I was considering the question from the wrong angle. 'We don't need words for ourselves,' he said. 'It's the living we're always watching out for.'

'What do you call us, then?' I asked.

He said that there were few names he would care to repeat – the kindest being 'bleaters'. 'Blood bag' is another. A buxom human female, in low circles, might be termed a 'claret jug'. He added that amongst those with better manners, the most wide-spread term for us is 'the Quick'.

Then he smiled – an effort made solely to discompose me. 'Not always quick enough, of course.'

17th August 1871

What I keep thinking of now was how <u>clean</u> Edmund was. He has grown adept. There was a spot of blood on his collar but nothing else, no other sign.

When he arrived at my rooms, I brought him tea as I always do; he told me what had happened.

Simple facts: he was on one of his night walks. He intervened – went too far. I am surprised that it did not happen sooner – it is killing, not wounding, which is in their nature.

I had never seen one of the victims before. Somehow I had expected something gentler. They grow savage at the very end, it seems. ~~The head was almost~~

I concealed my shock. We did what was necessary. The crisis has now passed, and Edmund is safe.

Must tidy things away, make certain that all is clean, in order, no signs left of what he brought here. Cannot stop going to check that everything is tidied away.

[A page is missing here]

Work is the best thing. Ready to begin practical experiment.

Verner will not be any use to me. His presence may alert suspicion, and he is far too likely to kill rather than capture. I will have to obtain specimen myself.

What do I know about the creatures at present?

They are far stronger and faster than ordinary men. They heal speedily from physical injury. If they choose, they can divine one's very thoughts. Holy water, according to most authorities, is poison to them. Subdues – sufficient quantity will kill. They have owl eyes, see best at night. (Mem. investigate these limitations more thoroughly. Some appear irrational, superstitious. They certainly appear to work – e.g., holy water – but why?)

It will have to be done discreetly. Night, a carriage following. A revolver ought to do something, will at least provide a few minutes' grace. Sabbatarians tend to prefer the axe – impractical here, cannot afford to risk permanent damage to the subjects. Also too obtrusive. Holy water, properly administered, would be the thing.

Perhaps – a device of some kind. Worn on the wrist, sharp. Strikes suddenly – acting like hypodermic, but with blade, delivers dose of holy water directly into a vein. One might have one on each wrist, to reduce possibility of mistakes.

25th August

He called today. I had thought perhaps there would be some awkward discussion of our last meeting, but he did not mention it. He carried with him a rosewood chest.

It was my instruments – most of them, anyway. Some tools will have to be especially made. They should be here within the month. For the meantime, I can acquaint myself with the instruments I already have – and practise, I hope, on an ordinary cadaver. I have done my best with an old 'anatomical Venus' of Verner's, but Michael and others are forever coming upstairs to play foolish jokes with it. Last week I opened one of my desk drawers to find a cunning tableau of blood (rat's blood, perhaps) and intestines – a pink-grey tangle of wax viscera. I have asked Edmund to take the model away.

Edmund, meanwhile, is to square the other arrangements with Kingstead. Then our investigations can begin in earnest.

The chest locks with a key – there is only one, Edmund said. Inside, the box is lined in blue silk velvet, and the instruments lie waiting, clean shining blades and smooth ebony handles.

I could not hide my delight. It was all precisely what I had requested. I have never had such a gift before.

'Rather a lot of knives,' Edmund said.

'All necessary, I assure you,' I replied.

He did not smile. He does not smile very much now. But I think he was pleased to see that I was satisfied. He took an instrument at random and held it out to me. 'What's this one for?'

'That is a metacarpal saw.'

He replaced it in the box, took out another instrument, and another, asked me their names. Between us we ended in taking everything out. He showed no sign of weariness as I explained each blade in turn. He said that he has also ordered the post-mortem case I require, as well as the stomach pump, syringes,

&c. Arrangements for regular delivery of holy water have also been made. He has thought of everything. The expense must have been considerable.

As I write this I can see the box from the corner of my eye, all that bright blue and silver. I have no further doubts. I am eager to begin.

5th October

It is not unfortunate as far as I am concerned, only it is unexpected.

The Alia being unacceptably numerous and disorderly of late, Kingstead made a decision to remove a woman named Price, who is their de facto leader. With the assistance of another woman (they call her 'Agnes'), who serves as a sort of lieutenant, she has gained control over Salmon Street. She is acquiring money and property. The club men find this particularly disquieting. I understand that she hunts chiefly about the Cremorne Gardens – has done since the place's fashionable heyday – and is noted for both her nerve and her ruthlessness. Kingstead has decided that her influence must be checked. He says that it is best not to allow the residuum to gather around any single authority – it makes them more difficult to manage.

Makeweight and four others set off to retrieve the woman and bring her back to the club. They planned to waylay her unawares, to be sure of finding her alone.

Eventually Makeweight returned – with Price, but without any of his companions. He looks dreadful – limping and bloodied, with a vicious cut down one side of his face. She must have gone for him with something silver; I could see a gleam of metal in the wound. A blade, I think – it had snapped, and his bone and skin had begun to heal over it. It might be dislodged, I suppose, but only with considerable pain. Since he is strong enough to bear the silver, perhaps he will not trouble to extract it. The injury will give him an additional standing, I believe, amongst his kind.

The others are dead. Verner was amongst them. So perhaps Price has saved my life, or at least preserved me from a grave injury. I felt sure Verner would do me some harm before too long, whatever Edmund might have said.

But it is a heavy loss, as far as numbers are concerned, and there is considerable anger amongst the club men – some of it directed towards Kingstead. Price is a notable fighter, and some believe that Kingstead ought to have sent more men to seize her.

Makeweight said that their struggle lasted for several hours. They had chased her down to the St Katharine docks, and there she hid herself amongst the warehouses, attacked her pursuers one by one until only Makeweight was left.

He said she did not attempt to surprise him but stood in the doorway to one of the warehouses and beckoned. They brawled across barrels of wine and bales of wool and crates of spices. They shattered bottles of perfume, kicked tea into the air. At last they came to the ivory house and fought there till dawn amidst the great rolling elephant tusks. He said it was a sight to see.

Kingstead initially envisaged a quick removal. But now, thanks to Edmund's intervention, they have altered the plan – she is to be delivered to me, as my first subject for experimentation.

No more now – must make ready.

7th October

She seemed so weak that I thought the cuffs would be sufficient.

[The rest of this page is ripped out. A number of subsequent pages are also missing. They appear to have been torn out carelessly, or with much haste].

and of course I am to blame for the escape. If I had only mastered my fear—

I developed the photographs today. She is smiling in all of them.

Continue researches – books. I will write something on them one day; it will stand on a shelf and name them by their right name, and they will see I am not afraid of them.

I will not abandon my experiments, I will be better than this. Must try again. Another subject, soon.

<u>Hansom</u> – Jebb & Co. Ask for Fisher. 1l on departing, 1l on return.

1st February 1872

Success. The worst of it was waiting until he was close enough to strike. I kept my nerve, however. In the end it was quite straightforward. Very satisfactory first use of the wrist blades. Holy water, too, proved most effective.

The subject is at the club, awaiting me. I could experiment now if I was not so feverish; weariness has already passed. I am ready, awake. I will try to rest a little, make myself some cocoa. Later I shall go to work.

3rd February

It is <u>fascinating</u>. To make an incision and see the wound close before your eyes – it is extraordinary. I made the same cut more than twelve times, and each time it closed within a minute or so. Their capacity for pain is a surprise to me. Much to learn.

Their strengths, abilities

- ~~Enhanced physical prowess?~~ Yes. But how much variation? Are males stronger than females, full-grown adults stronger than children? Further investigation required.
- Resistance to injury – ~~from knife wounds?~~ Yes (wounds swiftly healed)
    - ~~from bullets?~~ Yes (wounds swiftly healed)
    - from drowning?
    - ~~from fire?~~ To some extent. Will burn eventually
    - ~~From poison, infection &c?~~ Yes
- Flight? No
- Physical transformation – into bat, owl, wolf, &c?
- ~~Revive from death in moonlight?~~ No
- Immortality – they do not appear to age. Still some vulnerability to accident &c
- The 'mazement' – enter mind of victim, read his thoughts or communicate their own – may also be used to subdue/overpower victim's will. Unless making a deliberate effort to enter victim's mind, they will experience only vague impressions/sensations which may be ignored.

Their weaknesses

'Observances' – some seem insurmountable, some self-imposed, must test (demands caution – they do not like them questioned)
- ~~Sunlight?~~ They are weakened, half blinded, but does not kill
- ~~Holy water?~~ Yes, acts as poison. Test further
- ~~Gold?~~ No
- ~~Silver?~~ Yes, acts as poison. Proximity is bad, wounding worse. Must test further
- ~~Lead?~~ No

- Starvation?
- Electricity?
- ~~Music?~~ Appears to diminish effects of the 'mazement',
causes discomfort
- ~~Bright light, loud noises, pungent smells?~~ Cause discomfort,
possibly confusion
- ~~Running water?~~ No
- ~~Wooden stake?~~ No – injury is not permanent
- ~~Invisible in mirror?~~ No
- Decapitation?
- ~~Dismemberment?~~ Not fatal. No regrowth.
- ~~Removal of organs (heart, brain, stomach, liver, kidneys,
lungs, &c, &c)~~ = Inconclusive
- Unable to enter home of living without invitation? Yes, but
why? They never question this restriction, make no attempt
to challenge – investigate further
- ~~Antipathy to churches &c~~ = they do not seem to believe
proximity weakens, merely hold a dislike for such places.
Antipathy to holy symbols – again not fatal
- Cannot (will not?) transform another/take part in Exchange
with unwilling participant – in order to become one of
them, consent must be explicitly given

[Rough anatomical sketches, and diagrams showing the design of an
unusual box, omitted here]

• • •

16th May 1876

I must mark today – few others would understand my pride. Only
Edmund to sympathise. My pamphlet has been published: 'Upon
the Deleterious Effects of Pungent Odours.' Copy to the library.

I feel that this is the beginning of a long career, I may well attain distinction in this field.

• • •

[Loose page, torn from another notebook]

Addition for Ch. 4? or Ch. 5 beginning?

As some confusion still appears to exist – even amongst those who have undergone the process – about the nature of the Exchange, perhaps it will be best to make the distinction between Exchange and feeding quite clear at this point. When the creature feeds, he draws blood and life from his human subject. The subject may or may not die during this encounter, though it is quite likely that he will. It is sometimes possible for the more adept of the un-dead to feed upon a chosen victim a number of times before the attack proves mortal. With discipline, the period of grace may be expanded to months or years. These uncommon cases occur only when the hunter is skillful, and has a particular wish to delay the death – perhaps for motives of discretion.

Sparing the subject's life *entirely* is a quite different matter – it is seen as risible, almost shameful, amongst most of the un-dead, if a kill can be made without attracting suspicion. One who refrains from killing may well be accused of the vice of anthropo-philia, sometimes known colloquially as philanthropy – unnatural fondness for the living. This rare phenomenon is loathed amongst the un-dead, just as the perversity of necrophilia is abhorred by human beings.

The subject of a simple bite may, after death, evince certain suggestive symptoms – but will have no resilience and will endure only a short while, as the Exchange proper has not taken place.

Records of those dead who appear to have shifted about in their coffins after death may be attributable to this phenomenon.

For the Exchange to be accomplished, the human subject's heart must have stopped beating. Having seen to this, the subject's 'patron' or 'sponsor' (a member of the un-dead willing to initiate and oversee the transformation) must open a vein (no easy matter, since the creatures' wounds heal quickly), and force some of his own blood into the subject's mouth. Convention dictates that for the best chance of a favourable outcome, this must be done within a minute of the cessation of the subject's heartbeat.

Much interest is placed upon the willingness of the subject. Explicit consent must be given for the transformation to take place. As yet, little scientific enquiry has been made into the reasons behind this restriction. It may be that for a human being not sufficiently prepared, the physical and mental toll of the transformation is simply too great – the shock of an unexpected attack, combined with the rigours of the Exchange, may end in killing the subject.

If the patron has managed to introduce his blood into the willing subject's mouth, the Exchange is achieved. To the external observer, the subject will appear to suffer something similar to a cataleptic fit, followed by a period of fever and unconsciousness, which may last from a few hours to several days. The body should be watched closely and kept warm to avoid an onset of rigor mortis or other complications. Even with this care, it may be that the subject does not survive the Exchange, that his nervous system is not able to withstand the strain. If this does not happen, he will gradually awaken to find himself transformed.

Even at this point, he is not entirely out of danger. He is likely to be confused and agitated. It is possible that his reason may be in danger. He will require some days, at least, to adjust fully to his new situation.

———

By small, painful degrees, a sense of his own body returned to him. There was something bound tightly around his throat, and he smelled of blood. He was lying on a bed, limbs flung out care-lessly. He could not feel his feet or hands. He was cold and shivering – this must have been what woke him – and there was a fire burning nearby. He could hear it from across the room but was too weak to move closer to the warmth. His eyes were still closed, and yet the light hurt him.

There were other people in the room, talking.

'. . . know what he's like,' someone was saying crossly, voice full of needly dislike. A man with a careful, genteel accent, like a schoolmaster's. 'You might have thought to watch him, given the mood he was in.'

'I 'ad other things to do,' said a rougher voice, made for heck-ling and street brawling.

'It's the timing that's so awkward. And then to bring him *here*—'

'Well,' the second voice continued, 'there's no 'elping that now. I don't think this one'll live, so it's no matter, anyway.' Someone drew nearer. James smelled blood, beer. 'See. Doesn't look up to much, does 'e?'

'No.'

'You'll get some good out of 'im, though, won't you, all the same?'

The other man said something in reply, and his companion

gave a coarse, mocking laugh, but what they said after that James could not hear – he was slipping back into sleep or fever. A moment later and he was lost, his thoughts had all run away from him.

He felt time pass, hours and days, and yet it was still night, always night. In the darkness he heard a shout and the sound of running feet. Far away something broke; he could hear glass smash against wood. Someone was talking desperately, pleading for something. He was getting no answers, the man speaking, but he was not alone. They were dragging him somewhere – closer, James thought. He was screaming now, whoever he was. A door was opened, then shut, and locked again.

———

Chapter Eight

The Notebook of Augustus Mould

3rd December 1885

I had resolved to give this up. Have not looked at this book for years. There has been little to record. Days and months become uniform in this life, nothing but my research to occupy and interest me. But today it is necessary, I must settle my thoughts somehow.

I still cannot quite believe it – so angry it is difficult to sit still to write. Edmund is as astonished as I am. I should have foreseen this, but to make the change so sudden and absolute – how <u>dare</u> he.

It happened yesterday. Kingstead spoke to Edmund. I was not present (of course – I am growing so weary of hearing his edicts at second hand from Edmund). He has decided that my researches have continued for long enough, that they are unnecessary, expensive, unwise.

He said Edmund could pension me off, if he liked, or put my name in the club book.

I have never seen Edmund so disappointed. I think in spite of the way things have been, he hoped that Kingstead might be won round, he believed that they might combine their efforts and accomplish something worthwhile. For some time now, I have felt that some significant discovery is not far distant – we may begin to question the sources we have collected, to use the knowledge we have accumulated.

'What are we to do now?' he asked, when he had told me all.

'You don't propose giving up, I assume?'

'No. Certainly not.'

We both fell silent; I tried to reflect on what we ought to do next. Edmund could already see the obvious course, I think, but was afraid of taking such a step.

'Is Kingstead still popular amongst the club men?' I asked at last.

'Yes. Not as popular as at one time, perhaps.'

'Removing him would still be difficult, though?'

He does not show surprise easily – he seemed somewhat taken aback, however, to hear it spoken so plainly.

'Difficult, yes,' he said, after some consideration. 'It would cost us a great deal of time and energy. It would be a fierce struggle. But I think it could be done.'

'Well, then, I suppose the question is whether or not you are willing to make the attempt.'

'Of course,' he said. Such a change, once the idea was spoken aloud – his gloom was vanished. He was all decision, energy.

We are to make our plans, then begin to sound out the other club men. We will have to move carefully. If my idea of Kingstead is correct, the victory will not be an easy one.

18th March 1886

The club building has been surrendered to Edmund's party. Minimal damage to upstairs. Of course, I had taken all my instruments &c away. But it is a relief to have my rooms back. The struggle we have had to regain the building makes me wonder how long our endeavour will take. A long-drawn-out campaign seems more likely than ever.

7th June

Money at last – but he sent it by Makeweight. I know he is busy and that the business last week upset everybody, but I still do not see why my salary must be paid in this erratic fashion.

My head aches. Mazement. It <u>hurts</u>, I have told Makeweight again and again, but I don't think any of them really understand how it feels. Sometimes afterwards I find that memories are fainter or vanished completely. I wonder if the creatures could not leech one's very mind and spirit away, if they wanted, feed on the soul as they do on the blood. What kind of fearful strength would they gain from such nourishment?

Makeweight refused to leave until I brought him strong tea with brandy mixed in – a favourite beverage of his, when he cannot get blood. He sat there and stared at me over the china cup – which looked ridiculous in his big, garrotter's hands – and said nothing.

At parting, I thought – briefly – that I was in danger. Of course Makeweight saw my fear.

'What if it was the Exchange?' he said. 'Bier might've sent me for that.'

'He wouldn't.' Edmund and I have an understanding on that point. It will be he who acts as my patron.

Makeweight laughed. I believe he may have the most distressing laugh of any of his ilk. 'You know, 'e might not be going to 'change you at all.'

He always threatens like this – calm, almost genial, at least at the beginning. He will describe horrors as if they were the merest commonplaces.

'Bier might let you die of old age before 'e gets round to it. Or maybe 'change you when you've already gone soft in the brain and you're too weak to walk – just for the joke of it, to watch you crawl about. Might be funny, keeping you in the club for a bit, once you ain't useful no more.'

'You don't know anything about it,' I retorted.

'Maybe not,' he said. 'Or maybe, Gus, you won't ever get what you want. Thought of that?'

I told him to go – and he did go, with one parting gibe, which I ignored.

I am upset, in spite of myself. I read back over these pages and they are tainted by Makeweight – I cannot help reading as if he were there at my shoulder, forever mocking.

[A long tally of figures and dates, names and places, written, crossed out, and rewritten, has been omitted here for the reader's comfort]

9th November 1887

I had always thought it likely that our struggle would not be decisively settled in a matter of weeks or months. But it has now been nearly two years. The waiting and additional danger has been a terrible strain.

But there is some good news: I have another subject – alive this time. This study shall be on the effects of starvation. Definitive results will require no small degree of patience, I suspect. (Mem. ask E. again re. second table?)

Edmund and the others were reluctant at first to turn men of their own class over to me – considered this disgrace unthinkable. Fate suitable only to criminals and the lower orders. But things have soured between the factions since then, and though the violence is regrettable, it has brought me one benefit, at least. There has been little need to hunt for new specimens of late.

9th December 1889

Edmund insisted that Kingstead be hunted down. I don't deny it is more prudent, only Edmund will not give attention to any other matter until he is brought back. I hope he has not yet got out of England. Pursuit overseas would be difficult. (Though not impossible, if there were sufficient incentive.)

[Date and the first few lines of this entry obscured by a dark stain which looks like a burnmark]

afresh how few are left. There are many empty rooms in the club, more than half now left deserted. There are some corridors where only Treadwell walks.

But we are finished, at long last. I am exhausted, thankful. Edmund wants the operation tonight. He is to observe, along with some other favoured guests. I said I hoped I should have enough space to work; Michael said that gleaning knowledge was hardly the point. I wish

2nd January 1890

I am glad to have it over with. Shall not go back to the club for a few days; I feel ill, utterly exhausted.

Kingstead did not speak at all during the operation – which was necessarily a long one; Edmund would not have had it otherwise. He did not make a single noise of pain. Edmund stayed with me and watched. I did not leave the club for four days, slept little during that time. It is all dreamlike now. I remember standing, weary and blood-stained, with aching limbs, holding Kingstead's brain in my hands.

I had never seen Kingstead before that night. Strangest thing of all – I could not believe how absolutely commonplace he looked.

But then, Edmund says an unremarkable countenance is an asset to his kind. Most of them do not like the Quick to pay them too much attention.

One notable exception to this rule is Michael, who still thrives. Perhaps our opponents saw that his removal would be an absolute boon to Edmund's cause. He remains vain as a girl, peevish when he discovers fashions which are unfamiliar to him, and entirely self-regarding. Edmund is forever helping him out of scrapes of one kind or another.

6th January

Still tired but I must write tonight. It was worth all that we have endured, worth the years of struggle, to see him so happy. He was officially elected chairman tonight. Now we can go to work at last, unhindered. First thing is to build up numbers. (This may take some time. Admission to the club is still a slow and circuitous progress. Few applicants prove truly suitable. Club can seek out members – as Edmund was approached – but they must then secure agreement from such possible candidates before proceeding further.) The worst part of this long struggle with Kingstead and his people has been the number of fatalities on both sides. Club's numbers now barely twenty. 'Owlmen' all gone.

[A page is half torn out here. The remainder is scored over with fierce lines of ink, making it quite illegible]

'The laugh of the creature is an unequivocally bad sign. He has no real concept of mirth; instead, his laughter shows a lack of something human. He will laugh and smile only to instil fear in his human victim. In Polidori, we find the description of the fiend whose "stifled, exultant mockery of a laugh, continued in one almost unbroken sound" during an attack; as a description it cannot be bettered.'

G. P. Shadwell and A. Swift – 'Signs of the un-dead'

Yes, accurate enough, though cannot countenance quoting fiction as evidence. I have another pamphlet from the same authors; such eccentric scholarship is typical. Also, their insistence on innate rather than arbitrary power of holy symbols &c &c is quite mistaken, in my view. Must strive to distinguish between insurmountable limitations (inevitable part of creatures' condition) and those which I suspect exist only in the mind – 'psychological,' one might say.

(Might these be overcome? And is such a thing desirable, even if it is possible?)

I do wonder how these men have come to know so much about this subject. It is somehow a comforting thought that there may be those, like myself, who know these things first-hand.

• • •

[Scrap of paper – loose, undated]

I feel Edmund look at me differently – they all regard me differently. We were almost contemporaries, once. Now we are separated further each day. Sooner or later – if he does not spare me – people might mistake us for father and son. I feel myself rotting, and there they are, utterly unchanged. Perhaps they forget that every day diminishes me.

I do not think I even recorded our conversation, cannot now recall the day or the year of it, but early into our work he promised me that it would be done, I would be one of them. Before it was too late.

No use in these musings. I think it is only today – being my birthday – makes me morbid. Next year I shall be fifty.

• • •

6th December 1891

Something out of the ordinary happened today – a pity I cannot share the joke with anyone else.

It was when I made a mistake on one of my hunts for a new subject. I had been seeking the creatures for several hours without any success. At last I became reckless – I ventured further east than I had ever gone before, where the Alia were most likely to be found. The cabman was reluctant to drive far – at length I left the hansom waiting a few streets away and continued my journey on foot. I went armed, of course, and had attired myself as inconspicuously as possible. I was uneasy, aware of the great risk, and yet there was a sort of enjoyment to it, too.

I had strayed beyond Whitechapel, south towards the river – certainly the district presented no very edifying spectacle, particularly at that time of night. But I thought it a good place to obtain a subject, and so I continued my hunt. At length I spied a likely quarry – a man in shabby clothes, with the air of a sailor. It was his pallor that first excited my attention.

I saw him enter a public house and watched him consume an extraordinary quantity of gin with scarcely any apparent effect. (The amount required to intoxicate one of the un-dead is proverbial.)

Convinced that I had perceived his true nature, I followed him down a lonely street, until at last he slowed his pace. I had not been careful about concealing my pursuit – there is no point, when chasing the creatures – and he had noticed me.

He stopped and turned, and I approached him. His expression was hostile. I believe he was hoping for a fight.

'What?' he said. 'What d'you want?'

I had my weapons ready – but was not within two yards of him before I saw my error. He was one of the Quick, and I had wasted my time.

'Excuse me,' I said, somewhat chagrined by my mistake.

'What d'you <u>want</u>?' he repeated – pugnaciously, evidently meaning a challenge.

I saw that whilst he might be accustomed to strong liquor, he was still quite drunk. I doubted he would recall much of our meeting in the morning. I turned away.

He shouted after me – my continued silence appeared to incense him. 'I know you. Know your sort.'

In spite of myself, I stopped and looked back.

'Yes,' he said – steadying himself – his balance was not perfect. 'Yes, you'd better get out of it. Go on. Or I'll smash your face in.'

I turned away again.

Then he shouted, 'You go to hell, you old <u>vampire</u>!'

I was taken aback to hear the word spoken aloud, after all my years of tactful silence and allusion. It had become a blank space, even in my own thoughts. And then to have it hurled after me by that vice-wrecked old inebriate!

I realised that I had actually frightened him – I, who never frightened a soul in my life. As I departed, I heard him yelling still – vile slurred curses – until I was quite out of earshot. I cannot help wondering what he saw in my expression to scare him so.

8th December

Edmund called today. He had not visited for some time; I was pleased to see him.

Sometimes it is difficult to look at him and believe that any time has passed at all since that Christmas Eve when he came to my door.

He accepted tea, and we spoke of Michael (the situation is not good; he has found another 'Miss Lee' to persecute – this is the third), and the difficulties he is still finding in recruiting new members for the club. Then he sat back in his chair and asked me if I was content.

'Certainly,' I said.

'You don't wish for more? The Exchange?'

I do not like to appear impatient for this reward. I know I am more useful to him as I am, at present – none of the club men can assist him as I can. In spite of their superior strength, there are some tasks for which one of the Quick is best suited.

For this reason, I did not allow myself to sound eager: 'Naturally I wish for it. When the time is right.'

He nodded, and I thought for an instant that he was about to do it then and there – and I was suddenly afraid. I had not prepared myself.

Instead, he said, 'It won't be long, you know.' He was friendlier than he has been for quite a while. 'I do appreciate all your work, old fellow.'

I could have done without this last remark – it felt artificial. But I replied, 'You know I'm glad to help you.'

'The Alia have a name for you,' he said. 'Makeweight told me about it – he hears everything. They call you Doctor Knife.'

'Doctor Knife?' I did not know whether or not to be insulted. I have been called many worse things.

'They must have seen you on one of your walks, collecting. With your black bag.'

'Ah,' I said.

'Are you careful when you go out alone?'

'Of course.' I was a little touched that he had considered my safety. 'You know I go prepared. And the hansom follows.'

'Good,' he said.

A picture came into my head then – unbidden – of Edmund himself in the place of my current subject, his blind eyes gleaming with silver. I don't know why this should have come to me. If he saw these unwelcome reflections (he is used to my defences, and he can sometimes reach the edges of my mind without my noticing), then it amused him. At least, something amused him, as far as is now possible.

He left shortly afterwards. Sour mood now and out of tune. Shall take a long walk.

3rd November 1892

Tired and cannot sleep – always the way now – watching the snow fall. I have been wandering up and down my rooms, impatient and restless. If I do not calm myself somehow I will never get any rest tonight. The news will have to keep until tomorrow, anyway; there is no one here to tell.

I made the discovery during my work on Thomas Suttlee's 'Epistulae'. Edmund has at last found me a copy in the original Latin – I have been forced to make do with slipshod translations for too long. The 'Epistulae' date from the thirteenth century, and the work is, I believe, the first written by an Englishman which explores the observances &c in detail. Most later texts draw upon it – and yet there is a regrettable tendency to depend upon unreliable and incompetent translations. I believe this is due chiefly to the creatures themselves, there being so few notable scholars amongst them.

Today, in a crucial passage discussing the conditions of the Exchange, I found that a gross mistranslation had taken place. Amongst other bungles, <u>invitus</u> has been rendered repeatedly as <u>invited</u> instead of <u>unwilling</u>, leading to the misinterpretation of an entire passage.

If I am right, then the stress upon consent during the Exchange is, in fact, utter nonsense. That no one has questioned this before or thought to inspect the original is apt illustration of the club's opposition to change and tiresome dependence on superstition. Even Edmund is not immune to it.

What this means is that anyone, willing or no, may be transformed into one of the un-dead, if the conditions are right, and the proper exchange of blood is carried out. There is no prohibition at all.

14th March 1893

An end to all this deliberation. They have at last settled on a plan – Edmund and Corvish, I mean, with some suggestions from Michael, Maylie, and one or two others who are closest to Edmund. Next they must convince the rest of the club. They have elected to call this new endeavour the Undertaking. The name is not worth quibbling over, I suppose.

20th March

Michael has behaved appallingly. I cannot bring myself to recount the Temple Church affair in detail. Suffice it to say that he has caused no end of trouble and inconvenience through a quite unnecessary attack, which he neglected to conceal from the authorities. This may, most unfairly, prejudice the club against Edmund. The vote on the Undertaking is soon; the timing is very bad.

Things have not gone as well as I could wish for some time now. Edmund's position in the club is not as secure as it might be. Even Corvish – one of the most steadfast in Edmund's cause – has seemed less enthusiastic about the Undertaking of late. They all dislike change.

At least we do not have a large number to convince (they still number only twenty, excluding the two servants and myself). I have worked with Edmund on his speech; I am reasonably confident that it will be well received.

• • •

[Pages pasted into the notebook here. Written in a different hand, additions by Mould in pencil]

Speech for 14th April 1893

Mr Mould's researches have shown that it is, in theory, possible to bestow the Exchange upon an unknowing – or even unwilling – subject. I propose that we begin to test this theory immediately.

Pause for effect here.

There are those amongst you who may ask, why should we risk ourselves by changing the customs of centuries? What practical benefit can this course ~~of action~~ offer?

Too many questions? They are suspicious of rhetoric.

I say that we are threatened, and what I now suggest offers our best means of survival. We are endangered, and this ~~the Undertaking~~ is our route to safety. ~~Our predecessors would never have taken the course that I propose. But this is not the world that they knew; this is not the city they knew.~~

Possibly best not to remind them that this is unprecedented – they will have seen it for themselves.

Our numbers are diminished. ~~Our recent struggle has cost us all dearly~~. If we are to continue, we must increase our membership, and quickly. By omitting the need to persuade prospective members to agree to the Exchange, we can more rapidly grow in strength. We can choose the very highest calibre of initiate. Let us select the very best that our country has to offer; let us take men in the prime of life, blessed with intellect, force, personality, position or wealth – ~~let us give to the most deserving the gifts we enjoy.~~ Let us fill our ranks – even exceed our usual limitation on numbers, if sufficient men are found. It can only strengthen our position.

'Let us share our gifts with the most deserving,' perhaps?

How to accommodate these new additions? I suggest that there are hunting grounds in abundance, if we seek them out. The Alia have lived and thrived in London for too long. We have put them down before but never decisively. Let us recruit new members and use our new strength to eliminate the Alia for ever. We are all aware that their numbers are increasing as steadily as ours have declined. The city harbours a thriving group of the most degraded sort, resentful and brutal, ever on the watch for an opportunity to strike out against us. When they are removed, their hunting places could be given over to new members of the club. Our influence would be unchecked across the city.

There is another reason for what I propose, which is perhaps less obvious: I speak of the Quick. I believe they present a danger to us and to themselves.

Let me be clear: it is their frailty, not their strength, which makes them dangerous. I think it is well known that I underwent my own Exchange with the aim of using my gifts for the benefit of society. I know that some of you disapprove of this aim – what have <u>we</u> to do with the Quick, after all? Surely we do enough – preying, as we do, upon the most depraved amongst the human race. Are we not a natural curb to their vices and iniquities? I confess that after my Exchange, I quickly grew disillusioned with the Quick. I did not, however, abandon my plans for their betterment.

Now ~~I believe~~ I have found a way in which we can influence society for good, whilst also furthering our own interests. We shall be custodians of all that is best in this country and its people. No great man shall be suffered to die or decline into feeble old age; we shall never forfeit the gifts of any man of knowledge or talent. Can you not imagine what a wonderful stockpiling of ability we may achieve – for ourselves and this country, its empire? ~~No talent or wisdom need ever be wasted again.~~

Possibly elaborate practical ways this will benefit the club: e.g., industrial advances, financial profit.

~~I do not wish to preach at you.~~ I know that some of you share my opinions in this matter. I would say to you: whatever your thoughts, the power and influence which these new club men will bring us all ought to be sufficient argument in itself. Who can possibly object to our numbers being swelled, our empty rooms and places filled by such new recruits? ~~I would also say that at this time, and in this matter, the interests of ourselves and the Quick are united.~~

Do not think they will like the idea of united interests – possibly this should be struck out?

It is our way to concentrate upon our own affairs – but I think all of you will have seen that there are changes in motion in this country which may yet threaten us all.

Much has been written on degeneration; many in recent years have voiced their fear that just as man has progressed so he might regress and have warned us that improvement is not inevitable.

One need not read Lankester to see the truth in this. Some say that no people can develop beyond a fixed point of greatness, after which they are fated to decline – some of these believe that the English nation is about to reach this point. One might make comparisons between ourselves and Rome in its last days – men given over to effeminacy, feebleness, self-indulgence, a moral decline.

A short walk through the streets of our capital certainly offers us much to think upon. The city throngs with Jews and Irish. The half-starved and brutalised inhabitants of Spitalfields, the stunted and pallid inmates of the casual ward – do these specimens augur a long future for the nation, for the race? In a time of war, would such creatures last long as soldiers – would they even be permitted to enlist?

Nor need one venture into the worst parts of this city to find cause for concern. A decline is evident everywhere, in the upper as well as the lower reaches of society. In the young, especially, one finds a kind of morbid emotionalism – what is called the <u>fin de siècle</u> frame of mind. Everywhere the 'New' takes hold – we must have New Journalism, New Women, New Remorse, New Drama. Behaviour that would not have been countenanced twenty years ago is now accepted – son defies father, wife declares her independence from her husband.

On a larger scale, our country's influence is not what it was. Our military, our political influence in Europe, our economic and industrial might – these are all under threat. Decades ago, Mr Froude observed: 'English officers tell us that they can scarcely show their faces at a table d'hôte in Germany without danger of affront. English opinion is without weight. English power is ridiculed. Our influence in the councils of Europe is a thing of the past. We are told, half officially, that it is time for us to withdraw altogether from the concerns of the Continent' I do not wish to bore you with politics, gentlemen, so I will only say that Mr Froude was prescient in his fears.

Today our country stands without significant military allies, charged with defending and administering to a vast empire. The men must be found to protect it, and those who are worthy must be preserved at the height of their powers – for their own benefit, and for ours.

Possibly cut Mr Froude – I do not know if many of them will have heard of him. Perhaps a reference to current events instead – e.g., Egypt Question/France (raise possibility that situation may grow more serious), increasing military and economic might of Germany. Perhaps also a reference here to current 'depression' in commerce/ industry. Some of them still landowners, will have suffered from import of cheap American grain imports &c.

I will give you one further example. Not ten years ago, rioters marched on Pall Mall; stones were thrown at this very building, our windows were broken. Can any of you imagine such an insult being offered a century ago? Many of you witnessed the outrage; many more of you will know that there was widespread panic; the police were set to guard Buckingham Palace. A year later, and we saw socialists and Irish in battle with police in the Strand. Can this be our city? Can this be our country? Can we stand by and do nothing when such incidents are allowed to occur?

Yes, the Undertaking will bring to the club a return to strength. It will bring influence, a chance to rid ourselves of our enemies, and financial benefits which are not inconsiderable. But, more than this, it is a chance to make a difference in this country, to draw back from the abyss.

Yes, we may have scant sympathy for the Quick, and up to a certain point their behaviour need not concern us. But I put it to you that this point has been exceeded. It is time to act as guardians to this country, in order to secure its interests, at home and throughout the empire. For our own good we must do this. If we do not intervene now, I do not like to imagine what world we shall be left with before too many decades have passed. I do know that it is not one I should care to inhabit.

• • •

15th April

Voting took place at midnight, following the induction dinner for Mr Howland (American, exceedingly rich, Edmund says – valuable acquisition, especially considering the club's current difficulties in attracting new members). Edmund called later to tell me the verdict.

The night was cold. He forgets his gloves sometimes, and his hands were almost blue. I made him drink some brandy, having nothing hot ready for him. When he was recovered, he told me he had been successful. A test case had been selected.

I congratulated him and asked who the man was to be – I know there had been some debate on the subject. The difficulty is in finding someone worthy of the transformation but not so valuable that his death – in the case of an accident – would be irreparable.

'Have you heard of Edward Drebber?' he asked.

'No.'

'No,' he said, 'I don't believe anyone has. He's an MP, I understand, a rather obscure one. They've settled on him. If only we'd been in time for Mr Owen.'

I agreed that it was a pity the great scientist had died before the Undertaking was well in hand.

'Still, Paige says we can get some good out of Drebber,' Edmund added. Paige is a fresh acquisition (which makes him something of a *rara avis*, new recruits being scarce just at present). He is a conscientious and sensible young man – as well as being decidedly wealthy, and engaged upon a promising political career. Edmund is pleased with him.

'The only snag is that Michael's rather disappointed,' he went on. 'He had his heart set on us getting that playwright.'

'Oh, yes,' I said. I had doubted that Michael would win much favour – the man has some sway with the public, his influence might possibly be useful, but he is scarcely the sort of person Edmund would choose. 'Where is Michael now?' I asked.

Edmund did not answer. Michael has been in one of his very worst moods for some weeks. In these spells he is almost ungovernable, tending to childish spite and deliberate flouting of the club rules.

I asked when Drebber was to undergo the Exchange, and he said that it had not yet been settled. That is like the club – they are slow to take any decisive action. Still, in this case it is best not to be over-hasty. Drebber must be approached gently, to avoid unnecessary shock. The less distressing his Exchange can be made, the easier he will find it to adapt to his transformation. Edmund assures me that once the Exchange is safely managed, Drebber will acclimatise himself to his new life with ease – and gratitude for his new abilities will bind him to the club. I myself am curious to see whether he will react to the Exchange just as Edmund and the other club men did – will fever &c differ in severity, perhaps?

I kept Edmund for a little longer – until he was warmer – and then he had to leave. He was evidently still worried over Michael, who most likely has merely gone off to sulk. He is still in disgrace over the Temple Church affair, would not risk another transgression so soon.

17th April

Edmund has sent me home to rest. Of course it's impossible. Anyway, I shall have to go back soon, to see if there has been any change in our stranger's condition. He is through the worst; I suspect he will wake soon.

I think this must be the worst of Michael's infractions. Extraordinarily ill-timed, too, given our recent difficulties with Mr Howland. Edmund must act decisively if we are to limit the consequences of this catastrophe.

Yesterday morning, I was disturbed before dawn by a knock at the front door. Fortunately I am a light sleeper; I wake easily for these night calls and can slip downstairs before anyone else in the house is disturbed. Usually it is Edmund waiting for me. In this case it was Makeweight. Dressed up to the nines as usual – I do not know why he insists upon attiring himself like a gentleman when he is so clearly nothing of the kind. It galled me to invite him in, as no doubt he was well aware.

'You got to come to the club,' he said. 'Bier says. Quick as possible.'

'Why?' I asked. 'What does he want?'

'It's Michael,' Makeweight said. ''E's done it.'

'What?'

'The Undertaking.'

I did not understand him, but he was insistent that I make haste, so I went upstairs again and

The ceiling was decorated with seashells. He stared upwards, and eventually Christopher returned and told him that he should not look into mirrors for a while. He had been gathering shells, but when James looked, the sea was all gone, and there was nothing but sand and the shells were buttons, mother-of-pearl, like pressed moons, like tiny pale faces.

They will wear mourning, Christopher said. All of them, Eustace included. Incidentally you will probably have to kill him. Tell them not to distress themselves, these things happen, especially in the best-regulated families.

Somewhere a clock was ticking, each click of the second hand a needle-spike to his aching head, and still the night refused to end.

I'm going to die, he told Christopher, as the cold grew worse, and he felt himself sweat and shake, and his voice sounded like the harsh caw of a bird.

No, Christopher said. At least, not entirely.

I can't bear this. And he continued to shiver and could not feel his own hands, and when he looked, the fingertips were white. I can't bear this. I can't bear the cold, not if you are not here.

It will get colder, Christopher said. And I am gone.

Part Three

Chapter Nine

When he next awoke it was another day, another week perhaps. The sunlight was a shriek of pain in his right temple, so that he was forced to hide his head under the covers like a child afraid of the dark and then inch himself back into the world.

Even by these slow degrees, the light was almost intolerable, so dazzling that he could not distinguish much of his surroundings. Though he was heaped with blankets and still in his clothes, the cold remained, and the sounds from the street below were wretchedly loud, as if every passer-by were trampling over his head.

And Christopher was dead. James had wept, perhaps, in the long night; he had a memory of tears spilling into his mouth, sobs shaking him like laughter. Now there was only a dull tiredness. There seemed very little worth thinking of.

There was one thing: a flash-flicker in his brain like a snake's tongue, a livid red thought of making something die.

There were footsteps outside, and in came a butler or steward, some high-ranking domestic with a white bland face.

'Good afternoon,' he said. A well-trained servant, his voice showed as little as his expression. 'I am happy to see you conscious, sir. My name is Treadwell. I have instructions to see to your comfort.' He went over and drew the curtains closed so that the light was gone, and now James could see and think without pain. 'That's better,' he said. 'Shall I bring you some tea, sir? Gentlemen in your circumstances often find it refreshing.'

James opened his mouth – his throat still hurt, as if his voice had been cut out of him whilst he slept. He had no words to ask or demand or reproach or rage at this man. He could only stare.

'A difficult business, of course,' Treadwell said. 'But over now. I shall bring your tea directly.'

Before James could move to sit up or make another effort to speak, the man had gone. He returned shortly, bearing a tray. 'Can you sit up, sir? Here. I shall help you.' His hands were cold. 'Lean on me.'

James managed a question: 'Where is he?'

He wondered if anyone he knew would have recognised the voice as his – rasping, toneless, full of pain. It was as if he were speaking from somewhere underground, every sound dredged up from the depths of the earth.

Treadwell gave no sign of having heard him. 'I will leave the tray here,' he said. He drew up a small table – the only furniture in the room, save the bed and a single chair – and set the tea down upon it. 'Will you be able to reach?'

'Where is he?'

Treadwell seemed confused. 'Who, sir?'

'My friend, the man who was with me.'

'I'm afraid I know nothing of that, sir. I did not bring you here. I have only been ordered to see to your comfort.'

'The man who brought me here – he's a murderer.'

The servant's face did not change, but James sensed his disapproval. 'You are upset, sir,' he said. 'Perhaps you should drink your tea while it's hot.'

There had not been even a flinch at James's accusation – he merely appeared to think James somewhat ill-bred.

'He killed my friend,' James said. His voice was raw, harsh to his own ears, petulant as a child's. 'You have to call someone – police—'

'Please drink, sir. You're still weak.'

He felt sick and wrong, dizzy and unstable. He kept waiting for some adjustment, for things to right themselves, but the sensation only persisted.

'What happened to me?' he asked.

'Drink,' Treadwell said, and passed him the cup. The tea was a small comfort – a brief warmth. 'I shall inform the chairman that you are recovered. I do urge you to finish your tea. It is really the best thing that you can do before feeding.'

There was no use in asking him anything more. James watched him leave in silence.

His clothes were those he had worn when he left Egerton Gardens with Christopher. They had not even troubled to take off his shoes. He felt grimy; his things were creased, dank with sweat.

His fingers were unwieldy, as if he were learning to use another man's hands. Sitting on the edge of the bed, he felt uncertain of the floor beneath him, afraid that he would only fall if he tried to stand.

He heaved himself up, moved carefully, instructed himself from memories. Nothing felt natural now; every gesture had to be premeditated.

On his feet, his first instinct was to run. But he did not have enough strength for it. With difficulty, he picked up his teacup and went to the window to see where he was.

From a cautious glance through the curtain, he saw that the room was high up. He must be at the top of the building. The light still hurt; he could not bear to look for more than an instant. Below he heard cabs, carts, an omnibus go by – and there were people. So many of them, massing, hurrying in different directions. He heard something crack and looked down to see that he had broken his empty teacup – white pieces clattered against the dark wood of the floor. Then he leaned heavily against the wall and was sick.

'Ah. Well, that does sometimes happen.' Treadwell had returned. 'Please, sir, let me . . .' He took James's arm, led him back to the bed. 'I have informed the chairman of your recovery, and he will be up to see you directly.' He went to the door and then stopped, glanced back. 'Oh – and I should not touch that bandage.'

'Bandage?'

'Your throat, sir.' His hand strayed to his own throat, just above his collar. One would not have noticed the dressing there unless one looked carefully. 'It is natural to want to see. Gentlemen are often curious. But it is better if you do not touch.'

'But I don't . . .'

Futile to trouble finishing the sentence. The servant's face showed there was nothing more to be asked. 'I will bring you some water,' he said. He left in silence, returned with a glass of water, departed once again.

Alone, James's first impulse was to examine himself, to see what Treadwell meant. But the room had no mirror. Perhaps it was for the best: he would not like to meet his own eyes at present.

He sat and tried to steady himself but could not stop thinking of Christopher's head forced backwards, his attacker's mouth against his neck.

The stranger had turned to James, his eyes shallow-mad and his mouth stained. His teeth were slippery as they bit into James's throat. He had drawn back briefly and said, 'Sorry, old chap, we have a rule. Discretion, you know.'

He thought he might faint. He was shivering and could not stop.

With hysterical calm, he reasoned: he would need to get out of this place. That was the first thing to be done.

He thought to check his pockets and found that nothing had been taken. He had not had much with him. A little money. His door key, too – Christopher often forgot his, and so James always made it a point to remember.

His mouth was sour with vomit. He drank the water slowly, in uneasy sips, and dashed a little over his face. Though tepid, it chilled him painfully – but it also startled him into alertness. He stood again: more easily this time. If he were lucky, he would be able to find his way downstairs without collapse.

But he paused halfway between the bed and the door. There were footsteps again – heavier, and more of them than before. A knock, and then immediately the door handle turned. James quickly sank down onto the bed. Whoever it was, it would be better if they thought he was still too weak to move.

Two men stood in the doorway: one middle-aged, the other taller and younger. At the sight of the younger man's face, James started – too horrified, for a moment, even to cry out.

'Yes,' the man said, slightly rueful, 'there is a resemblance. You've met my brother.'

In fact, the likeness was not very pronounced. This man was a year or two older, his hair was sandy-coloured instead of blond, his features were rather more commonplace. The thing was, James thought, horribly tempted to laugh, the thing was he looked ordinary, *pleasant* – the sort of young man who organised charitable subscriptions for the care of lost dogs or injured war heroes, the sort of young man one hoped would marry one's sister.

'It's the eyes,' the man continued. 'Everyone says so. My name is Edmund Bier. You've met my brother, Michael.' Bier nodded towards his companion. 'This is Mould.'

Mould was a slight man with a neat grey moustache, perhaps in his early fifties. His eyes, in a woman, might have been described as lovely – they were very clear grey and unusually expressive. Here they merely seemed ludicrously at odds with the tidy asceticism of his face.

'And now you have the advantage of us both,' Bier went on.

They both waited, as if they really expected him to introduce himself. They did not look like madmen or criminals. And yet surely they were here to kill him. Why had they delayed this long?

He owed Christopher something before he died. Let his murder be spoken. Let Bier be charged with the crime.

'He killed him,' James said.

'I beg your pardon?' said Bier.

'Your brother. He murdered my friend.'

Bier looked towards Mould. 'He's lucid enough.'

'Evidently,' Mould replied. His eyes did not move from James's face. 'Still very weak, though.'

Enough. To hell with them. His time had come, but he would do what he could – for Christopher and for himself. He struggled to his feet.

'I should stay where you are,' Bier advised. 'You're still—'

James hit him. The effort took all the strength he had left. He staggered, thrown off-balance, heard Mould breathe in sharply.

Bier hardly flinched – a blink, a step backwards, nothing more. Then he struck in return, before James could steady himself: a quick, brutal smash across the face that had James reeling backwards, toppling to the floor.

James lay helplessly, all capacity for resistance knocked out of him, unable to do anything but stare confusedly at Mould's shoes – very black, gleaming with polish.

'I warned you he would be agitated,' he heard Mould say, his voice tight.

'Get him back to bed,' Bier instructed, 'or he'll freeze. It's all right, you can touch him, he's not dangerous at the moment. Come on.'

James was lifted onto the bed, deposited none too gently. They both looked down at him – considering him like a scientific specimen of indifferent quality.

'Well, how do you feel?' asked Bier at last. When James said nothing, he added, 'I suppose you're still suffering from shock. That happens, doesn't it, Mould?'

'It does,' Mould answered. He added, lower: 'Perhaps if he were moved to the other room—'

'No,' Bier said, 'he can stay here for the time being.' He turned back to James. 'You'd better feed immediately, though, or you'll have a bad time of it.'

James did not reply.

Bier turned to his companion. 'You don't mind, do you, Mould? Look at him, he's very weak.'

'No,' Mould said. He had his notebook out and was writing busily. James could almost feel his thoughts moving behind his face, like a mass of worms.

'Are you sure? You could wait outside, if you prefer.'

'No,' Mould said again. 'You needn't mind me. Unless you'd rather that I went?'

'You can suit yourself, Augustus. You know you're never in the way.' Bier looked at James. 'Sit up.'

James lay still and stared at him. 'Sit up,' Bier repeated. 'Or I shall have you held upright by force.'

Slowly, James sat up. The exertion was even more painful than before. His arms ached with the effort.

'There,' Bier said. 'Good.' He drew up the chair and sat opposite James, close to the bed – as if James were an invalid friend he was visiting. 'Now, I'll sit here, and we'll do splendidly. Of course, you're new to this; it won't seem so outlandish after a while. Please, don't be alarmed.'

From a pocket, he brought out a knife wrapped in soft brown leather – it was designed like a paper knife but with a smaller, sharper blade, not unlike a scalpel. With a slight frown, he rolled up his left sleeve, and – before James quite understood what he was doing – he made a shallow cut in the skin. 'You'll feel better afterwards, I promise you. Just drink.'

'No.' James drew back, horrified, as the other man offered him his wrist, the blood already welling up from the wound. Whatever madness this was, whatever else they might do to him, they would not induce him to play along with their vile performance.

Bier did not move, though, and then there was the smell of

blood blooming outwards through the room, and there was nothing lovelier in the world.

'You've needed this since you woke,' Bier said. 'You've needed it for days and gone hungry. Drink. Then we can talk more, if you're strong enough.'

James shook his head.

'Are you planning to starve yourself to death?' Bier asked. 'Because if you do, it will take a while, and it won't be pleasant.' He held out the knife, still covered with blood, a pretty colour against the silvery blade. 'Take what you need,' he said.

Surely James had never smelled anything so strongly; surely it would drive him insane in another minute. The blood was warm, even on the knife.

It did not feel new, this hunger and thirst. That was the strangest thing. It felt as if it had always been there. It was as if something had come into clearer view, a figure emerging from a heavy mist.

'I won't,' James said. His voice was strange, almost unrecognisable to his own ears – it might have been the cry of any desperate creature in pain.

There was silence, which was agony, no sound but the blood moving slowly, slowly, in his ears, the fire burning low. Mould took a step forwards.

'Prove me wrong, then,' Bier said. 'Go on. I won't make you drink.'

'I . . .' James found he had moved closer, reached out.

'There, I thought you'd see sense.' Bier held out the knife again.

'Please. Not the knife.'

'Very well.' Bier might have smiled then. 'Not the knife.' He put the knife aside, offered his wrist – James took it, palm upwards, raised the gash to his mouth, and drank.

It was too short a time until Bier drew away. His eyes were darker, glittering, and to James's astonishment he laughed, slightly breathless.

'Now you see,' he said.

James stood up, not knowing what he intended to do next.

He was growing stronger; already he was steadier on his feet.

'Sit down.' Bier said it scornfully. He did not seem at all alarmed at what James might do.

'No.'

'Oh, you want to *leave?*'

And Bier took him by the shoulder with a strength that could not be resisted, and led him to the window, and drew back the curtain all the way, letting the sunlight fall onto James's face.

At first there was pain and nothing else. He felt his skin scorch, his eyes burn. But slowly he became aware of something he had not observed before. He remembered smelling a dead mouse trapped under the floorboards a long time ago – that smell was there now, down in the street: from the people. A stench so vile that he thought he would vomit again. They were walking up and down and talking to one another, and he could hear something else, he could *see* it: the people thinking their thoughts and quietly hating one another.

'Really quite shocking when you look closely, isn't it?' said Bier.

A man and a woman, passing in the street. Lust, fear, vanity, hypocrisy, hatred, in a little dance of half a dozen footsteps. Wolves, all of them, pretending they were not meditating how best to eat one another.

'I think you'd go mad out there if you went before you were ready,' Bier told him. 'It's happened before.'

'What – what's wrong with them?'

'They're the Quick,' Bier replied, 'and they are what they are. You just see them more clearly now. You'll find them even less pretty close to. Fortunately one may work to better their existence without caring much for them in general.' He let the curtain fall back. 'You may even grow used to them, after a time. They surpass our kind in the matter of flavour, if in nothing else. Of course, if you're leaving now, you will have to develop a tolerance very quickly—'

'No. Not out there.'

'I thought not. You need to rest. Tell him, Mould, won't you?'

'You should certainly rest,' Mould agreed, his pencil still scratching at his brown leather notebook. He was like the ones outside, James saw.

He sat down – feeling worse again for the sunlight. There was still blood on his lips. Across the room, Mould's heart was beating – James could hear it, almost see it hanging there beneath his ribs like a red fruit. It twitched uncontrollably, obscenely. What would it be like to take it between one's hands and squeeze?

Again he felt nausea. It lurched within him at this thought, and suddenly the taste of blood in his mouth was vile. Better never to have been born. Better to be dead on the street with Christopher.

'What've you done to me? Is this a drug or—'

'A drug?' Bier sounded scornful. 'No.'

'Let him be, Edmund,' Mould said to Bier – quiet, urgent. 'Don't tell him anything more. Not now, at least.'

James could not speak. The room seemed to dip, the furniture tilted oddly, he could not keep things still.

'Do you think he'll take longer to mend . . . under these circumstances?' Bier asked Mould. They were still observing him with some interest; Mould made another note in his book.

'Maybe. He is a special case, after all.' Mould raised his voice and said to James, with a doctor's authority, 'You must rest. Do you understand? You're still weak, and we don't know how long you will need to recover. If you try to move before you're ready, you will end in injuring yourself.'

'You can rest quiet, you know,' Bier added, glancing quickly at Mould. 'Don't struggle any more. You're quite safe.'

The room was confusion, strange shapes swimming before his gaze. He was about to faint.

They were leaving, he realised. Talking in low voices.

'—to me,' Mould was saying.

'Not yet,' Bier answered. (They were outside now, walking away.) 'Give him a little time. If he doesn't come round, then we can try it your way.'

Chapter Ten

When he woke again, it was much colder. The fire was still burning – someone must have attended to it whilst he slept; it was piled high with coal. But in spite of the blaze, the chill of the room had intensified. Eventually his desperation overcame his weakness: he wrapped blankets around himself, inched out of bed and crawled gracelessly towards the fireplace.

He crouched as close as he could, arms outstretched to the flames: it was not enough. He could not stop shaking.

He sat by the fire for a long time. Every thought deserted him, and it felt easiest to let himself vanish. But each time he felt about to become lost entirely, he would be brought back – startled and irritated – by the sound from next door.

He could hear the solid footfalls of a man walking up and down, and there was a voice talking on and on, as if the speaker were desperately trying to reason something out. Finally the man lapsed into silence.

James stood up with a painful effort, clinging to the mantelpiece for support. Holding his blankets tightly about him, he crossed the room, approaching the wall that divided him from the man next door. He knocked, three soft raps. There was no response.

'Hello,' he whispered. 'Can you hear me? Can you talk?' His voice still rasped and hurt.

He could hear breathing from the next room. It was a half-muffled sound; the man must have a hand to his mouth. James ought not to have been able to make it out. If he listened carefully, he could hear more – he heard the man's blood moving, ceaseless as a tide.

'It's all right,' James said quietly, 'they won't hear. Do you know what this place is?'

The man stayed silent for what must have been almost a minute. 'The Aegolius Club,' he replied at last.

'What's that?'

There was no answer.

'Please,' James said desperately. 'I don't know where we are, I don't know what they want . . .'

'They want to make us like them,' the man said. 'Do you know what that means?' He was young, James realised, and not English – American?

'Yes.' James's head was clearing. 'We have to get out.'

'We can't. I've tried. You'd have to be as strong as one of them even to break through these doors.'

He remembered how it had felt, hitting Bier – like attacking a great cold mass of clay.

James hesitated. Then he said slowly, 'I think I could get through.'

'What do you—' The other man broke off sharply. James imagined him angry, feeling tricked, betrayed.

'I didn't choose it.' James pressed closer to the wall, desperate for him to understand. 'Listen, whatever they've done to me, it wasn't my doing, I didn't *ask* for it—'

'Of course you did. They all ask. It doesn't work any other way.'

'Did you ask?'

The man did not reply.

James said, 'Why would you *choose* it?'

'Because I was a fool. And now I'll pay for that, and probably it serves me right.' The man took a breath. 'Did it hurt? They said it doesn't hurt.'

'Of course it hurts.'

'It's not like being dead, they told me.'

'No. Worse.' James remembered the cool stone and the warm city air. 'I think they're going to kill me,' he said.

'They won't. Not if you're one of them now.' The stranger sounded bitter.

'They killed my friend. They know I won't forgive that. I'll go to the police the first chance I get. They're bound to kill me. Unless we get out.'

'All right,' the stranger agreed. James heard a new note of energy in his voice; he was relieved to have something to do. 'We'll try to get out. Won't lose anything by trying, I guess. See if you can get the door open.'

'It'll make a noise.'

'I'll drown you out. Stomp about or scream or something. I was screaming before and no one came.'

'Screaming?' James recalled the sound from his dreams. He had thought it was his own voice. 'You got out before,' he said.

'Yes. That's why they put me up here. I know the way out, if you can break the locks. But do you think you'll attack me if you get loose?'

The man was struggling to keep his nerve. It was strange to pity him and yet feel such revulsion. He disgusted James like the hordes in the street below. The sympathy *hurt,* seemed to make the pain in his head worse. 'I don't know,' James said wretchedly. 'I'm sorry, but I can't be sure.'

'Right. Well, that'll have to do. Let's try it.'

And he began to shout and kick against the floor like a man possessed. As he had predicted, no one came; they must be accustomed to the sound. James went to the door, still unsteady on his feet, tried the lock.

He shook at it, pulled against it – only to get an idea of its strength – but, to his astonishment, the metal gave way at once and the lock wrenched apart.

The stranger's noise died away, and James waited in silence to see if he had been overheard. No footsteps came.

From next door he heard a whisper: 'Did you manage it?'

'Yes.' He stepped out into the corridor. It was lined by four doors, two on each side, with another door at the far end of the passage. To his right, he could hear the stranger pacing up and down. 'I'll let you out,' he said.

'Right. More of a racket, then?'

This time James did not hesitate, and the door broke open even more easily. The stranger's shouts ceased instantly.

He was about James's age – tall and well built, clad in evening dress which was very much the worse for wear, marked here and there with stains of blood and pale smears of dust. At some point he had fallen and grazed his hands. He had neither hat nor gloves, and there was a splash of white paint across his black shoes. His eyes were bloodshot, his brown hair wildly dishevelled. He stared at James as if he were only the latest of many recent horrors. The room beyond him was darkened and empty of furniture, save for a curious chair, heavily built of metal and wood, pushed far back against the wall.

James was frightened then by his own thoughts. So much blood in him. So easy and pleasant and sensible to seize him, drink.

He took a step backwards, pressing a palm to his mouth, biting down.

The stranger stood and watched, waited.

At last James steadied himself, let his hand fall. 'I won't. They'd want me to.'

The man kept his distance – perhaps the instinct was involuntary. 'What's your name?' he asked.

'James Norbury.'

'Arthur Howland. How do you do.' He tried to smile.

'You said you knew the way out.'

'Yes. I think so. There's not much light. They've got eyes like owls, they can see in the dark. Though I guess that means you can, too.'

'Come on, then,' James said roughly. The blood was so close, it was almost intolerable.

'This way,' Howland said, nodding towards the door at the end of the corridor. 'If they see us, you have to run. You'll be faster. And one of us has got to get out.' He was scrabbling in his pockets. Finally he retrieved a folded scrap of card. 'If I get left in here – will you take a message for me? For my family.'

'All right.'

'There's an address.' Howland handed him the card. 'It's all there.'

James did not answer. Until he was certain of his own moral strength, it was better to ignore Howland as much as possible. Better not to think on the sound of his blood.

The door at the end of the corridor did not yield easily. Even as he touched it, James knew that it would not. It was sturdier, more carefully made. More than this, there was something about that it he disliked.

Howland was looking at the door handle. 'Silver.' He got out his handkerchief, wrapped it around the handle. 'Might help.'

But the door was still too strong; the lock would not budge.

James said, 'Perhaps if we try together.'

'All right.'

He put his shoulder to the door; close beside him, Howland did likewise.

'Don't touch me,' James warned, and Howland nodded, kept his distance.

After a struggle, they broke through – but not quietly, not without a wrench and a clash that had them both listening in dread.

The door opened onto a staircase, which led down to a long corridor. The candles were burning very low behind their green shades, but James found he could see clearly. Howland, following him downstairs, seemed to James almost wilfully loud. But they did not see anyone during their descent. Perhaps the place was generally deserted in the daytime. The corridor was very dark – James realised this only when Howland tripped and nearly fell, catching James's arm for support.

James shook him off – fierce, urgent: 'Don't.'

'Sorry,' Howland whispered. They were silent as they moved – carefully, carefully – down the dim corridor. Then the passage opened out, and they were on a landing. The place was built like a covered courtyard. From the bannister, one could see all the way down: another landing directly below theirs, below that a black-and-white-paved floor.

'That way,' Howland said. He moved forwards without waiting. He was desperate to be out – too desperate to remain cautious for much longer.

James took a step after him – and stopped. When he listened very closely, he could hear a steady sound, too slow and soft for the beating of a human heart.

Treadwell was standing on the other side of the landing, watching them with sombre, incurious eyes.

Run, James thought to say, though there was no need. Howland had followed his gaze: he had seen enough. They were both racing down the stairs as fast as they could. Behind them, someone shouted, there were doors opening. As they reached the black-and-white hall, Howland dashed forwards towards a great wooden door. It was locked, but James knew, or his body knew, that he would have strength enough to force it—

'Excuse me,' a voice behind them said sharply. Edmund Bier's voice, of course.

James turned. Howland did likewise, attempting to fathom the darkness with wide eyes. He could not see, as James could, the figures watching them from across the hall. It was as if they had been waiting.

Bier was quite unperturbed. And there was Mould lurking at the back. James had a brief inkling of his thoughts – watchful curiosity, a quick succession of mental notes. Treadwell was there, too, waiting at the top of the stairs.

The fourth man, standing beside Bier, was a stranger – a man obscenely large and obscenely tall, impeccably dressed. There was a mark from his forehead to chin – an old wound, a bruise with an unnatural sheen. There was metal in the scar – a line of glinting silver, driven into the man's face.

'You goin', then?' he asked. James recognised the voice from his dreams upstairs. And Howland seemed to know the man, too, for at the sound he shrank backwards. James could sense his dread, like chill water rising.

'I'm leaving,' James said to Bier. He had not taken his hand from the door handle. 'Mr Howland, too.'

'No,' Bier said. The others were waiting for his word to attack, James realised. 'I don't think that's a good idea. You certainly can't have Mr Howland. He's ours, you see. The papers have been signed.'

Howland spoke with an effort: 'I want to go with him. If you're gentlemen . . .'

Clearly his eyes had adjusted to the darkness, for when Bier smiled, Howland cringed backwards, his voice faltered.

'Makeweight,' Bier said. 'Would you mind?' He nodded to the tall man, who stepped forwards.

James wrenched fiercely at the door – it yielded as he had expected, letting in a sudden glare of afternoon sunlight. Bier and the others flinched away. James himself almost cried out in pain. Though the day was not bright, in his first shock he could hardly bear to keep his eyes open.

'Do you think that's wise?' Bier asked from the shelter of the shadows.

'You couldn't kill us in the street,' James said.

'I admit, it would provoke a certain amount of talk. However, it's irrelevant. You won't go out there. You wouldn't dare. The light would finish you.'

James knew that he was right. Even the sun on the back of his neck was hard to stand. Besides, there were people outside – what might he do to them?

'As for you, Mr Howland,' Bier went on, 'you may flee if you wish. I promise you we will find you again, before much time has passed. You may prefer to remain and spare yourself the torment of suspense.'

'If you come any closer,' Howland said, 'I'll shout for help. And people will see if you do anything.' He tugged at James's sleeve. 'Come on.'

'I can't. You go.'

'No.' With a desperate effort, Howland pulled James across the threshold, out onto the street. 'Come *on*.'

James looked back into the darkness, where he could see four pale faces, watching inscrutables. 'If you follow us,' Howland said, 'I'll call a policeman.'

Then something horrible: someone in the dark hallway was laughing. It was a skeleton sound, the outward semblance of mirth with no warmth in it.

'Come *on*,' Howland said again, pulling James by the elbow, forcing him onwards. And they fled – into the sunlight, the pitiless noise and brightness of the street.

Chapter Eleven

The Notebook of Adeline Swift

1st April

Good news, letter from Mrs Riggs – safe & out of country. Club dont care to pursue out of Eng at present. Numbers still to short for that thank god, Burke says theyre still struggling though pretend all as usual. Made good sale – 6s. Mama ill, insists is nothing, wont stop typing 2nd MS of TMEV though I said to leave it – if not better soon will call doctor. <u>NB</u>. buy: bullseyes, milk, tea, bread, candles, ?cheese, tooth pwder. Cartridges.

2nd April

No new information re. Club &c. Progress on TMEV going well, all should be ready for Rag&Bottle when they come (not long now – week mybe.) Information on poss Club man – Corvish, will investigate further, hope to add to Map – getting full now, have plotted 3 more since Jan. Shop made £1 6s 2d last month, pawnd Shadwell's watch for 6s, will have enough for rent most likely. Got 2nd axe mended. Will go out & bring back fish & chips, too tired to cook now.

4th April

Burke has no news on Temple Church, agrees w me leaving body to be found not typical for either Club or Alia – strange. Shadwell suggested ordinary murder, Burke insists was not, says something is up – bad – not sure what, worried. He took more than usual.

11th April

Mama will soon finish typing TMEV. Asked if she found interesting, she said never reads anything she types. Borrowed 3s, <u>NB</u>. pay back next week even if she says not to. Plan to follow Corvish, plot route – under way. Have found his addres. Shadwell worried, talked over plan agin. If Burkes right better to act soon. Shadwell tired out, sent to bed w cup of tea.

  False alarm earlier, thought someoned found us. Shadwells made arrangements for move soon – have started packing things up.

14th April

Burke announced new pamphlet from Mould, Shadwell cheered up, looks forward to refuting. Burke now certain Club planning something, doesnt know what. Porlock worried too, <u>slammed</u> door when we left. Shadwell doesnt see she hates us. He thinks too well of people always.

15th April

Mama better, made us borrow 6s.

Day after tomorrow will attempt following Corvish. Lives on Cromwell Rd so will begin there. Otherwise try City, he has connections there & its vry quiet at night generally so good hunting-spot, popular with Club &c.

16th April

Preparations ready for tomorrow. Practised w revolver downstairs this morning, neighbours angry, Shadwell angry. Will practise somewhere else. Or w knife.

<u>NB</u>. Pay baker, wont let us have more bread until account settled.

Chapter Twelve

It had been a month of nothing but frost and snow, and when Liza went out that day, Ma said be careful, there are men about, they're out of work and they want bread and they're liable to be violent. All the bakers may be closed, but see how you get on. And get some glue, too, we're short. They were always buying glue, the whole place stank of it. It was for the matchboxes, which were Ma's trade and Liza's, as well. There were drying boxes everywhere, they'd all got used to moving carefully so as not to knock them over or squash them. The wood and labels and sandpaper you got from the match company but the glue you had to buy yourself. Liza always fetched it. One time she'd been so hungry she'd et a lot of it and then she was sick, which had been a great nuisance.

Ma had said be back soon, it's getting dark. And Liza had nodded and bounded downstairs. She was hungry, eager to be out.

Outside it was colder than ever, but she'd got Ma's red shawl to wrap around her head and keep her ears warm. Far off she'd heard shouting. She'd steered clear of it, taken a different way,

down Old Nichol Street. Not that many people out, and the folk
that were had wrapped themselves up like Liza.

It wasn't natural, she thought. It was never quiet on these
streets in the day. There were all kinds of folk, foreign, lots of
them – lots of Jews, like Mrs Next Door, who had to pay Liza
tuppence every Saturday to light her fire for her.

The bakers were all closed. She'd walked about and even banged
on some of the doors in case they might open up, but nobody had.

She'd been passing Salmon Street then and had thought, what
if I try there? The men might leave Salmon Street alone, and
perhaps there's a baker down there that's open.

She had never been in Salmon Street before, though it was so
close. Ma said she had no business there, that Salmon Street people
were no good. They were a strange, wan, miserable-looking lot,
mostly, for all their rent was so low. People said that Salmon Street
had the cheapest rooms in London.

But the Salmon Street people never stayed long. No one ever
saw them leave, there was never a cart come to take any of them
away, they just weren't there any more, and then there was a new
lot come.

They had their song, though. It went to the tune of 'The Roast
Beef of Old England', and they sang it throughout the neighbourhood, in their cups or in the street, all chiming in on the last line
like it was a dirge.

> A pretty young maiden in London did dwell
> Just up past St Bath's, as the stories all tell
> She courted a gentleman and loved him well
> And he was a Salmon Street fellow
> And in Salmon Street lodgings is cheap
>
> They'd walk out each evening till quarter to nine
> The young man so pale and his sweetheart so fine
> But they never once halted to drink or to dine

And she never beheld him in daylight
(In Salmon Street lodgings is cheap)

My darling, please tell me, the lady she said
Why your skin is so white and your mouth is so red
Why your hands are so cold like the hands of the dead
And why you don't ask me to marry
Though in Salmon Street lodgings is cheap?

Liza didn't know any more – Ma didn't like her singing the song. It was disgusting, she said.

There was something else Liza knew about Salmon Street, though who'd told her it she didn't remember: they had no rats. Not a single one. Catch a rat, take it as far as St Bath's on the corner between Salmon Street and Mount Street, and let it go, and see what it does. You won't ever see any creature move so fast, it'll be gone before you blink.

Liza had done what Ma said and stayed out of Salmon Street – but she was hungry now, with that sharp hunger that ached and hurt, and Salmon Street didn't look much to be afraid of. So she'd walked past St Bath's Church, down a little way. Nothing to look at, really – except for one shop window, which was all lit up.

There were so many good things: cakes and sugar butties, and the suet and plum puddings that they called baby's heads, which were Liza's favourite. She waited for a while by the window, just looking.

A woman was standing in the shop doorway, and she saw Liza and smiled and beckoned to her. Though the shop must be warm, she was shivering in the draught. She had a beautiful red dress on and a black shawl and a black bonnet, and there were rings on all her fingers, and, the way she stood, you'd think she owned the whole street, every stone.

'Evening,' she said, nodding like Liza was a grown-up lady.

Liza said 'Evening' back and sniffed the air again. She could smell bread in the shop. It must have just finished baking. It would be crusty outside and inside almost too hot to bear, lovely soft in her fingers.

'My name's Mrs Price,' the lady said. 'You walked far?'

Liza nodded.

'You must be cold. Come in, you can have a bite to eat.'

Well, after all it was a *shop* – anyone could go into those and it would be all right. So Liza nodded, and she followed Mrs Price inside, out of the cold.

That was as far as she liked to go when she remembered it all later.

• • •

'You were brave as anything,' Mrs Price always said afterwards, 'didn't cry a bit. I knew you were going to be a big help to me, right off.'

Liza thought she remembered it, that second when her heart had gone still, but Mrs P said she couldn't have done, she must have imagined that part.

Afterwards she was ill for a bit and confused, but Mrs Price looked after her, and when Liza was better, Mrs Price explained it all. Liza was *undid* now, as people said around Salmon Street. The undid were strong and fierce and fed on blood, which Liza would find was the best thing of all to drink, better than coffee or lemonade or anything. There was a lot of undid in London, and quite a few lived in Salmon Street, next door to Mrs Price's shop. There had been undid in Salmon Street for more than a hundred years, though none of them had ever owned any of the houses there till Mrs P came along and bought up half the street. There were gentlemen mousing around, wanting to pull the place down because of slum clearance or something, but that would be the day, Mrs P said, they'd never tear down her shop. She had other places, too. She'd done well for herself and now she needed a bit of help, a smart girl to lend a hand, and she'd seen straight away that Liza would do nicely.

Of course, after she'd been 'changed, Liza had been a fool at first, wanting to go home.

'All right,' Mrs Price had said, 'if you think they'll have you back like you are now, off you go, then.'

Mrs Price took her to the door and pushed her outside, into the daylight, barefoot into the snow, and Liza had been so frightened she nearly cried, plunged into the street like that, with the light and the cold so awful, and quickly she was back, beating her fists against Mrs Price's door, crying and pleading to be let back in.

And Mrs Price had let her in and sat her down and rubbed at her bare feet until they stopped aching from the cold. 'That's right,' she said. 'You be a good girl, now.'

• • •

She did see Ma once more, though – passing in the street one evening, huddled in a grey cloak. Liza had been Mrs Price's girl for a long time, running her errands – carrying messages and other jobs where a child might go unnoticed. She was doing a job for Mrs Price when she saw Ma again – hurrying along Church Street, looking down as she walked.

Ma looked cold. She must miss her red shawl, Liza thought. Mrs P said the shawl had been lost. Liza never saw it again after she was undid.

Ma was different, Liza thought. What had happened to her face, why did she look like that now? How had she got old so fast?

Ma had seemed to know Liza was watching, had turned around, searching. Liza had darted down another street, ran and ran, hiding herself amongst the snarling alleys and courts of Bethnal Green.

At last, when she had been away for a while, Mrs Price came and found her.

'Come on,' she said. It was past dawn by this time. 'You got to come back.'

Mrs Price was the same as she had been twenty years ago – the day they'd met. She had new clothes, but she had them all made to look like the old fashions, and she still wore the same bonnet, though it no longer resembled a bonnet much at all. And Liza was just the same still, no taller or older than she had been that day in the shop.

'Don't I ever get old?' she asked Mrs Price.

Mrs Price shook her head. 'No,' she said. 'Never say die.' She had an odd look on her face, and Liza couldn't guess what it meant. 'We oughter be going,' she added. And they both turned away and went home.

• • •

Salmon Street was a busy place, Liza discovered. There were undid always about, and the Quick, too. Sometimes Mrs P would take Liza with her when she went round to see about rent. Liza liked that – there was always a drink in it, and she liked how polite they all were to her and Mrs P. Scared half out of their wits, most of them. Of course, they knew what Mrs P was like – they knew what might happen, but they were desperate, there was nowhere else they could afford, and they always hoped it'd happen later and they'd find money enough to leave before it was too late.

In time the street got busier – after Liza, Mrs P had decided to get some more kids in. First came Sally, who was pretty and yellow-haired, dainty as a china cup. Mrs Price had bought her off of the Imp Woman on Chambord Street – she had a gang of kids, all undid, that she rented out to theatres as imps and goblins and fairies. Sally had been a monkey once in the pantomime, but she hadn't much liked it. The Imp Woman was a nasty old witch, not at all like Mrs P, who had bought Sally for five pounds and said it was a bargain.

The next one Mrs P brought back was Nick, who had red hair

and was the same age as Liza. He'd lived amongst thieves until something went wrong, and he knew how to pick a lock and dozens of other things like that. He was fun but told lies all the time – he would even lie about seeing Doctor Knife, which was something nobody should joke about.

After Nick came One-Ear. One-Ear was really called Bill or something, but he had always been One-Ear to them, because as long as they'd known him he'd had no left ear, just skin that kept growing over and then blistering and peeling off. He never said what had happened to his ear, though they'd all asked him often enough. (Ears didn't grow back, mostly – fingers, neither, unless you were lucky. Legs and heads, not a chance.) One-Ear cried a bit and got upset if you made fun of his no-ear and he stuck to Sally mostly, Sally being the kindest to him. He was from the country, had been undid for ages before coming to Mrs P's. Before that he'd been in a mine, his whole family had worked there. He'd been something called a trapper, he said, and he'd hated it. Used to hate the dark.

After Mrs Price had got the kids, some of the grown-up undid who were in the habit of passing through decided they'd like to stay, and Mrs P put some of them up in houses she owned. Some of them even lived in Mrs P's house, which was next door to the shop.

There'd always been undid on Salmon Street, Mrs P said, but never so many. And they'd never answered to one person before until her. They were better for keeping together, Mrs P said – kept the club from bossing them too much. The rents she charged the undid were low, but there were rules: you had to behave, you couldn't attract attention.

One of these grown-up undid was Gil, who was sometimes known as Lamby Gil, maybe because he once lived in Lamb Street. *He* said they called him Lamby on account of his kindly nature. But Gil was never kind. Always smart, though – black satin necktie and shiny shoes and beaver hat, and under that his hair all shiny, too, with bear's grease. His trousers were cut in the very latest style – or it was the latest style once and, the way Gil wore them, you'd think it was still. Gil's real name was Gilbert Gil, that's what he said. Or Gil-but-Gil, because there was a tale that he had once led a Lady, a proper Lady from Belgravia or some such place, right into the heart of Salmon Street. She loved him, perhaps because she never looked right or left but followed him right down Salmon Street, which was no place for one of her sort. And when she was surrounded, the silly thing had kept saying – *Gil, but, Gil*, over and over. She'd broke inside like a clockwork toy and she wouldn't shut up until they gave her something else to think of. There were some, Mrs Price said, as *asked* for misfortune.

Like Tom Brimstone, who she had thrown out of Salmon Street last week, on account of coarse behaviour and him not paying the rent. He was old and grim and mean and dirty, and sometimes he left marks on the furniture. No one wanted his company. He was pickled most of the time (and it took a powerful lot of gin, Mrs P said, to souse one of the undid) and he was always foul-mouthed and stinking to boot. Worst of all were his teeth. Waterloo teeth, pinched from dead soldiers and other killeds, stuck into gums made of ivory. When Tom Brimstone smiled, it was white, white everywhere. He was a bully, too, and if he could catch any of the kids, he would knock them about and make them run errands for him. None of them missed him when he was got rid of.

Agnes was much nicer. She was old – so old her hair was white. She always looked tired. Everywhere she went, she had an umbrella with her, because she was afraid of rain. She said the damp made her bones ache. She'd worked in the fields when she was young, and that takes a lot out of you. Her skin was dry all over, flaking off. This happened sometimes, Mrs P said. Agnes was tough, though, and Mrs Price trusted her more than anyone to look after her concerns – apart from the shop on Salmon Street, there were three houses she let and two second-hand clothes shops on Turk Road. Agnes wasn't much good at chasing the Quick, but she carried with her a box of bonbons that were dosed with

something to make people sleepy, and these she would sometimes
give out to children if she met them walking unattended.

The other grown-up who lived on Salmon Street was Phossy
Lil, who'd been a matchmaking girl. Agnes was her friend, and
she looked after Lil when she was in her sad moods. Sometimes
Lil had nightmares, and Agnes would go and sit with her and
comfort her until she could sleep. Liza herself had a friendly
feeling towards Lil, on account of having been in the match
business herself. It was hard looking at her, though, because of
her face, which was all spoiled from phossy jaw, which she'd got
from working in the match factory. Then she'd been dismissed
and it had been bad for her until Agnes had met her. She'd been
'changed before the phossy jaw could kill her, but her face was
all swollen and et up on one side, and some of her teeth were
gone. At one time she'd taken to painting herself up to try and
hide the damage, but Gil had made fun of her for that and she'd
stopped, and then Agnes had got her a beautiful hat with a veil,
and she wore that so you could just see her eyes, which were
still handsome.

Gil plagued her less often after that, though from time to time
he'd make vulgar jokes and pull at her veil and Lil would try to
scratch his eyes out and Mrs Price would look at Gil with a terrible
look and say, *No more of that, Gil,* and everyone else would shake
in their shoes but not Gil, who was never scared of anything, not
even Mrs P. Perhaps that was why she kept him about, for he never
did much else useful, not as far as Liza could see.

Until the night when he did at last make himself helpful: he
brought dinner back. He'd never brought dinner for them all
before, and from the fuss he made about it, you'd think he'd
brought twenty back instead of just one.

He came home with something in a bag and said with a grin
that they would go to bed full that morning.

'What've you got there?' Mrs Price asked.

'Well, wouldn't you like to know,' Gil said, and he held up the bag and added, 'Smell – it's fresh as anything.'

'It ain't Quick, though,' Mrs P said, 'now, is it?'

'Well, it was a few hours ago,' said Gil . 'Strong and 'ealthy, too.'

'Where's it from?' Mrs Price asked. ''Cause we don't want no trouble.'

'I got it from a club man. Dog cheap, too. Five bob. Not bad for such a young one.'

It was a good bargain, but mixing with the club lot was a risk. Still, blood was blood.

Gil or someone else had made a right mess of stowing the body in the sack. It came out all heavy and broken odd angles and smelling of blood. Young feller, all dressed up smart, nasty yellowy-green scarf round his neck. Dead as dead, but they clustered round, anyway, and though there were some who said it wasn't nice, swigging from a killed like that, it tasted good enough to Liza, who was hungry.

They had thought that was the end of it – there was still the stiff to get rid of, of course, but that could be done later, when there was time. None of this fly-by-night, throw-in-the-river nonsense, Mrs Price always said. None of this careless stuff that gets the law on your back. That ain't our way.

There was the club to think of, as well. If you left bodies about, they'd be really shirty, Mrs P said. Wasn't safe to make them angry. And they've got worse recently, very high-handed, so we've got to watch ourselves.

The club scared everyone, even Mrs Price. A while back, Liza had overheard her talking with Agnes. It was noon and everyone else was asleep, and Mrs P and Agnes were chatting in front of the fire whilst Agnes mended one of Lil's corsets (Gil being out of the house at the time). Corsets had to be made special for Mrs P and Agnes and Lil, because otherwise they'd split and snap them in a second. It was on account of all the moving and fighting, Mrs P said, and then we're tougher than the Quick and our insides don't give as much.

'Burke says the club lot're up to something,' Mrs P had said. 'But 'e don't know what.'

'Well, we'll be careful,' Agnes said. But she was afraid, too, Liza thought.

Liza had never seen one of the club men herself – not until after Gil's bargain. They had drunk their fill and gone through the stiff's clothes, taken all they could, but hadn't had a chance to get rid of it yet. And that turned out to be a piece of luck, because not long afterwards the club lot sent Makeweight to get it back. Makeweight, who Gil always called a seven-sided-son-of-a-bitch. Or Makeweight the Bastard, he was sometimes known as. Bastard son of London, Mrs P said, he's been here longer than most, been here for ever maybe. Ain't no one knows where he came from, but he knows his way about.

Makeweight wasn't allowed on Salmon Street. None of the club lot was, but Makeweight was *especially* not allowed, Mrs P said. Liza had never even seen him until that day when he turned up, in the dead of noon, all fancy clothes and a bright red tie. He had short bristly hair and eyes that looked everywhere, a stare that went through to your brains. Worst of all was his face, a big gash of a scar at the corner of his eye right down to his chin, silver showing through. Would have corpsed anyone else, that much silver left in them, but not Makeweight.

When Makeweight turned up, Mrs Price said, 'Liza, you take the others outside,' and Liza had nodded and done as she was told. Then she came back quietly and put an eye to the keyhole and listened.

Mrs Price had asked, 'What do you want?'

And Makeweight said, 'Friend of yours had a piece of luck recently. You know what I mean.'

'You're late if you want breakfast.'

'What did you do with the rest?'

'That's our business, surely,' said Mrs P.

From the way they both stood, so ready and watchful, Liza had hoped they might start to fight – they had once before, she had heard, a long while ago, and it had been a sight to see. But now Makeweight just smiled and said, 'You've got no use for it now. Save you a job getting rid.'

'What d'you want it for?' Mrs Price asked. 'Unnatural, I call it, asking for one of them things.'

'You know I can't tell you that, Lucy,' Makeweight said, and Liza thought Mrs P might go for him then, because only Gil ever called her Lucy.

But Mrs P stayed calm and said, 'Two bob.'

'You're joking,' Makeweight said. 'You know what'll happen if I have to go away empty-handed. The gentlemen will be put out, and that won't do any of us any good.'

'Two bob,' Mrs P said, 'times being bad, which I'm sure you know 'cause it's your masters are the ones putting the squeeze on.'

And Makeweight replied, 'Oh we'll be putting the squeeze on more before long, and I look forward to squeezing you most of all, Lucy Price.' But he handed over two bob because this was Salmon Street, where even Makeweight the Bastard would be on his good behaviour, or as good as could be expected from Makeweight. Gil brought the stiff up from the cellar, and Makeweight went off, carrying the body – wrapped in a lot of sacking he'd brought with him, tied up so it looked like a carpet or something.

'Well, that saves a job, anyway,' Gil said, trying to be cheery because they were all a bit scared, even when Makeweight was gone. He sort of left it behind him like a bad smell.

'Yes,' Mrs Price said. 'Close the door, will you?' And they didn't talk about it any more. But for a while afterwards Mrs P seemed quieter than usual.

Chapter Thirteen

The laying out was done at last. Charlotte, assisted by Susan, the maid, had seen to it after the doctor's departure, washing Mrs Chickering's body and wrapping her legs in calico, folding her arms across her breast. When all was as it should be, they left Mrs Chickering alone in her bedroom, a handkerchief tied beneath her chin to hold her mouth shut. It was necessary, this last indignity, and yet it had struck Charlotte as grotesque. It was as if she had attempted to silence Mrs Chickering by fastening her jaw closed.

Even after Charlotte had washed her hands, she imagined that she could still smell sickness beneath the carbolic soap. She went downstairs, sat in the drawing-room with a cup of tea and for a brief time gave way to a feeling of absolute exhaustion.

They had been between nurses when Mrs Chickering died. The cook had given in her notice weeks before and had now departed. Susan would soon follow suit. Half an hour ago, Charlotte had sent her into the village to despatch the telegram to London, and now she was alone in the house.

She wished that James were here with her tonight. But he

would be back soon – the telegram would fetch him from London. She would have help and comfort.

Over the last few months, the drawing-room had gradually become Charlotte's domain – Mrs Chickering had been so infrequently downstairs of late. She had hung her maps on the walls and left her gardening magazines about without fear of reproach. Mrs Chickering had never quite approved of this hobby of Charlotte's – she held that sunlight spoiled the complexion, that earth was bad for the hands. Charlotte had brought Mrs Chickering fruit and flowers she had grown and let her find grudging praise for their sweetness.

Perhaps it was the self-evident achievement of Charlotte's gardening that Mrs Chickering had disliked. One could not defend oneself against accusations of plainness or an unprepossessing manner or a dozen other small feminine failures – but an apple was an apple. It was a tangible accomplishment which could not be taken away. Mrs Chickering had been afraid that the trees and flowers would be blighted or eaten by worms or killed in the frost, but they were not. Under Charlotte's guardianship, the garden at East Lodge had flourished.

Outside, it was almost dark now. Susan would have a miserable walk of it, trudging through the hall grounds in the rain.

Charlotte was not in the habit of thinking about the future. There had been little time for it, and it had not seemed sensible to brood over her situation. What leisure she had, she had tried to use wisely – reading or out of doors. Apart from this, her days were taken up with caring for Mrs Chickering, who had kept her too busy for much reflection. One was not unhappy, living like that.

But in recent months – as Mrs Chickering grew weaker – Charlotte had found herself reading over the advertisements at the back of their old copy of Bradshaw, turning over the ship passages advertised: to Vigo, Lisbon, Gibraltar, Australia, Zanzibar, Calcutta, to a score of other places. On cool fresh mornings she longed to leave with the autumn birds.

Now her occupation as nurse was gone, and she was not sure what would happen next. Would James want her in London? She dreaded being a hindrance; he was so evidently content as he was. But surely he would not let her remain in East Lodge alone?

In the quiet of the empty house, she saw what her life would be if she did stay here, and the prospect frightened her.

She finished her tea, reminded herself that there were many tasks still requiring attention. But instead of busying herself with something useful, she took from the bookcase a map which she had purchased only very recently. LONDON stood out brightly on the cover, printed in yellow-gold capitals.

She lingered over the map for some time – until Susan returned, wet and shivering and morose, but with the telegram sent. Charlotte was glad to think that it had gone.

• • •

The next day, she waited for James's reply. To her surprise, there was nothing. Nor did any communication reach her in the days that followed. She thought that perhaps he had set off for Yorkshire immediately, forgetting to send a telegram to let her know. It would be like him, departing late and forgetting something so important. But he did not return.

She went to the post office herself, sent another telegram and then, in spite of the expense, two more in quick succession – and still he did not write, and still he did not come back.

• • •

There was a limit to how long she could decently delay the funeral – this time had now elapsed. Charlotte had no acquaintance in London, so there was no one to help her discover what had happened to James – other than the police, perhaps, but it hardly seemed a fitting job for them. After all, he could easily be ill or out of London; he had written, not long ago, of wanting a holiday.

Mrs Chickering had left detailed written instructions for her funeral, which was to be economical in every detail, though Charlotte suspected she would secretly have enjoyed the lugubrious excesses of thirty years ago. Mrs Chickering had wanted to wear her hair bracelet (Charlotte must put it on her *left* wrist), and all her rings – her wedding ring and her engagement diamond, a mourning ring and the little pearl circlet her mother had left her.

Everything was arranged in advance save Charlotte's mourning clothes, which had to be managed in a hasty and unsatisfactory fashion. She had a black wool gown which was presentable enough, if growing a little shabby, another of black silk which had been made nearly ten years ago and which had been made over twice and had grown too tight. Silk for the funeral, then, wool for everyday. At least she would not have to endure it for very long.

Lingering at the graveside, half-choked in black silk, Charlotte thought that she would no doubt have disappointed Mrs Chickering had she been there to see. She stayed by the grave for some time: she felt that she owed it to the past they had shared. Their years together demanded some tribute, though there had never been much tenderness between them. Perhaps she had cared about Charlotte – she had preferred Charlotte's nursing to that of a stranger, certainly – but her affection and her pride had chiefly rested with James, though James had never noticed as much. She would have been grieved, Charlotte thought, to know that he would not see her buried. She would have said that it wasn't like him.

There was nothing in any of the papers – no accident or murder, no report of any disaster. But she imagined things all the same. James, with his gentle eyes and expressive face and his habitual air of being slightly lost – what might have befallen him alone in the city, which Mrs Chickering always said was full of vice?

Charlotte had made up her mind: she would go to London,

and find him for herself. That evening she took the London map down from the bookcase again and found Egerton Gardens. It was a strange comfort, to look down at the printed streets and buildings – it was like floating over the city from high above, watching over the place where James was sleeping, as if somehow this might keep him safe from harm.

· · ·

King's Cross was an assault on the eyes and ears, a scurry and bustle which almost bewildered her. Alighting from the train, Charlotte was struck by the noise of the place – dozens of voices, and above those the screech and pant of the engines. She found herself engulfed by a crowd of fellow passengers, hemmed in on all sides and borne helplessly forwards. She could smell dirt, sweating human bodies and damp wool and wet dog fur, a thousand other ripe and rotting things all blended together. The station was cold, and she felt insignificant beneath the high ceiling, as if she had dissolved entirely into the crowd. The taste of smoke lingered at the back of her throat.

She had never seen so many people gathered in one place. The women were almost as soberly dressed as the men, in dim tasteful colours from which the odd touch of brightness stood out sharply: an Indian shawl, a blue woollen scarf, a red cloak. She passed servants carrying travelling furs, an elderly couple struggling with a large picnic basket, a Scotch family with a pack of lively dogs, a little girl and her nursemaid – the woman reaching out a swift hand, pulling the child back from the platform edge as a train began to move with a wrench of metal and a billow of smoke. Charlotte's attention was caught by a man in a uniform: he had scrambled up onto the roof of a train and was examining something – what? – as soberly as if he had both feet safe on the ground. Watching him, she forgot herself and nearly tripped over a pile of luggage. By the time she had recovered her balance, a porter had retrieved the cases, passing her with a cold stare.

Clutching at her modest suitcase, her small handbag, she struggled towards a place where the crowd was thinner, where she could stand and recover her dignity and conquer the silly urge to cry. Beneath her half-panicked alertness, she was grimly tired. She had been awake since before dawn – too anxious about James to fall asleep again.

She had carefully written down the name and colour of the omnibus she would require to reach James's lodgings. She also carried her map of London but was reluctant to take it out – it was so large when unfolded, it would make her look such a visitor. She picked up her bag and walked out of the station.

She was not sure what she had expected, but the reality of it – people, horses, carriages, omnibuses – frightened her. She did not know which way to go or whom to ask. A porter would be the best choice, but those she saw seemed too busy to approach. One felt so conspicuous, she discovered, standing motionless in such a place. As she reached into her handbag for her handkerchief, a man passed close by. She heard a mutter – *Got another purse for you here, sweetheart* – and scarcely had time to flinch from the onslaught of tobacco breath before the man was gone. Already she could not recall his features. He might be anyone in the crowd. But he would have seen her look about her, confused and upset, and he must have laughed at her, a woman so thoroughly out of place.

Mrs Chickering had warned her about London. Take the wrong turning, choose the wrong side of Regent Street, and one was lost. The streets would soil one's shoes and stain one's skirts; there were pickpockets and foreigners and Irish dynamiters and who knew what else.

She would take a hansom, she decided. It would be quicker than the omnibus, and there would be less possibility of making a mistake. Engaging a cab proved less difficult than she had feared. After one failed effort, she at last attracted the attention of a porter, who took her in charge and managed the whole business with aplomb.

The cabman was quick, rather impatient with her detailed enquiries, but seemed good-natured enough. He would probably overcharge her shamelessly, but that was only to be expected, and it was worth the expense to be away from the crowd – even shut away in the rattling box, which sped down the busy street far faster than Charlotte would have liked. She would not mind if no one ever looked at her again.

The cab smelled strange. It took her a few puzzled minutes to realise that she must have walked through something before getting in. Of course – horse manure. A nice sight she would be for James when she finally arrived.

Don't make a fuss, she told herself. It's nothing much. Nothing we don't see at home, and nothing a little water won't fix.

She gazed out of the smeared window, trying to follow the quick progression of streets. Her spirits had lifted a little: the fact that she had managed two stages of her journey without mishap was encouraging. It was only when they had been driving for some five minutes that she recollected that Mrs Chickering had once said that it was not the thing for ladies to travel in hansoms alone.

To her relief, Egerton Gardens appeared quiet and respectable. James had said it was a pleasant part of London, but she had always suspected that he might have taken rooms somewhere dreadful by mistake and failed to notice his error. He had a tendency to miss things.

Her first ring of the doorbell went unanswered – as did her second. She checked the address she had written down, and tried again. But though she heard the bell sound shrilly within the house, there was still no answer.

It was too much, after coming so far, to be confronted at the last with such an obstacle. Where could they all be? What sort of household did Mrs Morris keep?

She waited, and thought, and rang the doorbell again. At last, in frustration, she tried the door. It was not locked.

She looked around. There was no one passing by to witness this shocking lapse of manners. She opened the door and went in.

'James?' she called – rather timidly, expecting that someone would bear down upon her unexpectedly and challenge her presence.

But no one appeared. She did not call out again. Something in the hushed air of the building made her reluctant to cause any noise.

When he had first moved in, when his letters were more regular, James had drawn for her a picture of the house and a little map of its inside. He and his friend had the second floor to themselves – a bedroom each, and a sitting-room between them.

His room was small but cosy, he had written. It was at the top of the stairs, the first door one came to. Charlotte stopped outside, knocked, and went in.

The room was unoccupied. The bed was made, and there seemed little of James about it. A Gladstone bag was standing empty on top of the table; another suitcase stood locked by the bed. But there was her photograph on top of the chest of drawers, a few other things she recognised lay scattered about.

She moved on to the sitting-room. The curtains were closed, daylight struggling through. It was warmer in here than the bedroom; there was a fire burning low in the grate. Someone had at least been here recently, then – she was obscurely relieved by the discovery.

The room smelled warm and dusty and unpleasantly sweet, like decay, and beneath that there was smoke and earth. But it could not possibly be earth.

What to do now? Was it best to wait?

On the table there was an empty bottle of wine and two dirty glasses, a jumble of papers, a bottle of ink left open. And so many books – perhaps some belonged to James's friend, whose name

Charlotte had forgotten. He was a rather dull character, to judge by James's letters. But then, James's letters had been unusually stilted of late, full of foolish jokes, never answering any of her questions.

It had been the same at Christmas, the last time she had seen him. He had always given the impression of existing in both the everyday world and somewhere else, a private country of which she saw only brief glimpses. But at Christmas he had seemed far more distant – his real life all elsewhere. She had pretended not to see it, and played at cheerfulness until he left. She had almost been glad to see him go.

She picked up a book that had fallen open, closed it and examined the spine: John Donne. She had an idea that James had told her about him. The men of letters had forgotten him for a time (why this should be, if his verse had merit, Charlotte could not imagine – it was as if poetry could rise or fall like the value of shares), but he was now coming into fashion again.

One page was marked by a grey-dappled feather. Here and there, phrases were underlined faintly in pencil. James's taste appeared to run mostly towards sacred subjects. The words of blood and devotion embarrassed her.

Religion was one of the things they did not talk about any more. She had not yet had the courage to tell him that her own faith, so stern and sturdy in her childhood, was gone: more than this, that she had wrenched herself out of it and could not wish herself back again. She had decided that it was better to suffer and see clearly.

She had wanted to tell him about the many things she thought now; she would have liked to discuss the few, carefully chosen books she had managed to get on the subject. But she had not been able to imagine his response, and this had made her uneasy.

She was about to set the volume down when another line snagged her attention:

License my roaving hands, and let them goe
Behynd, before, betweene, above, belowe.
Oh my America! my Newfoundland!

That was quite enough. She shut the book with a crisp snap, sending a little cloud of dust flying upwards.

As she set the book down on the table, there was a soft sound behind her. Someone was standing in the shadows, watching her.

She could not help gasping – but there was no need for alarm, for of course it was James. In her relief, she almost laughed.

'James,' she said, smiling, a little proud at having made the journey alone. 'James, how long were you standing there? The front door's open, and nobody answered, and I thought you were all *out*. I didn't know what to do . . .'

She stopped, waiting for him to speak, to embrace her, but he did not.

'Are you all right?' she asked. 'James?'

Still he said nothing. It was too dark to see his expression clearly – in the firelight it might have been a look of malice.

'James,' she repeated. 'I didn't see you.' It was a foolish thing to say, but surely anything was better than silence.

Trying for briskness, she went to the window and drew back the curtains all the way.

'There. That's better.'

The room was in a mess, worse than she had thought, and had evidently not been dusted for some time. There were papers on the floor by James's feet – some ripped into pieces or crumpled into balls, a pile evidently destined for the fire. As she took a step towards James, Charlotte felt something crunch underfoot – a piece of china, a smashed vase, perhaps. She had crushed a shard with her boot heel, severing for ever a blue-painted shepherdess and her swain.

'James,' she said. 'What's happened?'

He pushed past her and drew the curtains again, face twisted against the sunlight.

She was frightened now. But she went to him and put her arms around him as she had not done for years.

'James,' she repeated, as if speaking his name might bring him back to her.

He remained silent. He was shivering, despite being indoors and wrapped in his overcoat. For a moment or two they stood together. Then roughly, without warning, he pushed her away.

In spite of herself, she was upset – it was the unexpectedness of it, his sudden hostility. She went to the desk, turning over books and papers in a pretence of tidying up.

'This room is disgraceful. When did you last have someone in to dust?'

He wasn't even looking at her now. His gaze was on the fire, the faint remaining light.

'Don't you want to know why I'm here?' she asked.

No response. She kept on tidying up, making neat stacks of books, collecting the pages lying by the fire. It was when she stooped for a book lying face down on the hearthrug that he seized her wrist – hauled her to her feet. The strength of his grasp made her catch her breath. She pulled back, but could not free herself. There was a purpose in his look that she did not understand.

'You're cold,' she said.

He released her and stepped backwards.

'Please,' he said, 'it's not safe.'

'*Safe?* What do you mean?'

'You have to leave. *Now.* Please. I can't bear this . . .' He spoke quickly, urgently, as if they were about to be separated, as if time were short. But as he spoke, he again seized her hand and raised it to his mouth.

She did not understand what he was doing. All she knew, in that cool instant of terror, was that he was too strong for her; she could not pull away.

He pushed back the sleeve of her dress, pulled down the edge of her glove, and his mouth was cold on her skin – a kiss with teeth in it. She cried out in astonishment and sharp pain. She swung at him wildly with the book she still held, and he stepped backwards in surprise, letting go of her wrist.

She was bleeding. He had grazed the skin – a shallow cut, but enough to bring blood. It was there, running down her arm, smeared about his mouth. She looked at the book in her hand now and recognised it, familiar and unfamiliar, as if she were seeing it in a dream – it was the biography of Carlyle she had given to him.

He stepped away from her. 'Charlotte,' he said, as if he had realised for the first time who she was. His voice again became desperate: *'Go away.'*

Something had changed about his face. It was the same change she had seen in Mrs Chickering's.

She turned and fled, not daring to look back at him. She let the door slam behind her, careless of appearances, desperate only to be away from him, away from the house. She fled towards the staircase, breathless, half sobbing, holding her wrist tight to her chest.

She was halfway down the stairs when she realised that there was someone else in the house. A figure stood downstairs in the hall, staring upwards. In the half-light of the hall, she could make out a black dress, long loose white hair.

'You shouldn't have gone up.' The woman spoke flatly, in the voice of one who had suffered long illness or pain. There was a purple bruise on the side of her face. Before she averted her eyes, appalled, Charlotte thought she could make out finger marks.

'Mrs Morris?' she asked hesitantly. 'Are you—'

'Go away. Get out.' The woman swayed on her feet, about to faint. Charlotte caught her before she could fall, held her up as gently as she could.

'Please,' she said, 'can you tell me what's happened, what's wrong with him . . .'

Mrs Morris did not speak, and Charlotte realised that it would be cruel and futile to press her any further at the moment. She looked as if she had not eaten for several days. Her gown was smart but creased and stained.

Charlotte put an arm about her shoulders, guided her to the nearest chair, and made her sit down.

'Wait here,' she said. 'I'll get you some water.'

After a couple of wrong turns, she found her way to the kitchen. The range was out, and the place was a shocking mess – vegetable peelings strewn across the floor, a dropped plate lying in fragments where it had fallen. A fish was rotting on the kitchen table – the rank smell made Charlotte choke. In the scullery she found the sink piled high with dirty plates. She possessed herself of a clean glass and took some water up to Mrs Morris.

'Do you have any brandy?' she asked.

'Drawing-room,' Mrs Morris said. 'Upstairs. First door . . .'

In the drawing-room the blinds were shut, and Charlotte could barely make out her surroundings – only the faint light from the hall allowed her to look around. She discovered a decanter of brandy on a table. She carried it downstairs and made Mrs Morris drink brandy and water until a little of her colour had returned.

'Can you tell me what happened to him?' she asked.

Mrs Morris shook her head. 'He said I mustn't go upstairs. He doesn't like it.' She put her hand to her head.

'Did he—' Charlotte could not bear to finish the question. The idea of James striking a woman made her feel sick. 'Why didn't you leave?'

'It's not allowed.'

'I beg your pardon?'

Mrs Morris took a shuddering breath. 'He won't let me.'

'What about the servants?'

'I sent them away,' Mrs Morris replied. 'They were – it wasn't safe. He told me not to, but I couldn't just . . .'

James had done this. He had terrified her, left the mark of his rage stark on her face. How long had she been hiding downstairs in the dark, too afraid to leave? Charlotte thought fleetingly of madness, lunatics from novels who walked unrecognised amongst the sane until suddenly, unexpectedly, turning violent.

She said to Mrs Morris, 'I'll get you a hansom.'

Mrs Morris looked at her and did not seem to understand.

'You must go,' Charlotte told her. 'It's not safe to stay with him.'

'But—'

'I'm with him now. I'll get him away from here somehow, then things will be all right. Can you leave here? Is there somewhere you can stay? For a little while, I mean, just until . . .'

'What will you do?'

Charlotte did not answer. She was already guiding Mrs Morris from her chair towards the front door. Her outdoor things were scattered carelessly by the front door. Charlotte retrieved the cape and gloves from the floor, helped her to tidy herself.

'Thank you,' Mrs Morris said.

'I'm sorry,' Charlotte said, taking the empty glass from her. 'I don't know what's happened, but . . . I'm sorry. For this.' She was feeling sick again. Her wrist smarted where he had hurt her.

Mrs Morris nodded. 'There's a key,' she said. 'Mr Paige, he left it downstairs when he was here last.'

'Of course, I'll make sure everything's safe.' A thought occurred to her. 'But where is Mr Paige?'

'I don't know. They were going away, you know, for a holiday. I thought they must have left early. Then Mr Norbury came back—' She was struggling against something, tears or a scream. 'He came back different.'

Charlotte did not know afterwards how she managed to hail the cab – she had never thought she would have the courage to do such a thing, and yet she raced down the street after a passing cab without a thought, waving her arms in what must have been a ridiculous fashion. To her great relief, the cabman stopped and waited as she collected Mrs Morris, helped her down the steps.

When the cab was safely away, Charlotte went back inside and locked the door.

The house was still. She sat down in the hall chair and rolled up her sleeve to examine her arm. The wound was not very bad – the bleeding had stopped already. She took out her handkerchief and awkwardly tied it about the cut – the bite – pulling the makeshift bandage taut with her teeth.

She wished she had some water but did not like to go back to the kitchen. She was reluctant to move anywhere in the house, in fact.

Had she done right to send Mrs Morris away? It was surely for the best – until Charlotte found out what exactly had happened. She would have to take James somewhere, to a doctor of some kind.

The first thing was to go back upstairs and, if at all possible, convince him to rest. If he was safely asleep, she would be able to leave him to find a doctor.

She rolled down her sleeve, hiding her wound, and got slowly to her feet, preparing to face James once more. She had not reached the top of the stairs before the doorbell rang – sharp and loud in the quiet house.

Chapter Fourteen

The Notebook of Augustus Mould

18th April

Escaped. Howland, too. They have not even discovered his name (though Edmund revealed his name, and mine, and Michael's, which was hardly wise). Edmund is confident of retrieving both without much difficulty. He ought to have been moved to my workroom from the very start; his chief value is as a scientific curiosity, since he has undergone the Exchange without consent. But Edmund wanted to admit him – to mitigate Michael's mistake, I suppose.

19th April

Makeweight has showed himself useful for once in successfully retrieving the body – which Michael <u>sold</u>, of all things, to one of Price's gang. He brought it back and laid it out upstairs on my operating table, and we gathered round and looked at it. We were at a loss to begin with. I suppose we had expected there to be something in the pockets that would yield a clue, but Mrs Price's lot had been through his things already.

The body was in no very pristine state, of course. I pitied the dead man, as I could not pity his hysterical friend. Most likely he had deserved better than death at Michael's hands.

'Does anyone know him?' Edmund asked. (It was not so remote a chance. The man's clothes showed that he had evidently moved in the same circles as most of the club men – if not the upper ten, then close to it. That sort do tend to recognise one another.)

Michael was watching, more pleased with himself than anything else, I should say.

'What should we do, then?' Corvish said at last. I was about to reply that the body had nothing more to tell us, and had best be disposed of, when Paige arrived.

I should have seen the resemblance before, but the likeness was obscured by the corpse's injuries. Only with Paige in front of me did I see it.

Edmund prudently led him outside to explain, asking Makeweight at the same time to make sure that Michael went downstairs. It was a wise precaution. But Paige did not react violently.

The others left – Edmund asked them to wait downstairs, to determine what was next to be done. Only Edmund and I remained, whilst Paige went in alone to see his brother's body. They are not warm-hearted, the un-dead. Many are purely selfish. But they do have their affections.

After a little while we went in to see how he was. Paige asked me to remain, as Edmund went downstairs to speak with the others.

He asked, 'How did it happen?'

I told him. He did not say anything, perhaps for a full minute. I did not know whether to break the silence or not.

'Can we lay him out?' he said at last. 'I don't like seeing him like this.'

'Of course,' I said. 'I'll help you.'

Together we washed and laid out the corpse. There were many savage wounds, and the limbs were stiffened and broken; it was not easy to make the body decent.

Paige spoke of his brother as we worked. He was a flighty fellow, and Paige had always felt a slight resentment towards him, for when one brother is cheerful and irresponsible, the other brother must necessarily be grave and prudent, punctilious over every duty – particularly when there is no father alive to shoulder such burdens.

When we had done all that we could and the bloody water was taken away, he kissed his brother's forehead – forgetting, I think, that I was in the room. I was surprised at the bleak expression I saw in his eyes.

But when he straightened and turned to look at me, he was quite steady. I asked him if he knew who his brother's companion might have been.

'How old was he?' he asked.

'Young,' I said. 'Grey eyes, very dark hair, about middle height. He didn't look like a man who works for his living, if that's any help. Perhaps some sort of writer – Michael said he had a manuscript with him. Dressed like a gentleman—'

Paige raised a hand to stop me here. He was able to identify the man and has given us a name and address. He and Paige's brother lodged together, it appears.

Paige's distaste for the man was quite evident, and from his hints, I should say this is entirely justified. His name is Norbury, and he is a poet, or would-be poet, or professional idler, or something of the kind.

Later, same day

I was obliged to break off from exhaustion – I actually fell asleep at my desk, woke with a dreadful backache some hours later. Now I am refreshed.

To continue:

It was, by this time, long past midday. Paige, having told all he knew, said that he should like to take the body home. He will give out that there has been some accident. It will allow his family to bury the remains, which should be a comfort for them. I understand that Paige's mother and sister are already under his influence and are unlikely to ask many questions about what has occurred. Paige and two others left to carry out this sad duty. A party of others, led by Corvish, has been despatched to the address that Paige gave, in search of Mr Norbury.

Chapter Fifteen

W hen Charlotte opened the front door, she was relieved to discover the visitor to be a respectable-looking gentleman – middle-aged, with a serious, intelligent countenance.

'Good afternoon,' he said, and Charlotte saw that he was making an effort to smile – a twitch of the mouth only, not the slightest show of teeth.

'Good afternoon,' Charlotte replied. 'I . . .'

What could she say, how could she ask for his assistance? Tell him that her brother was ill, that he was suffering from some temporary disturbance of mind?

'I wonder if I might see Mr Norbury,' the stranger said. 'If he is at home. My name is Browne.' He was a Yorkshire man; the accent was a disconcerting touch of familiarity.

'He's unwell—' Charlotte was about to explain how she came to be opening the door and ask that Browne send for a doctor, but he cut her off:

'Unwell? Have you seen him, then?'

'Yes. I'm his sister.'

His expression did not alter when she said that. But something about him changed. She sensed a new alertness, a keen unfriendly interest. His eyes made her think of careful hunting creatures – the fox that kills daintily, without a trace of feathers or blood left behind.

She knew, without understanding why, that she should not let him into the house. No matter what reason she gave, no matter what rudeness it demanded on her part, she must not allow him past the threshold.

'I'm sorry to hear that he's not well,' Browne said. 'I wonder if I might be of assistance? I am a doctor, you see. I don't know if your brother's spoken of me, but we have a slight acquaintance. I'm sure he wouldn't object to my help.'

His gaze had already moved past her to the interior of the house, to the staircase that led to James.

'Thank you; I think we'll manage.'

'But Miss Norbury, if your brother is ill—'

'He only wants rest. Thank you.' She spoke almost at random now. 'I'll let him know that you called.'

And she slammed the door shut. She listened, not daring to move, until she heard him depart.

Immediately she regretted what she had done. She did not understand how she could have been so foolish. It was an inexcusable piece of silliness, to throw away such a timely offer of help, simply because she had disliked the man's manner. And what was she to do now?

See to James first, she thought; there will be time for self-reproach later. Without allowing herself to dwell upon what awaited her, she hurried upstairs, back to the sitting-room.

'James?' she called. But the room was quiet. The curtains were still drawn. The door had drifted shut behind her. She could see almost nothing.

Ignoring the darkness and her fear that James might approach her unseen, she felt her way to the window and opened the curtains. Then she turned quickly. The room was empty.

She went to his bedroom and did not find him there. She called his name – softly at first, and then louder. Then she stood still and held her breath and listened. The house was silent.

Mustering her courage, she went from room to room, higher and higher through the house, searching and calling. At last she found herself at the very top of the building, in a little attic room that must belong to the maid. It was empty, but the window was open; a draught stirred the faded curtains. The bed had not been made, and the drawers had been pulled out and emptied in haste. A single stocking lay forgotten on the floor.

The idea of James climbing out of the window was incredible, and yet where else could he have gone? She would have heard him if he had come downstairs; there was no other way he could have fled. She leaned as far out as she dared and looked upwards. Nothing moved on the sloping roofs above her. Beneath, there was a steep drop to the street, little in the way of guttering to provide a foothold. Could he really have managed such a feat?

Again she shouted his name – just once – ignoring the traffic, the people going past. If he heard her, he did not answer.

She closed the window and went downstairs – back to the sitting-room. She stooped to inspect the scraps of paper which littered the floor, some torn or burned. They were James's writings. It seemed pitiful to leave them scattered and uncared for. Because she did not know what else to do, she gathered together all the pages she could and piled them onto the table.

What was the best course to take? She could not remain in the house. That much was clear.

On the table, beside the pile of James's papers, she saw her telegrams. And a small green-edged card, with writing scrawled across it. It occurred to her that, amongst all the mess, there might be some clue to James's state – a letter containing bad news, something of that kind. In his room she had noticed a large suitcase, packed and locked, and an empty Gladstone bag. James had been going away, Mrs Morris had said – it would be like him to be lax in finishing his packing.

She fetched the empty Gladstone and forced papers and letters inside – not troubling to sort or read, eager only to be finished quickly. She took as much as she could carry. He would certainly want his writings again once he was recovered, and they would be safe with her.

When she was finished, she went downstairs. The Gladstone had a good weight to it; she would not be able to walk far carrying it along with her suitcase and handbag.

And where was she to go? She was eager to be out of the house, to be away from this absolute hush. A tea room, she thought, or a restaurant. There must be somewhere within walking distance. A place to sit and rest – think things over.

Outside, the air was cool. She was surprised to discover that the light was already failing. It would not be evening for some hours, but the sky had clouded over, and a fog was coming on.

It was an unnatural place, London. At home she could walk briskly, unhindered, through the grounds of Aiskew Hall or down to the village or across the fields, without fear of being looked at askance or of accidentally colliding with another pedestrian. But the city cared nothing for her – there had been thousands here before her birth, thousands more would walk these streets after she had died. And yet it was a relief now to walk amidst so much life. It affected one like a cup of strong coffee, she thought – a hectic energy and excitement, eventually succeeded, no doubt, by listless exhaustion.

She began to feel somewhat recovered; her wrist still hurt her, but the pain had lessened. The cold was bracing, now that she was walking more quickly. She had decided not to think about what to do until she could sit down and recover herself.

She strode on, faster and faster, so absorbed in not thinking that it took her some minutes to realise she had wandered into a subdued street of houses, rather less well-to-do than Egerton

Gardens. She had passed a few shops a while back, but now there was nowhere to ask directions, and there were no passing cabs. Perhaps she should stop and take out her map, but she did not want to make herself unnecessarily conspicuous.

Something else – she had sensed it a few minutes earlier and been reluctant to acknowledge it: she was being followed.

It was not her nervousness acting upon her imagination – there were footsteps, steady and deliberate. Close behind, and yet not so close that the stranger would be obliged to pass her. Guided by an instinct of which she had never before been aware, she kept moving, tried to give no sign of her misgivings. She changed direction twice at random, and still the footsteps continued. Heavy – a man's tread.

Her abrupt changes of direction led her to a quiet, respectable little street beside a church. There were houses all around but nobody outside. How could there not be one child playing, she thought, no women lingering outside for a confidential chat, no men hastening home from work?

She was frightened now, almost frightened enough to knock at one of the dark houses – some had lights in the windows – and say anything necessary to gain admittance.

As the fright grew, her pace slowed. Her bags felt very heavy, and her arm and shoulder ached from the weight.

Finally she stopped walking altogether. Anything would be better than to continue like this, listening to him come closer. She turned around.

Browne stood there, perhaps ten yards away. As she stood motionless, he came closer. She could see in his face that he meant to kill her.

'Stay,' he said.

It was as if a cold hand had reached behind her forehead and closed around the play of her thoughts. Things slowed and grew distant.

Then someone called out, words that Charlotte could not

distinguish. She heard running feet very far off, a hiss of rage. She fell and was lifted to her feet again – then there was pain: someone had slapped her hard across the face.

'You hold her, Shadwell. Get her away, I'll deal with him—'

'Can you hear me?' another voice demanded – a man's voice, tones clipped and urgent. 'Please listen, you need to stay awake.'

'Get her away,' the first voice repeated. 'He's mazed her already.'

Charlotte opened her eyes. Her vision was cloudy. A man held her by the shoulders – not Browne but a stranger, bare-headed and breathless.

He said, 'Can you walk?'

She opened her mouth to ask something – who was he, why should she not be able to walk – when something flew past her ear, clanged against the pavement. It was a knife.

That brought her to her senses, enough for her to understand what was happening.

She was standing on a cold pavement in an unknown part of London; an unknown man had taken her arm and was trying to drag her away with him. She tried to tell him to let her go – but found she could not speak.

'Don't look,' the stranger said. 'Come on . . .'

But he was not making much of an effort to lead her away, for all that – he was watching, too.

His gaze was fixed on another man, who stood a few yards distant, one arm raised. He could not be more than twenty, and was much slighter and shorter than Browne. His hat was pushed down low over his forehead. The boy regarded Browne with a peculiar intensity – Charlotte had never seen anyone so absolutely alert. But he was not afraid. In the half darkness, Charlotte thought she even saw him smile.

'You should've known better,' he said. 'It's not even night yet.'

Browne merely snarled and rushed forwards.

Something glittered in the half-light – another knife. It was beautiful, Charlotte thought, the boy's movement. The lad ducked away from his attacker, who stepped back abruptly, blood suddenly dark on his pale face.

Browne raised a hand, wiped the blood from his temple, leaving a crimson smear behind. 'You filthy little whore,' he said.

The man at Charlotte's side now released her and moved towards the other two. He held out a blue glass bottle, half filled with liquid.

'You know what this is,' he said as he approached Browne. 'There are two of us, and we know what you are. We *know you*, do you understand? And there are people living on this street. You know how many they are – you can hear them, can't you? Sooner or later someone will see, someone will come out. So go.'

Browne's face showed no reaction to these words. Instead, he stepped towards the hatless man – sprang at him, in a motion very swift and somehow entirely ugly.

Charlotte's scream was lost in the sound of a shot. The boy had fired a revolver, hit Browne in the face.

Browne was knocked off his feet – and Charlotte could not look away from the wound in his forehead, the horrible confusion of blood and other things.

Still pointing the revolver, the boy edged around the body of his victim, backed away until he was close to his accomplice.

'Come on,' said the man. He still held the blue bottle before him, as if it offered a kind of protection. He took Charlotte's arm. 'Come *on*. Before he gets up.'

Charlotte struggled as he snatched roughly at her other arm. She was about to scream for help – when she saw the dead man sit up.

He had a hand clapped to his brow, the other pressed to the back of his head. There was blood still rolling slowly down his face, a horrible soft mess of injury behind his fingers. But he was leaning forwards, attempting to stand up.

'Run,' the boy muttered. '*Now.*'

Charlotte offered no resistance – like the other two, she turned and ran. At the corner, a four-wheeler was waiting. She followed her companions inside without hesitation.

'Went well, did it?' the driver called from his seat.

'Shut up, Rafferty,' the boy said. '*Go.*'

There was a hoarse chuckle, but the driver obliged, and they were off.

For a few minutes neither of Charlotte's companions spoke.

'He won't follow,' the bare-headed man said at last.

'He was angry enough,' the boy observed.

He took off his hat, and as they passed a streetlamp, Charlotte saw his face clearly for the first time – it was unquestionably that of a young woman, with bright black eyes, her dark hair pinned back and bound fiercely beneath her hat. At any other time this would have been utterly confounding. Now it was just one minor uncanny detail.

'You shouldn't have shot him,' the man said. 'The noise—'

'Had to. He'd have killed you otherwise.' The woman turned to Charlotte. 'Are you all right?'

'Are you going to kill me?'

'No,' the woman said. And she laid one slender hand on Charlotte's. 'You can put them down.'

Charlotte realised that she was still gripping the handles of her bags. She was holding them so tight that it had been hurting her for some time.

'Yes, you're quite safe,' the man added. 'My name is Shadwell, and this is Miss Swift.' He held out his hand, and Charlotte shook it.

'Charlotte Norbury.' Probably it was unwise to give them her name – she knew little enough about them, and what she did know was not entirely encouraging. But then – and this fact was still difficult to take in – they had saved her life.

'She's shaking,' Miss Swift said. Charlotte caught a slight foreign note to her accent – the faintest note of French. 'Shadwell, did you bring any—'

'In the bag.' Shadwell did not appear dangerous, Charlotte thought. He was a plain, slovenly-looking man, but with a kind face. If pressed, she would have said he was a gentleman, though a rather ill-kempt one. His expression was intelligent, sympathetic.

Miss Swift had stooped, brought another bottle from the carpetbag and held it out to Charlotte. 'Here. Brandy. It'll do you good.'

'No, thank you.'

'Take this, then,' Miss Swift said. There was a rather tattered woollen blanket on the seat between them. She picked it up and laid it gingerly around Charlotte's shoulders. 'Keep that on. You've got to stay warm.'

'Where are we going?' she asked. They were now travelling too fast for her to make out any street names.

'A safe place,' replied Miss Swift. 'Do you know Wych Street?'

'No.'

'Well, we've got a shop there. Books, mostly.'

'The street has its reputation, of course,' Shadwell put in, 'but it's convenient for us.'

Charlotte pulled the blanket close about her. She did not know where Wych Street was or why it should have any kind of reputation. Nor did she care. A curious numbness had taken hold of her; she was not in pain or distress any longer. She felt nothing but a fervent wish not to speak or move or think.

When they at last rattled to a stop – it was an old carriage and must have had a long life before being given over to Mr Rafferty's tender mercies – Charlotte climbed out to find herself on a narrow street of shops, high, rickety buildings that ought to have been pulled down many years ago.

Miss Swift was paying Rafferty – who Charlotte now observed to be a middle-aged man with sharp dark eyes and a tragedian's mouth. He wore a sturdy bowler hat and a thick rough coat.

'You've ruined us,' Miss Swift said to him, when the fare was settled.

'Serves you right,' Rafferty replied, 'for being in such a bloody stupid profession.'

And he nodded and was off without a word of goodbye.

'This way,' Shadwell said. 'Just a few yards. Quickly.'

Miss Swift took Charlotte's arm. 'Keep the blanket round you.'

One shop was still open; a variety of lithographs were displayed. To scan the gaslit window was to get a rapid impression of sprawling naked limbs, bows and sashes coming undone, petticoats flung up in a flurry of white lace. From one photograph a reclining woman, naked to the waist, regarded the viewer with a strange, direct smile – Charlotte averted her gaze.

There were other establishments, too: a corset-maker and a butcher, a public house and a theatre. It was not quite Gomorrah, though it might as well have been. They did not speak again until they were drawing close to the last shop on the street. Through the window one could make out books displayed on shelves and on a table, but none of the titles could be distinguished through the grimy glass. The door was painted red, and instead of a written sign, the shop displayed a hanging board on which was painted an onion.

'Here,' Shadwell said. 'Miss Norbury, we can talk inside.'

'Why . . .' Charlotte began, looking up at the sign.

'Tradition,' Miss Swift replied. 'Come on, we'll—'

'Adeline,' Shadwell said suddenly, cutting her off. 'Look there.'

Charlotte saw it in the same moment: a human body – slumped face down on the street, just outside the door to the shop. Her first shocked thought was that it was James and that he was dead.

But it was not James – she told herself fiercely that it was *not*. This was a stranger, there was no resemblance between him and James. It was only that for a moment he had embodied her worst fears – a young man, lying prone and injured.

Shadwell stooped over the stranger, frowning. 'He's alive. Fainted, I think.'

Even as Shadwell spoke, the man stirred, struggling to raise himself out of the dirt.

'Are you hurt?' Shadwell said.

He opened his eyes now and stared blankly, then shrank away. He muttered something that might have been a question – a why, or where.

'Get him inside,' Miss Swift said. 'Not safe here.'

'Can you move?' Shadwell asked. He held out his hand. 'Come indoors, and we can—'

'No.' The stranger slowly climbed to his feet. His clothes were evidently second-hand, and fitted him poorly. His grey flannel shirt was too big; his jacket was conspicuously short on the sleeves, stretched uncomfortably across his shoulders. There was dirt on his face and straw in his hair and a red mark on his forehead that would soon be a bruise. On one of his shoes was a white stain that looked like paint. His eyes were dazed, and he did not look as if he had known peace or rest for several days.

'It's all right,' Miss Swift said. The man did not seem to understand. 'Shadwell, tell him.'

'You're safe.' Shadwell took the man by the shoulders. 'Do you understand? You're safe.'

The man stared at him. 'Shadwell?'

'Yes. That's my name. This is Miss Swift, my colleague. You're here to see us, aren't you?'

'. . . said you could help,' the stranger muttered.

'Yes,' Shadwell agreed, 'we can.' He had begun to struggle with the key to the shop door – hastily, urgently, glancing over his shoulder as he did so, searching the darkening street. He was looking for something he dreaded, Charlotte thought. But he spoke calmly, as if there were no hurry at all. 'It's all right,' he said to the stranger, who was still staring at him blearily. 'Come in and get warm, and then you can tell us all about it.'

Chapter Sixteen

James had driven Charlotte away, sent her running from him. It was what he had wanted, and yet he would have called her back again if he could, if it were safe for her to be anywhere near him.

His love for her was there as it had always been: he searched himself, like a man turning out his pockets to see if he had been robbed, and he could still feel how dear she was, how any injury to her would grieve him. And yet he had hurt her, he had tasted her blood and briefly felt her life and strength become his. He had been irked by the interruption – it was like an unfinished cadence. He had wanted her death.

The worst of it was that she drew him the most. Resisting her had been worse than resisting Howland or Mrs Morris. Perhaps he would never be free of it again, this horrible instinct; he would have to flee her for ever.

He could not remember very clearly when he had first returned to Egerton Gardens. He had a confused idea that he had pushed Howland away, told him to run. Everything had seemed too loud, too bright – even scents had been almost too powerful to bear. Somehow he had got himself upstairs. He had been very cold. He had lit the fire in the sitting-room and locked the door.

He had not stirred outside, and days had passed, and as his strength had returned to him his hunger had grown worse. He had begun to bite and scratch at his own arms, the blood was a feeble respite. The wounds closed every time, disappeared without a mark or scar.

Now there was Charlotte's blood in his mouth. He thought of that simple, horrible fact and listened to her downstairs (she was in the hall now, with Mrs Morris). She was saying something kind, doing her best to help.

He did not like to think about Mrs Morris, either. She had been so worried for him, so eager to fetch a doctor, and then she had asked where Christopher was and whether James would be joining him soon, and he had struck her to get her safely away from him, to stop her talking. He could not get away from the memory – her soft, gasping sob.

He put his hands into his pockets for a trace of warmth and found that his fingers brushed something he had forgotten: the note Howland had given him. It had been dashed off in pencil, scrawled over a printed card, one side of which bore the legend:

The Ægolius Club
8 Ormond Yard
London

On the back was a quaint device – a little green owl, over which Howland had scribbled some hasty message, the words almost illegible.

James let the card slip through his fingers onto the table, remembering where he had seen one identical to this – in Mrs Paige's house, the night of the dinner party. It had been displayed deliberately, he remembered, left in plain view on the mantelpiece.

Then he saw it: of course, Eustace was one of them. James's memory of their meeting now made sense – Eustace would have known what was between James and Christopher as soon as they entered the room, just as James had sensed the thoughts of the crowds in the street. And his wound, his pallor, his strange manner – it could be nothing else.

If Eustace belonged to the club, then it would have been easy for him to arrange for James's removal. Perhaps he had also intended for Christopher to be made to see reason, or even to be transformed as James had been. Only a mistake was made – James had been saved, Christopher murdered.

The fire was nearly out. James sank down in front of it, taking what warmth he could from the last of the blaze. After the coal was finished, he had begun to burn his own papers. They were strewn over the floor and he scrabbled about in the mess, dropped a few onto the embers. The work that had cost him so much time and effort now sickened him. He scanned lines and lines in his own hand without recognising anything of it. It was not only that it was bad, it was that it made no sense. It jangled. Good for nothing but kindling. He thrust a handful of pages into the heart of the fire, careless of the hot coals. The papers flared up rapidly, and he winced at the sudden brightness.

If he did not feed soon, he would have to destroy himself. He could not stand the death Bier had described to him, the slow wasting of famine. How long would it take for one like him to die of starvation? Would it be years, or decades, or longer still?

As a child he had trapped a spider in an empty matchbox, with an idea of making it his pet, and had afterwards forgotten about it. When he had finally let the creature out, it was grey-white where it had been black, a spindly, almost transparent thing. He had wept foolishly over it, he remembered. Would he become like the spider if he did not feed – would he simply fade away, turn the colour of dust?

From downstairs came the sound of the front door closing.

Had Charlotte left? The sitting-room window looked out onto the street. He went to it, pulled back the curtain cautiously, wincing in the faint afternoon sunlight. He saw Mrs Morris emerge, leaning on Charlotte's arm. She got into a waiting hansom and was gone. Charlotte was here alone with him. He let the curtain fall back but did not move from the window. He knew she would come upstairs again shortly – she would worry over him and refuse to be turned away.

He steeled himself to go to the door and lock it – then he heard the doorbell ring. Squinting through the window again, he saw a visitor waiting outside. The man looked up at the building, inspecting it – a stranger, and yet familiar. One began to notice the signs. Even at a distance, it was not difficult to see that there was something subtly amiss in the man's face, a peculiar dullness to his eyes. James saw the same quality in his reflection when he had the courage to look in the glass.

Carefully, he stepped back from the window and heard the man speak to Charlotte, heard her make a short reply.

James would kill him. If the man took another step towards Charlotte, if he so much as crossed the threshold, he would kill him. It would be easily done; he could be downstairs in an instant.

But the man did not come in. Charlotte had said something polite and firm and shut the door smartly.

So they were watching the house now. Somehow they knew James was here, and Charlotte would not be safe until he had drawn them away from her. They would be watching from the street, waiting for him to emerge.

Not the door, then, but the roof. He made his way to the top of the house, into the maid's bedroom. The window slanted upwards, a square of dark-blue sky in the whitewashed ceiling. It was only a slight effort to heave himself through and outside.

The windowsill was narrow; the angle of the roof made it hard to keep his balance. He teetered for an instant, then righted and hauled himself upwards.

On the roof, he had one instant of panic – not at the height, not at the thought of his pursuers, but at the fact of leaving this place for the last time. He had been happy here. He remembered it without conviction, in the same way that he remembered the warmth of the fire now that he stood in the cold on the roof.

There were several more houses in the row; he might get quite far before needing to climb down to the street. The daylight was already beginning to fade, but he could see his way clearly, his vision so precise that it almost hurt: every crack and spot of the slates was visible, every detail of the street below. It was difficult to comprehend all that his eyes had to show him.

He moved cautiously, eager to avoid notice. He knew with dull, absolute certainty that he would not lose his balance. He was strong and agile enough now. The knowledge gave him no joy.

At first he kept low, crouching close to the roof slates. After the first house, he abandoned this effort, stood upright again. If they spotted him, they would not see him cringing and terrified.

He was six houses along – seven – and then he could go no further. There was London, spread out below and around him, gas and electricity flaring in the shop windows and on the streets. And there were people, and he could hear them talking: the same babble he had heard from the street at the club. Already he was growing better at ignoring them. But at the back of his mind they were still there, the stinking rabble. They had tramped these streets for so long that the place echoed with them. They had seeped into every brick and slate; there was nowhere free from their thoughts and sufferings.

He must not delay. Someone would notice him, sooner or later.

Someone had seen him already. He felt a gaze on him, a cool, unfriendly notice, and then his ears picked it out: someone down on the street saying, with a delighted giggle, 'There, just look.'

There were two little girls staring up at him from the steps of the Brompton Oratory. They were sitting with their backs to one of the stone pillars and seemed to have been playing a game or sharing secrets. One was dressed with care in buttoned boots and a pretty blue coat. The other was shivering in a threadbare boy's jacket. The blue-coat girl was open-mouthed. Her companion's gaze was direct and unsurprised. A strange old look, James thought. Then she poked her tongue out at him.

In his surprise, he loosened his hold – before he could help himself he was sliding forwards, too fast to stop, toppling over the edge of the roof. He fell as he had fallen before in nightmares – slow and fast at once, a dreadful inevitable plummet, a pulverising smash.

The street hit him with such force that all he felt at first was astonishment. The breath had been knocked out of him; his very thoughts had been knocked out of him. All that remained was his pain. Surely this was enough, and now he would die.

Very, very far off, there were voices shouting. A horse whinnied in alarm and shied backwards.

Gradually, his senses returned enough to tell him that a crowd was gathered but that they were reluctant to draw near. He wondered if it was natural fear of a possible corpse or whether they knew, without understanding why, that he was not to be approached.

The traffic had stopped around him. There were complaints about the delay, suggestions that he ought to be moved. Someone else said he shouldn't be touched, not until the doctor came.

Had the doctor been summoned? (No one knew.) What about a policeman?

If he was dead, then he ought to be taken away, instead of being left there to impede the traffic.

'Not much blood,' someone said, 'considering.'

Already the pain was subsiding. He moved his head – something cracked, horribly, back into place. The crowd saw: someone gasped; one or two onlookers seemed about to be sick. He was mending. It was a useful discovery. He now knew that it would take a great deal of force to kill someone like him.

As James sat up, the crowd shrank from him. But they did not go away, and there was now one man crouched before him, perhaps a doctor. He carried a black leather bag. And they were all watching, white-faced, clerks and street traders and professional men. One of them – a fellow with a checked coat and a luxuriant red beard – said, 'Well, I'll be damned. He ain't dead.'

Someone chided the red-beard for his language, but the man had evidently spoken for the majority. They were amazed, and rather disappointed, to see James sit up.

'Sir,' said the man crouched beside him. 'Sir, are you – are you all right?'

'Quite,' James replied.

'But the fall . . .'

'Yes. I was lucky.'

They were all dissatisfied, he saw. They wanted an explanation, but they were unsure how to begin. It hardly seemed good manners to demand of a man why he wasn't dead and what did he mean by not having the decency to be dashed to pieces like anyone else would have been?

Seizing on the first explanation he could think of, he said, 'I'm with the circus. Trained, you know . . .'

More murmuring. It was an explanation of sorts. Some of them had seen magicians. Perhaps the whole thing was a stunt, though in very bad taste.

James got to his feet. His clothes had not survived the fall as well as his body had done. His coat was ripped, and there was blood – Charlotte's and his own – on his sleeves, on the collar of his shirt.

'Are you sure you shouldn't go to the hospital?' asked the doctor, who was still watching James closely.

'No, I'm quite recovered. Thank you.' It was a struggle to be gracious. And still the crowd would not leave or stop looking at him. As he left, they drew back, muttering, to let him pass.

Now he noticed the two girls again. Blue-coat was staring at James – astonished by the display and reluctant to move – but her shabby companion was tugging at her wrist, urging her away from the scene.

The ragged girl had the look of a London native, a scrawny sallow-faced little Cockney. He had braced himself to endure the thoughts of the crowds – their noise – but from her he suffered nothing. She was a small island of silence.

The children were already yards ahead. He pushed through the crowd and followed the route they had taken. They led him far from Kensington, twisting and winding away from the smart streets, taking unexpected turns down unprepossessing byways. He followed them down alleys, dead ends that were not dead ends after all.

At last they came to a street he did not recognise, where few turned to look at him and the ones who did averted their eyes quickly.

It was a street built on good intentions which had failed – whoever had designed these houses had envisioned respectability, prosperous self-confidence. Instead, something, had gone wrong, and now it was not the neighbourhood for a decent family.

He let them move further ahead, for he could hear them, he discovered. If he listened carefully he could pick out their foot-steps, even streets away.

Then he turned a corner incautiously and found the two of them halted a few yards in front of him. They were sitting together in a doorway, close as confidantes.

The house behind them was empty, windows boarded over, and looked as if it was about to be torn down. Though he thought himself hidden in the shadows, the girl in the shabby coat made him out quickly. He had been correct: she was a child and not a child. Her clothes were indeterminate, piled on top of one another as if she had wandered up to a second-hand clothes stall and thrown on as many garments as she could before taking to her heels. In spite of them, she was shivering. Her hair was dark and greasy, one lank lock hanging into her right eye.

The girl in the blue coat was slumped, unmoving, barely breathing. Her eyes were closed; there was a small wound on her neck. The air was full of the smell of blood.

James took a step forwards.

The girl bared her teeth. 'I ain't sharing.'

'I don't want any.'

That surprised her. She looked at him more carefully. 'Then you *are* green.' Another pause. 'Or mad. Some of 'em go mad. If you're mad, you won't last long. The Other Lot don't like yer to go mad. 'Tracts attention.'

'I'm not mad.' He nodded towards her quarry. 'You could let her live.'

'You could try an' stop me.' She must see that he was still damaged from his fall. She might well be the stronger.

'Please stop, then,' he said. He moved closer. 'Don't you see what you're doing? You'll kill her.'

She laughed – though it seemed to cost her some effort. ''Course I'll kill her. Or else I'll die. That's what I'm like, same as you.'

'I'm not like you.' The smell of the child's blood was impossible to ignore – James was cold and hungry and desperately ashamed. 'Please let it go.' He heard his words – corrected them swiftly. 'Let her go. Please.'

The child in the blue coat stirred slightly, moaned softly. The girl looked up at him, and, to his surprise and disgust, she spat onto the pavement – a gobbet of red saliva.

'Hook it,' she said. She turned back to her prey and gave the child a little shake. 'You're too late, anyway.' The girl let the child's body slide gently sideways, then eased off her blue coat and flung it over her own shoulders.

''S'nice,' she said to James, slightly defiant. 'Nice an' warm.'

James stared at her and was not sure what to do.

She had wiped the blood from her mouth, but there was a trace of it – or something else red – showing on her jagged and uneven teeth. She had a small knife with her, lying by her foot. Now she picked it up and licked it clean. Seeing that he watched, she held it up, showed him the blade.

'Makes it easier,' she explained. ''Specially if your teeth ain't up to much.' She considered him, her head tilted to one side. 'You fell off the roof,' she said. She seemed divided between amusement and disapproval.

When he remained silent, she went on, 'You shouldn't've fallen off the roof like that. There were people looking an' everything.'

'I know.'

'They almost nabbed you – the ones following.'

'Listen, I'd like to ask you some questions,' James said. 'I promise I won't harm you.'

''Course you won't. As if you could. You look awful.' She sounded a little younger when she was being scornful. But she was intrigued, he saw, by the novelty of his presence. 'What d'you want to know?'

'Do you know many . . . like us?' She considered him – head to one side again. He was reminded of Charlotte as a girl, scrutinising his mistakes in spelling.

''Course,' she said.

'How many?'

'Lots.'

'Where—'

'None of your business.' She tucked her knife away out of sight. 'You don't know nothing, do you?'

'No.'

'They should've told you, 'ow to feed and such. You got to drink, you know, for your 'ealth.'

'I won't,' he said. 'I won't do that.' The words sounded feeble. 'I didn't ask for this.'

Now she was interested. 'Why'd you do it, then?'

'Do what?'

'The Exchange.' *Ixchange*, she pronounced it, a violent snarl of a word.

'I didn't,' James said. 'They forced me.'

She spat again, licked her lips. Her mouth, he saw, was very pale, inside and out. 'Liar. 'Course you wanted it. Don't work otherwise.'

'What?'

'You got to say yes,' the girl insisted. 'Everyone knows that.'

'What's your name?' James asked.

She shook her head. 'You think I'm cracked? You could be one of the Other Lot, for all I know. Though *they* don't let the new ones wander about all stupid, like how you are.'

'I'm not one of them,' James said, 'but I'm looking for one of them.'

'You better stay away if you ain't one of them. Otherwise they'll send Doctor Knife for you.'

'Who's that?'

'You really *don't* know nothing,' she said – losing patience with him, it seemed. 'You'd better clear off if you've got any sense.'

'But—'

She snarled again – an inarticulate, animal sound. 'Clear off. We don't want trouble.'

Before he could respond, she had already gone, vanished into the gloom of the alley. Perhaps out of pique, she had left the body behind, as if he were to dispose of it.

The girl lay small and twisted, mud on her white frock. Her face rested against the pavement as if it were a pillow. Eyes open, straw in her hair. She had died without a cry, after that last soft moan of distress.

There would be a mother already searching, her pretence of calm giving way to shrill, impatient fear as the search continued and nothing was found. And nothing would be found.

It would be so easy to drink from her. But James would not let it happen. He would not let himself be a man who held a dead child in his arms and felt nothing but thirst.

He might preserve what remained of his better self and yet not go hungry. There was no real crime in preying on the men who killed without remorse, in drinking the blood of the murderer. He might reduce Eustace Paige and Michael Bier and all their club to nothing and feel no guilt. Revenge on those two killers and their associates would free the world from a terrible evil – it would be justice.

But first of all he would warn Christopher's family about Eustace – Christopher would want James to keep them safe. He would defend them against their son and brother.

He made his way quietly through the streets like a drifting fog. Few people appeared to notice him. He held the girl close to his chest, ready to say, if asked, that she was his child, who had fallen asleep, that he was taking her home. But no one did ask, no one seemed to wonder, and he went on his way into the evening.

Chapter Seventeen

Inside, the shop was very cold and smelled of damp paper. The odour reminded Charlotte of James's rooms – had he found somewhere warm to pass the night, or was he still out wandering the city?

Miss Swift busied herself securing the door. There were several bolts, and she struggled and grumbled over them in the near darkness.

'Upstairs,' Shadwell said. He took the stranger's arm – the man was still unsteady on his feet – and guided them through the shop, up a narrow staircase.

They were led into what looked like something between a study and a sitting-room. It was shabbily furnished, with ill-assorted rugs and chairs that must originally have been very different colours and patterns but had faded with age into an almost identical shade of uncertain brown. Two armchairs were pushed close to the fire. One had a great stain across its back; the other was adorned by a grubby-looking antimacassar, hanging crumpled and crooked.

Charlotte could smell tobacco and peppermint, coffee and book dust, and more damp. There were two desks, both covered in papers, and books everywhere – on the shelves and piled on the floor. Most of them were arranged in disorderly stacks, as if there had not been enough time to put them away; others were still inside wooden crates. The mantelpiece was dominated by a tarnished mirror and a hideous carriage clock, which had stopped at a quarter past twelve. Pinned to the wall was a large map of London – scrawled over in coloured pencil, in at least two different hands, the many crossings-out and corrections making a kind of duel, right to the paper's edge. The whole room gave the impression that its occupants were either moving in or moving out.

'Right. Yes, I suppose we'd better—'

Here Shadwell broke off and caught the stranger's arm. The man seemed about to faint again.

'Come on,' Shadwell said to him. He helped him to one of the armchairs near the fireplace. 'This way. Sit down.'

'Brandy,' Miss Swift muttered.

'Where is it?'

'Coat pocket.'

'Ah. Yes, here we are.' Shadwell produced the bottle and retrieved a glass from the top of the mantelpiece. He poured out a measure. 'Here.'

The stranger took the glass – almost spilled it. 'Thanks.'

'Do sit down, Miss Norbury,' Shadwell added. He was looking at her with some concern. 'I'm sorry it's so cold in here.'

Miss Swift went about lighting the lamps, and gradually Charlotte could make out her companions more clearly. There was nothing particularly sinister about them. Miss Swift, who appeared slightly younger than Charlotte, was dark-haired and slender and (in spite of her curious attire) what the magazines would call *chic*. Her eyes were tired, and there was a half-healed graze on her chin.

Shadwell was tall, perhaps in his early fifties, a powerful man just past his prime. His clothes were well made and ill cared for.

His hair was a mixture of grey and brown, rough and wild and conspicuously in need of cutting. He took off his gloves, and Charlotte saw that his fingernails were jagged, as if he had simply torn each nail short.

She seated herself in the remaining armchair. Her head ached; her hands and back hurt from carrying her suitcase and James's bag.

Shadwell set about laying the fire, and Miss Swift disappeared into the next room, muttering something about tea. Charlotte was relieved to be able to sit for a while and not say anything. Across from her, the stranger had finished his drink.

'Are you sure you won't have some brandy, Miss Norbury?' Shadwell asked. He was looking at her over his shoulder, face slightly worried.

Charlotte was about to make a polite demurral, when the stranger cut her off:

'Norbury?' He was scrutinising her with an urgency she did not understand.

'Yes,' she said. 'Why—'

'Do you have a brother—'

They both stopped, and she saw that whatever he had to tell would bring her no comfort.

'Have you seen James?' she asked. She saw Shadwell, still kneeling in front of the hearth, turn to listen to the stranger's reply. 'Please, do you know something? What's happened to him?'

'A few days ago. We were . . .' He paused, took a breath. He looked as if he was struggling not to be sick. 'I'm . . .'

She felt that she could have shaken the truth out of him in her impatience. But Shadwell interposed gently:

'I should sit quiet a little while longer.' He stood up, wiping coal-dusty hands on his coat. 'You've both had a great shock. We can talk with the tea.'

The fire had kindled into light; in a few minutes the room would begin to grow warm.

Shadwell took a paper bag from his pocket, offered it to Charlotte and the stranger. 'Would either of you care for a bull's-eye?'

When they both declined, Shadwell took a couple of sweets from the bag, crunched away in silence until Miss Swift reappeared from the next room. She carried a tray with plates and cups and saucers for four (none matching), a large brown teapot and half a loaf of bread.

'No milk?' Shadwell asked. 'Or butter?'

'Ran out yesterday. Don't you remember?' Miss Swift set a kettle rather precariously on the fire to boil. Then she took a slightly dented cigarette case from the mantelpiece. 'Either of you two smoke?' she added.

Charlotte shook her head, but the stranger nodded. Miss Swift took two cigarettes, lit both, handed one to her visitor – all with the ease of long habit.

'Now,' she said, 'I suppose we should talk.'

She sat down with her back to the fire – cross-legged, a posture Charlotte had never before seen a grown woman assume.

'If Miss Norbury and our other visitor are sufficiently recovered,' said Shadwell, looking from Charlotte to the stranger.

'Howland,' he said. 'My name's Howland.'

Shadwell nodded. 'I'm glad that you found us, Mr Howland.' He turned to Charlotte. 'Miss Norbury – perhaps I might begin by asking you some questions? It may be that we are able to help you. We're used to helping people who've had experiences like yours.'

She wanted to ask why they should want to help, who they were and what it meant that they pursued men like Browne and accepted an unconscious stranger on their doorstep as an almost commonplace occurrence. Instead, she nodded.

'Excellent,' Shadwell said. 'First of all, then, how did you happen across Mr Corvish? The man who attacked you, I mean.'

'Corvish? He told me his name was Browne.'

'We know him of old,' Shadwell said. 'Corvish is his real name.'

Charlotte explained briefly what had happened: James's strangeness, Browne's eagerness to see him, his later pursuit. About James's attack, she found she could not bear to speak – she skirted it briefly.

Shadwell nodded when she had finished. 'I see.'

He had been interviewing her, she realised. Like a detective or a journalist. The questions came easily; he had known exactly when to speak, when to let her pause.

'How do you know Corvish?' she asked. 'What – who is he really?'

Shadwell glanced at Miss Swift, who was finishing her cigarette. The firelight touched her dark hair with orange and red. 'We'll get to that.' He looked to Howland.

'My turn now, is it?' Howland said.

'If you're sufficiently recovered,' replied Shadwell.

'Yes. Sorry about before. Made a fool of myself.' He did not appear much recovered, in spite of the brandy. Charlotte was reminded of Mrs Morris – he had the same unfed, sleepless air. 'Where shall I start?'

He was American, Charlotte noticed. An odd memory came back to her – James, last Christmas, imitating a Chicago glass-eye magnate he had met in the National Gallery. It had been his first evening home, one of the better moments of his holiday. Strange to think of that now, with Mrs Chickering dead, James lost to her.

But then, nothing felt quite real. The room around her was like a set from a play.

'Who gave you our address?' Miss Swift asked Howland. She had set about slicing and toasting her way through the loaf of bread.

'Man in the police station. Constable – don't remember his name. Maybe he didn't say. I was a bit – well, I got upset, I lost my temper. Could have managed things better. They threw me out. But this man came after me, told me to come to you, said you sometimes helped people.'

Shadwell was apparently unsurprised at the mention of the police. 'Have you been in England long, Mr Howland?'

'What? Oh, not long. Two months.'

'And something has happened to you, and you need our advice. Can you tell us what has happened – from the beginning?'

'I'll do my best. I made a mess of it before, at the police station. Tried to tell them everything, but it didn't work somehow. I suppose that sounds ridiculous.'

'No, it doesn't sound ridiculous. How did you feel when you tried to talk about it?'

'Like I was being strangled. Like – like hands choking me, almost. Do you understand what I mean?'

'Yes,' Shadwell said. 'Don't hurry yourself. Tell us what you can.' And when Howland still hesitated, he added, 'Start at the beginning. Are you in London on business?'

'No. I'm here for a vacation, of all things. After I finished at Harvard, I thought I'd travel about for a bit, wait until I got tired of it, then go back and start at the firm. We're in clothes pins – you won't have heard of us over here, but we're fairly well known back home.'

'A family business?'

'Oh, yes. Father started out as a farm boy – built the company himself. He's senior partner now. Fred and Sam – they're my brothers – both work for the business, so does my oldest sister's husband.'

'And you were going to join them?' Shadwell said. He was keeping Howland talking on purpose, Charlotte thought. Howland sounded better the longer he spoke – his colour had returned, his voice was becoming clearer and firmer.

'Oh, yes, eventually. They aren't in any desperate need of my talents, you see, so I could please myself. I like travelling, reckoned there was no reason not to keep on, once I'd started. I went to stay with a friend out west, first of all, then some other places,

Canada for a few months—' He broke off. 'Look, are you sure you want to hear all this?'

'Yes, it may well be useful. Carry on, Mr Howland, please.'

'All right. I was in Europe for a while, France and places, and then I came here a couple of months ago, to see some friends, take in the shops and antiquities, you know.'

There was money in clothes pins, apparently. How pleasant to take in country after country so easily, travelling with only one's own whims as a guide. Charlotte was finding the long recital a great strain on her patience. It was almost intolerable to sit and wait for him to tell them what he knew about James.

'Then a little while back I met a man called Bier,' Howland went on.

'We know of two men with that name,' Shadwell said. He glanced at Miss Swift – who had been silent for some time, Charlotte realised. This must be a system between them – Shadwell would ask questions and offer kindness whilst Miss Swift watched, bright-eyed and thoughtful.

'Well, this man was called Edmund Bier,' said Howland. 'And I don't know that I *liked* him as such, but he was quite interested in me and introduced me to a lot of people. I suppose I was grateful. One night we went to the theatre, and between acts we went out for a smoke and he told me he was a member of a club here in London, called the Aegolius, and if I was interested in getting elected he could guarantee I'd get in, since he was chairman.'

'And what did you say?' Shadwell asked.

'I said I'd think about it. I didn't know how long I was going to be in London; it didn't seem worth the bother. I hadn't heard of the club, and even after I met Bier I was still pretty much in the dark. They were all so damned secretive about it. I guess that was what first made me interested – I wanted to know what all the fuss was about.'

The kettle had come to the boil. Miss Swift stood up to make the tea. Her every motion was harmonious, Charlotte thought, just as it had been when she attacked Corvish.

Howland continued: 'After that, I saw a lot more of Bier and some of the others from his club, as well. Not the most amusing company I'd ever been in, but they were fine people, all from pretty old families. I suppose I was a little flattered they'd taken me up so easily.'

He paused – raised both hands to his face, pushed back his hair as if his head hurt. 'I went to a dinner at Bier's. A lot of them from the club were there. I thought it was the wine, the way I felt at dinner. Bier asked me again if I had thought about joining. And then he told me what they were.'

Miss Swift glanced at Shadwell – Charlotte saw something in her expression, a certain wariness.

'What were they?' Charlotte asked, when no one spoke.

Silence but for the snapping of the fire. Howland looked questioningly to Shadwell. 'Shall I . . . ?'

'Tell her, Shadwell,' Miss Swift said.

'All right.' Charlotte sensed Shadwell mustering his remaining energy, preparing himself for an unpleasant duty.

His explanation was brief and as kind as was possible in the circumstances – he avoided naming the creatures, perhaps from distaste, perhaps from discretion, but told Charlotte very plainly what they were.

When he stopped talking, she could say nothing at first.

'Do you . . . Have you perhaps read about such creatures?' he added. He thought that she did not understand, she realised, that she was too shaken to take in his full meaning.

'I've read about them,' Charlotte said.

She was not sure if she was speaking the truth or not. Where did this idea come from – the stalking figure, the blood drinker? Had it been a bedtime story from some nurse or governess, or from a book she had read with James by the fireside at night, as the moon rose over the hall gardens outside?

'Well, they exist,' Shadwell continued, 'and they are here in London. The most powerful amongst them belong to the Aegolius Club. You've met Mr Corvish – he's one of them.'

It seemed too much, to have suffered the many tribulations of today only to be confronted with this now, at the end. They were mad or deluded, all of them. There was no hope of assistance from this quarter. Then she thought of James's face the last time she had seen him, the horror in his eyes, and what he had done to her.

'It's not true,' she said.

She expected that Shadwell or Miss Swift would press their case, try to argue her out of her incredulity, but they did not. Instead, neither spoke; Miss Swift busied herself preparing the tea. She saw that they were being patient with her, giving her time to get her bearings.

Shadwell returned his attention to Howland. 'What did you do when Bier told you the secret of the Aegolius Club?'

'I was pretty angry,' Howland said. 'I thought they were making fun of me – taking me for a sucker, you know. I said I wasn't going to stand for it. Then Bier said he'd prove it to me. He was enjoying himself, I could see that. And I said I'd heard enough, but he insisted, had the servant bring in a revolver on a tray. I wouldn't play along, so he did it himself. Put the barrel in his mouth before I could stop him.'

Charlotte remembered the man who had followed her in the street, saw again how he had fallen – shot at point-blank – and stood up again.

'Tea,' Miss Swift interposed quietly, and she passed a cup to Howland, to Shadwell, and last to Charlotte, who held the cup tight in both hands, letting the heat bring the sensation back to her cold fingers.

'I yelled out,' Howland said, 'but all the others just sat there. I was about to go for help but one of them told me to sit down, not to be a fool. Then Bier sat up again. He was wounded, but you could see him healing. In a couple of minutes he started to talk again, as if there hadn't been any break in the conversation. He said he'd live for ever and I could be like him, if I wanted. If I had the nerve. And he said they weren't murderers.' Charlotte had an idea that Howland had rehearsed this last detail in his mind – he spoke so eagerly now, with such haste to get the lines out. 'He told me they didn't hurt innocent people, and it was a gift, that I could do great things with it.'

'So you agreed to join?' Shadwell asked.

'I was impressed, I admit. And I wanted to know how he'd managed the business with the gun. I thought I'd go along with it all, see whether it was a hoax or not. I suppose I thought it'd be an adventure.

'And so he said, let's not wait, and they brought me back to the club that evening. They had me up in this room – all very nice and comfortable, they do things properly – and asked me to wait. It was one of their rules: you have to fast before. I waited, and once they'd left me alone I thought I'd take a look around, so I slipped out – wasn't hard, they'd left the key in the lock. I got downstairs to the cellar, there were things there—' He stopped. 'I'm sorry. I keep trying to push past it and I can't . . .' The look in his eyes as he struggled to speak was pitiful to see.

'Don't,' Charlotte said. 'Stop it, you'll hurt yourself.'

'Miss Norbury's right,' Miss Swift agreed. 'Don't try any more. What happened afterwards?'

'Well, they caught up with me, took me upstairs again – different room, it was in the attic. And they did something. Bier did it. He hurt me. He was – I don't know if this makes sense, but he was in my thoughts. I wanted him out of my head, but he wouldn't leave.'

Shadwell spoke gently: 'It's called the mazement.'

'Whatever it's called, it shook me pretty badly. I didn't know what was happening for a while. They said they'd bring me downstairs soon. I'd signed this paper they'd given me, and they said I could choose between honouring my promise or being killed.' He turned to Charlotte. 'That was when I met your brother.'

Tell me quickly, she wanted to say. It had become difficult to speak, difficult to hold her cup of tea without spilling it.

'His room was next to mine. He talked to me through the wall, and I told him why I was there. And he said he was one of them.'

She remembered feeling his hands on her arm – such alien strength, such a hostile look in his eyes.

'Are you all right, Miss Norbury?' Shadwell asked. 'We can leave the rest for later.'

They were all looking at her; she ought to say something to reassure them.

Miss Swift stood up. 'It's your wrist, isn't it? Where he hurt you. The left?' Charlotte could not answer. 'And if you try to speak of it now, you can't. That's the thing about them. Even if they don't kill you right off, you won't be able to tell anyone you were attacked.'

Charlotte opened her mouth to tell them that this was all wrong. 'He . . .'

With growing fright, she discovered that it was impossible to speak – to try felt like being smothered. There was no breath left in her. This was what Howland had felt. She forced back her tears.

Miss Swift laid a hand on Charlotte's arm, the one James had hurt. 'D'you mind if I . . .?'

Charlotte nodded her assent, not caring what she did, and Miss Swift pushed up her sleeve. Shadwell sat back in his chair with a sigh. Miss Swift nodded as if he had spoken. She let Charlotte's sleeve fall and returned to her seat by the fire, where she began to make toast again.

'He didn't choose it, though,' Howland put in. 'They'd killed his friend, Miss Norbury, he hated them. He—'

'I beg your pardon,' Shadwell interrupted. 'Did you say that he didn't choose it?'

'That's right. They changed him and he didn't want it.'

Miss Swift set down the toasting fork with a clatter.

'But that's impossible,' Shadwell said. 'The consent must be given, otherwise the human subject would die. Apart from anything else, the shock would probably be too severe without some preparation and understanding. All authorities agree that whilst the creatures can *persuade*, to actually force the transformation is quite out of the question.'

'In that case, they've changed the rules.'

'You can't simply *change the rules*, Mr Howland.'

'Well, they worked out a way to do it, managed it somehow. It's part of this new plan they've got. They can change people even if they don't want to be changed. They were talking about it at my induction dinner, saying they were going to pick out the best men in London and make them join. My guess is that Norbury got mixed up in it all somehow.'

The silence was more profound than any that had gone before. Shadwell and Miss Swift were staring at each other – Charlotte might almost have thought they were oblivious to their guests.

'Are you sure?' Shadwell finally said to Howland. 'Are you *absolutely* sure that's what you heard?'

'Yes. Bier's doing, apparently. It's a scheme of his to save society. There's some group they don't like—'

'The Alia?'

'Yes, them. They're going to get rid of them. Make space for the new men.'

'Do you know how many men they intend to add to their number?'

'As many as deserved it, Bier said.'

'We need to see Burke,' Adeline said to Shadwell. 'As soon as possible.' She stood up, took another cigarette from the mantelpiece, lit it. 'This can't wait. We'll have to go without an appointment.'

'Adeline, wait.' Shadwell sounded as if he was struggling hard to remain calm. 'Hear the rest. Then we'll think. You know we can't do anything tonight.'

Charlotte became aware of the noise of the traffic passing outside on the street, a faint sound of raindrops on the windows.

Shadwell turned back to Howland. 'How did you escape, in the end?'

'Norbury helped me. At least, we helped each other.'

'They didn't follow you?'

'Not right away. It was daylight, I don't think they wanted to be outside. Bier said it made no difference where we went, they'd find us both. I took him home.' He looked to Charlotte. 'I don't believe he could see very well in the light. He was so ill, he hardly knew I was there. I talked to him – it seemed like the thing to do, somehow, to keep him awake. I told him about myself and asked him what he was called and where he lived. I made him talk about things.'

'And you left him there at his house?' Shadwell asked.

'He wouldn't let me go in. I think it was a struggle for him to keep from hurting me.' He looked towards Charlotte again, almost eagerly. 'He told me about you. He was talking about you and it made him feel better, kept him steady.

'When he told me to go, I ran. It was strange. I felt all sick and shaky, but I had this thought that I had to keep moving, so I did. I got some second-hand clothes, hid in a doss-house for a couple of days till I got my nerve back. I'd left some of my things with a friend – passport, chequebook, that sort of thing – so I went back for those. He said there'd been people asking for me. He didn't— He asked me not to stay.' His voice was tight, uneasy. 'I understood, of course. Anyway. I thought the best thing to do was to go to the police.'

'All right,' Shadwell said. 'Thank you, Mr Howland. What you've told us is most useful.'

'And now we can help you,' Miss Swift added. She and Shadwell shared another glance; Charlotte envied them their closeness, their ability to confer with only a look. At another time, she would have been curious and disapproving about their living arrangements. Miss Swift's clothes and unconventional manner would have convinced her of the worst. Now such considerations seemed like half-forgotten rules to a game played in childhood.

Shadwell said, 'The club will still be seeking you both.'

'What do they want with me?' Charlotte asked.

'Your brother will be looking for you.' She could hear pity in Shadwell's voice. 'And so the club will want to use you as a lure.'

This poky little sitting-room was an island of safety, then. Outside, the whole city presented a danger she scarcely understood.

Miss Swift stood up. 'Toast,' she said.

Charlotte shook her head.

'Have just a piece. Toast's good to eat. It'll settle you.'

Too weary to argue further, Charlotte took a piece of toast. Howland followed suit.

'You still haven't told us who you are, what all of this is.' Howland gestured round him at the books, the shop, the disreputable street outside. 'Do you hunt them?' He said it as if it were a small matter either way.

'Of course not,' Shadwell replied. 'You have to remember, Mr Howland, that we don't know for certain how human they are. They've been viewed as men possessed by demons, a blessed elect, sufferers of a ghastly infection. They may, in many senses, be dead, and yet to kill them would be illegal and most likely immoral. You've seen them. You know one may look into their eyes and not be certain if there is a human soul staring back.'

'They're also much stronger than us and very hard to kill,' Miss Swift added. 'And once they're dead, you're left with a body, and what's to be done with that?'

Practical enough, Charlotte thought, though Howland did not appear convinced:

'What do you do, then, if you don't kill them?'

'We do our best to protect the living,' answered Shadwell. 'Those whom no one else will believe, who have come to the attention of the club – who've angered them for one reason or another. There are certain men and women – like the constable who helped you – who know enough to send people in our direction when they need our help. And when we can, we follow the club men – as we followed Mr Corvish this evening – and plot the streets where they hunt, ward people off. And we do our best to rescue their victims from their clutches. We get them out of the country, where possible.'

'What about the shop?' Howland asked.

'We specialise in literature on the creatures. We – Miss Swift and I – have published a couple of pamphlets on the subject. We've just completed a book, too, sharing everything we have learned. We'll have it ready for the Rag and Bottle Library when it comes.'

'The what?' said Howland.

Miss Swift poured Shadwell some more tea. 'Drink that. You've talked enough.' He smiled at her. Charlotte thought that this must be an old joke between them.

'The Rag and Bottle Library travels about Europe,' Miss Swift began. 'Maybe further.'

'The library *travels*?' Howland repeated.

'Yes.' Miss Swift did not elaborate on this point. 'It keeps hold of the rarest manuscripts, the ones that can't be replaced. Staying on the move keeps them safe. When the library comes to England, we return books we've borrowed for our researches, pass on any valuable manuscripts we've obtained. We tell them anything we've discovered. And if someone like us is killed, their books go to the Rag and Bottle.'

'Is there a cure?' Charlotte asked. She must have spoken abruptly, for they all turned to look at her.

'Please don't torment yourself with that hope, Miss Norbury.' Shadwell did not speak unkindly, but his voice was firm. 'The idea eats one up after a while. Many have tried to effect a cure, and no one's ever succeeded.'

'But in everything you've read, surely there must be some mention of someone being changed back?'

'The search for a remedy has ruined lives, Miss Norbury. There have been successful imprisonments, successful killings, but never to my knowledge a successful cure. I'm sorry to have to speak so plainly.' Charlotte saw him make an effort, adopt an easier tone. 'Now, you must stay here tonight, both of you. In the morning, we'll probably need to get you both out of London.'

'I can't go.'

'I understand your concern for your brother, Miss Norbury. But London is no place for you now. Besides – as I said, your brother will be looking for you, too.'

'They usually come for the family first of all,' Miss Swift added.

'But I want him to find me,' Charlotte said. 'How can I help him if I don't know where he is?'

'And what if he kills you?' Miss Swift demanded. She was too kind – perhaps she felt it would be ungenerous – to glance at Charlotte's injured wrist as she said this.

'But if there was a chance that he could be cured . . .'

'Miss Norbury,' Shadwell said. 'Please listen to me. You mustn't start down this path. It will bring you nothing but grief. I've seen this before. You must give up on this idea of saving him.'

She said, 'He's my brother.'

'Look,' Howland said, 'if you're staying, Miss Norbury, I want to stay, too. He saved my life; I should do something. I could help you—'

'You don't have the first idea about what that would mean,' Miss Swift interrupted. 'Either of you.'

'Why don't we leave this until morning?' suggested Shadwell. 'Besides, perhaps it would be better to consult with Burke before we make our final decision about what to do. We shall have to consult him in any case.'

How easily he said *our*, Charlotte thought. They were accustomed to this sort of thing, and she might be so easily borne away by their plans, which seemed to differ substantially from her own wishes.

'Who's Burke?' asked Howland.

'An acquaintance of ours,' replied Shadwell. 'He hears a good deal, and his advice is worth having. He'll know about the club's doings, if anyone does. He hears all the news of these creatures – the ones in London, at least.'

'Are there many of the creatures round these parts, then?' Howland asked.

'Yes, compared to most places,' replied Miss Swift. 'It's an old city, and very big. And the climate agrees with them.'

The fire was dying now, and Charlotte guessed that they would let it go out rather than use up more coal. The trade in occult books could hardly be a thriving one.

She stretched her hands closer to the red-glowing coals and thought of James. They came for the family first.

Miss Swift got to her feet. 'I'll take the plates. And then I suppose we should go to bed.'

Shadwell rose, too, before Charlotte could offer any help, and took the cups and the kettle from the hearth. 'Please don't get up, Miss Norbury,' he said. 'Rest a little while longer.' He followed Miss Swift out into the kitchen, leaving Charlotte and Howland alone.

'I suppose they need to confer,' Howland said. The food seemed to have done him good; he sounded considerably steadier and more alert.

'Yes.'

'It's strange, all this,' he added after a pause.

'I suppose so.'

She had been staring wearily at the carpet – now she looked at him. He was watching her attentively, half frowning. She saw that he meant well.

'Are you . . . managing?' he asked.

'I suppose I don't have any choice about managing. Any more than you do.'

'No. All the same. I just wanted to say, while it's only us here, that I meant what I said. I want to help. I think I owe you that, after your brother – after he saved me.'

'You needn't feel obliged to me because of what James did.'

'But I do feel obliged. I wouldn't have got away from . . . those men if it weren't for him. There's a debt there.'

'Well it's certainly not to me. And I'm not sure that knowing you were helping me would give James any satisfaction now.'

'Do you really believe that?' He seemed genuinely curious about her answer.

'They said he'd come after me. That he might want to kill me.'

'They haven't told us everything, though, have they?'

'Maybe not,' Charlotte replied, somewhat irritated. As if things were not bad enough without being forced to doubt their only protectors.

'I'm sure they have their reasons. Only . . . whatever happens tomorrow, I'll help you, if I can.'

'Well, thank you for the offer, Mr Howland.'

They did not speak again until Shadwell and Miss Swift returned a few minutes later. Miss Swift wore a slight frown, and carried a wavering candle.

'Will you mind sharing with me?' she asked Charlotte. 'I think Shadwell will leave Mr Howland his room and sleep down here.'

'Thank you,' Charlotte said. 'That's very kind of you.'

Her bags stood by the door, where she had left them – she picked them up, nodding a brief good night to Shadwell and Howland, who seemed as if they were about to begin a polite argument over who ought to take the settee.

'They might be a while deciding,' Miss Swift said softly. 'Best not to interfere.'

Charlotte was tired, and yet it was a wrench to move from the remaining warmth of the fireside. The landing outside the sitting-room was cold and dark, lit only by Miss Swift's candle.

'Our rooms are upstairs,' Miss Swift told her.

'And . . . the lavatory?'

'What? Oh, it's out back. Did you want to go now?'

'I – yes. If that's all right.'

'Leave your things here, then.' And she led Charlotte downstairs, through a back door, into a dank, ill-smelling courtyard where every sound seemed magnified by the walls of the buildings on all sides.

Charlotte could hear the noise of horses passing and voices coming from nearby, perhaps the next street. There were shouts, a woman shrieking, raucous laughter. Then a smash of glass. Silence – and then the shouting started again, a man and two women, all screaming at one another.

Miss Swift shrugged, as if to say, *Welcome to London*, or, *What did you expect?* 'It's there,' she said. The small structure she indicated did not look promising. 'I'll wait.' She handed Charlotte a sheaf of scraps, torn from paper bags and old envelopes, threaded together on a piece of string. She seemed to anticipate a certain amount of fuss on Charlotte's part. But Charlotte nodded, thanked her as gratefully as she could.

The door didn't lock and had to be held shut with one hand. She did her best not to breathe and got through the ordeal as quickly as possible. When she emerged, Miss Swift took her upstairs without further conversation.

At the top of the house was a narrow corridor with three doors. The rooms within must be very small.

'This first one's mine,' Miss Swift said. 'Next is Shadwell's – or Mr Howland's for tonight, if he loses the argument.'

Constrained by good manners, Charlotte forbore asking what the third room was used for. Perhaps – given what she knew of her hosts' occupation – it was better not to know.

Miss Swift's bedroom was small indeed, with a slanted

ceiling and a tiny square window. A tall person might stretch out an arm and a leg and touch the walls on either side at once.

Miss Swift drew the curtain and set down her candle. The room held three chairs, a bed, and a chest of drawers. There were clothes – quite a pile of them – folded over the back of one of the chairs. Charlotte caught her own reflection in a dark-specked mirror in the far corner, and wondered if she could possibly appear so haggard.

She looked away, around the room again, at Miss Swift standing by the window. The smell of tobacco was as strong here as it was downstairs.

'It's not very tidy,' Miss Swift observed. It might have been an apology or a challenge.

'You're very kind to let me stay,' Charlotte said, 'and I'm very grateful, Miss Swift.' It was an effort to remain standing. 'May I sit down?'

'Of course,' Miss Swift replied, and Charlotte sat down on the only uncluttered chair. 'You can call me Adeline, by the way. Silly to keep saying Miss Swift when we're sharing a room.'

'Thank you. And please call me Charlotte.'

'The bed's not big, but we ought to manage.'

'Yes. Thank you.'

'Don't mention it.' Adeline began to search through a pile of clothes. After a short hunt, she finally retrieved a nightgown.

'We've brought trouble, haven't we?' Charlotte said.

'You mean yourself and Mr Howland?'

'Yes.'

'There was always going to be trouble. There's always been trouble, since we started in this business.' Adeline shook the nightgown, to take the creases out. It looked as if it had rested there for some time.

'D'you want to wash?' she asked.

'Thank you, yes, please. Unless it's a nuisance—'

'I'll bring up some water.'

When Adeline was gone, Charlotte stowed James's Gladstone bag safely away in a corner. Looking around the room, she noticed that there was a hole in the wicker seat of one of the chairs, as if someone had put a foot through. The top of the chest of drawers was a great mess of ill-assorted articles – an empty scent bottle, a string of wooden beads, and a saucer and small paint-brush, both stained with the same peculiar flesh-coloured tint. Pinned on the wall nearby was a newspaper cutting, enlivened by several illustrations of a young woman holding a rifle. A head-line in capitals proclaimed: ANNIE OAKLEY, THE CHAMPION RIFLE SHOT, NOW WITH BUFFALO BILL.

She turned away, went to get her nightgown out of her suitcase. By the time this was done, Adeline had returned, carrying with her a towel, a chipped jug and a basin.

'I'll wait outside,' she said. 'Soap's on the shelf. Keep the water when you're done.'

The water was lukewarm and made Charlotte's teeth chatter. She was relieved to discover that the towel Adeline had given her was more or less clean, though it smelled of damp. Another small mercy was the fact that she had remembered her sponge.

When she was finished, she wrapped herself up in her coat as a makeshift dressing gown, stowed her discarded clothes carefully away in her suitcase. The black wool gown was the only one she had with her, and she did not know for how many days it would have to last. Fortunately, she had been prudent enough to bring clean linen and a few other necessities – including a bottle of rosewater. The smell was comforting. She thought of her flowers growing at home.

Opening the bedroom door a little way, she satisfied herself that the gentlemen were still downstairs before stepping onto the landing. Miss Swift was sitting at the top of the stairs, looking down. She was hunched forwards, resting her chin on her hands.

Charlotte said, 'I've finished. Thank you.'

'Right,' Miss Swift replied. Charlotte had an idea that her thoughts had been far distant.

'I could wait outside, if you like.'

'No need. You'd better get into bed. It's cold.'

Shivering, Charlotte retreated to the bed, which was rather narrow and hard. She huddled under the covers, still wrapped in her coat, blanket pulled up to her throat, and tried to ignore the smell of old smoke and unwashed hair, tried not to wonder about bugs.

Adeline had already unpinned her hair and was now caught halfway between lady and gentleman, an uncomfortable hybrid. As she began to unbutton her shirt, Charlotte turned away, stared at the wall.

After a few minutes she heard Adeline cross the room, heard her drop her clothes into a heap. When Charlotte turned her head, she could see her before the mirror, unplaiting her hair. In her nightgown she looked more like a woman than she had before but also rather like a ghost. Her feet were bare.

She got into bed with a muttered *good-night*, blew out the candle without another word. To Charlotte's envy, she seemed to fall asleep almost immediately.

Charlotte herself lay still, curled up against the cold, and for a long time could not bring herself to close her eyes.

Chapter Eighteen

There were patches of memory from before that day – a small cold room, something sparkling on a wooden floor, a man shouting – but this was the first thing Adeline remembered clearly: a thundery summer afternoon, dark-blue clouds heavy over the Thames. It was no day for the experiment, someone said. What if it starts to rain? Someone else, laughing, said, Well, she's got the river to break her fall. Everybody was in a cheerful mood. There were hundreds of people there, all pushing for space around Cremorne Pier. This was when the Cremorne Gardens were still open in Chelsea, when people still came down in boats or carriages for an afternoon's amusement or an evening's pleasure. Adeline remembered the coloured lanterns shining in the trees, music coming from far away. There was a man selling coffee, the smell mingled with the stench of the water.

High above the river they had strung a wire, supported by four narrow wooden ledges. About halfway across, just past the second ledge, a woman stood, holding a slender balance pole. She ought to have fallen, but Adeline had known from the way she moved – so light and easy, as if she were walking a steady pavement – that she would not. She had been advertised in the newspapers as the FEMALE BLONDIN, and a huge crowd had come to see her.

There was a breath of wind, and the wire swayed – the crowd murmured, but the woman showed no sign of dismay. Her dress was light white stuff, like a ballet girl's, and she wore a little red jacket that stood out brightly against the darkening sky. Adeline had never seen anyone who looked so free.

'That's your mama,' someone said. This was Mr Congreave, Mama's agent. Sometimes Adeline liked to pretend that he was her father.

People looked at her and muttered admiringly after Mr Congreave spoke. Adeline had been abashed at so much attention; she had stared down at her feet – at the pretty blue boots that were too large for her, which had been bought second-hand, like her frock and jacket and her tiny blue velvet hat with the white feather. There was a spot of grease on the hem of her dress, and it was a bit gone under the arms, but the jacket hid that. It was a splendid jacket, white velvet with a round collar and black silk piping. She had wanted to run and twirl about, to show everyone how fine she was in her new things – only Mr Congreave's stern warning that she was to be good (for Mama's sake) had kept her standing still. It was Mama's London *début,* and they had wanted to make a good impression.

Adeline was still looking down, wiggling her toes in her boots, which were beginning to let the damp in, when there was a noise from the crowd – a sigh and a groan. Afterwards, she was told that the rope was too loose, and it had begun to sway back and forth. The guy lines supporting the wire had been cut; a man had been trying to steal the lead weights which secured them. What Adeline saw was Mama letting go of her balance pole, which fell a hundred feet into the river below – she must have flung it from her, because it spun as it fell and hit the water with a decisive splash. Mama crouched and caught the rope with both hands, then seized one of the cords securing the wire. Sway ropes, they were called. Adeline had been proud of remembering.

Mr Congreave was holding Adeline's hand very tightly. Adeline had wanted to say that surely it was all right, Mama would not be hurt. They both watched as Mama made her way by slow degrees down the cord – down to the water, where a boat was moving forwards to meet her. Adeline could always recall this clearly, later: the slow progress of the boat, Mama's white dress caught in the breeze as she descended.

When she reached the safety of the boat, there was a cheer, rather subdued. On the shore, Mama bowed, acknowledging the muted applause. A man with a high shiny black hat and a loud voice – someone to do with the Cremorne Gardens – stood up and thanked everyone for coming to watch and said that Madame Fantine was grateful for their attention but exhausted from her ordeal. He added some words of explanation for what had happened, though it was clear that some of the spectators were disappointed not to see Mama either cross in safety or fall and hurt herself. A few minutes passed and it appeared that there was nothing more to see – the crowds began to move off; those who had been watching from boats started to paddle back to the shore.

Mr Congreave took charge of Mama and Adeline and got them into a carriage. He said, *It's all right, old girl,* to Mama – he had always called her that, though Mama was neither old nor a girl. And Mama nodded and smiled, too tired to speak.

Adeline remembered that when they were back at home – the two rooms they called home that fortnight – Mama, dressed in ordinary clothes, held her tightly, not letting go even when Adeline grew bored and began to squirm away.

There was a knock at the door – Mr Congreave had ordered his servant to run out and bring them back a baked potato each for supper. Adeline gobbled her potato so that it burned her mouth and then her throat and her belly. Only when it was all gone did she ask:

'Were you scared?'

'A little,' Mama said. She licked butter off her fingers.

'Will you do it again?'

'Of course.'

Adeline had been confused and cross that she did not understand Mama's matter-of-fact *of course*. She had not known then the pull of pure fear, the dizzying thrill of it. When you are up there, Mama once said, it's like love: there is nothing else.

'What about me?' Adeline had said. She was very young, jealous of everything Mama did that was not to do with her.

'Except you, of course,' Mama replied. 'I would never forget you. And, besides, you walked the wire with me before you were born, don't you know that?' This was her favourite story, the one Mama told over and over. 'You knew you were there before I did, hiding safe inside me. Many times I must have crossed with you before I knew you were there.'

'How many times?' Adeline always asked.

'Oh, dozens, for certain,' Mama always answered.

• • •

Mama's *début* earned her a season at the Alhambra Theatre in Leicester Square – and after that there were other theatres; they travelled to so many towns that Adeline sometimes had to stop and think before she could remember where they were performing that week. Later, her recollections of that time were even more confused – a succession of lodging houses and hotels, all very much alike. Mama could take as much as £8 for a single performance. They were happy and comfortable; they had everything they wanted. When Adeline began to perform, they did better still. She never had Mama's passion for the high places, but she enjoyed being looked at and took pride in her skill. It was a fine thing to be aloft, light flaring all around her, beneath her a great sweep of eyes. She never got tired of the murmur of expectation as she stepped into view. Mama was pleased with her, though she was strict, too, and ready with criticism – careful with your arms, your head, your toes. Adeline could never cross the wire without hearing Mama's voice in her ear.

She grew up pretty – and, what was rarer, she grew up prettily, without any intervening gawky stage. She was neat and dark and hid the beautiful muscles of her arms and shoulders beneath simple gowns, always made in as grown-up a style as possible. In most theatres she was not the handsomest girl on the bill, but she was the one people looked at. She walked with a swing, a clip of the heels of her neat black boots.

A few months before Adeline's sixteenth birthday, there was an accident. She had been performing alongside Mama (as MADEMOISELLE FANTINE, THE CHILD PRODIGY – from a distance she was still slight enough to pass as twelve or thirteen) when a cannon, fired too early, had startled Mama in the middle of her act. She had fallen. Adeline, waiting to go on, did not see it happen. Even much later, she was not sure whether seeing it happen would have been worse than her imaginings.

Everyone had thought that Mama would die; the doctor told Adeline to prepare herself – but Mama did not die. She was the sort who took hold of life and dug her nails in.

For many months afterwards, she could not walk, could not even sit up without help, and could not be left alone for long. She never complained, not of the pain or the loss of the profession she loved, not of her new helplessness. But she worried, Adeline knew, about what was to become of them.

Few things ate up money faster than sickness, Adeline discovered. It would have been cheaper if they had both had taken to dram-drinking.

They had done so well and saved so prudently that there was enough to get by, for a little while at least. But eventually Adeline would have to do something. In spite of Mama's insistence, she did not intend to go back to performing.

Mama asked her if she was afraid, after the accident, and Adeline said that she was not. She might have stepped back onto the wire at any time, cool as ever. But the life now repelled her. She was disgusted with Mr Congreave, who had shown little interest in Mama since her injury, whilst at the same time persecuting Adeline with messages asking when she intended to return to performing. She had begun to brood over other stories of falls and mischances and narrow escapes. She thought of the great Léotard, who nearly fell from his trapeze at the Alhambra when someone in the crowd shouted bad news to him across the theatre. Adeline didn't perform for the love of it, as Mama had – and without love, it no longer seemed worth the risk.

When it became clear that Mama would not die, there had been a subscription organised for her, and quite a lot of money was collected. The lady who had got up the subscription came to visit, sat gingerly on a wooden chair whilst Adeline brought her tea. The lady was very sorry for them both, in a superior way, and had asked Adeline what she intended to do now – how did she intend to support herself?

Adeline, sixteen and sullen, had said she was not sure.

'I know a few girls who have done well with telegraphy,' the lady began. She paused and looked around the room, at the dirty plates on the floor, at Adeline's sparkling costume laid out carefully on the bed, a cunning shimmer of green sequins, her tights folded nearby.

'Well, perhaps not,' she went on. 'Have you considered going into service?'

Adeline had not, and would not. And why could she not do telegraphy, anyway?

Well, there was a certain standard of spelling and writing required, the lady explained. There was an examination to be passed; it was not easy to get into at all. One needed arithmetic, geography. The girls who were successful. . . . well, they were not really of Adeline's class, to be blunt. There would be many of them fighting for a place, Adeline's chances were small.

Adeline nodded, outwardly humbled, and got rid of the lady as quickly as possible. She would become a telegraphist, she decided. She had arithmetic already. Mama always made her do the accounts. And she had French, better than any of the other telegraphists, probably; it would come in useful.

Becoming a telegraphist was almost as difficult as the lady had suggested. References had to be got – from respectable persons, no less – and Mama had to be reasoned with. She did not know why Adeline was so determined to waste herself working for the post office or whatever it was she intended doing. Pain made her irritable. Adeline nodded or shrugged at her arguments and carried on.

There were other girls training to be telegraphists – daughters of clergymen, or clerks, or tradesmen. They looked askance at Adeline at first, and some of them laughed at her spelling. But she passed her examination all the same. A year later she was working at the Central Telegraph Station, Blackfriars, with excellent prospects for the future.

Twenty-five words a minute, she boasted to Mama. Well, she'd always had steady hands, Mama said. This was the most encouragement that Adeline could expect.

There were women on the other side of the Atlantic, one of the other girls told her, doing the same job as they did. She liked to think of it, the lines stretched between them like thread, like great stitches holding everything together.

She had been at her job for five years, and was happy enough in it, when she met John Shadwell on an omnibus on her way back from work. He dropped a book, and Adeline reached down and picked it up for him. The page had fallen open at a diagram of a woman anatomised, every part labelled in black and white.

'Thank you.' He took the book from her without embarrassment. 'It's all right. I'm a doctor.'

He seemed rather lost, she thought, crammed in against the other omnibus passengers.

'Are you new in London?' she asked.

'Not exactly. I was born here.' Mama would have said he was too tall to have been born in this city. They were a pale, stunted race, your native-born Londoner; their bones grew crooked.

She glanced briefly at the book he still held. 'You know your way about, then.'

He returned her smile. 'You might say that, yes.'

He was just down from Edinburgh, he told her, where he had been studying medicine. They alighted on the same street and met again that evening, and the evening after. It was not a good time for either of them to fall in love, certainly not a good time to marry, and yet there they were.

Later she would remember him very deliberately – thoroughly, from crown to heel, to show herself that she still could. He was handsome – tall and with broad shoulders, which she liked in a man. Brown hair and brown eyes. She liked his hands, so much larger than her own; she would turn them over in comic wonderment. She liked that he believed the best of people and that he found it easy to be kind.

Mama had not been pleased to hear of the engagement, for all John was a doctor. For one thing, his family weren't Catholic and would certainly not approve of Adeline being so.

'There's only his father,' Adeline said. 'No other family.'

'Well, does *he* approve?'

'I don't know.'

'Why marry him? You earn enough with those telegraph machines of yours. Are you going to have a child?'

'No.' They had been very careful. Mama had made sure Adeline knew what was what, for all her sudden piety. And John was a doctor and not shocked by such things, as another man might have been. He had even bought the stuff for her on one occasion – she had kissed him and said, Now, this I like better than jewels, better than silk stockings or flowers or bonbons.

'This would never have happened if you'd only stayed performing,' Mama said, with absolute truth.

'You know I won't go back,' Adeline replied. She thought of Mama falling from the wire, sparkling in her costume, dropping like a gem from a snapped necklace. She had not seen but she had *heard*, waiting in the wings – the sudden silence, someone gasping in the crowd.

Mama said nothing. She could sit up for a few hours at a stretch by this time, and even walk slowly, as long as she used a crutch. This was as much as she could ever hope for, the doctor had said. Now she was sitting at the table, practising her typing, face tight in a frown.

Mama had a friend, a horseback rider whose eyesight had failed. She had come to visit Mama after the accident and told her that it was possible to make good money as a typewriter these days; one could even work at home. She had lent Mama her machine to begin with, and after a few weeks Mama had got a machine of her own.

The typewriter took up space, there was nowhere in their rooms where it could conveniently be kept, it ate up money for paper and ink, it weighed more than a baby and was awkward to move. It had come second-hand and still cost a dreadful amount – £9 at least, Adeline was sure.

But it had given Mama happiness, something to do – and soon she ought to be able to make money at it, with her friend's help. Adeline knew that not being able to earn her living was almost intolerable to Mama. She had taught Adeline that it was a pleasure to look around at your food and clothes, the roof above you, and know that you had put it all there yourself, that you had made your own place in the world.

The typewriter was beautiful, Mama would tell Adeline, showing her the shining black metal and the round white keys, the metal spokes like harp strings. She came to say that machines always did their best, they were not like human beings – never malicious or given to holding grudges. Adeline had not yet pointed out to her how unjust she was, to be so fond of this contraption and yet so scornful of Adeline's telegraphy.

'Look,' Mama said now. 'I'm getting better.'

She was, Adeline saw, looking over her shoulder. There were pages already spread across the table – lines and lines of CAT and HOUSE and JAM. There was also BONJOUR and EAU and SOL.

'I got you that little book,' Adeline reminded her. 'You're supposed to write the words that it tells you. There are sentences.'

'It's so dull,' Mama said. 'And all English words, Adeline. You ought to know better.'

'No one's going to pay you to type French.' This was not precisely true – there were lots of French people in this part of Soho; some of them might want Mama's skills sooner or later. 'Can I bring John to see you?' Adeline added, after a pause.

'Of course,' Mama said, and typed another line.

She took Mama at her word and brought John to see her a week later. He arrived more smartly attired than Adeline had ever seen him and paid Mama every possible courtesy. Mama took it all as a matter of course – she was sitting up for the visit and had dressed herself with particular care.

And she had her questions ready – first regarding John's present circumstances, then his prospects for the future. He took it all with good humour.

'Will you not mind,' she asked John finally, after a long interrogation, 'having a wife who was an acrobat?'

'Mind?' John said. 'No. Of course not.'

'And what if the other doctors – or your friends, or your family – what if they pity you for marrying someone like Adeline?'

'Then I will pity them for not marrying someone like Adeline.'

Mama nodded. 'All right,' she said. She was not entirely convinced, in spite of John's sensible replies. But he had charmed her in the end, as Adeline had known he would. He made her laugh, told her stories about his medical training, and paid Adeline many lavish compliments. Mama rarely praised Adeline but liked nothing better than to hear others admire her.

'He's not complicated,' Mama remarked when he was gone.

'*Tant mieux*,' Adeline said. She was French only with Mama now, or when she was angry or frightened. 'I don't like complicated people.'

'And he's handsome and good. I suppose he may suit you.'

'You do like him, then.'

'He likes you, which shows he has some sense, at least. Have you met his father yet?'

'No. I will soon, though.'

John's father had been an army chaplain, then a clergyman in London – one of those slum priests Mama despised. Worse still, he was a sort of socialist. He had quarrelled with his bishop over politics, and now he was a private tutor or something of that kind. From John's description, Adeline guessed that he had little enough to live on, but he would take nothing from his son. John had fallen out with him shortly before leaving for Edinburgh to study. Now they were reconciled, but things were still awkward.

'We're too polite with each other,' John explained. 'It's uncanny.'

Adeline thought of Mama, who had never, in her recollection, been polite to her. The idea of it was horrible. 'I see,' she said.

'Perhaps you'll help mend things.'

'Or start another row.'

He shook his head. 'No. I'll tell him we're engaged, and then we'll meet, the three of us. Once he meets you, he'll like you, there'll be no more bother.'

They were in Hyde Park, where they liked to walk whenever they could both spare the time. The breeze was warm. She had looked at him and thought, I mean to have this man, and with joy she saw how easily this would come to pass; there was nothing real to stand between them, nothing that could delay them for long. She had kissed him – a light kiss, she remembered afterwards, almost a tease. She had wanted him to think of her that night and the day after and all the days until they saw each other again, to long for her so that his father would not be able to persuade him against the marriage. Then they had said farewell, intending to meet in a couple of days at the same place. Two days later at the appointed hour, she had returned – he had not.

She was annoyed. Then, when days passed and she heard nothing from him, extremely anxious. Ignoring Mama's advice, she went to his rooms. He was away, and had been for several days, the landlady said.

Where now? There seemed only one place left to attempt. One evening after work, she went to John's father's house.

The address – she had it written in John's rambling scrawl – was Cowcross Street. It was close to Farringdon station, a disappointed neighbourhood, lots of lodging houses, more than a few undesirable types about. Suspecting that beneath the new skin of respectability she was still rather an undesirable herself, she felt a bit of fellow feeling for the tired-looking women and skinny children lingering in doorways, staring bleakly at every passer-by.

She knocked at the door. There was no answer, but she heard someone move in the room beyond. Adeline began to hammer furiously on the door. When this accomplished nothing, she called, 'You may as well let me in. I won't go away until you do.'

No response. Very well, she thought. She kept knocking, louder and louder. It felt good to smash at something. When her knocks went unanswered, she began to kick instead, thud after thud with her neat black boots – so carefully polished and re-soled for her meeting with John's father.

Finally she heard someone stand up with a curse. The key turned in the lock.

The man who opened the door was undoubtedly John's father. He was broad-shouldered like his son, slightly shorter, softening a little around the middle. His eyes were blue and bloodshot, his hair overlong and unkempt. He wore a shirt but no coat, and had the look of a man who had drunk too much the night before and fallen asleep in his clothes. His sleeves were spotted in blood, and in his mouth was an unlit cigarette.

He said, 'Where are they?'

'What?'

He looked at her and took the cigarette out of his mouth. 'Aren't you from the bookshop?'

'No. I'm engaged to your son.'

'What?' He blinked. 'I'm sorry, he isn't here.'

'Well, d'you know where he is?'

'Try his rooms.'

'I've tried them.'

'Then I can't help you.'

'He's *missing*,' Adeline said. 'Aren't you worried?'

'I beg your pardon. He isn't missing. I spoke to him today.'

'Well, where is he? Why hasn't he seen me?'

'I'm sorry,' he repeated, 'but I had no knowledge of his engagement, nor do I know why he should avoid you.' He swayed a little. 'I suggest you forget him, Miss . . .' She did not give her name. 'I suggest you forget him. He's fickle. I say it though he's my son. You're safer without him.'

He was the worst liar she'd ever come across. If she told him she knew he was talking a load of rot, would he tell her anything else, or would he just slam the door?

Adeline came to a decision. The man was exhausted, bleary-eyed, perhaps still half drunk. She had probably woken him up. She had seen her mother deal with nighttime visitors before, turning them out or sobering them up when necessary – all you had to do when they were like this was be firm. They were usually in too delicate a state to argue.

She said, 'Let me in.'

'You can't—'

'Let me in and tell me what's happened to John, or I'll come back here with the police.'

She thought he would close the door and call her bluff. Instead, he let her in.

The front door opened directly into some sort of parlour. As she had expected, it was a terrible mess. There were books and papers everywhere, and the room smelled of unwashed clothes.

Shadwell stood in the middle of the room, gestured about him half-heartedly. 'Will you sit down?'

There was no free chair, but he didn't seem to have noticed.

'No,' Adeline said. 'I won't stay. I only want to find John.'

'You said you were his fiancée.'

'Yes.'

'I didn't know.'

'He was going to tell you.'

'Ah,' Shadwell said. 'Listen, I'm terribly sorry, but I don't think he'll want to see you any more.'

'Why not?'

'He's . . . I'm sorry, but there are debts, and . . . and there's another lady; he must have thrown you over. You're better without him, I'm afraid.'

She did not pretend to believe him. Instead, she waited in silence for him to tell her the truth.

Shadwell sat down on the settee. Papers crunched under him, as if it were the sound of his legs giving way. And he sighed. 'I'm sorry. I'm not much of a liar. For your sake, I wish I were.'

He was on the verge of breaking down. Adeline had always found it horrible, seeing people cry.

'D'you want some water or something?' she asked.

'No, thank you.' He took a breath. 'I'm sorry,' he said again.

'For what?' When he did not answer, she repeated, 'For *what?*'

He sighed and stood up. 'All right. You're his fiancée. You have the right to know if you want to. But I'm asking you to go now and let this alone. You know he loved you. He wouldn't leave you of his own accord. Can't that be enough for you?'

'No.'

'No,' he said, and sighed once more. 'God forgive me.'

And he led her up a dark and evil-smelling flight of stairs to the rooms above. On the poky landing, he stopped, indicated a door. 'Here,' he said. 'Look. Then I'll tell you what I know – what little that is. I'll just see if he's . . .'

He crouched to peer through the keyhole – only to step back in alarm.

'He's got loose,' he told her. 'I'm sorry, but it would be better if you came back another time.' He carried on talking – to himself, she realised – planning, trying to remain calm. 'It'll be all right. He's sleepy towards noon. I'll go in then. Can't go in now.' He stepped back from the door, his gaze never leaving the keyhole. 'You must understand, he asked me to do it. He has times when he's almost himself, and the last time he told me to tie him up, lock the door. Just look at him, if you think I'm cruel.'

Adeline went closer to the door. As she approached, she became aware that the foul smell she had noticed on the stairs had grown stronger. She coughed, flinched.

'He has something there with him,' Shadwell said. 'He brought it back, wouldn't let me take it from him. I think' – he gripped his right wrist with his left hand, tightly – 'I think it was a dog.'

She knelt by the keyhole, her handkerchief pressed over her nose to keep out the smell, and looked.

• • •

She did not go home straight away. With others, with her friends in the office and strangers on the street, it would be easy to pretend that everything was as it should be. With Mama, she would want to cry. She did not return until she was certain she had herself under control.

She had prepared herself, but it was all for nothing, because Mama looked at her and immediately asked, 'What's wrong?'

Adeline had decided it was better not to tell her. She would surely not be believed. No one who had not seen him would believe what had happened to John. Even now she sometimes doubted that it could be real, what she had seen through the keyhole. In the day, when she was out in the street, away from him, it was easy to pretend that such things were not possible.

She said, 'Nothing's wrong,' and Mama made her sit down and let her cry and comforted her like a child.

'There,' she said finally, and gave Adeline her handkerchief. 'Now, what's this about?'

'You wouldn't believe me.'

'Try and see,' Mama said.

And so Adeline told her what had become of John.

When Adeline was finished, Mama did not speak immediately. She reached out and grasped her crutch, as she sometimes did when she was thinking.

'Well, you're not lying,' she concluded. 'If you were, you'd come up with something more sensible. And you aren't mad.'

'I don't think so.'

'And you saw all of this yourself. You're *sure* of it?'

'Yes. I'm sure.'

'So what are you going to do?'

Adeline stared at her. 'Do you *believe* me?'

'Yes,' Mama said. 'Why not? Strange things do happen. I've never seen a—' She stopped. She must have noticed Adeline wince. 'I've never met one myself, but who's to say they don't exist? And, you know, if it was going to happen anywhere, it would probably be London.'

Mama had always believed in implausibilities. Cards and

charms, premonitions of good luck or bad. Adeline had loved to hear her stories when she was a child – like the one about Mama's friend, a trapeze artist, who had been visited several times by the ghost of his grandmother.

'What will you do?' Mama repeated now. 'Will you see John again?'

'Of course.'

Mama sighed. She pressed both hands against her eyes, as she did when anything wearied or irritated her. 'How often?'

'I'm going to live there.'

'It'll be dangerous. If he's changed the way you say he has . . .'

'We'll be careful. We'll feed him somehow. Something.'

'And it will just be you and this father of his?'

'Yes.'

'You know what they'll call you.'

'I know.'

Adeline explained what Shadwell had told her, the little he had been able to learn so far:

At first he had known only that his son had returned to him changed and ill, shivering as if with fever. Later he had discovered the other symptoms, and he had gone searching for information. There had been one clue only – a red stain the size of half-a-crown on John's sleeve. A raw wound underneath. He had been bitten, Shadwell said.

Shadwell found references here and there, in the margins of old records. It seemed that such things had been happening in the city for a long time.

The books said that John would have asked to be transformed. Otherwise it couldn't have been done. Neither of them had speculated aloud about what could have made John agree to it. Had someone threatened him, or had he succumbed to curiosity? Adeline couldn't find a reason that tallied with the man she knew, who was brave but not reckless, who loved his life and loved her.

Shadwell was learning, he had told Adeline; he had got all the books he could find on the subject. He was going to cure John, if a cure were possible. And perhaps he could do other things, he said – he might help others who had suffered.

'I can help, too,' Adeline told Mama. 'Maybe other people, as well as John.'

'You'll be killed,' Mama said.

Adeline did not reply.

'Please, Adeline. I am sorry for John, and his father, but if you don't get out of this, you will waste your life. I want better for you than this.'

'I can't leave him now.'

Then Mama became angry: she abused Adeline, and John, and his father, and herself for allowing the engagement, all in the roundest terms. Adeline waited for her to finish.

At last Mama said, 'It's my own fault. I taught you when you were a child, do you remember? I taught you not to be afraid.'

Adeline recalled her training, from the age of five. You began by balancing atop a large India rubber ball; when you could stand up on it as it rolled at speed, you were ready for the wire. Mama had made her walk up and down a line strung a foot from the ground until she could do it blindfolded (it's your ears, Mama told her, that you really need for balance).

'This is another wire,' Mama said. 'Higher up still. These things may kill you. And you will let them try.'

'I want to help, to do something . . .'

Mama sighed. 'Well. Do you remember everything you learned? When you were a little girl? I taught you to somersault, and walk a rope, and throw a knife.'

'Yes.'

'Good. You aren't an ignorant girl that these creatures can make short work of. You'll need practice, though. Have you thought of that? You'll have to train again. Those machines have made you weak. And you're starting to stoop.'

'I don't stoop.'

'Go and see Nell. She'll help you.'

'See who?'

'Nell. You know, she's everywhere at the moment. All those posters they're making a fuss about. As if a woman with legs like that should be ashamed about showing them off.'

'D'you mean the acrobat? Fabula, or whatever she calls herself?'

'Yes. She knows me. She'll do you a favour, if you mention my name. Ask her to train you up, make sure you're in decent condition.'

It was, Adeline admitted, a good idea. She would have to be strong for what she was planning to do. 'Thank you, Mama.'

'One more thing. Bring me my hatbox.'

Adeline had never been allowed to touch the hatbox before. It was leather and very old; Mama had brought it over with her from France when Adeline was young. Now she fetched it from Mama's bedroom and passed it to her.

Mama opened it. From under letters and photographs and old playbills and a thick roll of butter-coloured paper tied with a red ribbon, she brought out a revolver.

'You used to go down to the shooting-gallery stall on Leather Lane, didn't you?' she said. 'Tim Younge used to take you. You remember him. The man-frog – that was his act.'

'Yes.'

'He used to swim about and eat and smoke a pipe underwater, in that tank of his.'

'I remember.'

'Not much skill in it, to my mind, but he was popular. And a nice boy, always kind to you when you were a child. He said you had a good eye and a steady hand, even when you were small.'

'Yes, I do remember.'

Mama handed her the revolver very carefully. 'I will show you how to load this. You should have no difficulty getting cartridges.'

'How long have you had it?'

'I got it during the war. It seemed safest. And then I brought it over with me. Galand. Fast to reload, the man said. I don't know myself – I've never fired it.'

'I didn't know you had a revolver,' Adeline said.

'Of course not,' Mama replied, 'or I would have had no peace until I let you play with it. Now it's yours. Take good care of yourself. Promise.'

'I do promise. Thank you, Mama.'

And it was not a lie, for she was always as careful as possible – as careful as she could be in the life she had chosen.

• • •

They never did discover under what circumstances John had been transformed. Adeline could only think that he had been tricked or had volunteered to protect someone else. He would never speak of it, even on his best days. On his worst days he scratched and bit himself and tore at his clothes. They starved him and dosed him with holy water so that he would not escape. To keep him fed they brought him birds – a pair a week, pigeons mostly. The floor was covered with feathers and light bones which crunched underfoot.

The holy water was obtained from a friend of Shadwell's – his only friend from his former life, a pleasant old clergyman from Farnham with a passion for white mice. He stared at Adeline and chaffed Shadwell good-humouredly and never asked any questions, and sent them on their way with gifts of hard bread and crumbling fruitcakes. He was one of the small group of people, mostly living in London, who knew what they were doing – who would sometimes give their names to people in need of help.

They heard rumours of Burke long before their first meeting. Everyone spoke of him. Adeline had feared attracting his notice, but when at last he did pay them attention, Burke brought them under his protection. There was a price for this, but it could not be avoided.

Burke took their payment, took their stories, too. He fed on them gleefully, grew young again on tales of hairbreadth escapes, of flights down narrow lanes and through decrepit old courts.

The first person they helped was a scullery maid – fourteen years old, with frightened dark eyes. Her master was a wealthy man, she said, so respected and important that she could hardly believe what he had done. And here she began to cry and removed her glove to show them both a messy wound on her wrist, which looked as if it had been made by human teeth.

She was called Alice and she was their first great success, for they got her away in time and her master never knew what had become of her.

Sometimes things did not go as well. But people thanked them whether or not they could do much to help, if only out of simple relief at having someone understand, someone who would see what they could not express.

They found a place in Wych Street where they could work and do business, as well – a trade in occult books. It was a sensible choice. They parcelled up piles of books, took the shop on a five-year lease, and went to work. The books were on many peculiar subjects – on certain outré uses of garlic and rice, on stakes and unburied dead and the strange afterlives of the bodies of suicides. Their customers were few but fervently grateful.

They were both careful about names. They catalogued the creatures' need for blood, their love of shadows, their hatred of silver, their unending youth and strength. But there were words that neither of them would speak aloud, though they might write them down; they avoided these because they preferred to think of John as ill, wounded, unlucky, insane – anything, so long as he was human.

In those first days, Shadwell would go out to drink in the evenings, leaving Adeline alone except for John, pacing back and forth upstairs. They had restrained him as best they could, but it was still only holy water and semi-starvation that kept him tractable. On one occasion he had begged her never to let him out, he was so afraid of himself. She tried to remember this at other times, when he cursed at her, spat out every insult he could think of. In this mood, he would tell them how he would soon be free and they would be sorry.

'You shouldn't go up there,' Shadwell said once.

'Of course I have to go up.'

'But it isn't right for you to hear . . .'

She shook her head. 'I don't mind it. I don't.'

After a few months, John changed, grew quieter. He stopped asking for blood, began to ask for something else. Adeline would sit at the top of the stairs, a little way from his door, and listen to him talk, his voice grown faint and thirsty.

• • •

It was two years after John's death when they helped a family named Riggs. The youngest Miss Riggs had bravely repulsed the strange attentions of a long-toothed baronet with ruddy dead hands. Now the whole family were in danger of suffering the consequences.

The family had hidden in the shop for some weeks, during which time the youngest son had proposed to Adeline. He was young and cheerful, and after refusing him she had brought him upstairs to her room, leading him gently by the hand. She made him undress her. He was so obviously at a loss that it felt like a kindness to teach him how buttons and corsets and petticoats could be managed. After this, she undressed him in turn. To reassure him, she made a joke of it, a mock lesson, naming each part of him as she went, as if he had never seen himself naked before. These are your hands, she said (a kiss to each); these are your elbows (another kiss); this is your mouth. Along with his laughter there was a slight wonder in his eyes, as if she were a witch slowly calling him into being. She was gentle, teasing, when she said finally, Of course, you know what this is, don't you? Know what it's for? And she stooped for the final kiss, the lightest of all, and looked up at him through her loosened hair.

She felt as if she conjured herself, too, in touching him. This part of her had been stunned for so long. He was sweet with her – really, he was very young – and so unspoiled. Years ago, she must have been like this. Afterwards he asked her if she was sad, and she shook her head and said no.

John was not the sort to mind. He had too much common sense for that. If things had happened the other way round, she would have wanted him to be happy. If she haunted his bed, it would be in sympathy, not jealousy. Adeline thought of herself as a ghost drifting above him, urging him on, a lewd spectre indeed.

She found that, far from being sad, she was laughing, and could not explain why to the boy who lay beside her.

• • •

In time, she got used to Shadwell. He would bring her ill-cooked food to eat when she had no spirit to fetch anything for herself. He had brought her sweets once – bull's-eyes, the kind he was fond of. He could crunch bags of them as he worked – it was hell on his teeth. She had tried one of his sweets once, made a face, and spat it out before she could stop herself. Mama had sometimes tried to teach her better manners, but with one thing and another, the bad habits had crept in.

'Sorry,' she said. The sweet had stuck to the carpet and could never afterwards be removed.

But he smiled at her, and she had found herself smiling, too, which she had not done for some weeks, and after that she was certain that they were friends.

After their success with the Riggs family, they became more

confident in their abilities. It was not enough to wait until frightened people came to them. Why not venture out, Shadwell
suggested, and seek those in trouble?

They would sit together after supper and smoke in silence
before heading out for an evening's work, and it was comfortable
enough. He would sit in his favourite chair, the one with the
pattern that looked like endless flowing moustaches; she would
sit in front of the fire, as close as she could get to the warmth.
If he objected to her cigarettes, he made no mention of it, apart
from the occasional aside about how expensive they were. Why
not buy the gold-tipped variety, since she was so determined to
ruin them both? She would usually retort with some remark on
the stench of his coarse tobacco, the disgusting condition of his
old briarwood pipe. After this they would lapse into silence again.
Sometimes she would imagine that she still heard John stir above
their heads. Perhaps Shadwell did, too.

He was always kind to her – this was nothing strange; he was
kind to everyone. He reminded her of John in that way. He was
good to her because it was the decent way to behave and because
John had loved her.

When things changed, she was not slow to notice it. When
Shadwell began to look at her differently, when he was warmer
and easier in her company, she had known what to think. The
girls at the telegraph office would talk together, giggling, over
their young men – those fascinating, neat-moustached fellows
who *might* be intending to propose. Adeline had enjoyed these
conversations, the girls' comradeship and good humour. But she
herself had never known either the pleasure of hope or the misery
of doubt. She always knew, one way or the other, whether a man
had an interest in her.

John had been so strong and new, full of hopes and plans. And
Shadwell was the same and not – older and a little scuffed from
life, a bit neglected, soft bits of grey in his hair, his face fallen
into friendly lines. He could swing an axe with a speed that was

wonderful to watch, and he could tell her something she didn't know without being tiresome about it.

He was *good,* too, and worried about not being good enough. He began to look guiltily at her, and his manner became uncharacteristically remote.

In the end it had seemed best simply to go to him, at night, after they had both retired. She took a candle and walked barefoot across the landing to his bedroom door. As she knocked, she had the thought that they had abandoned respectability already, living as they did. Mama often pointed this out. They no longer had anything to lose.

He answered so quickly that she thought he must have been sitting up in bed, perhaps reading. She wondered if he ate bull's-eyes up here, too.

'What is it?' he asked. He must have been undressing for bed, because he was barefoot too. They would both get frostbitten, she thought, if she was not quick. Frowning, he added, 'Has something happened—'

The kiss alarmed them both. He stepped backwards into his own room – astonished, words all lost.

She said, 'Please let me in.' She had not meant to say *please* – it suggested uncertainty, and she was not unsure of this now.

She thought, Why am I always the one waiting outside your door? It's hardly fair.

'Don't,' he said.

She took his hands, which were cold like hers. 'Why not?'

'Adeline, I know that you mean to be kind—'

'Never,' she said. 'Look at me. Not kind.'

He shook his head and drew his hands away; he would not smile at her. 'Then . . . that's worse. We can't just – Adeline, it's wrong.'

Of all the wrong things they had done together, Adeline thought, how like him to object to the only one which would be pleasant.

'Are you sure?' she asked.

'I believe it would damn my soul,' he said very simply.

It's late to be thinking of that, she could have said – peevish, because she had seen how it would have been with them, how fierce and unlikely, like blazing sunlight in this cold pea-soup city. And he would surrender this, give up an opportunity with a woman like Adeline, because of some quaint principle or other. Or because he was afraid or thought he did not deserve happiness. And we do deserve it, she thought, and if we do not then let us take it anyway, whilst we can.

She might have him now, in spite of his honour. But she saw that to insist would be cruel. She would only lose him to his guilt. He had set his limits, and however illogical they seemed to her, it would be selfish to push him beyond them.

'Promise me, then,' she said. She had been silent for perhaps half a minute, looking at him. 'Promise me we will always be friends. No more of this silliness.'

'Friends,' he agreed. He sounded as if he might laugh. 'We will always be *friends*, Adeline.'

'Good.' She took one of his hands, raised it to her lips. 'There. Friends. It's sealed.' She stepped back. 'I'm sorry I disturbed you.'

'No,' he said. She saw that he would hold this moment close, that it would be a kind of consolation. Perhaps he had not noticed before tonight how much she felt for him. It would have been clever of him to guess, when she had not wholly known herself.

'All right,' she said. 'Good night, then.'

Always, afterwards, she remembered the second kiss, not the first. It had seemed a pledge, though she was not certain, then or now, just what had been promised. Perhaps it was simply as she had said, that they would always be friends, until all of this was ended, until their work was done.

Chapter Nineteen

James was not quite sure of the street where he left the child
– perhaps he had walked as far as Holloway, perhaps not so far.
Distance meant little now; he did not feel as if he would ever
grow weary. Perhaps his kind did not tire easily. She was cold
when he set her down, curled up in as close an imitation of
comfort as he could give her.

He departed quickly, slipped away, back to the busier streets,
where night was diluted by streetlamps and shop lights.

He had never been able to find his way anywhere before. Now
he walked the city without doubt, without wrong turns.

The house was as he remembered, the same discouraging air
of grandness – but everything stood out more sharply now. Not
a detail escaped him. The fierce contrast of white house and black
railings was almost painful. All the curtains inside appeared to be
drawn; there were no lights showing within.

The door was opened by the butler, as plush-voiced and immacu-
late as he had been the last time James had visited the house.

'I would like to see Mrs Paige,' James said.

'I'm afraid she is not at home, sir.' He did not seem to remember James. But he was afraid of him, James realised. Just a small flare of alarm, somewhere towards the back of his mind.

It was past eight at least. They would think him rude, calling uninvited at such an hour, on such a day. Because, of course, they knew about Christopher. That was plain enough in the servant's face. It was there in the surface of his thoughts, too.

'I'm a friend of her son,' James continued, 'and I know that she would like to speak to me.'

'I'm sorry, sir,' the man repeated, 'but Mrs Paige is not at home.'

James gave up any pretence of politeness. 'Let me see them. Let me in.'

'Sir, I'm afraid I cannot—'

'What is it?' Someone else spoke from inside the house. 'Who's there?' Miss Paige appeared, the butler falling back respectfully to allow her space in the doorway. She was wearing black. It made her face look almost grey.

'Please let me in,' James said.

'Why? What could you possibly want?'

'Listen, there's something you must know.' Because he could do this, at least, however degraded he might be now: he could save Christopher's family. 'There's something wrong with him. Eustace. Please let me in.'

She said, 'Clarke, that will do.' And when the man didn't move, she added more firmly, 'Thank you, Clarke.'

The butler nodded and left them alone.

'Can we speak indoors?' James asked.

She hesitated for a few seconds. 'Very well,' she said finally.

Her superficial thoughts were easy enough for James to perceive. She was having difficulty reconciling her view of him as he had been – pitiful, by her recollection and by his – with what she beheld now. She felt that he was dangerous. She was as wary as the butler had been.

There would be other things in her mind – it was like a tree

covered in fruit; he might strip it bare of every memory of
Christopher, hoard the stolen past for himself. But he would not
do such a thing. He steered his thoughts away from hers, put up
every resistance he could.

'Wait here,' she said.

She shut the door and returned a few minutes later, holding
something wrapped in a silk scarf. 'Come in, then.'

The room to which she led him was familiar – the drawing-
room in which Mrs Paige had received her guests. But all the
curtains were now drawn; the clocks had been stopped.

Miss Paige unwrapped the object she held. It was some kind
of firearm. Rather old, though he knew little more than that. It
looked out of place in the fashionable parlour.

'This is loaded,' she told him. She raised it, as if she intended
to fire. 'It was my father's. He kept it in case of thieves. You can
probably guess that I've never shot in my life. But I think I could
hit you at close range, and Clarke is waiting outside. He'll hear,
even if I miss.'

'All right,' James said. 'I understand. But I don't want to hurt
you.'

This, for the moment, was true. There was, however, somewhere deep within him the conviction that it might be a good idea
to drain all of Miss Paige's blood from her body in one glorious
red swallow and leave her desiccated corpse sitting upright at the
piano, as if about to begin a long concerto.

'Talk quickly,' she said.

'Where's Eustace?'

'He's not here. What is it you want to tell me?'

He did not know how to begin, now that it came to it – how
to give her the news kindly, how to make her believe him.

'He isn't safe,' said James. 'You have to keep away from him.'

He waited for a protest, for anger or disbelief. Instead, she
smiled. It would have hurt Christopher to see her smile like that,
so sad and bitter.

'Did you really come here to warn me?'

If he had not been so fastidiously avoiding her mind, he would have seen it in her thoughts before – the fear of Eustace, of what he would do. Now he allowed himself to look closer, and in her mind he saw Mrs Paige, grim-faced, murmuring, *Not your sister. No, Eustace. No.*

'He's my brother,' Miss Paige said. 'Do you think I wouldn't realise?'

'Then you know you're not safe here,' said James. Had Eustace harmed her already? She had less colour than he remembered; her light was burning low. With discipline and restraint, Eustace might feed on her for years as she declined into sickness or madness. He was probably capable of finesse.

'He will be thinking of killing you. He won't be able to stop thinking about it.' James looked down at his own hands, stark white, his gloves lost or forgotten. 'Family's the worst of all.'

She did not reply immediately. At last she said, 'I want to know how he died.'

'What did Eustace tell you?'

'Nothing much. They just brought him upstairs and—'

'He's here?'

She nodded. She did not give him time to recover from this news. 'Tell me how it happened,' she said.

They stood opposite each other in the parlour, and James told her everything – the truth of that night was the only kindness he could do her.

When he was done, he waited for her to speak.

'Why should they spare you and kill him?' she asked. 'Why would they choose *you*?'

'They made a mistake. I should have been the one to die.'

She was trembling. He thought she would break down, but instead she said, in a calmer tone, 'You ought to go.'

'I want— I would like to see him.'

'You can't.'

'Just for a few minutes. Please.' It was necessary to beg, to refrain from striking her, to be better than the club men.

'No.'

In spite of himself, he stepped closer to her. She was startled; her face was briefly distorted – grief and fear and distaste. The pistol slipped from her hands, fell to the floor.

They both flinched, but there was only the soft thud of metal on the thick rug.

They looked at each other, at the pistol lying between them on the floor. Then James heard the front door open and close with infinite gentleness. It might have been anyone in the hall, had it not been for her expression. She looked like someone deep in a nightmare.

'You must go,' she said.

But he could not have left then, even if he had wanted to, for the drawing-room door opened and Eustace Paige came in.

'Hello, Lydia.' No anger in his voice, not much of anything – only indifference. James saw Miss Paige wince as her brother spoke, as if her name had become a chain about her neck, which he might jangle whenever he chose.

'I've just asked Mr Norbury to leave.'

'Very sensible of you. Is Mother any better?'

'A little.'

'Only a little? That's a pity. Make sure she's all right, will you?'

She nodded, and took herself away, closing the door behind her with an agony of quiet care.

Eustace Paige turned the key in the lock. 'I did wonder if you'd be fool enough to come here.'

'I want to see him,' James said – and then Paige hit him. James fell, striking his head against the marble of the fireplace. He was briefly stunned, unable to rise. A week ago, such a fall would have killed him.

'I don't know that you'll be in a position to *talk* for much longer,' said Eustace Paige, 'but whilst you still can, I don't want to hear you speak of him. Do you understand?' He stepped forwards and kicked James viciously in the ribs.

James felt bones crack; pain tore up his side.

'He's nothing to do with you now,' Paige said.

The lie – filthy, malicious – gave James a small measure of angry strength, enough to heave himself to his feet to face Paige. The hurt in his ribs was already beginning to subside.

'It went wrong, didn't it,' James said. 'Your plan.'

'What do you mean?' James had managed to shake him – his voice was sharp.

'You meant for me to die, not him. Your friend made a mistake.'

Paige laughed. To a human being – to the women upstairs – it must have sounded almost too horrible to bear. 'I was right about you from the start. You really are remarkably stupid.' And he sprang at James, who moved forwards to meet him.

Before, the contest would have been a brief one: Paige was taller and broader – the *sportsman,* Christopher used to call him. Now the fight was drawn out and ugly. Things broke and tore. A picture fell from the wall, books from the shelves. The beautiful symmetry of the place was dashed to pieces. Glass cracked under their feet.

James forced Paige's face into the mirror above the mantel, again and again, and there were shards in his eyes and in his hair and it was almost enough to wipe all likeness of Christopher from his face.

But in another moment Paige had pushed James away so forcefully that he almost fell again.

They both stood, expectant, a few yards between them. For about half a minute, neither moved. Eustace Paige was watching James warily.

James said, 'Christopher would be alive now if it weren't for you.'

Perhaps he would kill James for saying that, but it was worth it to see his face twist, grief struggling to show itself on that immobile countenance.

Paige said, 'What do you mean?'

'If you hadn't sent your friend to—'

'I didn't send anyone. Why should I?'

'To separate us. You told me to leave him alone.'

'Yes, I did. And I scared you off with a mere warning. I knew at the time that you weren't man enough to defy me. There was no need to go to the trouble of arranging an attack.'

'I would never have left him. We were going to get away from you.'

'You're a *liar*.' His voice was almost a snarl. 'You're a liar and a coward, and you left him to die.'

James moved to strike him again, but Paige caught him by the wrist, so tightly that he could not draw back. He heard himself speak in a hoarse, painful snarl, and his own words took him by surprise:

'Don't you think I wish it had been me?'

Eustace Paige let go of his arm. James was not sure how long they stared at each other without speaking. The house was hushed, without even the move of a clock hand to break the silence.

'Why did you come here?' Paige said finally. He sounded tired now. There was blood on his face, and he did not trouble to wipe it away.

'I thought your family ought to know that you aren't safe.'

'Very admirable. I suppose you hoped to have things out with me, too. Since you believe I sent Michael that night.' He brushed glass from his shoulders, wiped the blood from his face. 'But I didn't.'

Was he speaking the truth? If he were properly human, James would have seen the answer clearly in his thoughts.

'Suppose you had killed me,' Paige continued. 'What would you have done then?'

'Found Bier,' James replied. 'Both of them.'

'Of course.' Paige seemed to hesitate, and then added, 'It's tomorrow.'

'What?'

'The funeral. Kensal Green. I suppose he would have wanted you to know that.'

Was it a challenge? A trap? Did he really expect James to appear?

'Now you'd better go,' Paige said. 'You've already been here too long. I don't know if they've followed you or not. If they're waiting outside, we shall both be the worse off.'

'Is this your revenge on them, letting me go?'

Paige went to the door, unlocked it. 'Don't come back here. And don't speak to Lydia again, or my mother. Understand?'

'You're hurting them,' James said. 'If Christopher knew—'

Paige reached out, grasped James's throat – unexpectedly, and with some force.

'Don't come back here,' he repeated. He took James by the shoulder, steered him into the front hall. He opened the front door and paused briefly, listening for James's pursuers.

'Keep walking,' he said after a moment. 'Quick as you can. Go.' He thrust James outside.

The street was quiet. The door slammed behind him, and James was left alone in the street.

Chapter Twenty

The Notebook of Augustus Mould

20th April

Searches for Norbury and for Howland have not brought success thus far. Corvish went to Norbury's house and failed to apprehend him. He did make one discovery, however: Norbury has a sister, and she is here in the city.

Unluckily, Corvish failed to seize her – she was borne away by two strangers, most likely belonging to that aggravating class of persons who pit themselves against the un-dead out of some misguided sense of moral outrage. Shadwell, perhaps? I would give much to meet him and his associate – their know-ledge would be of use. (Of course, they have caused some inconvenience here and there – assistance has been given to various persons – still, a discussion would be interesting.) Corvish said he was attacked by two strangers: one a man of middle years, the other a woman dressed as a boy. We must investigate further.

Of Howland there is no sign. Has he, too, been taken up by

these people? Unlikely. How would they know how to find one another in a city this size?

Later:

Edmund is growing impatient, sharp with everyone. This has quite spoiled the commencement of the Undertaking for him. It is not an <u>insurmountable</u> problem, of course, but it is a tiresome distraction. This business must be finished with soon. I do not like to see him in this mood. There are times when I feel that he does not quite hear me.

Where would Norbury go?

I remember his grief when we first brought him upstairs. Merely a guess. He may not be so rash. But let us see.

Chapter Twenty-One

Eustace Paige had told him to keep walking, and James followed his advice.

Within the first hour, the wounds he had suffered during the fight had healed. He was pristine again – unmarked and undamaged, save for his clothes, which were in a bad state. He had enough money with him to purchase a clean shirt, if he could bear the ordeal of a shop or a stall, the proximity to so many people. The temptation might be too much.

He walked without any definite direction, anxious to keep moving. It was only after a few hours that he noticed that he was retracing journeys he had made with Christopher.

This was the thing about London, the fact he had always suspected. One left so little impression on the walls and pavements. In London, one's past was not safe; the roads were overwritten by a thousand histories, trodden by millions of feet.

He was sure they had walked here together once. Somewhere on this street they had argued about art, and the conversation had descended to minor grievances – Christopher had borrowed and spoiled one of his collars, James had been annoyed, until the absurdity of the discussion finally made him laugh.

But there was nothing to show for any of this. They might never have existed.

He retraced their steps through Trafalgar Square – busy, even so late – down to the St James's Theatre. He walked to Mrs Hyssops's house, stood outside in the rain for five minutes, growing colder and colder. The lights downstairs were all out. Upstairs, a single room was illuminated. He thought it might be hers; perhaps she had only learned of Christopher's death a few hours ago. If things had been different, he might have had the right to knock and go in, to grieve with her. Instead, he walked on. He could not help thinking of Charlotte: he wanted to find her, and he wanted never to see her again.

Some hours later, he was down by the river. It had drawn him in spite of himself, the slow, tireless ooze of it. The movement of the water troubled him obscurely. One might watch and watch for ever.

He was on Waterloo Bridge. Ahead were the lights of the Victoria Embankment. There were few passers-by at this time of night, and those who did go past hurried by him as if they knew what he was. But then a man stopped to enquire the time, and James said, 'Wait—' and reached into his pocket, as if to get out a watch, and had that same insistent flickering thought of hurt. It would be easy just then; no wonder he had been drawn to the river, for on a bridge, there would be no need to worry about the body. It could be done tidily.

The stranger – comfortable, forgettable face – looked at him oddly and said, 'Never mind.'

Things might have happened differently if it were just the two of them on the bridge in the cold, the man's breath visible against the distant dark of the water. (James's breath did not show at all.) But then another man hurried over, a friend of the one who had spoken, and together they left hastily, not looking back.

It was too cold to linger. He walked on, not knowing or caring which way he went, and found himself at last in a miserable little public house which had the one advantage of warmth. They gave him gin, the smell of which was so strong it made him feel ill. (Everything smelled stronger now. Odours were a kind of violence; he perceived them with painful clarity.) He sat there until the place closed, scraping a fingernail over and over the wood of the table. It took effort to ignore them, to keep their voices and their beating hearts to the back of his thoughts. The landlord came over to him – was it usual to send the girls into the back room like that? – and respectfully asked him to leave.

'We *are* shutting up,' he told James faintly. 'Sir. Sorry.'

James was hungry now, and it was worse than before: his appetite was sharp and the man standing over him was brimming with blood.

He found that it was quite easy, to put the man aside, go to the door, and push it closed. He said, 'I'll stay a little while longer, if you don't mind.'

• • •

It was not much, if one considered it objectively. The man would live, if the girls were not silly about blood. Though the thought of the unfinished kill nagged at James like an open door, a draught, he had at least kept some part of himself. He had held back at the very last.

Before he had left the place, he managed to wash himself a little, cleaned his face and hands, concealing as best he could the marks on his clothes. He had taken a clean shirt and collar, made himself decent again. Even in the fresh air he smelled gin and tobacco and blood on his clothes and in his hair. He wished he had thought to wash his mouth out. The taste of blood was pleasant and could not be ignored.

But he had saved himself. Or the thought of Christopher had saved him. That was what he must remember. He had not killed the man; he could go unsullied to Christopher's funeral.

• • •

He did not know what it was which finally brought him to Hyde Park towards the end of that long night – no design, certainly. He went quickly past the spot where he remembered meeting Margoyle, letting Margoyle insist on introducing him to his friend Mr Paige.

He had an idea that concealment would be easier amongst the trees. The gates were already locked, but this was no obstacle to him now.

He followed the paths of the park, not caring in which direction he went. The rain finished. There was a half-moon, which was a kind of company, and did not shine bright enough to hurt.

Passing a bench, he saw a man lying curled up, knees close to his chest. From the smell of him, it was easy to guess that he had been wandering for a long while out of doors. He had dosed himself with gin and he was on the cusp of sleep, though the cold clearly pained him as it pained James. He was old, and his bones were ill-covered.

As James watched, the man slowly opened his eyes and looked at him. He did not speak – perhaps he had drunk too much or he was simply too tired to make the effort. But he regarded James warily.

Stay whole – that had been his decision. He would remain himself.

James took out a coin, one of his few remaining shillings, and held it out. When the man did not move, James said, 'Here,' so that the man would see it was not a trick.

The man shifted, with some pain, and made a snatch at the coin. In an instant it was gone, vanished into a pocket. He did not thank James or look away. In the man's thoughts – they intruded in spite of James's efforts – James saw a heaviness, perceptions blunted by long suffering, a dreary endurance. Beneath that, there was suspicion. He had seen something about James he did not like. But he was tired and cold and hungry and he wanted the coin. Now that he had it, he would continue to watch until James left him alone.

James nodded, walked on. When he glanced back, the man seemed to have fallen asleep once more.

It would be all right, he thought. He had passed a test. He had helped someone – he was still capable of doing good.

For a while he walked under the trees, imagined that he was back at Aiskew. He thought of the way things had been and watched the moon curve slowly across the sky.

· · ·

By the time the sky was starting to lighten, he was already out of the park, making his way to Kensal Green.

He found the cemetery quite deserted. It was past dawn now, and yet no birds were singing. There was only James and the graves. Such a wide sweep of neat-cut grass, so many acres of dead lying beneath. They rested under smart black marble blocks, under mossy, crumbling memorials, under rueful angels and squat monstrous urns, walled up in family tombs.

It was a calm, quiet place to walk, to think and grieve. The size of the grounds made one feel that death was not at all exclusive – an everyday affair, an unpleasant obligation that no one might avoid. A visitor, walking alive beneath the sky, would always feel like one of a minority.

The funeral would start soon. He knew this was so and yet the fact still confounded him. Even now it seemed that there must have been some mistake. This was not the sort of thing that ought to occur.

As the sun rose, the sky became a shy blue, and James at last came to the chapel at the heart of the grounds. He thought that he would wait inside. Perhaps he might at last find the right mind to pray – for Christopher, if not for himself.

The chapel was built with broad stone pillars, steps leading up to a portico, a tall wooden door studded with black metal bolts. He reached the door and stopped, one hand against the wood. Was it a fit place for him? Of course he could go in, he reasoned, he had done nothing unforgivable – but, all the same, he did not like to enter. Shame or cowardice.

He turned left. Running sideways and behind the chapel was a cloister of sorts – a square of grass edged on three sides by a stone-paved corridor, bounded by pillars. He paced up and down there, reluctant to stand still, keeping to the shade as the sun rose higher.

He tried to remember Christopher. This was the day and the time to think of him. Remember, James told himself, remember how happy we were; hold fast to that. But as he walked, the memories slid away, his thoughts became empty – heavy, monotonous as the grey stone slabs of the cloister floor.

He had read about the cemetery a long time ago – Christopher and he had made some half plan to visit the grave of Wilkie Collins (one of the few authors upon whom they had agreed), but there had never been enough time. There were catacombs underneath the chapel, he knew, where the dead were neatly labelled and shelved behind metal grilles. He had not been able to decide whether this would be better or worse than being covered up in earth.

The sun grew brighter. It began to make his eyes smart. At last he heard the noise of carriage wheels, then the first footsteps on the gravel path. The mourners were arriving.

He hid himself in the shadows behind one of the pillars. From this side of the cloister, he could see everyone who passed on their way to the chapel.

Some of the people James must have seen before; some he certainly knew, though he could not recollect their names. He drew back sharply to avoid Soames and Bleasdale, who arrived together. They moved gingerly in the morning light, theatrically tender with their aching heads. They had held a wake last night, James guessed, and now the world tasted unpleasant and was spinning at a nauseous tilt.

After them came others, strangers to James – except one. In spite of James's concealment, their eyes met.

Margoyle. It seemed like a long while indeed since James had seen him last. He had not changed. Still florid with health and good feeding, still superior in manner, full of plumey self-importance. Though there was a trace of something sadder today – James supposed he had been fond of Christopher, in his way. Or perhaps the tragedy had brought to his attention the fact that neither he nor his smart new wife was immortal, and this knowledge had make him melancholy and irritable.

James would have moved away without speaking, but Margoyle made straight for him. He had no choice but to step out from the cloisters and shake Margoyle's extended hand.

'How are you, Norbury? Must have been a shock.'

'Yes.' Christopher's family would have settled on some story or other – a fall down stairs or under a 'bus. He resisted taking a glance into Margoyle's thoughts to see just what had been said.

'You look dreadful,' Margoyle observed.

'Yes. How are you?'

'Well enough, thanks. Sad occasion, of course. These accidents will happen, but all the same . . .' He sighed. 'Seems unjust, doesn't it? And so mundane, the whole thing.' He tried to smile. 'He wouldn't have liked that. Nor such a small funeral. I hear his mother insisted upon it, though.' He glanced behind him, then added in a softer tone, 'She's attending today. And the sister, too. Lord knows why Paige's brother is letting them. Call me old-fashioned, but . . .'

James nodded. There was someone else coming towards them now – a lady in neat black boots, stirring up the gravel as she walked. He knew her face, but it was becoming increasingly difficult to differentiate between the living; they were all so alike. For a moment he thought, quite irrationally, that it might be Charlotte.

It was Mrs Hyssops, in fact. He had not expected her to attend. Perhaps Miss Paige had asked her. She was carefully dressed – fiercely neat, like a soldier. Before he could stop himself, James saw her thoughts, saw her alone in her dressing room, trying first one pair of earrings and then another, her mouth a grim line. Her friend was dead, and this was all that she could do for him.

Margoyle, who appeared to have met her before, gave a bow, made a polite enquiry after her husband – she answered briefly, her eyes on James's face.

'James,' she said. 'How are you . . . ?'

He saw that she pitied him, guessed at his hurt. She was the only one who would know what he had lost, she was one who might see and suspect the change in him. He ought to have hidden himself better.

He did not speak, and the other two looked at him strangely.

'Have you been ill?' asked Mrs Hyssops.

James made a great effort: 'A little.'

'You do look ill,' Margoyle put in. 'Should you stay, do you think?'

'Maybe not,' James said, just as Mrs Hyssops asked, 'James, are you really all right?'

He nodded, and to his relief she turned to Margoyle:

'We ought to be going in – do you think you could help me retrieve my husband, Mr Margoyle? He went on ahead to look at some curiosity or other, and now I've lost him.'

Margoyle could hardly refuse her. As they left him, she turned her head and looked back at James once, raised her hand, and he waved in return.

He would not see her again. One by one the ties to his old, ordinary life were falling away. He had no more friends to lose.

He moved back into the shadow of the cloister. He would not be able to get closer than this.

Then the mourning coach arrived, followed by the hearse. The passengers alighted, stark and sombre in their funeral clothes, their smart black gloves. There was Mrs Paige, expressionless, and Miss Paige by her side, moving with weary economy, like one beginning to be ill. They did not see him, though he had edged forwards now, more than was prudent. Their clothes were caught in the breeze, crape fluttering. Already the blue was disappearing from the sky.

The coffin was carried behind them, draped in black velvet. Eustace was there amongst the pallbearers. So was Edmund Bier.

The clergyman met them at the gate, like a gracious host. James heard him speak from far off – *I am the resurrection and the life.* The procession moved along the path, up the steps of the chapel.

The clergyman knew his business well. He had buried enough men to voice the words clearly, to give them the weight they needed. He made them a statement, not a protest or a desperate cry against oblivion. He was certainty, solemnity.

– *and though after my skin worms destroy this body* –

More footsteps, funeral-slow, funeral-heavy. The chapel door closed.

He did not like to leave the shelter of the cloister – he was too afraid of being seen in the open expanse of the graveyard, afraid of the sunlight. Instead, he found the darkest corner, sat down with his back against the wall.

There were birds singing in the cemetery, louder than James had ever heard before. They hurt him as the bright morning sun had hurt him.

From within the chapel he heard music, words leaking out. It should have been a comfort, the ceremony, the grand old cadences of the service. Instead, he was shut out – there was no help for him now, not in heaven or on earth.

At last the service must have finished. He saw people leave the chapel – slowly, in small groups, talking softly. He saw Mrs Paige pass close by, leaning on her elder son's arm. The coffin was not brought out again. Soon they were all gone. James let half an hour pass. Finally the clergyman stepped out of the chapel with two workmen, who were both wiping their hands. The coffin was to be interred below, then, in the catacombs. Christopher would be coffined in lead and shelved away.

When the place was finally quiet, James at last left his conceal-ment and made his way towards the chapel door. Outside he hesitated, suddenly remembering part of a myth, a story he had heard once – could it be that his nature now made such places unhealthy for him? He had read as much – somewhere, a novel, a long time ago. But the door opened, and he passed through unscathed.

Inside, there was shade and silence, balm for his aching head and eyes. Perhaps it was foolish to imagine that the place would be barred against any who had need of it. The chapel was domin-ated by a catafalque – a great black box about the size of an altar, decorated in gold. There was no coffin. Christopher's body had already been taken down – the catafalque lowered through the chapel floor, the coffin removed, the catafalque raised once more. He imagined a slow, ponderous descent, wheels and chains straining against the coffin weight. It was so precarious, the dignity of the dead. He laid one hand on the gilt-and-dark-wood surface where the coffin had lately rested.

He would have stayed there for a while, had he not heard footsteps on the stone flags outside.

He moved softly to the doorway. It was the man with the grey moustache, the one who had observed James's sufferings in the club: Mould. He stood, slightly breathless, at the top of the chapel steps, his hands in his pockets and a book tucked under one arm. He took a step onto the chapel portico and stopped, looking through the open door. The shadows, to a human gaze, would be heavy after the comparative brightness outside.

'Mr Norbury?' Mould said. 'Is that you?'

James stepped forwards into the light and had the satisfaction of seeing Mould flinch. He could read the man's mingled satisfaction and dismay at having found him. The problem of hunting monsters was that one might prove successful.

'Why are you here?' James demanded.

'To talk to you. Naturally.'

'Alone?'

'Yes.'

'Aren't you afraid?'

'No. This is quite a public spot. And you don't *need* to kill me – I cannot overpower you, I present no threat. You have fed recently, if the blood on your collar is any indication, so you are under no immediate imperative to prey upon me.'

In spite of himself, James put a hand to his collar, found the mark. He had missed it in his hasty efforts last night. The stain had been there all the time, whilst he was talking to Margoyle and Mrs Hyssops.

'Also, if you kill me now,' Mould went on, 'you will miss hearing what I have to tell you, and we shall both of us be worse off for it.' He smiled briefly – quick as the flick of a rat's tail.

'How did you know I would be here?' James asked. Was this Eustace's plan? But in that case, why send Mould? What purpose could it serve?

'It's his funeral,' Mould said. 'Of course you'd be here.'

It was an unpleasant shock, to be understood – even slightly – by this man. At the same time it was an obscure relief, for someone at last to recognise aloud something of what it might mean for him that Christopher was dead.

As if to give James a chance to collect his thoughts – as if he were being kind – Mould turned away to glance back out over the deserted cemetery.

'Shall we go inside?' His gaze returned to James. 'I think it's about to rain.'

Silently, James let him go ahead, following him back into the chapel. When they were both inside, James closed the door, seeing as he did so that the key had been left behind – someone had been negligent. Following a sudden impulse, he locked them in. Mould watched him but said nothing. He was so quiet, James thought, so utterly unabashed.

'I suppose you want an explanation,' Mould said.

'Yes.'

'It's good that you're curious. I wasn't sure how well your mind had held up under the Exchange. As it happens, I want information, too. Perhaps we can agree to a trade.' He took a few steps further into the chapel, down the aisle, left James standing by the door.

After a pause, he went on:

'I suppose I can begin by telling you that what happened to you was unprecedented, at least as far as we know.'

'Because I didn't ask for it.'

'Exactly. You've been talking to Mr Howland, I see. You're a successful experiment, Mr Norbury, the beginning of something important – and I want to know all about you.'

'You're going to anatomise me.' The intent was clear enough in Mould's mind – James did not have to delve far to perceive it.

He moved closer to where Mould stood. They were both by the catafalque now – James on one side, Mould on the other. He was glad, James saw, to have some obstacle between them.

'They might have admitted you as one of them, you know,' he said, 'if you had been content to remain where you were.'

'I'll never be one of them.'

Outside, as Mould had predicted, it began to rain.

'You hold yourself to a higher standard, do you?'

'I haven't killed. And I won't. I won't be like them.'

'You've fed already,' Mould said. 'Do you understand what that costs us? What it really means?'

'But he's alive – I left him alive.'

'And you think he will simply recover? Just like that? You think what you did doesn't leave a mark? You think there isn't a price to be paid? You've taken some of his *life*.'

'I had no choice.'

'What do you propose to do henceforth, Mr Norbury? Starve yourself?'

'No.'

'It's revenge, then, is it? I suppose you believe that will exonerate you. Avenging your friend, combating evil? It won't save you, you know.' Their eyes met across the catafalque. 'You can stay alive for vengeance, but don't deceive yourself: it's a private matter. You represent no higher purpose. You will grow strong on the lives of others; you will drink their blood and profit from their suffering – or from their death.'

'No,' James said.

The rain had lessened; there was light coming through the stained glass of the chapel window now, turning Mould's face yellow and green.

'I know your sort, Mr Norbury. You want to hurt us because we hurt you, and you'll dress it up in piety because you want to continue to think well of yourself. You want blood and pain and that's all there is to it. So please spare me your moral outrage.'

Mould opened his notebook and jotted something down. He wrote hunched up, elbows close to his chest, as though he feared someone might try to read over his shoulder.

'Why was I chosen?' James asked. 'Why did they do this to me?'

Mould finished writing, and put his book away in his pocket. 'You weren't *chosen*, Mr Norbury. You are, in fact, no one special at all. No one even knew who you were.'

He was lying, James thought. Of course he was lying. But then he remembered their enquiries as he woke in that cold room – they had not known his name.

'The whole thing was a mistake, if you must know,' Mould continued. 'Michael thought you were someone else – or he's pretending that he thought you were someone else, one hardly knows with him.'

'What?'

'He thought you were someone else,' Mould repeated. 'An unfortunate coincidence, nothing more.'

'No,' James said. It must be more than this. He had lost everything he cared for, and there must be a reason; it must *mean* something. He moved round the catafalque, closer to Mould, and reached at his thoughts – forced a way in.

It was like striding a little way into a patch of fog – fog which resisted one's intrusion. They struggled together in Mould's mind, and James caught a brief glimpse of a woman's face and a thousand other small details which confused and revolted him, and then a very clear image of Mould: waiting in a lamplit room (a room at night), striding up and down before the fire, staring with displeasure at a black blot on his left finger, and forever *waiting* – then the thought vanished, as abruptly as a window slamming shut. The hostile pressure of Mould's brain – which had rushed to defend itself – repelled him, and he heard a low, dreadful humming that might be music.

'You're learning, I see,' Mould said, white-faced and trembling. He looked tired, as if James's brief invasion had affected him like a sleepless night. 'But you can rifle through my thoughts until you drive me mad, and you still won't find anything to contradict what I've told you.'

Outside, the rain had stopped completely.

'Perhaps I might ask you a few questions now.' Mould was cool, professional again.

'You know I won't help you.'

'One question only, then: are you much given to religion?'

'What?'

He tried to re-enter Mould's thoughts – to grasp the meaning behind this question. But the tune, the music or song or whatever it was, the noise in Mould's skull, had grown louder. James was distracted, kept at bay. And there was that closed door again, and beyond that . . .

'I merely ask,' Mould continued, 'because I have a suspicion that those with religious tendencies ought to prove more susceptible.'

'Susceptible?' Still the music went on. He thought of killing the man, if only to end the jabbing confusion the notes left in his mind.

Then Mould leaned forwards, moved as if he were about to strike James in the face. There was something gleaming at his wrist – something like a blade. It shone briefly in the dim light of the chapel, and then Mould plunged it into James's neck.

James cursed, pushed Mould away from him. The blade retracted, snapping back into place, hidden beneath Mould's sleeve. As James raised a hand to his throat, he felt the wound begin to heal.

'A knife?' he said. It seemed pitiful, such a flimsy choice of weapon. He took his fingers away from his neck – they came back unstained.

'No. An injection. Holy water. Perhaps you've read of its influence on your kind? One may debate the causes, but the effects are undeniable.'

James began to see what Mould meant. It was as if his veins were stirring to revolt against him. His entire body felt as if it were about to disassemble itself.

'You should lose consciousness within a few minutes,' Mould went on. 'Another dose would kill you. I suppose Edmund should have warned you about it – but, then, you hardly gave us time for instruction.'

The room shifted; James felt about to fall.

'It's a very effective tool, I find.' Mould had moved closer now; he was regarding James with an air of professional satisfaction. 'Though not without its drawbacks. The short delay in its effects can prove rather—'

James stumbled towards him and hit him as hard as he could. Mould's head struck the floor with a thud, and he lay motionless where he had fallen. Perhaps he had fallen unluckily and was dead – no, his pulse was there, a stubborn beat at the back of James's mind.

James did not have the strength to move far. But there would be club men looking for Mould – they might already know that he was here. There was a door to James's right. He forced the lock, discovered a shadowed stone staircase leading down to the catacombs.

Mould was no great weight. James dragged the body into the darkness below, shutting the door behind him.

He smelled stone and wood. The air was clean; there was not a trace of rot. There was little light, but he could see clearly. They were in an arched passage lined on both sides with metal grilles. Behind these were a row of coffins, lined close but not touching.

He thought of something: Mould's book. James knelt, carefully, painfully, and reached into Mould's coat pocket. It was there – a small, shabby notebook. Something had been spilled over it: the pages had dried out of shape, and the cover was stained. It was half full of memoranda that meant nothing to him. The last sentence Mould had scrawled read: *tendency towards self-aggrandisement characteristic. Does Tournefort mention this?*

James made a brief search of Mould's pockets and discovered another book, larger and rather older than the first. It was held closed by an elastic band, and when James got it open, loose sheets of paper fell out; there were pages and pages full of writing, which blurred into confusion as James stared at them. The holy water was taking effect, then. He read rapidly, choosing quickly, feverishly seizing upon any passage that might offer knowledge.

His last hope left him here – the book told him the truth, the same truth Mould had offered him. He read until his eyes began to fail. Then he crawled to the wall, clung to one of the metal grilles, and heaved himself to his feet. They would probably find him, even down here. Clutching the book, spitefully determined that Mould should never get it back, he staggered away from Mould's body, into the shadows, as far into the catacombs as he could manage. Close by was a loculus, sealed with a square granite tablet. A hole cut in the stone revealed the coffin within – an old precaution against grave robbers. It was easy enough to slip the diary through the gap.

He crawled onwards, further into the catacombs, until his strength was all gone.

So quiet in here, he thought. Thank God for the quiet and dark. He could rest here for ever. Somewhere nearby, Christopher was resting too.

Part Four

Chapter Twenty-Two

Charlotte did not sleep well. Throughout the night she had imagined footsteps on the stairs and in the corridor. Once she had started up in bed, certain that there was someone at the door – James, or Corvish, a pale man watching.

But there was no one. She slipped into sleep, dreamed in uneasy starts. At last she woke again, feeling only a little less tired than she had when she first lay down to rest.

She was curled up tightly, anxious not to crowd Adeline. This was the great disadvantage of having grown up tall, broad in the hips and shoulders, built to stand long walks and bad weather: one was always conscious of occupying too much space.

After a few minutes more, Charlotte gave up any further attempt to sleep. It was early morning, and there was enough light to dress. She was quick about it. Her dress was slightly creased and damp, but when her hair was put up and her boots were on, she felt better prepared for the day ahead.

She looked down to examine the wound James had left on her wrist – and found nothing. Impossible, and yet it was so. She would have to ask Adeline or Shadwell; perhaps this was usual in these cases.

Stepping onto the darkened landing, she could hear someone moving about in one of the rooms below. She carefully made her way downstairs, feeling each step in the dim light. Outside the sitting-room door, she knocked gently.

'Hello?'

Howland met her at the door. He was dressed in different clothes – shabby, but more decent than those he had worn previously. Shadwell must have lent him a suit. He looked much better than he had the previous evening, but the bruise on his forehead had darkened.

'Oh, I've had worse,' he said, seeing her wince. 'Used to fall off things all the time when I was a boy – trees, horses, fences. Anything, really. I was rather proud of it, I think.'

Of course he was that sort, the kind who are happiest out of doors. One could see that in the set of his shoulders, his fading tan. She found it difficult to imagine him in an office or factory, or wherever it was that his family's business would send him.

He stepped back to let her into the room. The fire had not been laid – last night's ashes were still grey in the grate – but it was warmer here than it was upstairs.

'Is Mr Shadwell awake?' Charlotte asked.

'He's gone to buy some food. I did offer to go, but he said they'll still be looking for me.'

He did not sound as worried about the possibility as she would have expected. Indeed, he already appeared somewhat recovered from his ordeal.

She could see now how he would be under ordinary circumstances. At home he was the favourite son, she was sure of it. He would do what he liked with his family – probably with most of his acquaintance. When he spoke, it was with the air of a man who is used to being listened to, accustomed to being charming. He was one of those whose life one observed from a distance, about whom one might think fleetingly, *How pleasant to be you.*

She moved towards the fireplace. 'This should be swept,' she said – more as a thing to say than because she expected him to have an opinion on the matter.

'You like being useful.'

'I suppose so.' As if he considered it a kind of weakness, she thought. 'It helps sometimes.'

She had picked up some practical knowledge of household tasks – with Mrs Chickering so ill, and the maids and nurses rarely staying for long with them, it had been inevitable. There were days when Mrs Chickering had not been able to bear having servants in her sickroom, insisting that they were too noisy. She had made Charlotte wrap each piece of coal in paper before it was brought into the room, so it could be laid in silence.

Howland sat down in one of the armchairs and watched Charlotte busy herself with the fire. She could not tell if he was amused, or curious, or not attending to what she was doing at all. At any other time she would have been self-conscious, *tête-à-tête* with a man she did not know – especially this favourite of fortune. She often reasoned to herself that it was best for a plain woman to be cautious with handsome men. Otherwise she might well make herself unhappy, brooding over some hopeless attraction.

Now, however, there was no need for awkwardness. The strangeness of their situation absolved her from the duty of making conversation, and there were so many other things to think of and plan for. She bent her head over her task.

'Why're you keeping those?' he asked after a few minutes.

'The cinders?' She had set these carefully to one side. 'You should always save them; they can be used for the next fire.'

'Ah.'

She began to lay the fire. He did not ask her anything else but merely watched, so quiet that she almost forgot he was there.

'There,' she said at last, when all was as it should be. 'That's done.'

'All right,' he replied, and before she quite realised what he was doing, he took a box of matches from his pocket and lit the fire.

He must have sensed that she was a little disconcerted. Turning to look at her, he asked, 'What is it?'

'I don't know. I suppose it doesn't – I only thought there might not be much coal left.' (She knew very well that there was not.) 'Mr Shadwell might have preferred us to wait.'

He shrugged. 'Never mind that. If we need more, I'll run out and get some.'

Wealth instilled confidence, of course. James was the same, on a more modest scale. Though most of the money was tied up in Aiskew Hall, it was still his. Such independence had allowed him to withstand Mrs Chickering's disapproval and come to London. Charlotte, with her more limited means, would never have had the courage to do likewise, even if there was anything for her in the city. She was used to habits of prudence, a sensible disposal of income.

But it would be nice, she thought, watching Howland, to have a good deal of money of one's own. One could make free with others' possessions then, because one would always be able to replace them, if necessary. And money had a kind of power; it would keep Howland from the worst of his experiences. Had he not already recovered his strength and spirits, whilst she was still anxious and exhausted? Last night she had thought of him as a sort of companion in misfortune. They had been washed up at Wych Street like two survivors of the same shipwreck. Now she saw that she was quite alone.

Downstairs, the shop door opened and closed; someone hastened upstairs with a heavy tread.

It was Shadwell, bringing with him butter and some fresh bread, wrapped up in brown paper.

'Half chalk, most likely,' he said. 'But it was all I could find close by. Miss Swift usually—' He looked towards the hearth, where the fire was now burning bright. 'Ah, that's good. We can have tea in a little while. Is Miss Swift awake?'

'I don't think so,' Charlotte replied. 'I didn't like to wake her.'

'We do tend to sleep quite late as a rule.' If Shadwell had any idea of the possibilities his words raised in Charlotte's mind, he seemed unconscious of it. 'I suppose it goes with the profession.'

'I'll go and wake her,' Charlotte said, and went back upstairs.

She ought to be better prepared, for the day before her, she thought. There had been half a wakeful night to think on what had happened, to plan what she would do next. But she was still stunned, feeble, at a loss. Her anxiety for James rose and fell like a tide. There were moments when she was certain that she would find him and make things better. At other times she felt that nothing could be safe or right again.

Upstairs, she found Adeline arranging her hair in the glass. A set of wooden dumbbells lay on the floor nearby.

'Good morning,' Charlotte said. 'I came up to see if you were ready.'

Adeline nodded. She added a final hairpin. 'Ready now.' She stood up, rolling the dumbbells under the bed with her heel. There were still shadows under her eyes, but her complexion, glowing from recent exercise, was lovely. Charlotte wanted to ask her if she practised every day. She ought to have guessed that such strength and agility were hard-earned. Surely something very odd must have befallen Adeline to have brought her to this hard, strange life.

To Charlotte's relief, Adeline was wearing a dress today (black, simply but elegantly made). Charlotte could acknowledge the undoubted practicality of trousers for a lady in Adeline's situation, without wishing to be seen in public with her whilst she was wearing them.

Adeline saw Charlotte's look, smiled briefly. 'Burke would sulk if I wore trousers. He's got views on that sort of thing. Did you sleep?'

'A little.'

'Better than nothing.' She glanced around her. 'All right, let's go downstairs.'

'What about the bed?' Charlotte asked. 'Should I—'

'Oh, leave that. I'll make it later. Come on.' Then she laughed. 'I'm sorry. You look so *shocked*.'

'Never mind,' Charlotte said – and she could smile back, she found, the frozen feeling lifted somewhat. 'Let's go.'

Downstairs, Shadwell had been busy making tea. Howland was gravely toasting bread over the fire, checking vigilantly every few seconds to make sure it did not burn. It ought to have been comical, Charlotte thought, to see two men so intent on domestic tasks – but it was not. Because of the privations of their accommodation, or because of the seriousness of their situation, it was rather like being in an army camp – how she imagined such a place, at any rate. They were endeavouring to be cheerful.

Adeline said to Shadwell, 'You went out?'

'Yes. No problems.'

'Good. It was stupid to go alone, though.'

'I know.' He smiled – something easier in his expression. He was younger with her, Charlotte thought. 'Good morning, by the way,' he added. 'Here.' He took up two cups of tea, handed one to Charlotte and one to Adeline. The tea was very hot: a comfort, a draught of life.

Howland eased a piece of toast off the fork. 'I think this is done.'

'We can eat, then,' Shadwell said. 'And talk.'

They did eat – all gathered close to the fire – but for a while no one spoke.

At last, Shadwell broke the silence: 'Now we must decide what to do. I think it's probably best to get you both out of London as soon as possible.'

'Excuse me. It isn't,' Charlotte said. 'I need to find James.' She saw Adeline frown, and added quickly, 'I understand everything you've told me. I know he may be a danger to me. But I've got to find him, even so.'

'Well, Burke will know, if anyone does,' Shadwell said. 'He knows everything that goes on in London. If we can get you away from here, he'll know the best way to manage it. And there's something else.' He turned to look at Howland. He was trying not to sound too anxious, or too eager, Charlotte thought. 'It's about what you said last night. About the club's plan. Transforming unwilling subjects. I didn't like to press you at the time – you were so exhausted – but it is very important. I wonder if you would mind coming with us and telling Burke what you know? We've suspected for a while that the club are planning something new. Anything you remember will be helpful. A description of the club building would be especially valuable – you're the only person we've ever encountered who's been inside and got out again.'

'And there's one more thing,' Adeline added.

Shadwell turned to look at her, eyebrows raised.

'Well, they'll both have to know,' Adeline said. 'If they're going to see him.'

He sighed. 'I suppose so.' She could see him choosing his words with care. 'Mr Burke is . . . unusual. In a way, he is one of them. One of the creatures, I mean.'

There was a brief silence. Charlotte set down her empty cup and saucer with a clatter that sounded very loud to her.

'I don't understand,' Howland said.

'He's an oddity. He's . . .' Shadwell sighed again. 'Adeline, can you not help me explain?'

He was impatient, perhaps thinking ahead to what they would say to Burke. Maybe he was distracted often. Charlotte thought it must be trying for Adeline. But then, Adeline herself – so brusque and restless and charming, and smelling so decidedly of tobacco – might not be easy to live with, either.

Adeline said, 'Mr Burke is Demetrius Burke, of Burke & Steadman, the publishers. He's the sole owner since the death of his partner. Mr Steadman was his great friend, until Burke killed him. It often happens like that.' (Adeline was not the sort for delicate hints, apparently – for here she gave Charlotte a significant look.) 'Burke never stopped grieving over it, which makes him unusual. Most of them get over it quick enough.'

'And so Burke took certain steps,' Shadwell put in, 'and imprisoned himself. He's bound to his guilt and his friend's memory, and he's no danger to any living person. He has gone to considerable lengths to ensure that, I assure you. He's an enormous help to us, because he hears everything that goes on.'

'He's a *gentleman*, Burke is,' Adeline added. 'Or he's a professional man, anyway, so the club can just about stomach him. He gives advice and lends money and acts as a go-between. They won't deal directly with Mrs Price – she's the one who rules the roost on Salmon Street. Nearest thing they have to a leader. Anyway, the club talk to Burke, and Burke talks to her. And sometimes he talks to us.'

'That's all very convenient,' Howland said. 'But what do you do when he kills someone?'

'He's not a threat any longer,' Shadwell answered. 'You can take my word on that.'

Howland was frowning, evidently displeased, but he made no reply.

'Right, then,' Shadwell said. 'It's past eleven now. I suggest we leave in the next half hour.'

Whilst Howland was upstairs, and Adeline was at the glass arranging her hat, Shadwell added softly to Charlotte, 'Miss Norbury. I beg you again not to cherish false hopes.'

'But—'

'You believe that there is still something of your brother left, that a cure may be attempted. If you decide to search for it, you could well waste your life in the search. I have seen what it can cost.'

'But I have to try.'

There was no opportunity for him to say anything else – the others were ready.

'Remember, you're both being looked for,' Shadwell warned Charlotte and Howland at the shop door. 'I haven't offered a disguise, because in daytime, light is your best concealment. Stay out of the shadows where you can.'

Outside, they found the city already busy. Looking about her, Charlotte saw how old the street really was. The buildings did not look as if they had known anything approaching care for many years. They reminded her of certain parts of York, the ancient buildings with their overhanging upper storeys which blocked the light. These were less charming, rickety rather than quaint.

She found a smudge of darkness – ash, most likely – on one of her cuffs and remembered James telling her how the air in London was full of smuts; one's collars and gloves were perpetual victims. Her lungs were probably full of smoke by this time; she was tainted from the inside out.

Shadwell managed to get them a four-wheeler (a growler, he called it – for a moment Charlotte had not known what he meant. She remembered James again, one of his letters; he had written that it had taken him a long time to imagine the *growler* as anything but an enormous black dog. He had pencilled her a picture of a shaggy, gigantic hound loping through a London fog, smartly dressed passengers riding on its back. That had been in the early days.) The driver today was not Rafferty – perhaps he was engaged only when things were likely to turn dangerous.

The journey wouldn't be a long one, Shadwell said. They would be there in next to no time, he and Miss Swift usually walked the distance, in fact. So the four-wheeler had been engaged solely as camouflage, Charlotte thought.

A few minutes into their journey, Shadwell – politely wrangling with Howland over who was to pay for the growler – suddenly stopped talking and sat back very quickly in his seat. The carriage had halted to allow the hansom in front of them to turn.

'Adeline,' he muttered. 'There.'

'Stay still,' Adeline said softly. 'Everyone. Don't talk.'

They sat in silence until the carriage started to move again – they passed a man in an ulster, walking close by. He stared in through the window as if looking for someone.

'Was that—' Charlotte began.

'Not sure,' said Adeline. 'You can't always tell.'

She did not sound unduly concerned – but Shadwell's hand had gone to the pocket of his overcoat. He was travelling armed. Adeline had reached for the carpetbag, the same one she had with her yesterday evening.

They were living on their nerves, both of them. Charlotte saw Adeline glance at Shadwell, with a look that probably meant, *Don't upset the tourists.*

Burke & Steadman's premises were on Fetter Lane, on a street that was all business, consisting chiefly of shops and offices. The carriage stopped outside a narrow, unremarkable building with darkened windows. From outside, it did not appear to be inhabited at all.

They were met at the door by a clerk – a young man with neatly parted hair and gleaming shoes, whose face appeared to have been positively *scoured* clean.

'Morning, Mr Shadwell. Miss Swift,' he said.

'Good morning, Lewis,' Shadwell replied. 'We have no appointment, I'm afraid.'

'I'll see if he's waking up yet. Will you wait here?'

The clerk went away, leaving them alone in a quiet office. All the furniture was dark wood; there were thick brown leather books on the shelves which looked as if they were never opened. It was difficult to make out much more of their surroundings: the gas was turned down low; the blinds were drawn. There was a desk, a pile of neatly arranged papers, a decanter half full of sherry, and two clean glasses. A clock was ticking on a high shelf. The room was remarkably warm.

No one spoke – the other three seemed as ill at ease as Charlotte was. A few minutes passed before Lewis returned. 'He says he'll see you, Mr Shadwell.'

'All of us?'

'Oh, yes. He said he was particularly eager to meet your friends.'

Now that the time was here, Charlotte found that she did not want to run. She was fearful but expectant, seized by the sick, giddy feeling she knew from high places, from steps taken in the dark.

'Thank you, Lewis,' said Shadwell.

'Go straight down, he said. You know the way.'

Shadwell moved towards the door from which the clerk had emerged, then turned back to face them all. 'Stay alert,' he muttered. 'Be careful with your thoughts.'

'It'll be very hot,' Adeline added. 'But you mustn't get faint in front of him, d'you understand? Say as little as you can. And don't interrupt him.'

'Why not?' Howland asked.

'He likes to talk,' Adeline said. 'Most of his sort do. Let him say his piece, and he'll be more likely to help you at the end of it.'

Charlotte was glad now that Howland was there – another who knew as little as she did. Though things must be different, easier for a man, she supposed.

No use thinking in this fashion. All that she could do was to push her small stock of strength and courage as far as it would go, and hope that it would take her far enough.

The door led to a narrow flight of stairs, quite incongruous with the office they had left. The steps were bare worn stone and led downwards, and as Charlotte descended she found herself hardly able to breathe. Well, Adeline had warned them of the heat.

'Are you all right?' asked Howland. Walking behind her, he had seen her sway forwards slightly before she caught herself.

'Thank you, yes,' she said – as softly as possible, for ahead of them Shadwell had reached the bottom of the stairs and was knocking on a rough wooden door.

'Mr Burke?' he called.

From the other side of the door, someone said, 'Come in.'

Inside, the heat was worse. The only light came from two sizeable fireplaces, one on either side of the room. The place was comfortably furnished, as far as Charlotte could tell, somewhere between study and sitting-room. They were walking over thick carpet, heavy rugs. There were hangings on the walls, too – woven drapes in a dim warm pomegranate colour. The effect was luxurious, smothering.

Before one of the fires were two armchairs, a small table, and a footstool – all symmetrically arranged. Beyond these, pushed back against the furthest wall, was a large walnut cabinet, half the width of an upright piano, brass hinges gleaming in the firelight.

One of the armchairs was occupied by a figure swathed in blankets, almost entirely hidden from view. Charlotte could just make out a man's head, eyes turned towards them. Behind him stood a woman, unusually tall and strongly built, dressed like a housemaid.

'Welcome,' said Mr Burke. His voice was very tired. 'I hope you will forgive me for not standing up. Porlock, say hello to Mr Shadwell and his friends.'

His companion nodded but did not speak. Her expression was sullen.

'Mr Burke,' Shadwell said. 'How do you do?'

'About the same, thank you, Shadwell. Come closer, all of you. Don't make an old man shout.'

They approached obediently – Shadwell first, the others following more slowly. Now Charlotte could make out Burke's face. His features were delicate, his expression one of great weariness and pain. He must have been around fifty when he died.

'Miss Swift,' Mr Burke said. 'How nice to see you here again. I hope you're well.'

'Yes,' Adeline replied, 'thank you.' Her eyes were not on Burke but on Porlock.

'And now things are happening,' Burke continued, 'and you want my advice. Such as it is.'

Shadwell nodded. 'We do require your assistance.'

'And this must be one of the young men who have caused such a stir. We wanted very much to see him, didn't we, Porlock?' Porlock said nothing, merely looked at Howland and then at Charlotte. She was human, nothing more, and yet her gaze felt heavy, like a stone pressing down on one's chest.

'Well, well.' Burke sounded increasingly cheerful. 'Bring him a little nearer, will you? I should like to see him close to.'

'You've heard, then,' Shadwell said.

'Yes, indeed. It's all over London. Two men escaped the Aegolius – one of 'em still Quick.' He looked at Charlotte. 'They didn't mention a lady.'

'This is Miss Norbury. She is sister to the other.'

'Sister, eh? Bring 'em both forwards.'

There was no helping it. She and Howland moved towards the fire, closer to the man swathed in blankets, to the woman standing behind him. She was stroking his hair as if he were a child.

Burke's eyes were red and sore-looking and never seemed to stop moving. His eyelashes and eyebrows were scanty and pale. 'It's Mr Howlett, isn't it?' he said.

'Howland.'

'Really. They're saying Howlett. Well, you know what rumour is, especially amongst my kind. Confounded old gossips, every one of us. And Miss Norbury. Your brother's name is already familiar to me.'

'What else have you heard?' Shadwell asked.

'For one thing, they've got Norbury. Just this morning, it was. They'll have him back in the club by now.'

Charlotte did not faint, though for an instant the room flickered, like a candle guttering. Adeline took her arm, held her upright. 'Steady,' she said softly.

'I understand,' Burke said to Charlotte. 'I do remember what it is like, you see. Being human and so forth. This must be very distressing.'

'How did it happen?' she asked.

'I don't know the particulars. I only know that he's been captured. Unharmed' – he smiled – 'at least for the time being. They'll be slow with him, that's my guess.'

Burke was there now in her thoughts, a sudden cold presence. There was no place to hide from him. He intruded into the raw pain he had caused her; he was gratified by what he saw.

'Leave her be, Burke,' Adeline said.

'I do apologise. I'm quite abashed. Forgive me, Miss Norbury. You know my nature, I presume.'

'Yes.'

'It is difficult for me to conquer my instincts, even now – but I assure you, you are in no danger.' He nodded downwards to draw her eyes to his own body. Now Charlotte saw what he meant, what the careful arrangement of the blankets had hidden from her: where his legs should have been, there was nothing – a mere fold of blanket. His arms, too, were missing, gone at the shoulder.

He watched her watching. She could see agony, past and present, in his face. He had not been born thus, and he had suffered no accident. Someone had stood over him with steady hands and a sharp weapon, and let the blade fall.

'My penance,' Burke said.

'Didn't you . . . Can't it mend?' Howland asked.

'Not wounds this severe. And so I would find it difficult to harm you, Mr Howland, even if I wished to.'

Charlotte understood then that his wounds were precious to

him, evidence that he suffered – and it struck her as futile. His pain changed nothing; it could not buy back the lives he must have ended. It made his existence tolerable to him. Shadwell had said that he was useful. Perhaps this usefulness, like the missing limbs, was merely something that enabled him to continue to exist.

'Please,' Burke said, 'will one of you ladies not sit down? Porlock, pull that chair closer to the fire. Ridiculous to have you all standing about like this. Miss Norbury, you look exhausted. Won't you sit down?'

Charlotte had no choice but to comply. Moving closer, she could make out Porlock more clearly: large rough hands, big dark cow-eyes, thin dry lips.

'You needn't be afraid,' Burke told her.

'I'm not.'

He smiled. 'Capital. Now, then, Shadwell, what precisely do you want to know?'

Shadwell moved nearer – closer to Charlotte's chair. 'How far has the news spread?' he asked.

'Oh, everywhere, I should think, by this time. Miss Norbury is in no significant danger, now that her brother has been captured. But the club are still in a stir about Mr Howland here.'

'What do you suggest? Should we risk getting him away?'

'I'll have to know all the particulars before I can answer that. And you've not told me anything yet. Why all this fuss over Mr Norbury?'

'It appears that he didn't consent to his transformation,' Shadwell replied.

'I beg your pardon?' Burke sounded incredulous. 'My dear Mr Shadwell, you are such a learned man. You must know that the consent is *essential*. It is one of the observances; one cannot get past it.'

'I do know. But, according to Mr Howland, they've managed to overcome this obstacle.'

'Has Mr Howland seen any evidence of this claim?'

'Bier told me about it,' Howland said.

'Older or younger one?'

'Older.'

'Hmm.' Burke made an effort to lean closer, to squint more thoroughly at Howland. 'And what did he tell you?'

Howland told Burke, very briefly, what he had heard: Bier's scheme, the plan to increase the club's numbers at the expense of the Alia.

'Well,' said Burke, when Howland finished. 'I shouldn't think Mrs Price will like all this. Not at all.'

'Perhaps she could be persuaded to act,' Shadwell suggested. 'If you were to tell her what's happened.'

'Do you want to speak with her?' Burke asked. 'I can easily arrange it. Your interests are united for once – neither of you would want London given up entirely to the club, would you? Of course not. So you'd better confer, as soon as possible. What about tonight?'

'Tonight?' Shadwell repeated. It was happening more quickly than he had expected, Charlotte thought.

'Certainly tonight. Talk to her. No doubt she'll have an idea or two. See her tonight. On Westminster Bridge, at seven. I'll tell her you'll be waiting.'

'What if she won't agree?' Adeline asked.

'I think she will,' Burke said. 'I'll tell her that you'll be bringing Mr Howland with you.' And when Shadwell opened his mouth to protest, Burke added, 'No, you'll have to, you know. She'll want to see for herself. From his thoughts.'

'We'll talk about that later,' Adeline interposed. 'But what about afterwards?'

'Oh, I'd get him out of London. No bolt-hole will be secure enough. If half what I hear is true, the club hasn't been this riled for a long time. Cross as two sticks, they are. They won't give this up in a hurry. You're best putting him on a train to somewhere very far away. But tomorrow morning. You must take him to see Mrs Price tonight. He's invaluable, he can tell her everything.' He glanced up at Porlock. 'She's got a soft spot for handsome young men, hasn't she, Porlock?'

Porlock said nothing.

'In any case, I shouldn't make an attempt at getting anybody out of London today. Club'll be expecting that.' He looked at Charlotte. 'I suppose you are getting Miss Norbury out, too? This is no situation for a nice young lady. Much safer away from here. Yes, go tomorrow morning, both of you. Near noon.' He looked towards the clock over the fireplace – its face too shadowed for Charlotte to make out.

'Now, how are we going to get you home? Walking's not safe. Better be a cab, I suppose.' He looked again to Porlock. 'Porlock, go and get these people a cab. A *decent* one, mind you.'

'A cab?' Porlock repeated.

'To drive in, Porlock. D'you understand?'

'Yes, sir.'

'Go to it, then, you silly sow. Don't just stand there and stare at me.' He spoke in a horrible mixture of irritation and joviality. Porlock did not make any reply but nodded grimly and stalked away upstairs. 'I'm sorry,' Burke said, 'she's a treasure, but *not* clever.' He said it loudly – Porlock would surely have heard. 'Now, Shadwell,' he added. 'Where exactly shall we send Mr Howland tomorrow?'

'Out of England,' Adeline said. 'France, to begin with—'

'Why you're so eager to send people there I can't imagine,' Burke interrupted. 'Patriotism? It can't be pleasant associations, you haven't been there since you were a child, have you, *Mademoiselle* Swift? In my time we told our children we'd send them off to France if they were naughty and Boney would make them into a *soup*.' He rocked sideways, making himself more comfortable. 'Well, let it be France, then. As good a place as any, under the circumstances. And, mind you, send word to me when you've seen Mrs Price. . . . I wonder, Miss Swift, if you'd be good enough to add a little wood to the fire?'

The heat was giving Charlotte a headache, her clothes felt stale and dirty, and she was conscious that she was perspiring with fear.

As the log Adeline flung deftly into the flames began to burn, Burke shivered.

'I hope you'll forgive me,' he said, looking at Charlotte. 'I do feel the cold.' He glanced up at Shadwell. 'Was there anything else you wanted to ask, Shadwell?'

'I wanted to ask something, actually,' Charlotte said. Throughout the talk of people and places she did not understand, this had been her one object. 'My brother. I want to get him out of the club. And I want to find a cure for him. Is there a way?'

'Ah. Yes. It's a pity, but I don't think there's a lot you can do for him now. Even if it were possible to rescue him from the club.'

'But . . .' She felt Adeline's hand, steady on her shoulder.

'Save yourself,' Burke told her. 'If Mr Norbury does ever cross my path – I'm afraid it's not likely – then I will advise him as best I can.'

Adeline, hand still on Charlotte's shoulder, said, 'Thanks for your help. We'll send word to you as soon as we can.'

'One last thing, before you go,' said Burke. 'Shadwell?'

'Yes,' Shadwell replied, 'I hadn't forgotten.' He began to take off his coat. 'Miss Norbury, Mr Howland, would you mind waiting outside?'

'What are you—' Howland began.

Adeline cut him off: 'Please. Wait outside. We won't be long.'

Charlotte stood up. 'Come on.'

When she spoke, Howland turned to look at her, and for an instant she saw again that bleak dead look in his eyes, the same one she had seen yesterday evening in Wych Street. His stare was drowned, helpless. He was remembering something too dreadful for her to imagine.

'Come on,' Charlotte repeated, and as Howland still did not

move, she put niceties aside and took him gently by the arm, steering him outside, shutting the door behind them.

'Shall we go upstairs?' she asked, when they were alone on the stairway.

'Better stay here, I suppose,' Howland replied, rather grimly. 'In case they need help.'

She had released his arm as soon as they were out of the room; now he stepped past her and sat down on the stairs. They were silent for a little while – from inside, they heard nothing.

'I suppose they have an arrangement,' Howland said.

'I suppose so.' She wished he would stop talking. It would be nice to sit and be quiet and still for a little while. It seemed the most she could hope for, at present.

'You don't think it's *right*, do you, feeding that thing?'

'I think they must know what they're doing. Besides, before you said that there might be some good left in them. The creatures.'

'Maybe.' He looked away. 'I'm sorry about your brother.'

She wished they had gone upstairs; it was too cramped for two of them on the staircase.

'You don't have to go to see this Mrs Price tonight,' she said at last. 'Not if you don't want to.'

'What, and have them think I'm a coward? Not likely.'

'They'll want to . . . look inside your thoughts. That's what Burke said.'

'I know. And I know there's a risk in going – but I guess I'll see this through.' He was resolute again, already recovered from that moment of unpleasant recollection – if she had not known better, she would have thought he did not understand the full significance of what they had both witnessed. 'And it's bound to be interesting,' he added. 'It'll be an adventure, won't it? Beats shooting bears, that's for sure.'

Of course he would not allow himself to be swayed. He had decided that he was to be brave and heroic, and if it meant risking his life, he would not mind that. Perhaps he really did enjoy the danger. Some people must be naturally inclined to seek out adventures.

'Are you tired?' he said.

'A little.'

He stood up. 'Would you like to sit down?'

'No, that's quite all right.' Her dress would surely be spoiled – or at least dirtied further.

He took off his coat, laid it out on the steps. 'There. Rest a while. I guess they won't be much longer.'

She thanked him, sat down.

Burke's news was like an injury, a disfiguring burn that one could not help looking at again and again. She knew – she had known as soon as Burke told her of James's capture – that she could not leave now. Whilst there was a chance of finding him, she would keep searching. And if it ended badly for her, then it would be better than living safe and healthy, knowing that she had abandoned him. Either both of them home again or neither. No other way out of this. It came to her then that she did not even know where the club was, in what part of London James was imprisoned. He might be mere streets away from her, and yet she could not reach him.

Her mind would not be still. Her thoughts took up Burke's words – *they'll be slow with him* – and began to show her, in imaginings vague and horrible, what this phrase could mean.

Chapter Twenty-Three

[Piece of paper in Augustus Mould's hand, dated 20th April 1893]

I still cannot comprehend this loss. Years of my notes and thoughts are now destroyed – or worse. Without the book, I find it difficult to think, and it becomes easy to slide into panic, confusion.

So I shall write down my thoughts and I shall burn this when I am finished; it is the only safe thing to do. I cannot believe my own stupidity. <u>Decades</u> of idiocy – I could have suffered similar disaster at any time.

I am so angry with myself that I have scarcely any rage left for Norbury.

We have retrieved him. He injured me and took my book during the struggle. Where he has hidden it I do not know. One of the loculi in the catacombs, I suppose. Only he could tell me which.

He is imprisoned now. Edmund has decided to wait a while before subjecting him to experiment, allow him to reflect upon his mistakes – and to heal. The effects of the holy water will weaken him for a little while longer. He will be useful, a novelty – unwillingly un-dead – a suitable subject for experiment.

They are still hunting for Mr Howland. Once he is seized, we can continue. Edmund insists that the Undertaking will proceed as planned.

In the club, they are less enthusiastic. Corvish says this business has spoiled things. I daresay he's right. And Paige's tragedy has been another blow. Edmund attended the funeral, has expressed his regrets. Paige was gracious in accepting his condolences. He has been gracious about everything, after that initial shock.

Well, we will proceed. It ought not be too difficult now to set everything to rights.

Chapter Twenty-Four

When Shadwell emerged from Burke's parlour, he was significantly paler, leaning on Adeline's arm.

Lewis, Burke's clerk, was waiting for them at the top of the stairs. 'Cab's ready,' he said, with a supercilious expression, and opened the office door. With almost bewildering quickness, they were ushered out onto the pavement.

The return journey was a quiet one. Back at Wych Street, Charlotte followed the others into the shop and upstairs, sat down as Howland began to pace back and forth and Adeline lit the fire and heated water and tended to Shadwell, who was still weak from his ordeal. She ought to do something, she thought, she ought to help – but even standing up was too much for her at present.

'There,' Adeline said. She had finished bandaging Shadwell's wrist. There was a blood-stained rag on the floor by the chair. Charlotte looked away. 'Sit and don't move,' Adeline ordered. 'I'll get the tea.' When Charlotte tried to get to her feet, Adeline added, 'Don't *you* move, either.'

When everyone had been provided with tea, Adeline poured a cup for herself, sat down on the arm of Shadwell's chair, and began to drink, pausing from time to time to give Shadwell a watchful look.

'How long have you been feeding that thing?' Howland asked.

'A few years,' Adeline replied, and Charlotte saw that she was not offended by Howland's abruptness – on the contrary, she seemed to like his being direct. Perhaps they were a little alike: both so un-English. 'Some things we've got to pay for.'

'What'll you do if this Price woman won't help you?' Howland asked.

No reply from either of them. Howland looked from one to the other but did not press his enquiry.

At length, Shadwell spoke: 'One thing to consider is what you will do tonight, Miss Norbury. Would you prefer to remain here?'

'I'll come with you,' Charlotte said. The decision was quickly made. Perhaps it would help Howland, to have another companion.

Shadwell stood up, appeared to grow dizzy, sat down again. 'Very well. Then I suppose we could make our plans for tomorrow. The train, I mean. Have we got a Bradshaw anywhere?'

He began a discussion of trains with Adeline – a conversation into which Howland was drawn, debating the merits of one route over another, the time it would take to travel from London to Paris. This was how they were going to overrule her – they would disregard her objections, proceed with their plan step by step, until eventually it would be too late to resist. She would be out of London tomorrow, if they had their way, and would never see James again.

'That's decided, then,' she heard Shadwell say from the other side of the room. He shut the Bradshaw with a snap. 'Now, what about lunch?'

As they ate, Shadwell lectured them on the nature of the creatures they were to encounter that evening – in preparation for the dangers to come, and also to fill the silence. At one point – when he embarked upon the story of one of his and Adeline's adventures, a tale which began with a herd of sheep and a stolen waxwork – Adeline checked him. Otherwise she let him continue uninterrupted. The discussion outlasted the meal. Neither Shadwell nor Howland appeared to notice when Charlotte went quietly to the sitting-room door. Adeline, departing on a visit to her mother (and what sort of woman must Adeline's mother be?), saw her go but said nothing.

In Adeline's room, Charlotte found some relief in making the bed. When this was done she sat down, shivering slightly. For want of anything better to do, she retrieved James's Gladstone bag, pulled out the books and papers she had gathered from his rooms, and spread them out on the bed. Slowly she began to sort through them, ordering them by date and by type – theatre tickets, a bill for new gloves, another for six linen collars. A letter from Mrs Chickering. An illegible scrawl of poetry, creased as if it had been kept for a long time in someone's pocket. An hour passed, then another, and still she continued her work – breaking off frequently to read.

Caught between an old theatre ticket and a page of what must be character names for a play, she found a card, green-edged, bearing an address: the Aegolius Club.

This was where he was, then. Now she knew the very street on which he was imprisoned. She stared at the brief lines of writing until they were scored into her memory.

The other side of the card bore the picture of an owl, partially obscured by scribbles of pencil – someone had written in haste, careful of the limited space available.

The message was difficult to puzzle out – when at last she managed it, she discovered it was a farewell letter. Perhaps there was only one such letter, she thought, differing merely in choice of phrase – for the message had in it all she would have said to James, if there had been time. Love and gratitude, and a promise to return, if return was possible.

And there, at the bottom of the card, pencilled very small in the same hand, was another address. *Mrs Howland. Boston, Massachusetts.* Charlotte dropped the card, feeling like a spy.

She heard footsteps on the stairs and started in spite of herself, foolishly guilty. She scarcely had time to put the card safely away before Adeline entered, back from her mother's and still dressed in her outdoor things, carrying a brown-paper parcel.

Charlotte saw Adeline's gaze turn to the bed, the papers spread all over it like a second eiderdown. 'I'm sorry – they're James's. I'll move them.'

'Doesn't matter,' Adeline said. Charlotte felt herself scrutinised. 'D'you think you could sleep? Might be worth trying.'

'I don't think I could.'

Adeline sat down on the other side of the bed, brushing James's papers out of her way like fallen leaves. 'You do have to leave tomorrow,' she said abruptly.

'And where would I go? France?'

'It's not so bad.'

'I'm sorry. I didn't mean it like that.'

'But you don't have to go there. Why don't you go home? You'd be safe. They don't want you any more. They've got your brother, they don't need you to lure him out. It's just Mr Howland they're after now.'

'I can't leave James here.'

'What'll you do, then? Try to get him out?'

Charlotte was silent. It was her only plan, and it sounded ludicrous when spoken in Adeline's dry tone.

'You'll be killed,' Adeline told her.

'Perhaps not.'

'He's probably already dead, and if he's not, you'll die trying to get him out, and if you do get him out, he'll kill you, anyway.'

Charlotte could not muster any anger – the brutal truthfulness had stunned her. She got to her feet; the papers went everywhere—

'No, listen.' Adeline took her hand, and though Charlotte could hardly bear to be touched, she sat down again on the bed, no spirit left to argue. 'Please. Understand, one way or another, it's suicide.' Her accent, which Charlotte had noticed before, was stronger now – she made *suicide* elegant, long-drawn-out, tight light vowels and a hiss. 'Go home,' she said.

'You don't understand.'

'If you get him out, you'll regret it.' She was looking away from Charlotte now, towards the tiny smeared window, the little square of London sky. 'You'll try every cure you can find, you'll hope every day that this will be the day he comes back to you, and he'll never come back. And he'll beg you to let it end, to keep him from doing something terrible. And in the end you'll stop him. D'you understand?'

'Adeline—'

'He'd want you to live,' she said. 'You've got to remember that. He'd want you to live, be *happy*. You've got to get out of this—'

Here she was interrupted by Shadwell calling up the stairs. Time was passing, soon they ought to be making their preparations to leave.

• • •

Before them was Westminster Bridge, stretching over the dark river, the lights wavering on the ripples like floating stars. The bridge was busy with traffic and pedestrians. Rafferty deposited them on the pavement a little way from the bridge, sent them on their way with a gibe about the pitcher returning too many times to the well.

Dusk had come slowly. Adeline wore her man's clothes again. In the dim of the evening, few people gave her a second glance. She had made Charlotte borrow a hat – smart and simple, with an artfully tied black-and-white-striped ribbon and a veil (there was no harm in being cautious). With her face covered, Charlotte found the passers-by became frighteningly indistinct, their faces blurred. Only those closest to her were clear – Adeline and

Shadwell, carrying the carpetbag, and Howland, his face half hidden in a thick woollen scarf, a dusty Homburg hat of Shadwell's pulled down over his face. It made him feel like a secret agent, he'd told them.

Adeline said sharply, 'There,' and pointed ahead of them.

Shadwell followed her gaze. 'Yes. I think so.'

'Where exactly . . .' Charlotte began. Then she saw them. They stood halfway along the bridge and were extremely – unpleasantly – still. There were two of them waiting. One had the appearance of a commonplace woman somewhere between thirty and forty, wearing a long cloak and a ridiculous old bonnet which might have belonged to her mother's mother. As Charlotte studied her, the woman looked up suddenly and seemed to meet her eyes, and Charlotte could not help flinching. The woman's eyes must have been a very light blue, but from a distance they looked almost white. It was like gazing into the eyes of a panther and finding oneself confronted with human intelligence, a mind which calculated.

The man looked some ten years younger than his companion. There was a penny flower in his coat, and he wore an old-fashioned beaver hat. If he had not been what he was, Charlotte thought, he might have been handsome, in a flashy, vulgar way. He stood as motionless as the woman, save for one detail – as he watched them, he licked his lips with a repulsive thoroughness.

'Come on,' Adeline said. 'They're waiting.'

'If anything goes wrong,' Shadwell muttered, 'run to where it's busiest.'

'They don't look so dreadful,' said Howland. He had grown more cheerful as the hour of their departure approached. Now he was perhaps the calmest of the four of them.

When they were within speaking distance, they stopped and waited, watching. All Charlotte's instincts told her to run.

'Good evening,' Shadwell said, addressing the woman.

'Evenin',' said the woman. Her voice was low, rather rough. 'While since I seen you, Shadwell.'

'Indeed.'

'Not a very nice occasion, *was* it?'

'Well, there's no need to dwell on that now,' Shadwell said. 'Our interests are united, after all.'

Mrs Price's companion sniggered.

'This is Mr Gil,' said Mrs Price. She looked at Charlotte and Howland. 'Who're those?'

'Mr Howland and Miss Norbury,' Shadwell replied. 'You may have heard the names before.'

Mrs Price smiled – an expression which made Charlotte feel sick.

'Heard of a Norbury,' she said. 'The one that escaped, wasn't 'e? One of my kids ran into him yesterday. They say 'e's back with the Other Lot now.'

She was watching Charlotte with a mild interest, a slight distaste, nothing more. Charlotte fought a desperate need to ask questions.

''E was in a bad way, Liza said.' Mrs Price turned to Shadwell. 'An' 'e's got the club all riled up, so I've heard.'

Her companion, Mr Gil, was staring at Charlotte, never blinking. She felt his mind steal closer. Then that same horrible sensation, as if someone had placed a cold hand against her forehead – *behind* her forehead.

Mrs Price looked towards her companion with a slight frown. 'Gilbert, you're distressin' the lady.'

'Both of you keep a distance,' Adeline warned. 'Remember where you are.'

'Oh, don't you worry, pet,' Mrs Price said – she had a special voice for Adeline, as if she found her a little more contemptible than any of the others. 'We'll be *polite*.' She turned to Shadwell. 'Burke said you know something. 'Bout what's going on. Burke said the club got a plan. An' you know what it is.'

'We do,' Shadwell said.

'An' why should we believe you?'

'Mr Burke believed us,' Adeline said.

'Well, 'e's a distinguished man, Mr Burke. Don't mean 'e can't make a mistake.'

Now Howland spoke, his eyes steadily fixed on Mrs Price: 'I can prove it's true.'

'*Can* you?' Mr Gil said. He had an insinuating voice – oddly fluid, the sort of voice which found its way into fissures and weak places. Listening to him made Charlotte feel unclean. 'Shall we look an' see, then?'

Mrs Price moved closer to Howland, then muttered, without turning her head, 'You can put that away, *Miss Swift*.' Adeline's hand had gone to her coat pocket. 'I ain't going to hurt him. I only want to see. *Properly* see. And unless I see for myself, it's no go. You can deal with the club on your own.'

Mr Gil chuckled.

Shadwell looked at Howland. 'Are you still prepared . . . ?'

He was solicitous of Howland's feelings, but he was determined for all that, Charlotte realised. He was willing to put Howland through this ordeal to achieve his object. Adeline was, too. Of course, their profession must require a degree of ruthlessness. Still she almost told them to stop; it was cruel, what they proposed to let Howland do.

'Yes. It's all right,' Howland said. 'Let her look, if she needs to.'

'That's a good lad,' Mrs Price said to him. 'It'll go easier if you don't struggle.' She turned to Mr Gil. 'Don't let me stray too far.'

Perhaps what Mrs Price was about to do held a degree of danger for her, then, as well as for Howland. It was a comforting thought.

'You've got one minute,' Adeline told her. 'No longer.' Her hand had not moved from her coat pocket.

'That's all I need.'

Watching closely, Charlotte could see the exact instant when Mrs Price reached Howland's mind. His calm gaze was troubled by an expression of such pain and horror that Charlotte was forced to look away for a moment.

'Good lad,' Mrs Price said. 'Let me in.'

And he must have done so, because Mrs Price's eyes brightened. Her lips were drawn back over her teeth. She gave the impression of an almost savage concentration of mental energy.

Howland mouthed something. 'No,' he murmured. And then, louder: 'No.'

Mrs Price laughed softly. 'Silly boy.'

'No,' he repeated, and at last Shadwell stepped forwards. 'That's enough.'

Mrs Price released Howland. He swayed and took a faltering step over the kerb. If Charlotte had not caught hold of his wrist and pulled him back, he would have stumbled into the path of an advancing omnibus – emblazoned with coloured advertisements, crammed with passengers, clattering along at a rapid pace. A few seconds later and he would have been crushed beneath the high grinding wheels.

'Are you all right?' Adeline asked, looking at Howland in concern. 'Did she hurt you?'

'No. Not hurt.' Howland was leaning on Charlotte; she did not like to let go of his arm just yet – and Mr Gil was still watching them both. She could sense him circling her thoughts like a murder of crows, drawing nearer a little at a time.

She remembered some advice Shadwell had given at lunch: think of music. But looking into Mr Gil's eyes made her feel as if she had never heard a tune in her life.

'Keep awake,' Shadwell was saying to Howland. 'Whatever you do, you must remain conscious.'

'Keep awake,' Howland repeated. 'All right. Fine.'

'Watch him,' Shadwell told Charlotte. To Mrs Price, he said, 'I trust you have seen enough.'

She nodded. Her eyes were dull, as they had been before she interrogated Howland; all expression was gone from her face. It was impossible to see what she thought.

Charlotte noticed an odd thing: the pedestrians on the bridge skirted around Mrs Price and Mr Gil without appearing to be aware that they did so. Not one of them turned to look at the little group, though they were taking up much of the pavement.

'If we're to assist each other . . .' Shadwell began.

'I'll need to consider,' replied Mrs Price. 'We'll let you know later tonight.'

'Through Burke?' Adeline asked.

'No. We'll send a messenger direct.'

'Out of the question,' said Shadwell.

'Why? Tell us where to find you. Show of good faith, it'll be.'

'No,' said Adeline.

'Then you can deal with the club lot on your own.'

Shadwell glanced at Adeline, then back to Price. 'You should know that we are likely to be moving very soon,' he said, 'but, yes, as a show of faith, I'll give you an address.'

'Write it down.'

'No,' repeated Adeline. 'You'll remember it. A piece of paper's easy to lose.'

'All right,' said Price equably. She had scored a victory, Charlotte saw, and was prepared to be gracious about the details.

Adeline repeated the Wych Street address, and Price nodded. 'I'll remember.'

'Good,' Shadwell said. 'We will await your message.'

Mrs Price turned to go. Mr Gil made them a showy bow, and then hastened after her. 'Spot of breakfast, d'you think?' he called.

It was nearly dark now. They stood, the four of them, and watched as Mr Gil hastened after Mrs Price and offered her his arm. For a minute or two it was possible to see them moving through the crowd, like two rapid fish through a stream. Then they were gone, and Charlotte could scarcely believe that they had been there at all.

Chapter Twenty-Five

Back at Wych Street, Shadwell and Adeline went upstairs, shut themselves in one of the bedrooms, and had a furious argument. They had evidently been waiting for it throughout the journey home. From the floor below, their voices were audible though not distinct.

In the sitting-room, Charlotte sat down, too weary to take off her coat and hat. Howland began to pace about the room, turning over books, wandering to the window to look down at the street.

'Ought you to be doing that?' Charlotte asked at last. 'Someone might see you.'

'Pretty unlikely, I'd say.' But he let the curtain fall back, moved away from the window, sat down in the chair opposite Charlotte's. 'So,' he said. 'What're you doing tomorrow?'

At first she did not quite understand the question, asked so lightly, as if they were both guests at the same hotel, debating the merits of one local attraction over another.

'They keep telling me to leave,' she replied. 'I suppose it's the best thing I can do.' The conviction she had felt at Burke's office was beginning to fail her. It might be that the others were right, that even James, if he could, would have told her to flee.

'Well, let me know if you change your mind. You'll need help, if you decide to stay.'

How wonderful it would be to believe him, she thought – how wonderful to take advantage. To have someone with whom she could share all of this.

They said nothing more for a while, listening to the dim sounds of the argument upstairs. In a few minutes the voices above them grew quieter and then fell silent.

'I wouldn't mind something to eat,' Howland said. 'What about you? Are you hungry?'

'A little, I suppose.'

'Well, wait here, and I'll go and fetch us all something.'

'I beg your pardon?'

'I'll fetch us something,' he repeated – he was trying to make it sound sensible, reasonable, and yet he must know quite well that the suggestion was both ludicrous and stupid.

'You can't go outside,' Charlotte said patiently. 'They're still looking for you. You might be seen.'

'I'll chance that. Anything not to be cooped up indoors all evening.' He was already putting on his coat, gathering up his gloves and the borrowed Homburg. 'D'you think I'll need the scarf?' he added.

She could have thrown it at him. 'You can't go out. It's absolutely senseless—'

'Look, I'm not going far, and it's a very big city. They won't find me.'

She sighed. 'Wait, then.' She picked up her gloves.

'What, are you going to protect me?'

'No, Mr. Howland. I merely want a walk. If the club find you, they're welcome to you, as far as I'm concerned.'

He smiled – quickly, eyebrows raised. 'All right, then. What would you say to baked potatoes? I think there's a stand not far off.'

'I've never had one from a stall before,' Charlotte said, rather dubiously.

'Oh, they're good, you'll see.'

They would be safest in a crowd, Charlotte thought. Luckily, the streets were still busy – with people bound for the theatre or public house, with barristers and lawyers' clerks, with tired-looking women on domestic errands, with costers and other street sellers, with dozens of shabby, fast-walking strangers whose lives were a mystery.

'It's up this way. I saw it when we went past this morning.' Howland pointed in the direction of the Strand.

'Turn your collar up,' she said shortly.

'All right.' Now that he had his own way, he was all compliance. He offered her his arm with a smile.

They did not speak as they made their way down Wych Street. Howland was quiet, more thoughtful than she had seen him before. It was a relief not to feel called upon to talk or think but only to walk, to become part of the crowd.

'Here,' Howland said, and there was the baked-potato stand, as he had said it would be. The man was old, face roughened by wind and rain. His oven glowed hot in the dusk. They were not his only customers – waiting also were a cluster of rough-looking children and a sallow man without a coat, wearing corduroy trousers and a waistcoat. In any other circumstances, Charlotte would have given the stall a fascinated glance and a wide berth, but now there seemed nothing better and more delicious than the smell of the food.

Howland bought eight potatoes before Charlotte could even retrieve her purse.

'Want 'em salted?' the man asked, and Howland nodded, let the man put butter on also, though his knife was far from clean.

'Thank you,' Charlotte said, when the potatoes were wrapped and they had turned back.

'It's my pleasure,' Howland replied. 'This ought to do us good, I think.'

'Yes.' She looked up into the night sky – never properly dark here but tinted dull red by the lights of the city.

She would not think of tomorrow, she decided, not until she had gone back to Wych Street and eaten. Until then she would only walk and take comfort in the bracing cold of the air and the warmth of the food she carried, the life continuing around her. There was so much of everything, so many people – of every degree and condition, all elbowing for space in the ridiculous tangle of old streets.

'Rum place, really,' Howland said.

'I suppose it is.'

At the sign of the onion, they halted. It was starting to rain. The door to the shop had locked behind them, and they were obliged to knock.

Adeline admitted them with a quizzical expression. 'You shouldn't have gone out.'

'That's what I told him,' said Charlotte, stepping inside.

'It's true,' Howland agreed, shutting the door behind them. 'Miss Norbury warned me, and I didn't listen. She only went to keep an eye on me.'

Adeline looked at the parcel Howland carried. 'What's that?'

'Dinner.'

Adeline smiled. It made her look more tired than before. 'Well, let's eat, then.'

In the sitting-room, Shadwell was crouched by the fire, warming his hands.

'I hope you understand how reckless you've been,' he said without preamble. 'You might have been killed.'

'I know,' Howland said. 'I'm sorry.' He held up the parcel of food. 'Would you like a potato?'

'I must insist you don't repeat the experiment. Or at least that you refrain from placing Miss Norbury in unnecessary danger.'

Howland glanced briefly at Adeline – that lady whom Shadwell seemed signally incapable of keeping out of unnecessary danger – and said mildly, 'I thought we'd all be better for a square meal.'

Shadwell sighed – gave up trying not to smile. 'Well, that's true enough. Thank you.'

He fetched three plates (either the only three in the house or the only ones which were clean). The potatoes were shared out, two apiece, Adeline and Shadwell eating from one plate, as cordial as if their disagreement had never occurred.

The potatoes were very hot, fluffy and pale yellow inside, and tasted rather better than Charlotte had expected. When she had finished, she folded the skins in half and ate them with her hands, forgetful of manners.

The meal was almost over when the interruption finally came: a knock on the door. All four of them flinched.

'That's good,' Adeline said. 'No more waiting.' Another knock. 'Will you go, or shall I?'

'Better be me, I think.' Shadwell took a last bite of potato skin, then stood up. A thud from downstairs; whoever it was had grown impatient and was kicking the door.

'Both of us,' Adeline said. She turned to Charlotte. 'Keep the door locked till we come back. No matter what happens.' She looked at Shadwell. 'Ready?'

'Yes.' Shadwell had taken something from beside the desk – a cricket bat, of all things. 'I was right, you see,' he said to Adeline at the door. 'We did well not to have a bell put in. They'd have rung the thing off the wall by now.'

'If you say so, love,' Adeline muttered very softly.

It seemed foolish, childish, to wish them good luck. Before Charlotte could even tell them to be careful, they had gone.

'I should go, as well,' Howland said.

'Of course you shouldn't.' She had no intention of being left alone to listen and wait. She locked the door.

He sighed. 'I feel like I haven't done a damned thing, so far. Excuse me.'

'You helped tonight, on the bridge. And you helped James.'

There was no sound from downstairs. Then they heard the front door closing. Footsteps on the staircase followed, then a knock on the door to the sitting-room.

'It's all right,' Adeline said from outside. 'Unlock the door. Then get back.'

Charlotte unlocked the door, stepped backwards to let them in. They were not alone – with them was a little girl in an ill-fitting blue coat.

Charlotte's first thought was that she had never seen a child so thin. Then she heard Shadwell repeat Adeline's instruction: 'Get back, please, both of you – stay well back.'

One saw the truth of the girl in her eyes. Charlotte retreated until she was some distance from her, an armchair between them. Howland did not move.

'Why'd you let her in?' he demanded.

The girl gave him a long stare and then laughed sharply. It was only a brief noise but loud and sudden, like the bark of a dog. Charlotte could not help wincing.

'She insisted on coming upstairs—' began Shadwell.

''S cold out there,' the girl interrupted, rather sullenly.

'And she's going to behave,' said Adeline.

'I *promised*, didn't I?'

'Please do move back, Mr Howland,' said Shadwell. 'We don't want any accidents.'

Slowly, Howland took a few paces away from the child. He did not avert his eyes from her for a moment.

'Now you're inside, like you wanted,' Adeline said to the girl. 'What's the message?'

'Still cold,' the child said. She went to the fire, put her hands out to the flames – into the flames.

'Talk.' Adeline moved closer. 'Or you'll have to go out in the rain again.'

The girl turned round. The fire had done her no damage: her hands were still white; the dirt under her fingernails showed starkly. 'All right. *Fine.* Mrs Price says she don't want no trouble with the club. She said it's more than her life's worth, going up against the Other Lot. Gil said they might send Doctor Knife on us – he's been about again lately, everyone's sayin'.' She scowled at Shadwell. 'Some of 'em say he's you.'

'What's your name?' Shadwell asked.

She said nothing – smiled again, a smile against which something cold pulled in resistance – and shook her head.

'Very well,' Shadwell said. 'Very well.' He was trying hard not to show disappointment, Charlotte thought. The child would carry it all back to Salmon Street. 'Tell Mrs Price that if she changes her mind, she can speak to us again.'

'Mrs Price said you might give me something. For my trouble.'

'No,' said Adeline.

'Remember your promise,' Shadwell interposed, as the child scowled at them all. 'And remember what Miss Swift told you outside.'

''Bout the gun.'

'Exactly,' said Shadwell. 'You go home now, and we'll say no more about it.'

'Fine.' The girl grinned, a horrible look that took in all four of them. She slipped past Adeline and Shadwell and vanished down the stairs. The shop door crashed shut behind her.

'Well, that's that,' said Adeline.

Shadwell sighed. 'It was our best chance.'

'What are we going to do now?'

'We'll have to leave Wych Street as soon as possible. As to the rest, I don't know.' He sat down, leaned his chin on his clasped hands. 'Perhaps Mrs Price will reconsider.'

'No. I don't think she will. I don't think she'd fight them unless she had to. Too canny for anything else.'

There was silence. Charlotte did not like to speak – both Adeline and Shadwell seemed absorbed in their own reflections. Neither of them looked as if their thoughts were very agreeable ones.

'Who's Doctor Knife?' Howland asked at last.

'It's a story of theirs,' Adeline replied. 'They've made it up themselves.'

'You know they wouldn't,' Shadwell said. 'They only tell stories about their own deaths. And the Seraph, of course.'

'Well, Doctor Knife is a story of theirs, wherever they got it from,' said Adeline. She sat down, close to the flames. In the firelight her face looked less tired, and her voice had softened. Charlotte remembered James comforting himself over his child-hood grievances with fairy tales. 'They say he's a man with a big black bag, who catches them and takes them away, cuts them to pieces. I say it's made up.'

'But they simply don't do that.' Shadwell spoke as if this were a long-running argument between them. 'You know they don't like any story that isn't true.'

'What about the Seraph, then?'

'Maybe the Seraph is real. It's not impossible.'

'What's the Seraph?' Howland asked – in the tone of one who knew his part, who had heard stories told around faraway camp-fires before now.

'They say – the un-dead say – she's one of them,' Shadwell explained. 'The oldest in London. She is mentioned, fleetingly, in a number of histories, but most of her story has never been written down. And the tales contradict one another. Some say she was brought here from another country – China or the West Indies or Africa; I've heard people say all of these – and some say she was born in London and has never taken a step past Southwark. Some say she couldn't, even if she wished to. Some say she is fashionably dressed, others that she goes in rags. But she's always barefoot, no matter how fine her clothes. And she's always dressed in grey.

'They say the Seraph is kind, as the un-dead are never kind. If there are living men and women who suffer, whose lives have become wretched, then she will release them. If a woman is starving, the Seraph will cut her agony short. If a man is to be hanged in the morning, she will visit him at night and cheat the hangman. If a child is born unwanted, into a family that cannot feed it, then the Seraph will knock at the door and take the child away with her.'

'When the creatures see her,' Adeline put in, 'it means that they're going to die. I mean die for ever. That's what they think. Sometimes they go looking for her.'

'They go looking for her?' Charlotte repeated, uncomprehending.

'Yes, indeed,' replied Shadwell. 'Many of them seek her out sooner or later. It's a terrible thing, being preserved beyond your time – and it's so difficult for them to truly die.'

'They get very tired in the end,' Adeline said.

'Lonely, too, I think,' Shadwell added. 'They are stranded outside their proper time. Everything they know will slowly pass away.'

Charlotte could still hear the rain falling. She had never known such a dismal spring. The curtains had not been properly drawn. She went to the window and closed them. The street below was very quiet.

Then Adeline said, 'Let's drink something.'

'More tea?' Charlotte suggested.

'No. Something stronger.'

'I think we have brandy left,' Shadwell said, 'perhaps some sugar. Surely we can do something with that.'

Adeline heated water over the fire, added brandy and sugar – the last of the sugar – and poured it into the teacups. Charlotte thought to refuse, but did not. The mixture was sweet and searing hot, and they drank in silence, without any toast.

Chapter Twenty-Six

They'd all eaten by the time Liza got back, but Mrs P had saved her something. When she was fed and had told Mrs P all that she'd done at Shadwell's house, Mrs P said *good* and told her that there was something else she'd need to do, tomorrow morning early. Important message to take.

Liza didn't like the sound of *early*, but, then, Mrs P never asked any of the other kids to do important stuff, so she didn't grumble. Nick was jealous, but *he* was no good for anything except larking about and telling stupid stories. Of course Mrs P would choose Liza. Lisa said as much to his face, and he hit her and they were about to have a good fight, when Mrs P had got angry and sent them all up to bed, saying she'd box their ears if they weren't quiet. So they were quiet.

'She's cross tonight,' Sally whispered, as they lay in bed – all of them tumbled up together like a box of kittens, trying their best to stay warm.

'It's since her and Gil got back from seeing Shadwell,' said Nick. After her return from Westminster Bridge, Mrs P sat for hours in front of the fire, talking with Gil and Agnes. And that nasty old man Tom Brimstone had showed up unexpected, gin on his breath, asking for his room back, and instead of sending him off with a flea in his ear, she'd let him stay.

Mrs P came and fetched Liza around dawn. Liza left the others sleeping – Sally and Nick still curled up together, One-Ear on the floor. Nick had kicked him out of bed for some reason or other.

She took Sally's boots with her – they were much newer and nicer than Liza's, and Sally never let anyone borrow her things when she was awake.

She put them on downstairs, and Mrs Price looked at her, looked at the boots.

'Those yours?' she asked.

Liza shook her head.

'Well,' Mrs P said. She smiled a bit. 'Always best to stay warm, if you can. You ready?'

'What've I got to do?'

'You know Mr Burke, don't you?'

Liza nodded. Distinguished man, Mrs Price always said. Liza had never met him.

'I need you to go to his place on Fetter Lane. You know where that is? When you get there, knock and ask for him, tell them that I sent you and it's urgent. All right?'

'Yes.'

She handed Liza an envelope. It was sealed, and there was something written on the front. Burke's name, probably.

Liza held it carefully so as not to smudge the ink. 'Is it about Shadwell? And what 'appened yesterday?'

'Never you mind what's in it,' said Mrs Price. 'It's to go into Mr Burke's own hand. That's all you got to remember. And don't you be going nowhere else but Fetter Lane. You go straight there, an' you come straight back. Understand?'

'Yes, Mrs Price.'

'Good,' she said. 'You're a good help to me.'

Outside, there was already enough light to hurt, and the Quick were abroad in swarms. Liza kept to the shadowed places, where a child might slip by unnoticed.

It was nasty and chilly. She hated the cold, it made her cross. Nick had told her that sometimes the undid would freeze solid if they weren't careful.

'Saw a feller once – one of us,' he'd said, 'jus' fell over, all frozen like. Couldn't wake 'im up. They 'ad to leave 'im there in the end.'

'What 'appened to 'im?' Liza had asked.

'Doctor Knife came. Took 'im home and cut 'im up.'

Liza had shuddered. 'Doctor Knife ain't real.'

''E bloody is real. You ask Mrs Price if you don't believe me.'

Nick had told all the kids the story of Doctor Knife. He was a small and greyish fellow – nothing out of the ordinary until you got up close.

'Then you see his eyes,' Nick had said.

''E's one of the Quick, though, ain't he?'

Nick nodded. 'Makes it worse. Means 'e don't want us to eat, whatever 'e wants us for.'

'But how could he catch us?'

'No one knows, do they? Them as could tell ain't ever seen again.'

Rubbish, she thought now, and ran quicker. Fetter Lane was easy enough to find, just off Fleet Street, no problem at all. She knocked on the tall black shiny-painted door, as she had been told. No one answered. She knew that Mr Burke had a woman called Porlock looking after him and the way they went on wasn't natural. Liza thought Porlock might come to the door and was interested to see her, because the Quick who lived with undid were always a bit peculiar, but she knocked and knocked and got no answer.

She was starting to worry that she might be attracting notice

– from the Quick or from the Other Lot or from any others who might want to know what she was about. She knocked harder still, harder and harder.

Then her fist splintered the wood – mistake a *baby* might make, not someone trusted by Mrs P with an important message to deliver. Liza stopped dead, expecting that Porlock or Mr Burke would sweep down and shout at her for breaking the door like that.

But there was silence. No one seemed to be at home. Well, she'd go inside, anyway, have a look. It wasn't like a Quick place. With undid, you could go straight in.

It was dark inside, which was a mercy – meant she could see everything very clearly. She was in an empty room with a desk and lots of papers in it. Everything was tidy and polished; there were big dark books and high dark shelves. Green leather chair left empty, umbrella stand full of black umbrellas, four at least.

There was a clock ticking in the corner of the room. Liza hated it straight off, its big smug face and its loud *tick-tick-tick* like a horrible chuckling.

She heard another noise, too – someone was moving about downstairs. She slipped slowly across the room closer to the sound. No mistake, there was someone there. She felt all the warmth from her boots and coat disappear. Perhaps she would be frozen stiff – perhaps Doctor Knife would find her and cut her up to see her insides.

Then the noise stopped. Liza wondered what she should do now. If she went back to Mrs Price without doing what she'd been told, Mrs Price would be mad. Liza quailed at the thought. But to go downstairs, where Doctor Knife might be waiting—

She balanced the two fears against each other, Doctor Knife against Mrs P: Mrs Price was real, Doctor Knife might be just a lie – and if Liza didn't go downstairs and look, she would have to go back and face her punishment and the scorn of Sally and Nick.

She had seen a doctor once – not Doctor Knife but a different

one, an old feller with a big black bag. He had come to look at
Liza's ma, and when he left there was a baby, perhaps brought
out of the black bag, though it could hardly have been comfortable in there, even for such a small creature. The baby had a
name, but Liza couldn't remember it now. It would never stop
wailing. Doctor Knife had a black bag too. He'd have his work
cut out fitting Liza into it, though.

She went down the cellar steps, quiet and careful as possible.
There was a smell of blood – funny, though. Something thin and
tinny about it. Not Quick blood.

The door at the bottom of the steps was ajar. Light was coming
from the room beyond. That was bad, Liza thought. Someone
had turned the gas right up. She crept forwards and peered through
the door.

Now she saw where the blood smell was coming from – a
body on the floor. Spilled and diced, chopped up in a way that
would finish off even an undid. Someone had torn his arms and
legs off, which was out of the ordinary. Why someone would go
to the trouble, she didn't know. She stared at the stiff and thought
that she would go closer to have a look, see if there was any good
blood left in him.

But that was a mistake, because there was someone else there
buttoning up his long dark coat. He was standing under the gas,
in the brightest part of the room. She'd missed him before because
she'd been staring so hard at the killed. He had a hat pulled down,
bag by his feet. Doctor Knife, after all. He heard her, and his eyes
turned sharp towards her.

She scuttled backwards, and in her panic she tripped up the
stairs, hitting her head as she fell. Before she could right herself,
he had rushed through the open door and was standing over her.

'What are you doing here?' he asked. Not angry but trembly-
voiced, like she'd given him a shock.

Liza pulled herself to her feet. The bang on her head had given
her a turn, but she could still fight him off.

'Listen,' he went on. 'I must speak with you. Mr Burke—'

She took a step, preparing to spring at him, but he saw what she was about and grabbed something out of his coat pocket – something metal, with a jewelleryish shine to it. Then there was a sound so loud that Liza cried out with pain, clasping her hands to her ears, and at first she was so shocked that she didn't realise she'd been hurt. It was a revolver, and he had shot her twice, once in each foot.

She sank back against the steps and began to cry. The pain was bad enough without knowing that this was the end, that Doctor Knife was about to cut her up into pieces.

He stepped forwards. 'I'm very sorry, but I need you to stay. I need to ask you some questions.'

She swore at him, using all the bad words Nick had taught her, all the ones that Gil used when he thought she wasn't listening.

Doctor Knife took another step towards her. Nick and Sally and Mrs P would never know what had become of her. She wiped the tears from her face and bared her teeth, hugging her knees to her chest. 'You come near me, I'll rip your bloody head off,' she snarled, fierce as she could.

Doctor Knife stopped moving. 'I'm sorry,' he said, 'but—'

'You going to cut me up now, ain't you?'

'What on earth would I want to do that for?'

'Ain't you Doctor Knife?'

'Of course not,' he said, all disgusted. He really seemed surprised. Look at him, all white and shocked. In fact, he was shaking – another sec and he'd be crying like a girl. Then he squinted at her. 'Aren't you Mrs Price's little girl?'

'What?'

'You came to my house last night. Don't you remember?'

Of course it was him. Shadwell. In her fright and with the light shining on him, it had been hard to tell. Now he pushed his hat back and undid the top of his coat, like he wanted to prove it was him. She could make out his sad old face, his wild, brownish-greyish hair.

'Oh,' she said. 'Didn't recognise yer.'

'No, I see you didn't.'

'You lot all look alike, mostly.'

'I've heard that said. Listen, would you like to sit down? Away from' – his face went odd, and he glanced over his shoulder – 'away from this. Then we can talk.'

'You ain't going to cut me up?' It wasn't likely, but, then, she had two bullet holes in her feet (though the pain was already better). Shadwell had done bad stuff before now, too. That business with the sheep and the wax head, for instance. Mrs P always said, Keep an eye on Shadwell, he ain't safe.

'I promise you, I'm not going to hurt you. And how could I, anyway? You're far stronger than I am.'

'You *promise* not to cut me up?'

'I do. Will you give me your word that you won't bite me?'

Liza considered him for a moment. 'Yes.'

'Will you let me carry you upstairs?'

'All right.'

He knelt before her and took her into his arms in one quick movement, picked up his black bag, too. 'Put your arms around my shoulders,' he said, and Liza did. He wasn't so very weak, for one of the Quick – and oh he was warm. Disgusting but a bit interesting, like something messy and mangled in the street that you might poke about with a stick, if you were bored enough. Liza leaned into him – his neck was bare above his collar – and he stopped walking.

'No.' He placed the gun against her forehead, all cold and horrible.

'All right,' Liza muttered sulkily, and lay still and enjoyed the heat from his body, the noise his blood made in her ears. He carried her upstairs – easy, like he was used to carrying kids – and when they were at the top he took her into the office, put her in a fancy chair that a clerk or someone might sit in, and then went to the front door and locked it. When he saw the hole Liza had left in it, he did an odd sort of smile, as if half his mouth wanted to grin and the other half didn't want to trouble itself.

'No one answered,' Liza explained.

He came closer to her. Leaned on the desk like he was tired or something. 'The place is quite empty, except for ourselves.'

'Where's Porlock?'

'I don't know,' Shadwell said, frowning. He still had the gun pointed at her, didn't trust her a mite. 'Perhaps she has fled.'

''E's been murdered, hasn't 'e? Mr Burke?'

'I'm afraid so. I had just found the . . . the body when you arrived.'

'And everyone else's run off?'

'So it would appear. What I don't understand is who could have done such a thing. Mr Burke had so much influence amongst the living and the un-dead.'

'The what?'

'The un-dead,' he repeated. And he explained, looking sad for some reason, 'Like you.'

Perhaps he was all right, for one of the Quick. With that skew-whiff smile and all that funny hair. And with a big man, you got more blood, and you could keep him alive for quite a bit whilst you took it all. They'd be pleased with her back home if she brought him along with her. Mrs P might not mind Mr Burke being dead if she had such a meal to comfort her.

'Un-dead?' she repeated.

'Yes.'

'Ain't never heard that one before. We calls it undid, mostly. That's what Mrs P told me I was.'

'How long have you known her?'

'Well, she brung me up,' Liza said. 'D'you want to come back an' talk to her? I'm sure she'd want to see you and hear about poor Mr Burke.'

He shook his head. 'Thank you kindly, Miss . . . What is your name?'

'Liza.'

'Thank you kindly, Miss Liza, but I had better not.'

He'd guessed what she was thinking, Liza realised. She had ignored the nasty press of his thoughts up to now – it could be useful, rooting in people's heads, but it always made her feel ill. It made all of them ill, actually. Sally had slipped into a shop-keeper's head once, to get him to let her have a yellow ribbon she fancied, and she had got the ribbon and gone outside and been sick in the gutter, and then they had had to run for it, because a child sicking up blood in the street attracted notice.

Shadwell was thinking that if he went along with her, she and Nick and Sally and Mrs Price would kill him. And there were some other pictures – she saw two ladies, one pretty and one plain, and a young gent with a bruise on his face. She'd seen them all before, last night.

Then Shadwell said, all breathless, 'That will do, Miss Liza,' and there was music – that's what the Quick called the horrible *mess* – and Liza forced herself away from the din of his thoughts, back into herself.

'She's pretty,' Liza said, 'that dark lady.'

'Yes.'

'Is she your sweetheart?'

'Will you take a letter for me to Mrs Price?'

'A letter? What for?' She was turning into a bloody *post office*, she thought, all the letters people wanted her to deliver for them.

'I think Mr Burke has been murdered by a group of un-dead who have become very dangerous. The club. Do you know about them? Mrs Price will certainly be worried to hear what has happened. Will you carry a letter to her? I would be most obliged to you.'

'You got anything to pay with?'

'I beg your pardon?'

'If you want me to take a message, you got to pay.' Really, how green did he think she was?

'Listen, this message is *extremely* important—'

'Then tell 'er yourself.'

He sighed. 'If I pay you, do you promise faithfully that my letter will reach Mrs Price and no one else? That you will neither open it nor destroy it?'

'Promise,' Liza agreed. 'An' what would I want to open it for, anyway?'

He looked tired. 'Will a mouthful suffice?'

'S'pose.' She stepped up from her seat, came closer. 'Better be your wrist,' she said.

But Shadwell shook his head. 'Far too risky.' He fetched a glass from the high desk – someone had left some sherry there half drunk. He raised it up to the light, then got a little leather case out of his coat pocket and opened it.

From inside he took an odd device, metal and glass, with a long needle. He took off his coat, rolled up his sleeve, and spiked the needle into his arm. The glass thing began to fill with a lovely dark red. Then he took the needle out of his arm and held the sherry glass beneath it and pressed down. And then – this was wonderful, almost as good as magic – the sherry glass filled up with his blood. When it was almost full, he handed it to Liza. He looked a bit white, and his hands weren't steady.

'There,' he said. 'Drink while it's warm.' His voice shook, too. Maybe he'd hurt himself. Liza took the glass – blood from a glass was a bit odd, but the smell of it was as good as ever, and there was the new taste of sherry mixed into it – and she drained it in a swallow. If all of them would take the trouble to put their blood in glasses for drinking, how much nicer things would be.

'Now, will you take the letter?' Shadwell asked, and Liza nodded.

He took pen and ink from the desk and wrote rapidly for a

couple of minutes, whilst Liza watched him in silence. The scrawl on the paper meant nothing to her. Even a quick glance into his thoughts didn't tell her anything – it was all words, Shadwell could see them in black and white inside his head.

'There,' he said, when he'd finished. He folded up his letter and glanced at Liza's feet. 'You seem recovered. I apologise for injuring you before.'

'You spoiled my boots,' Liza said. Sally's boots were now speckled with blood and had identical bullet holes in the toes, and no doubt Sally would go crying to Mrs P over it.

'I'm sorry about that, too.' He handed the letter to her. 'Remember. To Mrs Price only. Understand?'

Liza nodded.

'Then I will bid you goodbye. And thank you.'

Liza hesitated. It might still be worth at least *trying* . . .

'No,' he said, and she saw that he had both hands on the gun now, holding it steady, pointed straight at her. 'We will all suffer unless that message is delivered. Goodbye, Miss Liza.'

She'd once killed a man who had a gun. It had been easy enough, because he was an idiot and careless. Perhaps she could kill Shadwell, too – if she leapt swiftly, she could break his neck before he had time to fire. He was breathing fast, which meant he was scared. But he backed away to the door, gun still aimed at her.

He said calmly, 'Good morning. Now, off you go.'

Well, he was a funny one. She smiled at him, wide as her mouth would go, and left.

It was still cold outside, but she was cheerful as she headed back to Salmon Street. She'd done quite well. There was Shadwell's blood in her now, she could taste it when she ran her tongue over her teeth. And she'd delivered Mrs Price's letter, or as good as – not as if Burke would want it now – and she'd got some news to tell the others, and no mistake.

Chapter Twenty-Seven

Charlotte woke to find the bedroom empty. From downstairs she could hear raised voices. Though the bed was not comfortable or clean, she was reluctant to leave it. She sat up, shivering in the cold. Outside, it must be another grey day.

Her dress was grubby from travel and from London. Though she had brushed it scrupulously before she went to bed, her hair felt lank under her fngers – as she pinned it up she could not help imagining invisible particles of grime, a smell of smoke.

In the corridor she was briefly alarmed by a soft noise close by. There was something stirring inside the room at the end of the passage. A curtain, most likely, blowing in the breeze.

She found Adeline in the sitting-room. She was kneeling in front of the fire, toasting some bread. Shadwell was standing by the window, looking out into the street. Howland was sitting in one of the easy chairs, a plate in one hand, eating in determined silence.

'Good morning,' Charlotte said, and Shadwell turned briefly from the window to mutter a reply.

Unsure what to do next, she sat down in the other easy chair.

A glance at her watch showed her that it was almost nine. She could scarcely believe that she had slept so long, and yet felt so weary still.

'There's food next door,' Adeline told her. 'Help yourself.'

'Thank you.'

'We have Mr Howland to thank for this feast,' Shadwell said, making an obvious effort to sound like himself.

'That's not quite true,' Howland said 'I just gave the money.' (At least he had not been foolish enough to venture out a second time.) 'And it was about time I chipped in, after all you two have done.'

Silence again. Charlotte went into the next room – a dreary scullery–pantry–kitchen, she discovered, with one tiny window, a small, stained sink, and two empty shelves. A brown-paper parcel was open on the kitchen table, bread and cheese laid out. Nearby was a plate of fresh-cooked bacon and sausages.

She took a plate, found a fork – almost clean – prepared a breakfast for herself, though she was not hungry. The atmosphere in the other room had puzzled and worried her. What was wrong, and why would no one speak of it?

Returning to the sitting-room, she sat down opposite Howland and began to eat.

'There's coffee, too,' Adeline said. She took the cups, served them all in silence. No one spoke throughout the meal. When they had finished and the coffee was all gone, Shadwell moved his chair a little closer to the fire.

'Are you going to tell them?' Adeline asked.

'Tell us what?' said Howland.

Shadwell sighed. 'I went to Mr Burke's office this morning,' he began. 'I wanted to ask his advice after our disappointment yesterday.'

'Tell them what you found,' Adeline said.

Shadwell spoke shortly, not looking at any of them: 'I found Burke dead. He has been murdered.'

Charlotte did not immediately comprehend him. Then she was taken aback at how little the news shocked her.

'Was it the club?' Howland said.

'It seems likely.'

'Then they must know that he was assisting us,' Charlotte said. 'But why would they leave . . . leave him to be found? Is it a warning?'

'I cannot be sure. But there are bound to be consequences. He was well respected. Especially by the Alia.'

'Will they attack?' Howland asked.

'It's probable. If they do, they will want every possible means of assistance. Even us.' Shadwell stood and went back to the window. He moved very slowly, as if every limb ached. It must have been a ghastly shock, discovering the body. Charlotte was surprised that Adeline was not making any effort to comfort him. Instead, she had been brusque with him throughout the conversation. 'We must get both of you away from here as soon as possible,' he added.

Charlotte remained seated as the others set about getting ready – Adeline gathering up plates and crockery with a clatter, Howland disappearing upstairs to fetch his things. She finished her cold coffee and gave herself another minute – two minutes – to stay still. She had never felt so tired before.

In the corner of the room, Shadwell busied himself with a revolver. The weapon was opened, unhinged so that one could see its very skeleton. He was frowning, intent over his task, worry showing in the tight set of his mouth.

'I suppose you'll need to gather your luggage, Miss Norbury,' he said, without looking up from his work.

She stood. 'Yes, of course. I won't be long.'

Her suitcase was soon dealt with. James's papers were already packed – she had bundled them back into the Gladstone yesterday, had not had the heart to read them since. She looked around Adeline's room, and saw that she had left nothing behind – it was time to go.

There were footsteps outside – clipped, deliberate. Adeline came in, carrying a brown-paper parcel. She walked over to the bed, and sat down next to Charlotte.

'There's something I want you to take with you,' she said. 'If you don't mind.' She held the parcel out to Charlotte. 'It's our book. All our work's in there. There are only two copies – this one, and the one with Mama. She finished typing this one yesterday, she says it has the fewest mistakes.'

Charlotte took the parcel from Adeline. Without covers, the manuscript was a loose, yielding weight. Deprived of the protection of paper and string, it would go spilling everywhere. Such a fragile thing, Charlotte thought, so much work so easily lost.

'But it's precious,' she protested. 'Isn't there anyone else who could . . . ?'

'No. No time. Will you take it?'

'Of course. And when this is over, I'll send it back to you, and you must write and tell me how you're managing.'

'If that happens,' Adeline said, 'I'll send you a published copy.' And to Charlotte's astonishment, she embraced her – suddenly, fiercely. 'Thank you. You've made this easier.'

'If I go . . . Will you look after him, if there is any chance? If he escapes again—'

'If we can, we'll help him. Now, hurry.'

Charlotte put the manuscript carefully away in the Gladstone. Then Adeline took her to the mirror, made her put on the hat with the veil that she had worn the evening before. 'Just in case,' she said.

'I couldn't possibly, Adeline. It's too smart for me. And it's yours.'

'Yours now. Come on.' She ignored Charlotte's protests. 'Rafferty will be here soon.' She glanced towards the window. 'Me and Shadwell will probably have to stay here, in case Mrs Price sends a message.'

'I understand.'

'Remember, always keep alert. I think Shadwell will give Mr Howland his other revolver.'

'Can you spare it?'

'We've got others; we'll manage. But don't depend on it. It can go wrong, using a weapon against them. You can get too sure of yourself and forget to protect your mind. And if you do that, they've got you.'

'All right,' Charlotte said. 'I'll tell Mr Howland, if the need arises.'

'Good. He'll probably listen to you.'

In the sitting-room, they found Howland and Shadwell waiting, Howland in his coat and Homburg. His face was serious. Perhaps Shadwell had already given him the revolver.

'Rafferty's here,' Shadwell told them. 'Are you ready to leave, Miss Norbury?'

There was still a chance, she thought. Here was her opportunity. She could still insist upon staying.

Instead, she nodded. 'Yes, I'm ready.'

'Come on, then,' said Adeline. 'Can't dawdle. You know how Rafferty gets.'

They found Rafferty waiting outside, looking as surly as ever. He tipped his hat to Adeline but made no greeting other than to remark that time was getting on, and traffic was likely to be dreadful this time of day, 'specially on the Strand, and they'd have to go quick if they wanted to take a roundabout route.

Charlotte found that she could not manage a farewell. As the carriage drew away, she looked back, saw Adeline nod briefly, raise her hand.

The traffic was as bad as Rafferty had predicted. After a little while they came to a complete standstill – a cart bound for Covent Garden had been knocked on its side, vegetables spilled. Yelling – two men, at least – and the whinny of a scared horse. From outside came the sound of Rafferty swearing.

Howland was swinging his hat between his fingers, clearly ill at ease.

'Well,' he said.

And now – suddenly and at last – she was quite certain of what she ought to do.

She opened the Gladstone bag, drew out the manuscript, and passed it to Howland.

'Please look after this. It's very important.' She began to struggle with the carriage door. 'It was . . .' She could hardly say that it had been nice to meet him, given the circumstances. 'Good luck, Mr Howland.'

'What are you *doing?*'

She made no answer – and he swore and scrambled out of the carriage after her. She did not look around but continued to stride as fast as she could down the street.

Howland followed, overtook her after a few yards, kept pace with her as she walked. 'Are you going back for him?'

She stopped to stare at him as the crowds and the traffic continued to move around them. And he nodded as if she had spoken.

'Of course,' he said. 'Should've known.' She saw him reach a decision. 'Well, all right, then. If you're staying, so am I.'

'This is *serious*, Mr Howland. It isn't some game you can just—'

'I know. I know what's at stake, and I want to help.'

She searched his face but could see no trace of doubt or irresolution.

'I see you're impossible,' she said – touched, in spite of herself, that he had made such a gesture.

'Apparently so. Shall we see if Rafferty will take us back? I warn you, he won't be very pleased with us.'

They returned to the four-wheeler, which was still ensnared in traffic. 'What's goin' on?' Rafferty demanded.

'We've changed our plans,' Howland told him. 'We're going back.'

'To Wych Street?'

'Yes.'

'Well, you're a couple of damned fools, then.'

Howland nodded. 'Yes. I'll pay you the same, of course.'

''Course you will. Get in, then. Traffic ain't much better the other way, you know.'

'Thank you,' Charlotte said, as Howland helped her back inside the carriage. She might have said more, if she had been able to choose the right words, and if Rafferty had not turned the four-wheeler about with a manoeuvre both sudden and violent. The driver of the hansom behind yelled an insult, to which Rafferty replied in kind.

'We'll be a while yet,' Howland said, glancing out the window.

'They won't be glad to see us.'

'Maybe not.'

'I'll explain that it was my fault.'

'Do you know what you're going to do?'

'Get into the club somehow,' she said, doing her best to make this sound feasible, 'and get him out.'

They lapsed into silence and did not talk again until they reached Wych Street.

As Howland settled their fare, Charlotte picked up her bags with a struggle (the suitcase and Gladstone were heavier than she remembered, and she felt she might drop her handbag at any moment), and walked closer to the shop. There was nothing visible from beyond the dirty windows, no sign of movement. The sign of the onion was swinging slightly in the breeze.

An instant later she was dashing back to the carriage, her pace so hurried that the men stared at her in surprise.

'Wait.' She heard her voice come out strained, unnatural. 'Please, Mr Rafferty, will you wait?'

'Why—' Rafferty looked past her, his face changed. 'Oh. Go on. I'll stay here.'

No need to explain further. Both of the men had now seen just what Charlotte had: the door to the shop was ajar.

Chapter Twenty-Eight

The master would sometimes say, Porlock, what'll I do when you're dead?

Always this when she was washing him or tidying his hair, or cleaning the fireplace or bringing in his supper, or busy with some other task that only she knew how to do right.

What'll I do when you're dead, he'd ask. Who'll look after me then?

You could get someone else, sir, Porlock would always say, and the master would say, No, I can't, you silly woman, you know I can't. All very well for *you*, you'll be under the sod, nothing more for you to worry about. But what's to become of me?

Please don't talk so, she would say, and stroke his hair, which was the only caress he could ever stand. Don't talk about that horrible day. I can't bear to think of ever leaving you.

That would quiet him usually. He would get dozy, and she would feed the fire until it was a good strong blaze and then wrap him in blankets and hug him to her like a baby, let him grow warm. She was big and strong, used to hard work, and he was no burden to her. He'd had her weighed and measured once, one of his whims. She came to five foot ten with her shoes off, and he'd said, Well aren't you an Amazon, Porlock, what a marvellous brute you are. Whenever she carried him, she thought about that.

He would never bite her, of course. He was a gentleman. No 'changing, neither, and she'd never asked – that wasn't her place. She'd not be as useful if she was like him.

You might get ideas, he would say, sly-faced.

He'd never fretted over what might happen if he died first. It had never seemed likely. There had been a plan, though – he'd had a plan for everything, he was so clever with things like that. There was the walnut cabinet, locked with a key. He'd had it made special, he said, and inside there were dozens of little drawers, and each one held a secret.

She'd seen inside some but not all of them. He'd made her take things out for him to look at once or twice – papers mostly, old letters. Sometimes money. In the top drawers there were stranger things: a stained yellow ribbon; a single collar stud; a brown-dappled bird's wing. Master would have her take this out sometimes and show it to him. She liked the soft feathers, the light bird bones.

Porlock knew her business and knew her place. She'd never asked about anything in the chest, she opened drawers and fetched him things and never said a word.

He said once, If I'm ever killed, Porlock, open the middle drawer. Five along and five down. Can you remember that?

Five along, five down, she repeated dutifully.

Open the middle drawer, he said. There's money there, addresses, a few other things all sealed up in an envelope. Enough for you to get away safe, if you ever need to.

There were two keys. One he had with him always, though he could never have used it without her help. The other he made Porlock wear, on a chain round her neck.

She'd never looked in the middle drawer, not even when he

slept. He had never lied to her, she had no doubt that he would want her looked after. All the un-dead in London had known not to touch her. She could have walked into Salmon Street or the club itself, if she'd wanted.

She found him when she came down to see to the fires. Butchered to a great pitiful mess, dead on the hearthrug. She didn't cry over him, she thought how he would have chided her for that – he hated crying women worse than almost anything, and she'd never cried when he could see.

She was used to the dirtiest tasks, the ones that left stains and smears on her hands and clothes and filth under her fingernails. She knelt on the floor and put him back together. The ones that had killed him had left him without any care, hair all bloody and teeth knocked out and that great gash across his waistcoat. He had struggled, probably tried to shift himself or call for her, and someone had held him down and gone for him with an axe or a knife. Thank God it was something sharp – must have happened fast. She laid him out properly, set his head right above his shoulders.

She had left him alone for such a short time. He was usually at his quietest in the early morning; he'd sleep from dawn, sometimes didn't even wake when Lewis got in at nine. Once or twice a week she'd slip out then and get some air, get some light, do her shopping early. He sometimes forgot she needed to buy things to eat, she liked to do it when he was asleep. She left him comfortable, his chocolate all drunk up. He always liked a cup of chocolate last thing – disagreed with him but he had it just the same. She told him she'd hurry back, just as she always did.

If she'd been cleverer, she might have killed the murderer herself. She was strong enough for such a job. If she'd taken him by surprise she would have managed it. Instead, she had watched him leave – dull with surprise at seeing a man with a black bag come out of the front door she had left locked. She thought it might be one of the master's secrets – he had visitors at times that she wasn't to know about.

He had been a long way off, this gentleman. She didn't guess quite who it was until she'd been downstairs, seen what he'd done to the master. Then she remembered the shabby coat, the striding walk, the untidy hair – she felt the name rise in her mind like a body rising in the river. Shadwell – he'd been there only the day before, with that Howland man the master had found so interesting.

There was a story that Shadwell had killed the master's kind before. She knew this, but the master had always said he was safe and let him and his tart visit whenever they wanted, stuffing themselves with news and paying only grudgingly, mean little gulps of blood.

She left the place tidy. All clean, it was always clean. There was never anyone like Porlock for hard work, and she liked things done right. Lewis would find the master, and he'd scarper, no doubt. It didn't matter – the master had made arrangements for this sort of thing. Someone would come and sort out all his things, look after his poor savaged body.

He took up such a small space, lying still on the floor. No quick hectoring voice to talk to her now, no more of his sharp eyes.

She left him for the last time, shut the front door, though the lock was broke and there was a hole cracked in the wood. There were instructions in his letter to her. He had told her to get away, to run as fast as she could. He'd told her exactly what to do, where to go to be safe. But there was nowhere she wanted to go, now that he was gone.

Or maybe there was one place. There was one thing left she could do.

Chapter Twenty-Nine

Shadwell did not believe in long-drawn-out farewells. When Charlotte and Howland were safely into the four-wheeler, he turned and went indoors. Adeline waited longer, watched until the carriage had turned the corner.

It was good that they were gone. They were out of danger, and so was the book. She and Shadwell had managed something worthwhile, whatever happened next.

The sitting-room was quiet with the others gone. She would miss Charlotte. It had felt for a while like being back at the telegraph office, the same sort of camaraderie.

Now it was just Shadwell and Adeline again. He had taken off his shabby old coat and was standing in the middle of the room, looking as if he didn't know what to do next.

They hadn't yet finished their argument about what Shadwell had done that morning. Now that they were alone, it would have to be resumed. Shadwell sat down in his favourite easy chair. He had been neglecting himself again of late. He was almost as shabby as when Adeline had first met him; his hair needed cutting. And he *stank* of tobacco, Adeline thought spitefully.

'I'm sorry,' Shadwell said. 'I know it seems—'

'It seems to me that you did something stupid without telling me first. Don't you trust me after all this time? Or did you think I'd have hysterics?'

'I didn't want you to know. I didn't want you mixed up in it.'

'But you thought it was the right thing to do.'

'Yes.' Something horrible was reflected in his expression. He looked away from her. 'But he was so frightened. I hurt him.'

'You've killed before.'

He sighed, and she saw that she had pained him without meaning to. She wished that she were better at offering comfort.

'That was different. Before . . . With that there was no alternative. We couldn't keep him here to suffer.'

Adeline remembered it clearly. John staring up at them, eyes wide and mad and dazzled in the light. Afterwards, Shadwell had sat up for days without sleeping and would not rest or be comforted.

'This was different,' Shadwell went on. 'It was my choice. And it was murder.'

She might have been angry for longer – she had been saving her rage jealously, waiting until they were alone – if she hadn't seen his face then. So pleasant and guarded with everyone else, so open with her.

'Perhaps it was the only way,' she said, and maybe she did believe that. Burke was a small loss. He would have cast them aside easily enough if it had suited his plans. No sense mourning him. She thought of him struggling, helpless, on the floor, Shadwell standing over him – he had not told her how he did it, and she had not asked. He had brought his axe back wrapped up in his bag, cleaned the blade before the others awoke.

'I gave Charlotte the book.'

'What?'

'She'll look after it. Mama's got the other copy. Good to have both of them safe.'

He drew her to him then, his chin rested on her shoulder, and they stood so close that their shadows mingled on the floor. He had been waiting to do this, she thought. Now there was no one to see or mind. The fire was out; the coal was all gone. They would have to stand the cold or start burning the furniture.

'You know, don't you . . .' he began.

'What?'

When he did not reply, she twisted about to stare into his eyes, and finally he said, 'You must know. How much it's mattered, having you here.'

'Oh.' Such a small secret after all the other secrets they had shared. 'Of course.' (My love, my accomplice, my dearest friend. I am glad of you, too.)

They might have remained together – embraced, saying nothing – for a long time if something downstairs had not shattered. Someone had forced the door. By threats or bribery or the mazement, they had sent one of the Quick ahead of them into the house.

Shadwell rushed to the door of the sitting-room, turned the key in the lock. Hastily, Adeline went to the cupboard where the weapons were kept and brought out all that she could find – her revolver and Shadwell's, her knives, his axe. There was the cricket bat, still leaning against the side of the desk; she took this, too.

Something else smashed downstairs. And they could hear the footfalls now – there was a pack of them. They were already on the stairs. No one to call for help, no chance of getting past them.

'John's room,' Adeline said. Shadwell nodded. There was a heavy thud – the slam of a body against sitting-room door. It was a good strong lock. They might have about a minute.

Shadwell went to the curtains and ripped them down. The sunlight would fall onto the bookcases – perhaps it would hide them from the creatures downstairs, who saw clearest in the dark.

No more time. She followed him upstairs, past the bedrooms, to John's room.

Shadwell unlocked the door, and they both stepped forwards into an onslaught of sunlight.

This was how, when it had become impossible to do otherwise – when he had begged them for months to be laid to rest – they had finally killed John. The place was full of light: from the skylight, reflected from the mirrors that were fixed to every possible part of the walls and ceiling.

They might have a fighting chance in here. She locked the door. Then she went to Shadwell, took his hand. She heard the door to the sitting-room give way. Heavy feet. They were in a hurry, not troubling to conceal themselves.

'I hope they spare the books,' Shadwell said. 'Some of them are very rare.'

'I know. Expensive, too.'

Revolver in one hand, knife in the other, she put her arms about him, stood on tiptoe, kissed him on the mouth.

He looked at her and nodded. Little time to wait now. Then the footsteps stopped.

She couldn't help holding her breath, as if it were possible to hide. The door began to rattle.

They looked at each other once more. She managed to smile at him. 'It'll be—'

The door shook again and then crashed open. There were four of them, all blinking, furious-eyed in the light, blind for a second or two. Her hands were quite steady.

The first was easy enough, a careless fellow, too confident of his own invulnerability: it was done with two shots to the face, then Shadwell's axe was through his neck.

She would never be able to tell Shadwell that it was a compliment to them both that so many were sent to deal with two mere *Quick*.

It was not long before her bullets were gone; there were only the knives left. The knives were enough: slice, duck into the sunlight, aim for the eyes, for the soft places that are still almost human. Keep your balance, she told herself, you're the rope-walker's daughter; it will take a lot to topple you even now.

But though the creatures were half blind, they were still fast – they listened for your heartbeat; they smelled your blood. She did not see Shadwell killed, only heard him fall. His axe struck against the floorboards with a thud. Outside there was sunlight, bright on the mirrors, bright on the walls and the floor.

Then it was quiet. Adeline stopped, breathing quick and raw, and looked around her. The creatures were dead, all four of them. She stumbled, dizzied and bleeding, something wrong with her neck and her head, blood in her eyes now and her weapons falling from her.

Last man left standing, she thought dully, before she fell. Only now, at the very end, would she close her eyes, and then there was brightness behind her eyelids, there was sunlight—

Chapter Thirty

At the top of the house, they found the first two bedroom doors closed. The third was open.

Neither Charlotte nor Howland called out. The silence was too absolute. Howland gently pushed the door. It opened a little further, then stopped. There was something on the other side, blocking it. He tried again, with greater force, shifted the door enough to peer through.

What he saw made him step backwards immediately, almost colliding with Charlotte. 'Keep away,' he muttered.

'Is it . . . ?'

'They're in there.' He leaned against the wall of the corridor, his eyes closed. He looked as if he might faint. 'There are things there, too.'

'Things?'

'They're dead. *Old.*' He gave a shuddering breath. 'Withered.'

'Come away,' she said softly. 'Come on.'

She led him downstairs to the sitting-room – but at the door, she stopped short. The room was no longer empty. There was someone sitting in one of the chairs before the fireplace. The chair was turned away from them; Charlotte could see only a pair of thin legs in torn black stockings, a pair of boots with holes in the toes. The feet were swinging back and forth, kicking a rhythm against the fender.

Then the movement stopped, and an instant later a face peered at them over the back of the chair. It was the girl from last night, the one Mrs Price had sent.

'Where's Shadwell?' she asked. 'Got a message for him.'

Charlotte laid a hand on Howland's arm to keep him still. 'Why are you here? Did you – are you responsible for this?'

The child tipped the chair backwards, letting it fall onto the floor with a crash. She scrambled upright with a grin.

'For what? I ain't done nothing. Told you, I got a *message* for Shadwell.'

'Have you been upstairs?' Howland said. He brought out the revolver Shadwell had given him, pointed it at her. 'Did you kill them?'

'I ain't killed no one. I just got here now.' She scowled at the revolver. 'An' Mrs P says you shouldn't use them indoors, it makes a smell.'

'If not you, then who?' Howland demanded. 'Who broke in?'

The girl shrugged.

'Very well – what's your message?' asked Charlotte.

'This midnight we're goin' to the club.'

'What?' Howland said. 'D'you mean some sort of attack?'

'Gonna happen tonight, Mrs P says. 'Cause of Mr Burke. An' she said Shadwell were meant to be there, too, to 'elp, but now I'd better go an' tell 'er that 'e's dead.' She frowned. ''E is dead, i'n't he? *Properly?*'

'He's dead,' said Howland.

The girl looked between them, one to the other. 'Is the other one dead, too?'

'Yes,' Howland said. 'Tell your guardian—'

'What?'

'Tell Mrs Price that Mr Shadwell and Miss Swift have been murdered. By the club. Do you understand?'

''Course,' the girl replied, and was off before Charlotte or Howland could say anything else, slipping away with speed that was not human.

'We have to get out of here,' Howland said, when her footsteps had faded from earshot. 'They might come back.'

'Yes.' Suddenly anxious, Charlotte looked about her. 'The books, though, the papers. We can't just leave them . . .'

'No. We'll take what we can. But quickly. Can you gather everything together? I'll go downstairs and tell Rafferty—'

'And Adeline, Mr Shadwell. We can't leave them up there. Not like that.'

She fetched water from the kitchen, and together they went upstairs again.

Howland pushed the door open. At first all Charlotte saw was the brightness, almost painful after the dim of the corridor. There were mirrors on every wall, all reflecting Howland and herself.

Their friends were reflected, too. Their *friends*, Charlotte told herself, biting the inside of her mouth. That was all that was important. Their dead enemies, putrefying in the sunlight – these could be pushed aside with one's foot. There was no need to look at them. She turned away from the decaying limbs, ignored the sweet stench of rot. What mattered was that their friends should be cared for.

With Howland's help, she moved them so that they lay side by side. Shadwell had few visible injuries – it was only from the dreadfully wrong set of his head that one could tell what had happened.

Howland arranged him gently, left him looking as if he were asleep. There was blood at Adeline's throat and on her face; her hair had come loose. Charlotte wiped her mouth with water, made her pretty again. They gathered up the weapons and left them within their friends' reach, as if they might want them again. Howland muttered something over them – a prayer or a word of remembrance and thanks.

'Come on,' he said, standing up. 'We have to go. We've done right by them.' He had seen what was in Charlotte's mind: the thought of flies, unnameable indecent decay. 'I'll send money,' he told her. 'They'll—' He could not bring himself to say that they would be all right, but she saw what he meant. Such comforts as could be afforded the dead – they would have these.

He led her out into the corridor, and she did not look back until he had shut the door.

In the sitting-room they collected papers, bundled them together haphazardly, and piled the most important-looking of the books together. They made a large parcel, tied with string.

There was the carpetbag, too – Charlotte did not have time to go through its contents, but Adeline and Shadwell had taken it with them when there was danger; surely it would hold something useful. She picked it up, struggling a little under the weight.

'I'm not sure we can carry all of these,' she said.

'We can get them to the cab, at least.'

'Then where will we go?'

'I don't know.' He glanced at her over the pile of books he held. 'What do you think? A hotel? We can rest there, think what to do . . .'

'Yes. I suppose that's best.' In the normal way of things it would appear very bad. But that did not matter now.

Outside, Rafferty was waiting. He looked at them, and the great parcel of books and papers they carried, and his expression was grim.

'Caught up with them in the end, then,' he said.

Howland nodded.

'We . . . took care of them,' Charlotte told him. 'They're upstairs.'

Rafferty nodded. 'Right.'

'We need to get away from here,' Howland said. 'Can you alert the police? Or . . . someone – they can't be left there.'

Rafferty gazed up at the windows of the shop. The curtains in Adeline's room were half drawn. 'I told 'em it'd end like that, you know.'

'They weren't the sort to listen,' Howland said.

'No.' The horse stirred, and Rafferty turned back to the street as if the creature had spoken to him. 'Where to, then?'

'The Langham, if you don't mind,' Howland said.

'Fine. In you get.'

When Howland spoke, it was not to ask Charlotte how she did. She was grateful for that. He said, 'I hope you don't mind the Langham. It was the first place that came to mind. We can take a room. Rooms. Then at least we can be private and rest a little while, decide what's best to be done.'

'I suppose that's sensible.'

'You'd better be my sister,' he said. 'At the hotel.'

'I beg your pardon?'

'When we give our names.'

'Oh, I see. Yes.'

The journey was not a long one. When they reached the Langham, Rafferty took his money in silence.

'What'll you do?' he asked, when the fee had been duly counted.

'We'll be going tonight,' Howland told him. 'To the club.'

'You're as stupid as they were, then.'

'I s'pose we are. We're leaving at around eleven, and we'll be needing a driver.'

'Will you, now.'

'There'd be a good fee in it.'

'Would there, indeed.'

'And you'd be doing us a good turn.'

He looked from Charlotte to Howland – at last he sighed. 'All right. But it's the last thing, you hear me? I ain't doing any more of this stuff after tonight. I'm bloody sick of it all. It ain't right.' With that he drove away, leaving them alone outside the Langham.

The hotel was grand and glittering. Charlotte had an impression of polished wood, brilliant lights. It had become difficult to make sense of things. The details of her surroundings were oddly indistinct.

Howland offered his arm at the door. 'You must be tired. Aren't you, sister?'

She glanced up at him, realising suddenly that she would not be able to speak again until they were in private – her accent and Howland's were so ill-assorted, so many thousands of miles apart, that anyone hearing would know immediately that they could never be siblings. He must have seen her thought, because he nodded and said distinctly, 'Don't talk. Save your strength.'

He managed everything. They were Mr Alan Shaw and his sister, Helen, just arrived in London and exhausted by their voyage. There were two rooms – Charlotte was quite sure these were the most expensive to be had. They had electric light throughout the hotel now, Howland remarked. All so civilised and modern. The elevators were wonderful too, weren't they – he'd heard they had made a minor sensation, back when they were introduced. He was talking too loud, breathing too fast, Charlotte thought. He gestured with his hands in an unnatural, stagey way. The man with their things looked at him oddly.

It seemed a long time before they were alone in the room which had been taken for Charlotte – a gilded chamber so alien to her that she could hardly bring herself to remove her coat and hat.

'Shall I have some tea brought?' he asked.

'In a little while,' Charlotte replied, though she would have liked tea immediately. With mild interest, she saw that her hands were shaking.

'Miss Norbury—'

Then he was holding her up and the room was spinning.

'The shock,' he said. 'You're faint. Sit down.'

'Thank you.' And when he did not release her, she repeated, more steadily, 'Thank you,' and he let her go. She crossed to the bed and sat down.

'You must have some tea. Or wine. Or brandy. Or some water, at least. What can I bring you?'

'I'm quite all right now.'

'You're not. I'll bring you some tea.'

'But—'

'I'll fetch it myself. I'll say you're ill and don't want to be disturbed, which is the truth, anyway, and you won't have to see anyone.' He went to the door. 'Lock it behind me. I'll knock four times. All right?'

'Yes. Thank you. You're very kind.'

'Try to rest. I'll be back soon.'

When he was gone, Charlotte locked the door and began to wander about aimlessly. Finally she went into the bathroom. At another time she would have marvelled at the luxury of the room, the great white bath with its gold clawed feet. She washed her hands and face and tidied her hair. There was a spot of blood on her sleeve – she wetted her handkerchief, sponged at the mark. It did not disappear.

She was cold. For want of anything better to do, she went to her bag and took out her possessions and laid them on the bed. Her nightgown, her hairbrush, her little bottle of rosewater. A small bundle of clean linen. The novel she had brought to read on the train but left unopened – New Grub Street, the last book James had sent to her. He had said he did not much enjoy it but perhaps it would amuse her.

She looked away, turned her attention to the manuscript, which Howland had placed on the chest of drawers.

She told herself to be useful. She sat down on the bed and opened the parcel carefully. There was a comfortable weight to it. Inside, she found a title page, neatly typed:

THE MODERN ENGLISH VAMPIRE
By G. P. Shadwell and A. Swift

It was a shock, reading the word. None of them had uttered it, and yet it must have been in their minds, just as it was in Charlotte's.

She turned over pages, reading sentences at random. Gradually she was lulled into a sort of calm. The first chapters dealt with legends and myths. It was not until the fourth that the book turned to more practical matters.

It cannot be emphasised too often that it is unwise to pursue or attempt to kill a vampire. In England, attempts to eradicate the creatures rarely produced very favourable results. It was often remarked in earlier times that our custom of dealing with witches (and under this head we must count revenants of all kinds) was ineffectual in the extreme – hanging, rather than burning, was the preferred method and almost uniformly failed to despatch the vampire permanently. (Fire is a far more effective weapon – not only does it destroy the creature's body, but he will be fascinated by its warmth and may be unable to flee. More than one of them has died simply by refusing to relinquish the pleasant sensation of immersing himself within a blaze, even though his natural resistance to flame is eventually overcome and his body reduced to ash.)

A direct confrontation, then, is generally unwise. However, it may be that this cannot be avoided. Perhaps, in order to defend oneself or another, it may be necessary to fight the creatures, perhaps even to kill. This is not desirable, nor is it easy – but it is possible. Those who are driven to this extremity are greatly to be pitied. All the assistance that this book can offer them will be found in Chapter Five. The advice there, if followed correctly, will be of some use – and may God defend all those who have need of such knowledge.

She found tears in her eyes, for it was Shadwell's voice, as clear as if he were in the room with her. Chapter Five was entitled *'Attack and Defence: Apotropaics, Deterrents, Possibilities of Cure.'*

> *While a cure has never been satisfactorily achieved, it has certainly proved possible to detain a vampire – alive – for a period of time. It must be emphasised that this imprisonment is a difficult and uncertain process and one which profits a mortal little, unless there is some definite scientific end in view. The vampire may be kept alive and conscious simply by depriving him of nourishment and subjecting him to a degree of careful restraint. This method is unreliable and untenable in the long term. An alternative is to keep the vampire in a state of unconsciousness – a sleep which is like death. This may be achieved using a ritual long practised in Hungary and Silesia. Though primitive, this process has been shown to work in a number of cases. Full details are given in Appendix A.*

They had not told her of this possibility, because they had guessed exactly what she would do.

The ritual, she learned from the appendix, was difficult but not unfeasible. It would be awkward to accomplish alone – the instructions advised that five persons should be present, all men of strength and proven courage, at least one of whom had taken holy orders.

Four knocks sounded on the door, and Charlotte jumped. She wiped her eyes and went to let Howland in.

'Sorry it took me a while,' he said. 'They thought I was some poor confused foreigner. They can't have many people wanting to carry up their own tea.'

'No, probably not.'

'Is that Shadwell's book?' he asked, setting the tray down on the table.

'Shadwell and Adeline's.'

'Find out much?'

'Yes.'

He poured some tea. 'Drink,' he said, and pressed a cup into her hands. He was calm again, she noted wonderingly. Level-voiced and practical.

'Are you still determined to go with me tonight?' she asked.

'Couldn't let you down now.' He seated himself in one of the room's many gilded chairs, poured himself some tea, held the cup tight in both hands, and did not drink.

Now she remembered something – the card from James's rooms. She took it from the Gladstone bag and passed it to him. 'I found this with James's things.'

At first he did not seem to recognise the card. Then he took it from her. 'Thanks. I'd forgotten about that.'

And at last Charlotte saw that he was terrified. It was all there in that brief grin he gave her – gallant, full of suppressed fear.

All this time he had taken risks and been cheerfully reckless and pretended to be quite all right and somehow kept himself steady, though he was still horrified by what he had seen in the club – by whatever had been done to him there. He was even more frightened than she was. Perhaps he was playing out a child's adventure story in his mind, she thought – the hero unperturbed by peril and mystery, one of those dashing fellows who could sit and smoke his cigar on a barrel of gunpowder, the sort who would face his enemies and resolve to sell his life dearly.

'I wouldn't think any less of you if you wanted to leave,' she said slowly. 'You've already escaped once.'

'No. Can't leave now. Besides, you're the only one left who knows.'

She saw what he meant. There would be such loneliness, going through the world alone, with no one to share these horrors.

She was not sure how to make things better with him or how to express her thanks.

'At least drink your tea,' she said.

He nodded, drank. 'I'll draw you a plan. All I can remember of the place. It's so dark in there, you know – difficult to find your way around.'

She found him some paper – the back of one of James's poems – and he drew rapidly.

'That's the atrium.' He drew a square. 'It's on the ground floor, runs all the way up to the second floor. Sort of like an indoor courtyard. You've got stairs up to the first floor, then you're on the lower gallery, which is a corridor running around the side of the atrium. Upper gallery's the same, but on the floor above. If you're standing on the corridor on one floor, people can hear and see you on the floor above or below. Then there are corridors branching off the galleries on both floors. Lots of rooms.'

'Where do you think James will be?'

'Maybe in the attic. That's where we were before.' He added a corridor branching off the landing of the second floor. 'This is where the stairs lead. If he's not there, he'll be in the cellar.'

'That's where they caught you before, isn't it?'

'Yes.' He held up one foot, showed her that strange white mark still on his shoe. 'It's pretty dark, full of paint cans. I tripped over one.'

'Could we get in that way?'

'It's the only way we can try. Front door's no good. With the cellar there's a little window and a back door, steps leading down. Maybe we could force the lock.'

She studied the plan he had drawn. 'Where are the club men most likely to be?'

'The library,' Howland replied. 'Door's on the first floor there. Or the smoking room. Those are the most popular places. There are other rooms, on the second floor – private rooms, I think. They're not in regular use, not since the club fell in numbers.'

'I had better learn this by heart.' She took the plan gently from him.

'What shall I do?'

Charlotte pushed the manuscript towards him. 'You could read that, if you don't mind. We should know all we can.'

They both sat in silence, trying to read. More than an hour passed.

At last Howland put the manuscript aside and said, 'We could leave these with Rafferty tonight.' He nodded towards her bags and the bundle of papers they had rescued from Wych Street. 'That way we won't have to come back here. We can go straight to the station. You'll want to get him home, won't you?'

'But what about you?' she asked – grateful to him for speaking as if they might conceivably succeed.

'I guess I'll come along, if that's all right. I might be useful.'

He ought to go abroad, not to Yorkshire. But, then, it hardly seemed worth debating the matter. It was not likely that they would even reach the station.

'I think we ought to eat something,' Howland said. 'Shall I ring?'

'All right.'

Charlotte went back into the bathroom. She drank some water, washed her face again. She thought, I shall probably die tonight. It did not seem quite believable.

She remained in the bathroom until Howland knocked lightly on the door, told her that the food had arrived.

Howland had chosen wisely – good hot soup, soft bread, fruit and cold meat. She sat on the bed with the tray, Howland on the chair at the dressing table, his back to her.

'D'you mind me keeping the revolver tonight?' he asked.

As if she would be any use with the thing. 'Of course not.'

'I'll hang on to it, then. Only thought you might feel safer with it. You'd better take something, though.'

She nodded – although it was on secrecy, rather than force, that she hoped to depend. (She remembered how Adeline had used her weapons – that exquisitely balanced movement, the effortlessness of long discipline. She could not yet believe such fierce grace had been stilled for ever.)

Howland had finished eating. Now he knelt and opened the carpetbag. 'Here,' he said. He held out a folding knife with an engraved handle.

It looked like silver – Adeline had carried something similar.

'Might be useful,' Howland said. 'I'd be happier if you kept it with you.'

'Very well, thank you.' She took the knife from him. 'Is there anything else in there that could be useful?'

He began to sort through the bag methodically. 'There's not much in the way of modern innovations, I warn you. We have a box of matches, three candles, a dark lantern, a syringe, a bottle labelled *holy water* – not much left – what looks like a torn-up petticoat—'

'Bandages.'

'Thank you, yes, bandages. We also have a bottle of brandy, half full, a flask of water, completely full, an empty jam jar, string, another knife, a cartridge box – empty – another box of matches, and a Bible. That's all.'

'Some of those ought to come in useful,' Charlotte said. She began to tidy away the remains of their meal. 'How long do we have?'

'It's seven now.'

Still hours to wait. At present, nothing seemed worse than this enforced inactivity.

'Listen,' Howland said, 'I'll go to my room – I'm just next door – and you can rest. I'll call back here at ten. We can make our last preparations then.'

When he was gone, she tried to rest, until it became intolerable to lie still without doing anything.

Then she went – feeling very strange and unlike herself – into the bathroom again. She let the water run very hot. There were bath salts, soap.

She kept the knife with her, set it on the floor beside the bath after she undressed. She could not quite shake the fear that they had been followed to the hotel, that their enemies might rattle the bedroom door at any moment.

She sat in the hot water – the hottest and highest bath she had ever taken – and stared fixedly at the door. Reckless, her head aching, she had pulled out every hairpin. Her hair was warm and heavy on her bare shoulders. She let the ends trail in the water.

There were towels laid out in readiness; she had never known such luxury. Such a luxury of time, too – these hours were her own; no one would begrudge her them. She dried herself carefully – sentimental now towards the body which had carried her so far. She was grateful for her strength, which had brought her through the past few days' ordeal, which would take her further, until her task was accomplished or until she failed.

The mirror in the bathroom had clouded – she could see only a blurred image, a smudge of pink and white. Did they believe she was Howland's sister, in the hotel? Or did they think she was something else?

In the bedroom she dried the ends of her hair with the towel, rubbing fiercely, as she remembered someone – she could not remember who – doing for her as a child. She noticed her face in the glass above the dressing table. The bath had left her flushed, as if with anticipation. She watched herself, and wondered: Is this how a woman should behave with a fate like mine ahead of her? Am I being brave?

At last she was dressed and ready. The clock showed five minutes to ten. She sat at the end of the bed and waited. She had the bags packed and her handbag beside her on the bed, the silver knife in the pocket of her coat.

She jumped at the sound of Howland's knock, though she had been anticipating it. She went to the door, admitted him without a word.

He went over the route in the club with her one last time

– cellar, atrium, staircase (quick past the library door), top floor, corridor, staircase again, attic.

'We'd better go downstairs,' she said finally. 'Rafferty may be early.'

'Very well.' He was dressed for the street, hat and gloves on already, scarf tied carefully about his throat.

She went to the glass to put on her gloves and hat – Adeline's hat. She had left her own behind in the confused exit from Wych Street. She was slow, because this was the worst part; her nerves had almost overcome her. Her hands were so unsteady that she could not manage the veil, and the hat was crooked. The gloves were impossible.

Howland approached the mirror. 'D'you mind if I . . . ?'

Charlotte shook her head, and Howland took her hands in his, buttoned each glove in turn. 'Look up,' he said. She felt him fasten a bow, adjust the hat slightly to the left; he stepped back to examine his handiwork. 'There. Lovely.' He was as nervous as she was. 'Shall we go?'

Nothing left to wait for. She took his arm, and together they went out.

Chapter Thirty-One

James woke inside a coffin. There was velvet beneath him, a wooden lid close to his face. Outside he could hear horses, people walking past. When they were close he could sense their curiosity, sympathy mingled with enjoyment – one always did turn to look at a hearse, somehow. If he screamed, would they hear him? Would they pretend not to hear?

Perhaps the club had a sense of humour of sorts, to transport him in such a fashion. Or perhaps it was simply a matter of convenience: a hearse was mobile and practical, its purpose was self-evident, and it would invite few questions.

He had been dragged, almost unconscious, up the steps of the catacombs. They had been in a hurry, uncomfortable at being abroad in daylight. At the top they had let him fall onto cold stone. He did not remember being placed in the box.

For a while James lay without moving and considered confined spaces. Such prisons made one aware of oneself, the square inches one's body took up. One could not move one's arms or legs; it was like paralysis. There was no escape from one's thoughts.

The coffin swayed slightly as the hearse turned a corner. He wondered if they intended to destroy him without ever releasing him from this prison. He had tried pushing upwards at the lid but had been unable to move it. Perhaps he was still weak from Mould's attack – or perhaps the coffin had been altered to imprison his kind more effectively.

He recollected something of Mould's mind. There had been strings of numbers, wheels of steel and silver. He saw that it had given Mould pleasure to sit with a pencil and paper, devising prisons and scourges.

The hearse came to a halt. And then his coffin was being lifted, carried up a few steps, and then downstairs again. He could smell paint. The odour nauseated him.

At the bottom of the steps, the coffin was brought a little way forwards and then deposited unceremoniously onto a hard surface. The drop jarred his bones, rattled his teeth. But he did not feel as if he lay on the ground; he had not been dropped so far. A table, maybe? There were footsteps again, this time departing. He was left to silence.

• • •

They had chosen his punishment wisely. If they did not release him, he might lie here for ever. He did not know if he had the strength to destroy himself: it would mean tearing his own body to pieces, limb by limb. It would be a slow business, for he had barely any space in which to move. And there would be terrible pain, and perhaps after all of that he would not die.

As he reflected on this, he heard footsteps drawing closer, then the lid of the coffin was thrown open and he was dazzled by a sudden influx of light.

James squinted up at the face above him. Mould – prim and composed as ever, but with the beginning of a black eye, which made James smile faintly. Mould flinched at his expression.

He said, 'You've been singularly inept in your attempts at revenge, don't you think?' James could hear the man's heart beating fast. 'You failed even to kill *me,* which must be rather embarrassing.' And Mould held up both hands, as if to demonstrate to James how little strength lay within their compass.

James did not speak, but he forced himself – briefly – to reach out towards Mould's mind. The contact was terrible for both of them. James thought he would faint.

Mould stepped away, breathing heavily. 'I have an offer to make,' he said, composing himself. 'A bargain.'

James looked insolently at Mould's bruised eye and said nothing.

'It was originally our intention to keep you here indefinitely, to use you for purposes of study. But there are some in the club who think you ought to be removed more decisively. Ordinarily, I would press for the former course. But, to be frank, you're rather in the way, and it would be safer if you were dead. If you're cooperative, I will request that you are killed immediately, with a minimum of additional punishment.'

He waited, and James did not ask him what he wanted in return.

'The book,' Mould said at last. 'Where is it?'

'If you let me go, I'll take you to it.'

'And what will you do if I don't agree?'

'It can stay where it is.' Something came to James then. The book was secret to Mould alone – it was not to be read by any other. It held things which should not have been written down. 'Or I can tell someone else where to find it.' He thought quickly, made a guess: 'Makeweight.'

Mould's expression did not alter. He clung to appearances, as if a calm veneer were any defence against James when his thoughts had become so livid and passionate. James could sense his dismay – it was something like the smell of smoke and the taste of metal and the cold of a winter morning before the dawn.

Mould stepped back, looked James squarely in the face. 'I do believe you will rot in that box, Mr Norbury.' And he slammed the coffin lid shut, so loud that it hurt, and James heard his steps – hurrying, hurrying – across the room and up the stairs.

• • •

It was necessary to think of something other than his suffering. James thought of Charlotte. He remembered childhood: the terrace outside the library; the letters drawn crooked and random on the flagstones.

Then another spasm twisted him, and he vomited blood in a horrible helpless surge, a burning in his mouth and nose. The mess was thick and foul.

As he lay waiting for his shudders to pass, the coffin lid was lifted a second time – though he had noticed no approaching footsteps. Michael Bier stood over him.

'God, you look awful,' he said. He sniffed, grimacing at the bloody slime which James had vomited. 'Smell awful, too. Holy water, I suppose. Beastly stuff, isn't it.'

He was just the same, absolutely unchanged since the night James had seen him last. Cheerful, lifelessly handsome – eyes curiously empty, entirely lacking in shame or guilt.

'Thought I'd come and have a look at you,' he went on. 'Seeing how much trouble you've caused.'

James said nothing, but Bier continued as if he had made a reply:

'Oh, yes. Your escape. Made a frightful row – Edmund was very angry. And of course it was all of it *my* fault.'

James had wanted a kind of grandness, an enemy worthy of his vengeance. Instead, here was this inane, degraded creature, who neither understood nor cared about the damage he had done. Mould was right. Christopher's death meant nothing.

'They won't let me out, you know,' Michael said, interrupting

James's thoughts. 'I'm not safe, they said. It's such a bore. And I'm hungry, but there are rules about bringing the Quick here. They don't like too many corpses on the premises. And you're no use, not in the state you are now.'

He brought something out of his pocket. A roll of black velvet, tied with a cord. Inside, a bundle of shining things. They looked like nothing so much as knitting needles.

'Have you seen these before?'

'No.'

'Not surprising. They're Mould's.' He held one closer for James to look at. 'Silver. Very bad for our sort. Hurts like the devil.'

James wondered if he had the strength to sit up. 'They'll be angry if you kill me now.'

'They'll forgive me. Everybody always forgives me, eventually.'

He held a single needle up to the light, enjoying its shine. Then, with shocking speed, he stabbed it down through James's throat.

James opened his mouth in a scream that failed: the silver had murdered his voice.

Michael smiled at him. 'Told you, didn't I?'

Slowly, and with great difficulty, James moved his hand up from his side and drew the needle carefully, painfully, from his throat. The metal hurt his hands so that he could hardly bear to touch it. Michael watched his struggles, making no move to stop him.

'They don't heal,' Michael said, 'the wounds they leave.' He struck again, another needle, this time through James's shoulder. James heard himself make a noise – not a scream, a sort of gurgling.

His attacker paused, looking down at James, musing perhaps on the question of silver, or the prospect of James's agony. Or maybe he thought of nothing much at all. 'Or *do* they heal? I'm not sure, now I come to think of it. I knew once but I've forgotten. Edmund would know. I'll do your eyes next – let's see what happens.'

And again he smiled. The worst thing was that there was nothing adult or sane in his triumph – instead James saw the wild delight of a perverse and backward child. He knew – the monster which was in possession of him knew – how Michael would strike, the precise force that he would use. He was weak from the poison in his blood and the silver piercing his bones, but he had enough strength to do one last thing.

As Michael raised his arm to strike again, James clawed himself forwards, upright – sprang at him. The coffin crashed against the floor.

They fell together, and the needles fell, too, each jangling like a little bell as it struck stone. James reached out – quicker than Michael Bier – took a needle, and stabbed it down, very quickly, into the other's chest.

Bier made no sound. James had pierced his heart, but he was not dead. His eyes were open; he was watching James. One of his hands stirred.

There was no weapon in the room except the scattered needles, nothing but James's own hands and the last of his vile strength. He forced himself to loosen Bier's shirt and unfasten his necktie. He tilted the man's head slightly and then put his teeth to his neck.

His blood was cool, and it came sluggishly. It took a while, several minutes, to finish with him. Even when the blood was gone, James feared he might be revived. So James did not loosen his hold but bit down harder and at last took his hands to the task. For the next few minutes, he ceased watching himself.

Finally he was alone, mouth full of silver-tainted blood.

There was no joy in it. There was no respite in his craving after revenge. The walls around him were red-on-white, smears and splashes. The colours blurred together.

He might have run then, attempted some sort of escape. Instead, he sat in the dark with the body, the silver needles scattered over the floor, and thought of nothing particular until – he did not know how long later – the door was opened and someone else came in, halted at the top of the cellar steps.

It was Edmund Bier. In the gloom James saw him clearly. Fine, pale, pitiless features. He looked at James – whose mouth must be dark with blood – and then he looked at the floor and saw what lay there.

Before James could stand up, Bier was down the steps, standing over him. He took James by the collar and threw him against the wall.

As James lay where he had fallen, Bier came forwards and seized him again, tightened his grip around James's throat. Bier would kill him, James thought, scarcely caring; he would break and twist and tear until James was nothing but shreds.

But he did not – instead he loosened his hold and dropped James to the floor. And James found himself laughing, though it did not sound like his own laughter at all. It was a horrible noise, rough and canine. He laughed until the mirth had bled away, and then he lay back on the floor and wished that it might be the end now.

When he had strength enough to raise his head again, Bier was gone. Makeweight had taken his place. He lifted James to his feet with careless strength.

'Ready for you upstairs now,' he said, and smiled and smiled.

At the doorway, Treadwell was waiting, looking around at the mess.

'Needs a bit of a clean-up, eh?' Makeweight said. 'Better get the buckets out.' Treadwell made no answer.

Makeweight dragged James up two flights of stairs, into a room with walls covered in books, a high ceiling, cunning wooden ladders positioned against the shelves.

One light only in this room – another of the candles behind green shades – and two great fires burning. There was an empty chair facing away from one of the fires – its wooden back stained dull red in splashes – and around it, in a semicircle, sat the club men.

There were about fifteen of them. Most he did not recognise; most he could have passed in the street, in his old life, without sensing anything remarkable about them. Gentlemen, all of them – unless one counted Makeweight, who stood now by the door. Pallid faces, conservative in their dress. Most had been transformed at the prime of life; few appeared older than forty. They were perfectly still as they watched James, and yet James caught a sigh or a hiss, expectation held in check. They knew what he had done, and they were waiting for him. He felt them look at his wounds, still healing, at the mess his attack on Michael Bier had left on his clothes. They would smell the blood on him.

Makeweight hauled James to the chair before the fire, flung him into it. He was not restrained. They must have seen that he was too weak to run.

Eustace Paige was sitting close to Edmund Bier. He did not look at James. His face was calm, slightly bored. But to James's eyes he had a satisfied, well-nourished look, like a great cat that had recently fed. He must already know that Michael Bier was dead.

Mould sat closest to the door, holding a notebook – the small one, the one James had discarded in the catacombs in favour of the diary. He held it very tightly.

No one spoke immediately. James heard a clock ticking close by.

At last Edmund Bier got to his feet.

'Gentlemen,' he said, addressing the club men, 'you all know the regrettable events which have led us to this situation. My brother Michael's error of judgement has – has now met more than ample punishment.' He pressed a finger against his mouth. There were words that must be forced back, grief and recrimination. 'Mr Norbury has murdered him.'

There was a little stir at that.

'I don't have much more to say on the subject. I now propose that we bring this regrettable episode to a close.'

On the other side of the semicircle, another club man spoke – a man of immense corpulence, with lips the colour of glue. 'And what about your Undertaking, Bier?'

Bier frowned. 'We'll discuss that at a later time, Morton. For now we must press on.'

One of the club men – perpetual gentle frown, hair slightly

grey – added, 'Oughtn't we to wait for the others to get back?'

'No, we needn't wait,' Bier said. 'They may be some time yet. I asked them to bring back Mr Howland alive, if possible – it will take a little longer to manage that discreetly.'

'Don't see why you sent so many, Bier,' Morton observed. 'It's not much of a job, after all.'

A murmur of approval – they all agreed on this point. Bier ignored the remark. 'Makeweight,' he said, 'if you would like to begin proceedings.'

Makeweight rose from his seat next to Bier. He was still smiling. Alone amongst his kind, it seemed, he could maintain the expression with ease.

Then the library door was opened gently. It was Treadwell, blank-faced but moving hurriedly.

'What is it, Treadwell?' Bier asked.

'The Alia, sir. They're here.'

'How many?' Mould asked.

'Five. Price is with them.'

'Let her in, Bier,' the grey-haired club man called. 'Let's see what she wants.'

'In here?' Morton said. 'But what about the *rules*, chaps? Most *irregular*, letting females in.'

'That's not what I heard,' said another of the club men, with a ribald laugh.

'Oh, Burke's nursemaid doesn't count,' Morton replied.

Makeweight grinned from his corner. The room grew loud with dispute. Some of the club men were for inviting the Alia in and dispensing punishment for their presumption in calling in this fashion. Others considered it beneath the dignity of the institution to allow such low characters inside. Bier ignored all discussion and went to the window, pushed the drape back a little way, and looked out into the street.

'Is this over Burke, do you think?' he said quietly to Mould. He let the drape fall back.

'It must be.' Mould was frowning. 'Perhaps you ought to have spoken to them. If you had explained to Price that the club were not responsible—'

'We hardly need justify ourselves to them, Mould.'

Mould sighed. 'The others ought to be back by now.'

From downstairs, James heard something crash against wood, again and again. One of the Alia had seized the doorknocker and was making as great a din as possible.

'Gentlemen,' Bier said, 'I suggest we invite our guests inside.'

Applause, approval. Some of the club men were already on their feet. They were eager, hungry, ready for blood.

'What're you going to do with this one, then, Bier?' Morton called, indicating James.

'Kill him now, Edmund,' Mould muttered. 'We can't afford a distraction.'

'No,' said Bier.

A mutter from the other club men.

'Kill him *now*, Bier – we don't have time for this,' said another of the club men – tall, dark in his hair and garments. Like Bier, like most of the club men, his appearance was conventional. Only his eyes failed to harmonise with the respectable whole – hungry like those of a hunting bird. James recognised him as the one who had come to Egerton Gardens, who had spoken to Charlotte on the doorstep.

'No, Corvish,' Bier said. 'No swift execution. He deserves nothing so easy. Let Mould examine him – make his punishment useful.'

Mould sighed. 'I can manage without him as a specimen. Under the circumstances, you'd do better to kill him now. I understand that after Michael—' Whatever he was about to say was lost in a gasp of pain. Bier had caught his wrist in a sharp hold – a nice measurement of pain, enough to bruise but not enough to break.

Then he released his grip, as if Mould had ceased to interest him, and nodded to Corvish. 'Bind him. Take him upstairs. The other room.'

'It *is* a risk, Bier,' warned Corvish.

'Let his blood, at least,' said Morton.

A low laugh from another club man, with hair the colour of dust. 'There's always time for that.'

'Yes, very well. Do it upstairs, though. We can't be distracted now.'

'I'll do it,' said a man with red hair and a pleasant, unremarkable countenance. He spoke as if volunteering to play lawn tennis or partner someone at whist.

'All right, Maylie. But hurry.'

James was seized unceremoniously, forced to stand by pale-lipped Morton. When he attempted to resist, Morton struck him twice across the face, so hard that for a moment he could not see.

'You shouldn't have any difficulty,' Bier told Maylie. 'He is rather weak, for one of our sort.'

'Strong enough before,' James said. He spat out blood, a tooth. 'I killed your brother, and it was *easy*.'

A stir – Bier seemed about to speak. But Mould stepped forwards, holding his injured arm against his chest.

'Don't waste any thought on him, Edmund.' And to James he said coldly, 'That's quite enough.' He drew something from his inner pocket – a revolver.

He fired – twice, three times – and James was thrown backwards, hurt and blinded.

Mould was standing over him, giving instructions. 'Be careful with the chair up there. It's new, you mustn't—'

Someone cut him off with a coarse laugh. James was lifted to his feet and dragged away.

Chapter Thirty-Two

Up on the roof, Liza danced without rhythm or tune, a staggering jig that threatened to send her toppling into the air. The slates were cold and skiddy under her feet. She had left her boots hidden a few streets away, because it was best to climb barefoot, to dig your toes into each crack in the stone. There was a knack to it – dig in too hard, and the stone crumbled away, too soft, and you lost your grip.

She heard Mrs P in the street below, knocking on the front door. She'd been there awhile, watching the building, waiting for the others to arrive. They'd travelled from Salmon Street in small groups, not wanting to be conspicuous. Now they were all there, Lil and Agnes and Gil and Tom Brimstone.

Someone answered the door and let Mrs P and the others inside, just like she'd said they would. Time to get a move on.

'Slow, ain't you,' she jeered, when Sally and Nick and One-Ear reached the top at last.

Nick grinned at her. 'One-Ear was scared.'

'Shut up. We got to find a way in,' Liza said, before Nick could make One-Ear start crying. One-Ear had been useless all day, whining that he'd had a dream he saw the Seraph – as if she'd bother with the likes of him.

'Careful with the bags,' she said to the others. They each had a bag strapped to their back – Liza's was the nicest, a heavy leather satchel Mrs P had secured with a belt. Inside were bottles of paraffin – mustn't break them, Gil had warned her.

There were four skylight windows – all small, they'd have a job getting in. One was papered over on the inside. The others looked ordinary enough. Liza went to the closest one, pressed her face to the glass. She could see an odd sort of table down below. Didn't seem to be anyone in there.

'What if Doctor Knife's there?' Nick said. 'Waitin' to cut you up.'

'I ain't afraid of Doctor Knife,' Liza said. She shifted over to the closest skylight. 'I'll go in, then I'll call to tell you I ain't been got.'

She crouched closer to examine the skylight. The best thing would be to open it as quiet as possible, rather than smash it. She got out her knife, began trying to force the window open.

Nick muttered, 'You're so bloody *slow*, we'll never get *anything* to eat at this rate.'

Liza snapped, 'You watch your mouth,' because Mrs P always said there was no need for language.

'You got to slide it into the corner of the glass an' twist it,' Nick said. He knew these things. He had lived amongst thieves and other no-good types in New Cut before he was 'changed.

'I'm *doing* it.' But the window wouldn't open.

Nick nudged her. 'Let me do it.'

'No.'

'Go on.'

'*No*.'

Nick nudged her harder, and they struggled briefly. She was stronger, but Nick was quicker, and they fought and bit at each other as Sally drew back and watched, fascinated, and One-Ear whined over his wound – ought to have been born a *girl*, that one ought – and then Nick ducked quickly out of the way, too fast for Liza to follow. She fell against the skylight, and it all cracked in bits and her foot went through the glass.

They stopped, waited to see if anyone had heard the noise. But no one came up to see.

Liza pulled her foot out, and more bits of glass fell. 'That was your fault, Nick.'

'Go to hell.'

At least they could get in now. Liza wriggled through the gap – quick as possible, the glass was still sharp round the edges – and dropped onto the floor.

Looking around, first thing she saw was the table. She'd nearly fallen right onto it. It was wood and nasty silver, with holes in it, and its legs were clamped to the floor like someone was afraid it might try to run away. Underneath was a tray of clean sawdust. There were two desks, too. One was covered with papers and books and had a dirty plate on it. It smelled of bread crumbs and marmalade. On top of the other desk was an empty jug, and a bowl of bloody-smelling water.

There were drawings and photographs pinned up all over the walls. The drawings showed people with their skin taken off – all labelled, with names pointing to every bit of them. The photographs showed other things, and the folk in them must be undid, Liza thought – because they weren't dead, and the things that had been done to them would've killed one of the Quick.

'Liza? What's in there?' It was Nick, calling from above.

She said nothing. Let him worry a bit longer. She went closer to the table. There were cuff things that looked as if they might be for holding people down. The silver set off a horrible chime in her head, made her cold right to her stomach, cold to her bones. There were chains, and there were spikes that closed together like vices, and they were sharp.

'Liza?' Nick called again. 'What's in there?'

'Hurry up, all of you.'

Sally eased through the hole in the glass and landed gently. 'I'm all right,' she called to the others. 'Come on.'

There was a sound of a scuffle from above – One-Ear didn't want to come down. In the end Nick shoved him through the window, following a second later. He looked around, sniffing, and asked, 'What's this place?'

'I dunno,' Liza said. 'We need to get on, anyway.'

Sally was staring at the table. 'This is for us, ain't it?'

Nick went to the table, reached a hand towards one of the chains, drew it back hurriedly. 'That's nasty.' He glanced at Liza, and she knew he was thinking what she was – Doctor Knife. *He* might have tables like this one.

Liza pushed past One-Ear and went to the door. It was locked. Heavy, too, like doors weren't meant to be. Made to stop undid getting through. Without looking, she knew the others were watching, beginning to be afraid.

'Nick,' she said – calm, like Mrs Price would be calm – 'you got to help me with this.'

Nick rattled the door a couple of times, then inspected the lock.

'Can you open it?' Liza asked impatiently.

'Think so. It's an old one. They should've got a Bramah.'

'Hurry up,' Sally said, watching with a frown. They'd all edged closer to the door, not wanting to be near the table.

Nick went to work in a show-off sort of way, lots of flourishes, holding his picklocks up to the light like he was a conjurer.

'I want to go home.' One-Ear sounded as if he was about to start crying again.

'Well, you can't,' Liza told him.

'We can go home soon,' Sally said. She took One-Ear's hand. 'But we've got to help Mrs Price first. Then we can have something to eat, an' then we can go home. All right?'

One-Ear nodded, a bit cheered up at the thought of food.

Nick gave a cry of triumph. 'Done it.'

'Good,' said Liza.

'Good? You tell me who else could've done that so fast. You just tell me.'

Liza scowled at him. 'We ain't here to listen to you boast. Let's get on with it.'

The door led into a long corridor, dark enough for Liza to see clearly. There were five doors. Two on each side and one at the very end of the passage. From what Mrs P had told her, she knew that this was the one that would lead downstairs.

'Is it all right?' Sally whispered.

'Yes.' Liza stepped out into the corridor. 'Hurry up.'

Nothing to worry about in the corridor, nothing bad like in the room they had left.

Making towards the furthest door – quiet, cautious, in case the floorboards creaked – Liza heard a sudden noise, soft as a breath. It came from the last door on the right.

'Wait,' she muttered to Nick without turning round, and she went to the door and listened. Something in there, someone moving.

This door was locked, too. Might be worth a look. Mrs Price had said to keep an eye out, you never knew what the club might be up to.

'Nick,' she said quietly. 'Come an' open this.'

'Why?'

'Just do it. Now.' When he wouldn't, she added, 'Might be something inside.'

'Like what?'

'Ain't you hungry?'

At that he went to work, quicker than he had on the last door, and they were in.

There was a chair, with silver chains like there'd been on the silver table, and there was a man in the chair, and the chains went through his wrists and ankles and his neck, and there was blood – red and silver – dribbled onto his clothes where the chains were.

'What . . .' Nick began, pushing against Liza to see what she was looking at. When he saw the chair, he swore and went closer to see better.

The others were already behind them in the doorway, trying to get a look. And that wouldn't do, Liza thought – they'd panic if they saw the man sitting there.

'Get them back,' she said to Nick. 'They'll only fuss.'

'Fine.'

Nick shoved Sally away, One-Ear, too. Liza could hear them in the hall – complaining, the lot of them. They'd be fighting in a minute and she'd have to go and sort them out, but for the moment she just stood and stared.

He was a right mess, which made him harder to recognise. But then, he'd been a mess the last time she saw him, too.

'It's you, ain't it,' she said. 'The one that fell off the roof.'

There was blood-sick all down his front and blood at the corners of his mouth and where the chains went through him. He must be nearly silverfied – he'd be dead before long.

'What did you do?' Liza asked.

Maybe he was too weak to talk. They'd bled him, she could smell it in the air under the silver stink. He couldn't move anywhere unless he got some blood – and catch *her* giving him any. Probably he was half silly from pain. Mind you, he'd seemed a bit cracked the last time she saw him, hadn't he. Going crazy did you no good, Mrs P said. The ones that go mad don't last long.

Obviously got no notion of how to look after himself, the great baby. *One-Ear* probably had more sense.

From outside, Nick called, 'Shall we go, then?'

'You shut up,' Liza snapped back. 'Stay there, I'm letting him out.'

'What? Why?'

She ignored him. You could break silver, if you really tried. Wasn't that it was strong so much as that it *hurt*. The chains burned cold on her palms, but she pulled at them till they snapped, then let them fall with a clang.

'There,' she said. 'You can get out now.'

But he still said nothing, never even looked at her.

She shook him. 'Wake up.'

Nothing. Didn't even seem to hear her. Well, to hell with him, then. She could tell Mrs P what she'd seen – that'd be enough.

In the corridor, the others were waiting. The door to the stairs wasn't locked, which was something. Somewhere below, someone was talking.

'I'm *hungry*,' One-Ear whined.

'We're eatin' soon,' Sally said. She looked at Liza. 'Ain't we?'

''Course. We got to do what Mrs P told us, then we can go and eat.'

They all went downstairs, soft as possible, careful so no one would hear them, not even old Treadwell, wherever he was. Mrs P had told Liza to watch out for him.

The club was silent as could be – Liza couldn't hear the talking any more. It was a smart place, richer than anywhere Liza had ever been before, nicer even than Mr Burke's house, with soft green carpets and green-and-gold walls.

'You all got bottles?' she asked.

They did. The bottles were full of paraffin, to be poured over curtains and rugs and furniture, and they all had matches, too.

'Right. Let's burn it up.'

They all smiled – they'd been looking forward to this part.

'Sally, you and Nick go one way, an' me and One-Ear—'

'Don't call me that!' One-Ear snapped.

'All right,' she said. 'Keep your wool on.' No point getting him all miffed. 'Me and Bill will go this way. An' when we're done, we got to go down quietly an' see what's goin' on. Make ourselves useful, Mrs P says. Have a snack.'

Nick grinned at her. 'Don't go letting any more of 'em out,

Liza,' and him and Sally went off, and it was just Liza and One-Ear standing in the corridor.

The first rooms they found were bathrooms – three in a row, black-and-white-tiled, great shiny tubs so big that her and One-Ear and the other two could have all fitted inside at once.

'Not much to burn in 'ere,' she said, and stopped One-Ear messing about with the taps and bullied him onwards into the next room. This was a parlour or something – lots to burn. Carpet, tables, books.

They poured paraffin everywhere – Liza warned One-Ear not to use too much, they had to make it last. They drizzled it over papers and the rug by the hearth, and Liza no longer thought it was a shame that so much expensive stuff was going up in smoke, because there was that fine sight when she first struck the match and the paraffin flared up like a firework. What a lovely warmth it made. And it spread so clever, fast as the undid themselves, carpet to chairs to curtains, lovely live running thing.

When the carpet went up, even One-Ear looked a bit more cheerful. 'Come on,' Liza said. 'We got a couple more rooms to do.'

She led the way into the next room, cuffing One-Ear in irritation when he struck five matches without managing to light one. It was an office, and so dusty that the air tasted of it. Tasted of paraffin, too. Dark drips all over the curtains and carpets, like it was raining indoors.

'Won't they smell it?' One-Ear asked, at the doorway. There was smoke on them already, in a minute it'd be drifting downstairs.

'Not till it's spread.'

She paused, listening to see if there was anyone outside, if anyone had given the alarm, but there was no sound in the corridor – Sally and Nick must already be out of earshot. How big this place was, when you were actually inside. Like a bloody maze, almost.

Outside on the landing, it was quiet. Still quiet, though the flames were spreading behind them.

'You stay put,' she told One-Ear. 'I'll see what's goin' on.'

She went tiptoe by tiptoe down the broad staircase. The bannister would have been fun to slide on, if there hadn't been other things to do right now.

At the foot of the stairs, there was another square landing like the one above, and a big squarish bit below that. It was like a courtyard, only inside. Looking up, she could see One-Ear staring at her over the bannister. She made a face at him.

She could hear voices now from behind a door quite close by. Must be the library, where Mrs P had said they'd be. She crept towards the door, carpet soft and bouncy under her feet. She thought of herself curled up on such a carpet like a cat – how nice and warm. Closer, and closer – there was nobody watching. She went right up to keyhole and pressed her ear against it.

She heard a man's voice: 'The difficulty you present is so negligible.' He said something else, a bit softer, and Liza strained to hear.

Then, all at once: a noise behind her. She had forgotten to keep an ear out. Stupid girl.

She turned to face him, the one who had discovered her, and he reached out for her, too fast for Liza to do anything but flinch away from his grasping hands.

He wore a servant's uniform. Must be Treadwell. She shrank back, but he got her round the neck. He held her up above the ground, at arm's length. She snarled at him, twisted a little, testing his grip, and he said nothing but knocked twice at the door, tightening his hold as she struggled.

'Mr Bier,' he called.

'Treadwell?' someone called back from inside. 'What is it?'

'Forgive the interruption, sir,' Treadwell said. 'But I've found something you ought to see.'

Chapter Thirty-Three

Howland asked Rafferty to stop in Regent Street – they would walk the rest of the way.

'How long d'you want me to wait?' Rafferty asked. He must know that there was small chance of them returning.

'Let's say until two,' Howland replied. 'We shouldn't be longer than that.'

Rafferty nodded. 'I'll stay till then.'

Howland paid him, for their journey and in advance for the wait. 'Just in case, you know.'

''Course,' Rafferty said, counting his money. 'Luck to you both.'

He let them go without any gibe, which was unsettling. Charlotte turned once to look at him before they were out of sight. He had wrapped a scarf around his hat, had given his horse its nose-bag.

She was calm. Leaving the Langham had been the worst part. Now everything would soon be over.

'Here,' Howland said. They had turned a corner onto Jermyn Street. 'That one.'

It was a tall, pale building, rather narrower than she had imagined. The streetlamp caught the dull gleam of the metal plaque on the wall. In each window, blinds or curtains had been drawn tightly across.

If Mrs Price's girl had told them the truth, Price and the others would surely be approaching soon, if they were not there already. Charlotte did not dwell on thoughts of what should be done if Mrs Price and her gang failed to appear. Howland led her away from the house, down another street and then another corner, and they were at the back of the building – which looked out onto Ormond Yard. There was still a little traffic here, even at this late hour, and some people were walking up and down on foot, most of them bound on pleasure.

'There,' Howland said in a low voice. The back door was below the level of the pavement, reached by a short flight of steps. It did not look especially daunting or remarkable in any way.

A street away, the church bells struck the hour. It was midnight.

A moment later two figures passed them: a man and a woman. The man she recognised – it was Mr Gil, Mrs Price's companion on the bridge. He had a red flower in his coat; his shoes gleamed. His smile was wide. The woman Charlotte had never seen before. She was dressed in chocolate brown and black and deep violet, all draggled feathers and napless velvet. There was dirt on the hem of her dress, and her pale-yellow gloves were stained. She wore a hat with a black-spotted veil – beneath that, Charlotte glimpsed something rotting within, a face that was strangely and pitifully disassembled.

They gave no sign of noticing Charlotte and Howland, though they passed only a few yards away. They turned the corner and were gone from sight. Howland was gripping her arm tightly. If he had not been there, she might have turned and run.

Gazing upwards at the club, Charlotte thought she saw something – a shadow – moving on the roof.

'Cellar door?' Howland muttered.

'Yes. Let's go.'

Howland had to exert all his strength to shatter the wood, kicking with such a din that Charlotte almost called to him to stop.

At last the door gave way. Both of them halted, scarcely daring to move, and waited to see if they had been discovered.

Nothing changed. The building was as quiet as ever.

Howland steadied himself and pushed the door open. Charlotte could see a little of what lay within. A stone floor, walls whitewashed. Tins of paint piled about, just as Howland had told her.

Again they both stopped, but there seemed to be nothing waiting beyond the narrow square of light which fell through the doorway onto the flags.

'Slowly,' Howland whispered. 'Can't rush. Or they'll hear.'

She followed him into the cellar. It was cold inside, as she had expected. She had never liked being underground.

'No one here,' Howland said.

'No. Can we have some light?'

Howland held up the dark lantern and let a faint beam shine out.

There were hooks hanging down from the ceiling, others were hammered into the walls; this must have been a kitchen once. The walls were peculiarly, unpleasantly white. There was a strong smell of paint. The stone floor was wet – it looked as if someone had been washing the flags very recently.

'Look.' Howland spoke softly, and she turned to see what he was staring at. Something lying on the floor, knocked over on its side: a coffin, though of a most peculiar design. The sides were unusually thick, and fashioned not only of wood but – she went closer, leaned over, and laid a hand on one side – of metal. Steel, perhaps. The weight of the thing must be incredible. Inside, it was lined in velvet the colour of black grapes. There was a faint smell of blood.

Howland took her hand. 'Come on.' He drew her away, because they both knew who must have been lying there.

The lantern showed a dark splash on the floor, another red stain on the white wall. Whoever had been cleaning the room had made a small oversight. Howland drew the lantern away quickly.

On the far side of the cellar were steps leading up to a door. Howland went first, put his ear to the keyhole. Then he shook his head.

'Nothing.'

He slid the panel across the dark lantern, hiding its flame.

Then he tried the door – and swore under his breath.

'Is it locked?' Charlotte whispered.

'No. That's what I don't like. Stay back.' He had the revolver out now, held it openly as he put his shoulder to the door. It opened forwards into silence and darkness – but not absolute blackness, as Charlotte had feared. There was soft green shadow. Somewhere within there was a light burning very low.

At the top of the cellar steps, she followed Howland into a tiled corridor – the one which led to the atrium. She saw that the light was coming from a candle burning behind a green glass shade.

'Go left,' Howland said very softly.

He took a step forwards – then stopped so unexpectedly that she narrowly avoided colliding with him.

There were footsteps; someone was moving on the floor above them. They might not come this way, she thought. Of course they will come this way. Another step and they will smell us out.

Then more footsteps, quicker, heavy on the soft carpet above their heads. Someone moving fast. Then a little gasp, the sound of a struggle.

She heard a man say, 'I've found something you ought to see.' At the sound of the voice, Howland flinched. She did not dare move, even to take his hand. Above them, there was a smothered cry.

Then a door was opened and closed, and it was quiet again.

Howland touched her wrist very lightly. Under the faint green light he looked sick and strange. They moved onwards. Their cringing steps led them across the black-and-white-tiled floor, then up a staircase to the landing from which they had heard the voices a moment before. Above them was another landing, more stairs, all precisely the same. More green shades. If she got out of here she would dream of them, she thought, endless stairs and lights.

She could hear noises now – voices behind the door to the library. She was uneasy with her back to it; every time she turned her head she imagined it opening, someone looking out. They pressed on.

They reached the second landing. A corridor leading off the atrium and another staircase would take them to the attic.

'Almost there,' Howland whispered. He took a step forwards, and halted abruptly.

There was wavering yellow light not far off. It was coming from the corridor they were to take. From the rooms beyond, she could smell smoke.

'Wait here.' Howland slipped down the corridor towards the light. In the silence, Charlotte could hear something close to a dull roar, a crackling of flames.

She was about to follow when he returned – breathless, smelling of smoke.

'Are you all right?'

'Not singed, I promise,' he said. 'There's a fire in a few of the rooms, spreading quickly.'

'Can we get upstairs?'

'If we're quick.'

She followed Howland across the landing – they were almost running now, less careful about being discovered.

From beneath them, in the depths of the house, came the sound of laughter, which gradually became a long shriek.

And something worse. Hurried feet, coming closer. Someone running frantically downstairs from the attic, not caring for stealth.

At the far end of the passage, a figure rushed into view, then came to a rapid halt. He had already seen them.

The light from one of the green-shaded candles fell on his face. Such an ordinary-looking man, Charlotte thought, to be the death of them.

The stranger came closer. A small man, perhaps fifty or so – prim face, grey moustache the colour of mouse fur. A mark on his face, as if someone had struck him recently. His expression was mobile, human. She opened her mouth to call out to Howland that this was a mere man, that they could deal with him—

The sound of the shot was so loud, so utterly unexpected, that she did not at first understand what it meant. As she stopped short, bewildered, Howland pushed her roughly out of the way, only to crumple a second later, sinking to the carpet before she could reach out to hold him up.

The man advanced slowly on Charlotte, revolver raised.

Howland lay still. He stared at her, and though his face was tight with pain, his eyes were clear: she knew then what she would need to do. Quickly – she did not know she was capable of such speed – she reached into Howland's coat pocket, armed herself.

The stranger fired again, missed – she was not sure how close his aim had been. He took another step, considered her with his head to one side. The effect was unpleasantly birdlike. He looked at the revolver which she held gingerly in both hands. She had found the trigger and did not like to move her fingers now, in case she fired by accident.

'You must be the sister,' the stranger said.

Charlotte said nothing.

'I'm afraid you're wasting your time. It would be kinder to let him burn.'

The gun was an unfriendly weight. She was afraid that she might drop it.

They stared at each other. 'Well, then.' The man's revolver was still pointed directly at her. 'What do you propose to do now?'

'If you don't hurry, the place will burn down before you can give the alarm.'

'And your brother will die.'

'Then you'd better let me pass.'

She saw his lips twitch, once, as he looked at the revolver she held. 'Or else you'll shoot, I suppose?'

Then, quite suddenly, his expression altered. He had glanced upwards. In spite of herself, Charlotte followed his gaze.

It took her another second or so to understand what she saw: there was something crawling along the ceiling.

It was a child. A little girl with soot smeared across her face. If she had been clean she would have been pretty, Bo Peep-ish – she had golden hair hanging in ringlets and wide blue eyes. She regarded the scene with her head tipped backwards, face upside down. Then she let herself drop to the floor.

''S'all right,' she called. 'They're Quick.'

A scuffle, and then two figures showed behind the bannisters – two little boys with dead faces. One was redheaded; the other had a hand clasped to the side of his head, as if his ear ached. They had a kind of alertness that Charlotte had seen before in wild animals – the rat and stoat – but never in human beings.

'Let's 'ave these,' the redhead said. 'Before we go downstairs.'

'But what if Treadwell comes back?' asked the other boy, without taking his hand from his head.

''E won't,' red-hair answered.

'I want this one,' the girl said, ignoring them, pointing at Charlotte.

'Why d'you get to choose?' Red-hair scurried closer, spoiling for a fight.

Charlotte said quietly to the stranger, 'These are no friends of yours.'

'Evidently.' He had moved backwards into the mouth of the corridor, and they were now standing side by side. 'Are you suggesting we collaborate?'

'Yes.'

'How many shots do you have?'

'I don't know' – she struggled to hold the gun steady – 'how many do they usually have?'

He sighed. 'Try to hit something, at least.' He raised his revolver and fired, aiming at the little girl. She darted out of the way, cursing him. The other boy was moving towards Charlotte – and looking past her at Howland, still crumpled on the floor.

They're children, she thought; though this won't kill them, it will hurt, just as much as if they were alive. But she had seen it done, and it was no great matter, in the end, to raise her weapon and fire.

She had expected a jar and a shock of noise, and though the shot frightened her, she did not drop the gun. The redheaded boy jolted backwards with a howl. She had hit him.

Beside her, the stranger fired again, shot the girl in the face. She screamed and fell back, her hands over her eyes. The one-eared boy ignored his companions' distress, began edging towards Charlotte.

'Kill 'em now!' the girl called. Her voice was steady, in spite of the blood on her face and hands, the dark red mess where her eye had been. Charlotte looked once in spite of herself – at the eye socket that welled up with blackness, the stare that came from nowhere.

In spite of the girl's command, the other two children were growing wary, though; they did not want to approach.

The stranger took a step forwards. 'Do you know who I am?'

'Breakfast!' one of the boys jeered. The other laughed.

'I'm Doctor Knife. You've heard of me, haven't you?'

'You ain't 'im,' the girl scoffed.

Deftly, still holding his revolver, the stranger pushed back both his sleeves to reveal two straps around his wrists – Charlotte glimpsed a sharp spike, metal wheels.

'Try and see,' he said.

To Charlotte's astonishment, the children retreated a little way.

'Come on,' the redheaded boy muttered to his companions. 'Who cares 'bout this lot? Better fun down there.'

They followed him towards the stairs. After a few paces, the boy turned back. 'You'll roast to death up there, anyway,' he called, voice full of malice. Then the three of them slipped downstairs, leaping four or five steps to a stride. They moved in a horrible way, unnaturally agile. The stranger's gaze followed them into the darkness.

The dark lantern was lying close to Charlotte's feet, where Howland had dropped it. Before the stranger could turn to look at her, she seized the lantern and struck him as hard as she could. He fell forwards and did not move.

At first she thought she had killed him. But he was still breathing. He would be discovered soon enough; someone would attend to him. The important thing was Howland. She stumbled to him, crouched down, gently touched his shoulder.

'Mr Howland?'

He was ashen-faced, but he opened his eyes and nodded.

'Are you – is it bad?'

'No,' he said.

'Can you move?'

'Yes – think so.' She helped him slowly to his feet. He leaned on her shoulder, the weight almost painful. 'Left leg. Grazed me, I think – shock more than anything . . .'

She took the scarf from around his neck. 'Let me bind it.' She tied the scarf as tight as she could about his leg. It would staunch the bleeding, at least. 'Do you think you can get downstairs?'

'Not yet,' he said. 'Still a job to do.'

'Are you sure? Can you manage?'

''Course I can manage.' He was gripping her wrist hard, still struggling to stand.

A scream from downstairs. A low, sobbing howl. Something fell, smashed.

They walked – half staggered – towards the door to the attic stair. At the bottom of the steps, Howland stopped. 'You go on,' he said, looking down at his leg. 'I'll wait here. I can call if the fire spreads too far.'

'You'd better have this.' She handed the revolver to him.

'No.'

'Of course you must have it. You're injured.' She took a breath; her throat was already sore with the smoke. The screams from downstairs were growing louder.

'Be careful, then—' The crash of what sounded like falling timber in a neighbouring room interrupted him. 'Hurry.'

It was quiet in the attic, the din of the chaos below was muted. The smell of smoke had not yet reached this far. There were candles lit even here, guttering in the draught. The door to her left was ajar. She went in – heedless, reckless.

The room was empty save for a single chair. A man sat there, his head bowed. She had found him.

His eyes were closed. In the faint green light from the hall, his features seemed touched with silver – gleaming in the corners of his mouth, shining like tears beneath his eyelids. There were wounds on his wrists that made her catch her breath. The room smelled of blood and vomit.

'James,' she said.

He opened his eyes. He was so pale, as if there were no blood left in him. It took an effort, but she went to him, put her hands in his.

'James, I'm here.'

She wondered if he was able to speak. The chair – she did not like to look at it – appeared designed to restrain or torment its occupant; there were chains on the floor between his feet. He must have broken his way free before losing strength.

'We have to go,' she told him. 'It's not safe here. Can you stand up?'

'Charlotte,' he said at last.

There were tears in his eyes. She kissed him on the forehead.

'Lean on me. We must get downstairs.'

Still he did not move.

'James, you're ill. But you can recover, I'm sure of it. I'll find a way. But you must get out of here *now* – the place is on fire.'

He spoke with a struggle: 'You've got to leave me.'

'I won't leave you here.' She was already pushing up the sleeve of her dress. 'If you need this, then take it.'

But he shook his head.

'You have to, James. Take it now. We need to get out.'

She still had the silver clasp knife which Howland had given her. The blade was small but very sharp. She had bared her arm to the elbow. There was hardly anything to show the place where James had hurt her before. She could see the mark only because she knew it was there. Quickly, before she could think about the pain, she passed the blade over the skin, reopening the wound.

With the pain came fresh blood. She held her wrist out to him. 'Please, James.'

He stared at her, his face so distant and empty. He hesitated – in spite of herself, she felt relief – and then he took her wrist, lifted it to his mouth.

She counted. Thirty seconds, one minute. A small time. 'James, that's enough.' He did not stop.

'James. Enough. We have to go.'

But his grip tightened. He was drinking deeper than he had before.

In her panic, Charlotte raised the knife and stabbed at his hand, surprising him with pain. She wrenched her wrist free from his grasp.

He slumped backwards in his chair – trembling, confused. He did not want to believe what he had done, she thought.

'It's all right,' she said. 'It's all right.'

He wiped his mouth. It was *her*, she thought, suddenly appalled – it was her blood in his mouth, her blood which he licked from his fingertips.

Hastily, almost ashamed, she pulled down her sleeve.

'Stand up,' she said. 'Come on.'

He was strong enough now; the blood had acted quickly. He got to his feet at last – slow and awkward, eyes cast down. 'Lean on me.'

And he did lean on her – so cold and heavy, it was like supporting a fallen statue – and slowly they made their way out into the corridor.

Howland was sitting at the bottom of the stairs. When he saw them he stood up – awkwardly, checking an exclamation of pain.

'He's all right,' Charlotte called. 'Weak. We've got to—' Then she stopped. They had delayed too long.

The flames were now climbing the wall – lividly orange, dark smoke rising. The heat was a concrete thing: it pushed them backwards, searing their faces. To their left, the bannister had caught alight. As they watched, a picture hanging on the wall went up in flames with a foul smell of burning oil.

There was no sign of the man who had attacked them, nor of the children.

'Come *on*,' Howland urged, and Charlotte pulled at James's hand. He was staring fixedly at the flames. The blaze was about to reach the stairs. Another minute and there would be no way down to the first floor.

Suddenly, sharply, Howland called out a warning. But before Charlotte could understand what he meant, James had already reached out with both hands, crushed the ember that had fallen onto her hair.

She saw Howland yell something, guessed rather than heard what he said – *run*. They fled downstairs, the flames crackling in their wake. The air was nearly gone. On the landing below, Charlotte found herself crouching closer to the ground, James still leaning against her. The smoke made her eyes water, and she was choking, could scarcely keep moving. The fire was following them down, quicker now. The landing was barely passable.

She stumbled, almost tripping over something.

'Don't,' Howland said, coughing. 'Don't look.'

It was the body of a child. Feeling faint, she stepped towards the bannister. They were closer to the screaming now. Charlotte could make out occasional figures, male and female, moving behind the flames and the smoke. She saw the woman who had passed them outside – no longer veiled, blood in her eyes and smeared across her face, her hair burning as she clawed at an attacker. As Charlotte watched, the flames spread from the woman to the large, pale-lipped man who held her; neither appeared to notice or care as their clothes began to blaze.

That descent, the terrible struggle to balance secrecy and speed, had an odd unreal quality to it, as if she were suffering from fever. Shapes seemed close and then very distant in the growing smoke. People were running about – Charlotte could not tell if they were trying to save the building, or trying to escape, or had no thought but of killing. James leaned on her, heavier and heavier; she struggled not to fall forwards, to send them both toppling to the bottom. Howland, now walking behind them, sounded as if he was struggling, too, but she could not look back to see how he managed.

They were on the landing of the first floor; there was not much further to go. Just as she thought that they might slip by unseen in the confusion, two figures passed close by. One stopped, turned to stare at the small procession: two injured men and an exhausted woman. He was a young-faced man, from the club perhaps. He had a cruel slicing wound across his forehead, close to his left eye. As he stared at Charlotte, she saw the skin begin to heal.

'Leave . . . alone . . .' James muttered. But the man had forgotten his quarry – he was moving towards them; there could be no escape. There was blood on his hands, blood in his hair.

'Leave them,' someone said. Not James, not Howland. The voice came from the landing behind them – a cold clear voice, which carried easily through the noise and the shouts. '*Leave* them, Maylie. I'll deal with this.'

The man was only a few yards away. He stood as if unmoved by the blaze, though the flames were almost crackling at his ankles. He was tall and broad, half hidden in smoke. Her eyes were stinging, full of tears – she could just make out dark hair, a stern face.

'Leave them,' he said for a third time. The man he had addressed as Maylie stopped and turned to argue. It was difficult to make out what he said – not much air left now, and the screaming had not stopped. The other man made some reply. Maylie seemed to hesitate, then nodded. He stepped past Charlotte and the others, past the other club man, and vanished upstairs – indifferent to the horrible scorching air, the smoke which had almost obscured the upper rooms.

The stranger looked at James. He said something that Charlotte could not make out, held out his hand towards James, and she shrank back, yelled at him – she hardly knew what.

The man took James from her grasp as if it were no effort at all. He put his arm around his shoulders and pointed towards the door to the club – in sight now, though half hidden in grey smoke.

From above them came a snapping sound: the roof was about to give way. Charlotte went to Howland, helped him towards the stairs.

She saw James look at the man who held him upright. 'Paige . . .' he said faintly.

'Yes.' The man's face revealed nothing. 'Come on.'

He led them forwards, Charlotte and Howland struggling in his wake. She was coughing helplessly now, throat raw, her eyes full of tears.

One last staircase – the atrium – the front door. They were outside.

Chapter Thirty-Four

Liza had ruined everything. The club would know the others were up there before the fire had a chance to spread. What would Mrs P say?

The library was a big place – the shelves all full of books, so neat it was as if they had been measured to fit, and they were all bound in green leather that still looked brand-new. Mrs P was standing near the fire and didn't turn her head when Treadwell and Liza came in. Gil was standing beside her, Agnes and Lil a little further off. They'd probably never been in such a room, any more than Liza had. Tom Brimstone – with his teeth polished specially for the occasion – was in the corner, watching everything with a thinking look.

There was a man sitting across from Mrs P. He was young and light-haired and stuck-up, and when he saw Liza he sneered. Must be Bier. Everyone said that the boss of the club was a high-nosed bastard. And there were others like him, sitting and standing about, gentlemen all. Quite a lot of them between the Salmon Street folk and the door.

Treadwell let go of her neck and pushed her forwards, into the middle of the room.

'Whatever have you got there, Treadwell?' Bier asked.

'I found it eavesdropping outside, sir.'

'One of your brats, Price?'

Mrs Price said nothing.

Then Bier said, 'Mould.'

A man came over – keeping as far as he could from the Salmon Street lot. 'Yes?' He was *Quick*. Nasty thing.

'Go home, would you?' Bier didn't even trouble looking at him. 'We shan't require your assistance now.'

Mould stared at Bier and the others. He seemed to be thinking something, but Bier just shook his head. One of the other club men – young face, red hair – said, 'Shut the door, Mould, would you, when you go?'

Mould went off, and most of the gentlemen laughed because of his thoughts, which were all in a huff from being sent away like that.

'Treadwell,' Bier added, 'you'd better make sure that there are no other infants on the premises.'

Treadwell went out, and the door shut again.

And then one of the club men – fat and pasty-lipped – looked at Liza and sniffed. 'Bier,' he said, 'it stinks of *smoke*.'

'Smoke?' Bier repeated, turning sharpish to stare at Liza.

The club men had stopped talking. The ones that were sitting down got up quickly – Bier, as well. And Bier frowned and said, 'Gentlemen—'

Mrs P had stepped forwards, and Lil and Agnes, too, and Brimstone had glanced up, a bit more awake. Gil had took off his gloves – he was always picky about keeping them clean. And Mrs P looked at Liza and didn't even need to speak: Liza knew she meant *now*.

She screamed then in delight – and to hear her voice slam against the marble pillars, the goldy ceiling – and all of them laughed, Gil and Agnes and the gentlemen – they all laughed, tipping their heads back, all those teeth glistening. They all laughed except Mrs P and Bier. Maybe there was something worrying them both, but there was no time for that now.

Must be funny, she thought, to see all these people – nothing much to look at, nothing out of the ordinary unless you were paying attention – trying their best to tear one another to bits. Must seem ugly and strange, unless you felt the blood hunger redding your thoughts, singeing away the rest of the world.

She leapt forward, her bare feet sure and easy on the polished wood floor, and her long nails were at a club man's face, *in* his face, soft slippery stuff giving way under her fingers, and she was lost in the delight of it, her ears rang with the sound of her own laughter.

When she came back to herself she wasn't in the library any more. Her hands were all sticky, her thirst was mostly gone. The place was burning properly now, she noticed. She hadn't done so badly.

Only thing was that the other kids might be dead. The only one she'd seen was Nick, racing past her, yelling some silliness about Doctor Knife.

Somewhere up above, wood splintered and something went *bang,* and she swayed back and forth with delight. She was perched on top of the bannister, poised to jump forwards – or backwards, maybe, down to the floor below – and watching as one of the gentlemen went for Lil, whose hair was on fire. She was clawing at his eyes, making a right to-do – she'd blind him in a sec. It was hard on the men, Liza thought, having such short nails as a rule.

Then Gil rushed up – all messy and black with smoke, and he was in a horrible temper. He'd lost his hat, and someone had cut him all down his face.

'Where is she?'

Liza jumped down from the bannister and said, 'Who?' and giggled – still a bit silly with blood.

Gil hit her, harder than Mrs P ever had, harder than anyone had hit her since she became undid.

'Where *is* she, you little bitch?'

It was Mrs P he meant. Of course, he'd never worry himself about where anyone else had got to. 'Dunno,' Liza said. She'd staggered when he hit her but didn't fall. She was pleased with herself for that. 'She was in the library with the big feller – Makeweight.'

Gil swore again, using the sort of language Mrs P said there was no call for. And he ran off into the smoke pouring out of the library. She spat at his retreating back.

Then she heard someone say, 'Liza,' quite soft. It was Agnes – lying close to the wall, huddled under her cloak. Agnes asked, 'Where's Lil?'

'I dunno,' Liza said. 'Think she ran off outside.' Agnes might be mad if Liza told her the truth. Especially if Liza said she hadn't helped Lil when she was on fire. 'What's goin' on in there?' And she pointed to the library, because Agnes looked a bit confused, like she might not know what Liza meant.

'You got to go now, Liza.' Agnes was talking like she was hurt somewhere. Yes, under the cloak she was all torn up. What a mess. Liza would have seen before, only she smelled of blood so much at present that it was hard to notice it on other people. 'Take the others an' go,' Agnes said with a gasp. Liza was afraid Agnes might ask where the others were, but she didn't. She looked around and blinked, and Liza didn't think she could see anything, her eyes were funny. 'You sure you ain't seen Lil?' she added.

'Ain't seen her.'

'Well. Get out, anyway. That's a good girl.'

'But what about Mrs P and the others? I thought—'

Agnes snarled at her – Agnes, who was never cross like the

others. 'Get *out*,' she said. She closed her eyes and her head fell back.

Liza knelt down and shook her, and shouted, and kicked her hard, but Agnes didn't move again. They'd ripped her almost in two. Her neck was gashed through to the bone, which was a low way to treat an old lady.

Find Mrs P, Liza thought. She'll know what to do. She went back into the library.

The room was wrecked. Someone had pulled all the books off the walls and chucked some into the fire, the lamp was smashed.

It was quiet in there, too. Just the jumpy snapping flames. Liza didn't like it. Everyone else seemed to have run off.

Oh, wait – not everyone. There was the big feller. Makeweight the bastard, and he was striding through the bookcases – he'd seen her.

He was all cut up, and he was carrying a bonnet, and didn't it look odd in his hands. But it was Mrs P's bonnet, and Makeweight's shirt was torn and his coat was gone, and his arms were red past the elbow, and he was working something out of his teeth with his tongue.

Liza turned and ran for the door, quicker than fire, back out onto the landing.

Makeweight was coming after her, grinning. She found herself by the bannister again. Black-and-white floor below, no time to be careful. She jumped.

Not too far, but she landed badly. Hurt herself. No time to think about that now.

Run, Liza, she thought, trying to make it sound like Mrs P's voice. The front door was already open – pulled half off its hinges. Three big strides and she was free. Barefoot on the pavement.

Outside, there were lots of the Quick come to stare, and Liza slipped through them all as quickly as she could. Behind her, the club groaned like it was a live thing burning.

On the corner, she stopped and looked back. The flames had

begun to waver playfully along the roof, onto the next building. She was *burned,* she realised, close to tears – her skin was sore and her feet stung. Her hands were black and red, ash and blood in the lines of her palms.

She picked up a stone from the pavement and flung it as hard as she could at the club. It smashed through one of the upstairs windows.

There was a sudden billow of dirty grey smoke, a blazing flare of light. Crowd didn't like that – some of them gasped and elbowed each other backwards, trying to get away from the heat and the flying shards of glass.

Liza turned away, and started to run.

Part Five

Chapter Thirty-Five

Mould was not dead. For a minute or so, as he lay helpless on the pavement, gathering his breath and watching the club yield to the flames, this was all he could think of.

Gradually, he became aware of other things. He was in considerable pain; his arm was probably broken. He was also very cold and soaked with rain. He had fainted almost as soon as he left the club – it was a wonder he had not been trampled.

Above him, timbers were giving way, and the whole building looked about to come down. The fire brigade had been sent for; a crowd had gathered. Already some of them had begun to stare at him – he must be a peculiar spectacle, injured and covered in soot.

'You all right?' someone asked.

Mould stood up. It was a struggle to keep his balance, and it hurt to move. 'Yes,' he replied. 'Thank you.'

The man nodded – evidently preoccupied with the scene of destruction before them.

'Awful,' he said, with some satisfaction. 'All that waste. Terrible shame.'

More people clustered to the scene now, chattering and pointing. Where had they all come from so quickly, and at this time of night? Some were gentlemen, out in pursuit of amusement of one sort or another. Others, less salubrious in appearance, might have been disgorged en masse from a nearby public house, eager to see the destruction.

There was a collective gasp – or a sigh of pleasure – as the flames spread, passing from the roof of the club to the next building in the street.

The man who had spoken to Mould before shouted, 'There's people still in there!'

There was more pointing and more shouting; some claimed they saw figures moving against the flames, others insisted that the place was empty. Insults were exchanged, but it was all quite amiable, though there might well be a scuffle before long. Some of them had clearly been drinking.

Mould heard glass break, then an explosion, a fierce exhalation of smoke and flame. The crowds moved backwards, calling out to one another – what a lot of heat, what a lot of noise. They were scared and delighted at once.

He must get to safety, he knew. But it was difficult to look away from the flames, and in spite of himself he watched, dazed and stupid, for a few minutes more as his hopes and Edmund's were destroyed before his eyes. The full extent of their disaster left him unnaturally calm.

He cast about for some plan, some solution, something to do now, and for the first time could think of nothing.

His journey home was long and miserable – a struggle to find a hansom in the rain, another battle not to humiliate himself by losing consciousness inside the cab, the final indignity of having to be helped out of the carriage by the cabman on arrival. The man looked at Mould's hurt arm and injured face, and pocketed his money and said nothing, not a word of interest or concern. Then he rattled off in his cab, and Mould was left alone.

It could not be long until dawn. This was one of the things he had always hated about his connection with the club. They had no regard for proper times and seasons; association with them threw off one's own sense of time, so that he would find himself collapsing into bed at dawn, exhausted and quite unable to sleep, or eating breakfast at seven in the evening. Years ago he had settled into a dull, continuous state of semi-tiredness, never quite exhausted, never fresh.

He unlocked the door with haste, limped inside. Climbing the stairs, he was afraid that he would fall, thought he saw a figure standing on the landing, peering at him through the bars of the bannister. One of the dead children.

Upstairs, his room was cold and slightly damp. He lit the gas, poured himself some brandy, and took the glass to the desk.

He did not like to look at his arm just yet. He sat at the desk, emptied and refilled his glass.

He felt his mind clearing. The brandy gave a little warmth, enough energy for him to realise that this stunned calmness would not last for ever.

Another moment, he thought. I shall take five minutes' more rest, then I shall do something. He was shivering.

Perhaps he ought to have left the club earlier, as Edmund had told him. But he had feared for his notes – what if the chit in the library had confused or destroyed his papers before Treadwell caught her? Of course, his care had profited him nothing. The books and photographs were all gone now – there had been no chance to save anything from the attic.

Worse still was the library. He had discovered Edmund there, covered in blood but mercifully uninjured. He seemed weary but composed – apparently unmoved by the chaos around them.

'Mould,' he said. 'I thought you went home. Are you here to save the books?'

The flames were growing fiercer; in a short time they would envelop the place. These beautiful volumes, the ivy-coloured bindings, their pages gilt- or black-edged – they would soon be gone. The glorious smell of the place, paper and damp, this was gone already.

Sitting in the quiet of his room, Mould could not forget what he had seen: the place beginning to burn, the pages curling languidly, like flowers blooming. The paper breathing out smoke like a departing ghost.

He had been seized with a desperate wish to rush to the shelves, pile books into his arms, fling them out of the window, somehow save as many as possible. But there was Edmund, motionless beside him. He did not appear to understand what was happening.

Mould had shouted at him – told him that they must flee. He had not seemed to hear.

He was still downstairs, Mould had thought. In his mind Edmund was standing over his brother's body. He had not been the same since coming out of the cellar.

Mould had taken Edmund by the shoulder, attempted to bring him to his senses, tried to direct him towards the door – and Edmund had caught his arm, held tight and twisted.

Mould's wrist blade fell away, leather tearing, and there was sudden, hideous pain. The bone was broken. Edmund pushed him away, sent him falling.

He didn't speak. Even then, it was as if he scarcely saw Mould at all.

By the time Mould had righted himself, Edmund was gone, and he was alone in the burning library.

The screaming had stopped. All he could hear was the noise of the fire. He might be the last one left alive inside.

Outside the library, he found the landing deserted. There was no time to reflect. He staggered downstairs – coughing and blinded with smoke – and made a desperate rush to the front door.

He saved himself by the slenderest of margins. A few minutes more, and the door would have been unreachable.

Edmund must have left the club before him. The stairs to the second floor had been impassable by the time Mould made his escape. Edmund would not have lingered.

Please let it be so, he thought now. Let me not have abandoned him to his death.

Ordinarily he would have taken his book and written something. He felt the loss of the diary afresh – his quiet friend, buried under Kensal Green. How many months' searching would it take to find it again?

He could not bring himself to move, even to pour more brandy or change his soiled clothes – until he became aware of a noise coming from downstairs. Someone was ringing the doorbell.

His window would not yield at first. He wrenched it open left-handed, with an effort that nearly sent him toppling over. He leaned out and stared down. Someone was waiting in the street below, half visible in the dawn light – a man, looking up at him.

'Edmund,' he said – a whisper; his throat was still dry and sore from the smoke.

Edmund's face was shadowed, too distant for Mould to read. But it scarcely mattered, for he was there, he was safe.

'Wait,' he said. 'I'll come down.'

On the doorstep, Edmund was as Mould had last seen him – though with a cut across his face that was already healing.

He looked at Mould, then at his arm, which he held protectively, close to his chest.

'Is it very bad?' he asked.

'It will mend,' Mould replied – club men were impatient of human weakness. Even Edmund would not understand what the injury meant. (He was still in the habit of doing this: separating Edmund from the rest of them, as if there were a crucial distinction.) 'Come in. Get out of the cold.'

Edmund stepped inside, shut the door behind him.

'Who got out?' Mould asked.

'Just Corvish. And Makeweight, of course.'

Mould struggled for composure. 'No one else?'

'No,' Edmund said. 'And the Alia are all dead, apparently. Stop that, Mould, it's ghastly.' He must have felt something of Mould's gathering despair, and he sounded rather sickened. Mould made an effort, forced his thoughts back into some kind of order.

'Was anything saved? Do you know?'

'There was that crowd. You know how the Quick are. I doubt they'll leave anything of value intact.'

'Ah.'

'I'll buy you more books. No need for the tragedy airs.'

It was dreadful, unnatural. He simply did not sound interested – not in the destruction of the club or in the failure of their hopes.

'The important thing is that Makeweight saw Norbury escape,' he went on. 'Howland was there. And a woman was with him, too – the sister, one presumes.'

'How could they have found a way out?'

'Paige helped them.'

'Paige?'

'Don't worry, Corvish went after him. He won't present us with any further difficulties. What matters is that we find Norbury before he manages to leave London.'

He was lost – there was nothing in him now but thoughts of revenge. Mould had believed that the night held no more horrors, that there was nothing left to lose. But now he saw that something of Edmund was gone – the fine mind, the dedication to a high ideal.

The pain of Mould's wrist was growing worse; his head ached. He leaned against the wall for support, ashamed of his weakness.

Edmund watched, and made no effort to assist him. 'I need your help,' he said. 'There's a job I need you to do.'

'I need a *doctor*, Edmund . . .'

'You won't for long.' In spite of the night's violence, he was clean, shirt and collar irreproachable. Not a mark, not a smudge of blood. He stood close to Mould, and Mould thought how easily Edmund might kill him and walk away without a trace of the crime on him.

'This will be a reward for you, as well. You've waited long enough.' He looked at Mould, and Mould imagined himself in Edmund's gaze – drab, dry, middle-aged, feeble. 'Maybe for too long. Your arm won't hurt you any more. Not as much, at least.'

'You're hungry. You won't be able to stop.'

'Of course I will. And this is what you want, isn't it? I promised you that I would be the one who did it.'

Mould faltered. 'I wanted . . . I always imagined that it would be you.'

'Well, then. Let me pay my debt.'

It was possible to say no. Even then he could have refused. But if he did refuse, Edmund might easily kill him – or perhaps press forwards without Mould's consent. They knew now that it was possible, and who was to thank for that but Mould?

In the end, he only said, 'All right. But please do it quickly.'

'Good,' Edmund said. 'Move your head – no, the other side. There. Try to stay still.'

Mould's life ended in a deplorable confusion, a distant knowledge that his knees were giving way, that he was slumping forwards with a cry of pain. Edmund was holding him up.

His last human thought was a pang at the lack of concern in Edmund's eyes. He looked a little bored. He was counting under his breath. Mould heard *one, two* – and that was all. The pain took him fiercely, quick like a lover.

Chapter Thirty-Six

She wanted to go home straight off, but Mrs P would have said, Don't. Think, girl. Wait a while. It seemed good advice, even if she was only pretending, so Liza didn't go back to Salmon Street until a few hours later. If there were any of the others left, perhaps they'd be there, too, by this time.

Liza's key – she was the only one of the kids allowed one – was still hanging round her neck on a bootlace. But she didn't need it in the end, because when she got back, the shop door was wide open.

She called out hello, but no one called back. And the place was messed up something awful. They hadn't left it like this. She remembered Agnes telling them to make sure everything was tidy before they went off. Someone else had been there, turning things over, looking. Someone from the club, probably. So she couldn't stay, not even here. She would wait a bit, to see if anyone else turned up, and then she would go.

Seemed odd, all the quiet at Salmon Street. She didn't much like it, she decided. There was nothing better to do while she waited, so Liza tidied the place, keeping an ear and an eye out for visitors, and when she finished it was dawn. She wasn't sure what to do next.

Then there was a knock at the door. Liza crept to the window, the only one left unpainted so you could see who was outside. She hoped that it might be Mrs P, come back and all right after all. But it was only Tom Brimstone.

'What d'you want?' Liza asked, when she opened the door.

'Mrs P about?' Brimstone smelled of blood and dirt all mixed together. Filthy old man, Lil called him.

'No,' Liza said.

'She dead?'

'Dunno. Maybe.'

'What about the rest?'

'Dunno.'

He looked past her, trying to see if she was lying or not.

'Ain't *none* of 'em come back?'

'Only me.'

'And 'ow'd you manage that, then, Miss Liza?'

'Ran.'

Tom Brimstone said, 'Well, lemme in, will you? I'm about done in.'

She let him in, grudgingly. He sat down at the table and took off his shoes, began to rub his feet, one at a time.

'Been walkin' for hours. Thought they was after me.'

'Most of 'em are dead. In the fire and that.'

'Plan worked, then. Sort of.' He raised a foot to his face and sniffed, like he was smelling a fish to see if it was fresh or not. It was one of his nasty ways. 'We're ruined, you know. If Mrs P's gone.' He lowered his foot. Must be wet through to his socks, because there was a hole in the sole of his shoe – a great big one.

'She might not be gone.'

'She'd be back by now,' Brimstone said. 'No, they've done for 'er. An' now we're fucking *ruined.*' He put his shoes back on, brought out a flask he always carried – Liza had seen it before, a shiny thing made of pewter that he must've pinched from somewhere or other. It had brandy in it – brandy went the best with blood, Gil had told her once, if you can get it.

'You got a glass?' Brimstone asked, opening his flask.

She brought him one, and he bared his wrist – grimy enough, too – and sliced one of his nails quick across, drawing blood. It was a neat trick. Brimstone let blood drip into the glass, red like Liza remembered cherries, pretty little beads rolling down the inside of the glass. He poured in a bit of brandy, then a bit more, sloshing it inside the glass to mix with the blood.

'Why?' Liza said, when he'd finished this business and was drinking.

'Why what?'

'Why're we fucking ruined?'

'Language, Miss.' Brimstone wheezed to himself. He wheezed when he was trying to be nasty, it was how he pretended to laugh.

'Why, though?'

Brimstone stopped wheezing. 'She were something, Mrs P. You know we 'ad words every so often an' she'd sling me out of here an' tell me not to come back.'

Liza sniggered, to pay him back for wheezing at her. She remembered when Mrs P threw Brimstone out ten years back, and hadn't he looked stupid, chucked out of the house on his arse.

Brimstone said, 'You shut up, you silly slut.'

She made a face at him, but he didn't notice. He was already talking again. Fond of his own voice, that was Brimstone all over.

'But I 'ad respect for that woman, all the same. It were Mrs Price that kept us safe, you know. They didn't give us as much grief after she came along, 'cause they was scared. 'Cause she was *organised*.

They weren't used to that from our sort. An' she planned things, like how she planned yesterday.'

'But it went wrong,' Liza said.

'Aye. An' now we're finished.'

'What'll happen?'

'Well, p'raps with the fire an' all, there won't be any more club for a while. But there won't be any more of this, neither.' And he waved his hand round at Salmon Street, at the little room that Liza had just put in order. 'It'll be 'ow it was before.' Agnes said once that Tom Brimstone had been undid longer than any of the rest and remembered a lot of things. And wherever he went, his memories nipped him like fleas. 'We'll manage, mind, but it won't be the same.' He paused. 'You got 'alf a crown for an old man?'

'No.'

He looked about him. He was looking for where Mrs P kept the money hid.

'Ain't your money,' Liza said.

'It ain't yours, neither.'

'Yes, it is. Her and me was going to be *partners*. So there.'

Brimstone wheezed and swore, and then he stood up and put his flask away and went to the door.

'What about the shop an' all that?' Liza asked.

He shrugged, mean-looking. 'Ruined. An' that's an end of it.'

'But—' No point in arguing, because he'd already stalked out, letting the door slam, leaving a stink of filth behind him.

She thought of swearing or throwing something at the door, but she'd just tidied and this was Mrs P's house still, and Mrs P hadn't liked language.

It was quiet as anything, with Brimstone gone. It wasn't so much that she missed the others, only that she didn't much like being the only one left. And she was tired and cold, and there was already horrible grey light outside. She could feel it even through the black-painted windows. There was paper pasted over the paint to keep as much light out as possible. Lil and Agnes had stuck up pictures out of a magazine, beautiful ladies in the latest fashions, with pink faces and dainty waists. Mrs P had added a picture of the queen, because she'd always liked her. It would all peel off before long.

She lit the fire. Mrs P had left it laid, ready for when they got back. She'd only ever let Liza know where the matches were kept. Liza sat close to the flames, on the rag rug that Agnes had made. Whenever they had dinner at home and there were clothes left over that were good, Mrs P would sell those. When the clothes weren't worth selling, Agnes would keep them, rip them up for dusters, or make them into rag rugs, and soon there was one in every room.

Liza lay down, though Mrs P had always said, Don't lie in front of the fire – if a coal rolls out, you'll catch alight. She thought now it might be nice, in a way. They'd had hot bricks when she was small and still Quick, when she'd shared a bed with her sisters and brother. The brick was wrapped in an old petticoat, and you had to fight on cold nights, kick the other feet away, if you wanted to touch it at all. It burned your toes but in a nice way.

Now she curled up, as close to the fire as she dared. She cried a bit then, like she was a silly slut just like Brimstone had said, and then she went to sleep.

When she woke again, the fire was dead and it was dusk. She got up, and brushed down her dress, and tidied her hair. Mrs P or Lil or Agnes would plait it usually, but she could do it herself well enough. Her hands and face were still bloody and sticky, though she'd licked off all that she could. Her dress was bloody, too – it was just as well she'd worn her oldest, the one she'd worn when she first met Mrs P. It was all patched up and shabby now, but she'd never throw it out. Agnes said we all keep things like that. There was Mrs P and her bonnet, or Gil and that beaver hat of his.

She went out back to the pump and got some water. Then she

went into the kitchen and washed herself off as much as she could, shivering under the cold water. Imagine being plunged into it all the way, Nick used to say. Horrible, wouldn't it be? Not if it were warm, Sally would always say. Imagine if it was *boiling*, think how nice it would be then.

She alone knew the secret of the money box. It was Mrs P's money, though not all of it, just the emergency hoard – banknotes and goblins, which was what Gil called sovereigns, and shillings, too, every sort of money you could want. It lived under the sink, in a tin box with bright red dragons on it, which used to have tea inside. It was the size of the church Bibles that Liza remembered from when she was very small: she'd thought that perhaps if you were bad, they'd crack you over the head with one and down you'd go, stone dead. She'd never seen the box opened. It didn't rattle when she picked it up. Inside was just paper – notes, which were good, easier to carry, though she'd have to be careful spending them, because people would ask how would a chit like her get banknotes.

She put on a clean dress and took Sally's good shoes, the leather ones she'd been saving. They were a bit small, but they took the cold off her feet, that was something. And she took her nice blue coat.

Outside, it was dark enough. She would manage very well. She went out, and locked the door, and hung the key around her neck. Never could tell, she might come back one day.

• • •

She began to wander, almost aimless, through the city. If there were any of the club about, she didn't see them. There were other ones of her sort, but they gave her a wide berth. Something about what had happened must have got out – they were all frightened, suspicious. One time she was chased by a couple of louts, couldn't have been dead more than ten years between them. They threw stones and yelled, You're Mrs Price's girl, ain't you? Where's she gone to, eh, and where's her money?

She hoarded the money carefully, because it would have to last. But it was good to pay for a bed every so often when it got cold. There were places you could sleep, where you paid for a bed in with a lot of others, thirty Quick to a room. They made a racket, the noise of their thoughts and the stink of them so bad at times that she thought she'd kill them all or go mad with it, but there was nothing else to be done, she'd be miserable out there in the cold.

Most of them looked at her oddly on account of her being young, but they had sense enough to leave her alone and not touch the box she carried, though Nick had always said they were dangerous places, many lodging houses, the poor ones fenced stuff, often. No one fussed much in these places if you slipped over to someone else's bed in the night and took a sip or two – not enough to leave a body, nothing that drew attention.

There was one woman she ran into in a place on Lower Keat Street, though, who asked Liza for it. She had a rattish face, all bones, jerking like a puppet when she moved. And her eyes were horrible, all sad. Her thoughts made Liza ill, but she'd said, Please, please take it. Probably there was something wrong with her. Liza didn't much care – it was a meal. It was a kindness, too – like what the Seraph would do.

She'd slipped away and not gone back to that place, in case they knew her. Too kind for her own good, she was.

One time, years later – much later – she was in Hyde Park, watching the big crowds gathered, the troops going by. Some war or other had just finished, Liza'd heard, though nobody seemed able to explain it so it made sense, and none of the undid she ran into cared or understood much more than she did. She'd been standing, watching, because, though the crowd frightened her, you could take a bite and slip away without being seen, and it was much more convenient when you were only one. She was watching the crowd when she thought she saw Lamby Gil, opposite side of the parade, watching her. He was grey and sunken, not as cheerful, almost nervous. But she looked again and it wasn't him at all, not even one of the undid. She'd started seeing people like that – Gil or Mrs P or Nick or Sally, once even One-Ear. She kept a lookout for the club men – especially for Makeweight, because of what he'd done to Mrs P – but she never saw any of them. People said they were all dead or scattered. Undid in London weren't what they used to be.

The city wasn't what it used to be, either. There were streets gone – sometimes people forgot that they'd ever been there at all. Salmon Street was pulled down to make way for a new road with houses. There were Quick families living there now, clerks and their wives where Liza and the others had been. It won't never stop, she thought, this changing and changing. There's only me left.

She thought it would be good to find a place to hide, where there might be others like her. She hadn't had anyone to play with since the club: there was no Nick or Sally or even One-Ear left.

Bit by bit, she found that she didn't like to wander as far. Stuff kept happening, and once or twice she got lost. One of those big rushing motor buses nearly hit her, and a man *laughed*.

She followed him a long way afterwards, planning to pay him back for that. How could anyone be so stupid, to laugh at one of the undid. She followed him down into the Underground. She'd been a few times – it was handy having somewhere out of the sun like that, it was almost as good as the Adelphi Arches had been, back in their day. Though you had to be careful because a couple of the stations had their own undid and didn't like you pushing in on their bit of the line.

Her man went into Down Street station – it was quiet at that time of night, and Liza seized on him easily as he waited for the train. Not much blood in him, though enough booze to make her giddy, and it was a quick thing to finish him off and push him forwards onto the tracks. He fell with a slumpy thud, forwards on his face. The train would come and that would be him dealt with; they'd never notice the marks she'd left once he'd been squashed open under the wheels.

She had a thought: Well, isn't this a good place to stay? Where could be better?

It was warm enough, and there was no sun, and the Quick kept coming and going, busy and heedless.

She stayed, and after a while she made friends – kids who'd wandered away from their parents or nurses. They learned quickly, and there were games now – they could play forever, they would never get old. Perhaps one day she would go up again, to see if Makeweight was still around, pay him out for what he'd done to Mrs P. For now it was best to wait.

She heard that Down Street got a name – not as many people used it any more. It didn't matter, really, you could race between stations, skidding along the tracks, if you fancied a change. The trains went faster than she could run, but they took longer to speed up. It was a game, sort of. If you were slow, you'd be killed. Sometimes Liza wondered what that would feel like.

Then one day Down Street station was closed. They were happier there afterwards – there was no need to hide amongst the Quick, and it was quiet and warm. There were other places to go, if you wanted. There was Brompton Road station, dead like Down Street. Or the live stations, bustling with the Quick. Accidents here and there didn't attract much notice.

She looked out for Makeweight, but she never saw him. She didn't see any of the others, either. She didn't know if the club were still going, even. There weren't many except Liza's gang and a few wanderers, and Liza was the boss of the ones that were left. She decided she would stay here and have fun. And she stayed underground for a long time.

Chapter Thirty-Seven

W hen they reached Regent Street, they stopped running. They were filthy and gasping from the smoke; Howland had to lean against Charlotte's shoulder to stay upright. James was shaking, face set in a blank blind look.

Rafferty inspected them one by one – giving James a particularly careful stare – and put his pipe away. 'Langham, is it?'

'Yes,' Charlotte replied.

'No,' said Howland.

'Of course we must go back. Your leg—'

'It's not that bad. They'll catch up with us if we stop.' He caught his breath in pain. 'We've got to keep going.'

'All right.' She turned to Rafferty. 'Please keep driving.'

'What?'

'We want you to keep driving, please. Anywhere, just away from here. Change direction as often as you can.'

He sighed. 'Get in, then.' Under his breath, he muttered a curse on his own folly.

She pushed James gently forwards, towards the four-wheeler.

'Quick, James.' It was as if she could still boss him about, as if they were children again. 'We have to go.'

At first he did not move, and she was afraid he would refuse – but then he did as she told him, climbing inside without meeting her eyes. She had an absurd longing to take him by the shoulders and shake him, to make him see that it was *her*, that she was here now to take care of him. Inside the carriage, he turned his face to the window.

Even as the carriage started to move, Charlotte saw a man pass them – tall and thin, a smear of ash on his right temple. It was Corvish. James was leaning forwards in his seat, watching the man without moving, poised in a desperate kind of alertness.

Corvish turned, as if sensing their dismay. He hastened towards the carriage – but Rafferty had seen him, thanks be, and had already forced the horse into a trot. They moved away with a rattle of windows and a clatter of hooves. Rafferty took them swiftly down two streets, into a busier part of town.

Charlotte opened the window a little way, called out to Rafferty: 'We need to keep moving as quickly as possible – there may be others.'

Rafferty muttered some response – perhaps that he knew what was what without Charlotte's interference. She closed the window again.

'What happened to him?' Howland asked suddenly. 'The man who helped us?'

'I don't know,' Charlotte said. He had vanished as soon as they got out of the club, leaving so quietly that she had not seen him go. There had been no chance to thank him.

For a while they drove in silence. James, sitting beside her, was so still that he might have been asleep, but his eyes were open, staring into the darkened streets. Perhaps the blood she gave him had not been enough to bring him back to full strength. She was glad of the fact. It had occurred to her that she had left the cruel silver chains lying on the floor in the club, and there was little else she had to hand that would allow her to restrain him, if it were necessary. Howland had closed his eyes. He was taut and still with pain.

Her handbag was on the seat where she had left it hours before. The carpetbag was in the carriage, too. Blessing the foresight which had led her to leave it where she could reach it, rather than strapped to the roof with the other luggage, she opened the carpetbag and began searching for the water. It was difficult to make out the bag's contents in the uncertain light flaring into the carriage from the streetlamps they passed. Finally she was obliged to kneel on the floor between the seats.

She heard James move then – he had turned towards her.

'Sit still,' she said, calm as one could sometimes be at the very worst moments. 'Rest yourself. We'll be going home soon.'

He said nothing but did not move again, and she turned her attention back to the carpetbag. Her hands were feeble, unsteady; it was difficult to sort through the bag's contents.

'Find anything?' Howland muttered.

'Brandy, and water.' A sudden sway of the carriage almost caused her to lose her balance and drop both bottles. She stood up with difficulty and shifted to Howland's side. 'Here,' she said. She raised the bottle to his mouth and helped him to drink a little of the brandy, then some water.

The next thing was the leg, she thought. Her hands were dirty – she wiped them as best she could on a handkerchief soaked with brandy. Then she knelt and unwrapped the makeshift bandage gently. It was soaking with blood.

She bit her lip, kept her hands steady. Her distress would not help him. In the fleeting light of the streetlamps, she could make out a bloody graze, like a scarlet finger daub of paint. She could not tell how deep the damage went. The bleeding had not yet stopped. She wiped the dried blood away, cleaned the wound as best she could. Then she bound it with clean bandages.

Howland's eyes were closed, and he had a feverish look she

did not like. He seemed to be trying to stay still, but the pain clearly made rest impossible.

'We should stop,' she said. 'Find a doctor—'

'No. Got to keep going. Got to get out.'

Across the carriage, James was staring at the bloodied red scarf, lying on the floor where Charlotte had dropped it.

'Please don't,' she said. 'Please, James. Just a little while longer—'

With alarming suddenness, he reached out and snatched the scarf, then collapsed back into his seat. She averted her eyes.

'Rest,' she told Howland softly. 'Or I'll have Rafferty drive us straight to the hospital.'

He seemed to smile, briefly, at that, and he did close his eyes. She saw the pain go out of his face – he had fainted.

James held the scarf to his mouth. She looked to the window, the lights flashing by. The world seemed shrunk to the carriage, the three of them, this one night.

She said, 'We'll get the train as soon as we can, we'll be back in Yorkshire soon, and then I can take care of you. It should be all right. Don't you think?'

She was so tired now and sickeningly aware of Howland's blood on her hands, and James had let the scarf fall onto the floor of the carriage.

She kept talking, as one talked to distract a child from pain or fear. 'You haven't been home for a while, have you? It's spring now, of course. The cherry tree's out. And there are daffodils.' James stirred, and she spoke louder. 'But you never liked daffodils, did you? They used to make you sneeze.'

He moved to stand up, and she said more sharply, 'No, James, not yet. We're not there. It won't be long now.'

She saw his short struggle. After a pause, he lowered his head. The energy went out of him. He had conquered himself, at least for a time.

'It'll be all right,' she repeated. 'We'll get back. You'll be all right.'

'Keep telling me,' he said.

So she kept talking. She told him how it was once – the green-mossed garden statues, the great copper beech tree they had both loved, the shadows of the clouds moving over the wide untended lawns. She told him about the strange old world they had shared – the dust-sheeted furniture, the quiet welcoming library. She told him how they had sat out on summer evenings, barefoot on the terrace, and watched the sun set over the gardens. She told him how the air smelled green in spring, and smoke-grey in autumn, how on April mornings the mists would lift slowly, leaving a blue haze behind.

She talked, gripping Howland's hand tightly, and James closed his eyes and sat and listened.

Finally she lapsed into silence, hoping that the danger had passed.

James opened his eyes but did not stir. Together they stared through the window and watched London move past them, watched the light return to the city.

At last he spoke, in the same dull voice he had used in the club. 'You should have left me.'

After that he was silent again. He bit down on his hand, so hard that it ought to have drawn blood.

The streets were still full of fog when they finally arrived at King's Cross. Morning was coming on slowly, pallid and reluctant.

She woke Howland as gently as she could. She was relieved to see his eyes open. Outside, King's Cross was waking, as well. The same rush that had previously alarmed her was now welcome: these people were so alive and so utterly uninterested in them. It was a relief to see life going on as usual. That's the thing with horrors, she thought: they reconcile one to the ordinary. She would never complain of boredom again.

Rafferty helped them out of the carriage without being asked, got down the luggage, and nodded as Charlotte thanked him.

When she paid him, he blinked at the amount – generous, even considering all he had done.

He handed her the carpetbag – she had almost forgotten it – and drove away without another word.

'Come on,' she said to James. 'Stay close.'

During their rush from the booking office to the train, there was little time to reflect. Only when they had gained the privacy of their first-class compartment could she think at leisure again. Even then it was impossible to feel at ease. There were three minutes left until the train departed. Charlotte sat at the carriage door, fearful of other travellers choosing their compartment or of stealthy watchers in the crowd. They might take their opportunity, she thought, to clamber onto the train as it departed. But though she watched anxiously, starting at every approaching footstep, no one else came to their compartment.

There was a whistle – so loud that it hurt her ears – and at last the train began to move; she saw smoke drifting past the window. She imagined she heard shouts as they departed – a commotion on the platform, someone calling loudly. But the station was now behind them, they were safe.

Distantly, she realised that she was close to tears, and she was angry with herself, because it was not the time. She couldn't afford to rest yet. There was James, hunched in one corner of the carriage, staring at her as if she were a stranger. There was Howland, sitting across from her. In the morning light he looked dreadful, worse even than he had on the first evening they'd met, in Wych Street.

'We got away,' Howland muttered.

'Yes. We can rest now.'

The train was gathering speed; soon they would be out of London entirely. It seemed a long time since she had seen fields. It would be a pleasant day; the sunlight was already warming the carriage. James had shifted away. She thought of lowering the blind, then thought that it might be prudent to allow the light in. It would never feel decent, thinking of James in such a fashion.

'James,' she said. He didn't look at her. 'James, I'm going to see if I can do anything more for Mr Howland. There'll be blood. Can you stand it?'

He turned to stare at her.

'You mustn't hurt him. Do you understand?'

She hadn't expected a reply, but after a struggle, he spoke: 'Don't let me hurt anyone else.'

'I won't.' If only she were not such a coward, she would embrace him. 'It'll be all right,' she said. 'Just don't look.'

He turned away. Charlotte moved across to Howland, giving him some more brandy and attending to his wound. When this was done, he allowed her to clean his face, wipe the soot away. He had a fever.

Charlotte drenched the handkerchief in the last of the cold water, held it to his forehead, and made him lie back and try to rest.

She was exhausted, her mouth was dry and foul with thirst, and the motion of the carriage made her feel nauseous. She did not close her eyes. She was so tired that she did not trust herself even to blink without falling asleep. There was country outside their window now. She sat and watched the empty green and brown-gold fields.

Perhaps she slipped into a half dream in spite of herself, for the arrival at York was a shock. She had to struggle to get them all out of the carriage in good time.

To her relief, James followed her without resistance, and she was able to leave the bags to the porter and give her attention to Howland, whose fever was worse.

The station seemed altered, though everything was exactly the same as it had been a few days ago – the high arching roof, the cold gusts of wind, the curve of the platform, which hid the departing train from sight. So much more space than in London, she thought. Far fewer people to jostle and stare. There was sunlight coming through the glass.

'Always planned to visit . . .' Howland mumbled.

He must be looked after immediately. Aiskew would be too far – the journey was more than five miles. Better to get him to a doctor first of all.

The station was so busy at this hour. It was madness to keep James here, in public, where he might so easily lose his self-control.

'James,' she said, 'we're going home, but we must take Mr Howland to the doctor first. And if you need – if you're hungry then, I'll make it all right. Do you understand?'

Once more would hardly hurt. If it would keep him from attacking an innocent stranger or Howland – so weak, and still smelling of blood – it was worth the sacrifice.

'Can you wait until then?' she asked. 'Can you wait without hurting anyone?'

James nodded.

'Good,' she said. 'Come on.'

Later she would wonder how she managed it, getting them all to the doctor's office. Necessity had made her bold and full of purpose – she had asked questions, given tips, hired a carriage (Howland being too weak for the tram), somehow got them there without mishap.

She had to help Howland out of the carriage. 'Not much further,' she said. 'We can wait inside.'

But he shook his head. 'You've got to stay with him.'

'I can't leave you here,' she said.

'I'll do well enough. Go on. Get him safe.'

He was right, she saw. 'I'll be back soon,' she told him. 'Do what they tell you.'

'Of course. Be careful.'

She turned away – best not to look back at him – and returned to the carriage, disliking herself. James was still waiting, watching listlessly out of the window.

'Are you all right?' she asked.

He looked at her. 'Where are we?'

'York,' she replied. 'Don't you remember? We were here long ago. Mrs Chickering took us to the Minster, and then we had tea. Look, we're going by now, you can see—'

'Where are we going?'

'Home. Do you feel any better?' He already looked better, she thought. A little colour had come into his face.

He said, 'Why did you bring me here?'

'To be safe.'

'For how long?'

'I don't know. Until you can get well.'

'I need something. You said.'

'I know.'

She let him take what he wanted – submitting quietly, staring away, watching the Ouse pass the window, the Minster far off in the distance. He was quick this time; in a minute or so he was done.

'They'll come after me,' he said. Already he looked more alert. 'If any of them are left.'

'Then we'll hide.'

'Like we used to.'

'Yes.'

She moved to take his hand, then realised that he had shifted away.

• • •

East Lodge, when they reached it at last, was just as she had left it – empty, clean and neat. It was just after noon; there were hours of sunlight left. She took James upstairs to his bedroom, which had been his ever since they had moved to East Lodge with Mrs

Chickering. Their great-aunt had always kept it ready; she liked to think that James could return at any time. Somewhere a fly was buzzing. Otherwise it was quiet. James stood and looked at Charlotte until she told him to lie down on the bed and rest. He obeyed her without comment, without removing his coat or shoes.

Then she went into the bathroom, washed herself, scoured her hands and face, scraped the London dirt out from under her fingernails. She put on a clean dress and got some water to drink. It was unnatural that she did not feel hungry, she thought. It had been a long time since her last proper meal.

She was cold in her clean things, and felt weaker, more tired than she had before. She went to the dining room, retrieved Adeline and Shadwell's book from her luggage, and spread it out on the table, read through again what they had written.

There was no sound from upstairs. She kept breaking off at intervals as she read, expecting to hear his footsteps. Was it a self-punishment, this silent passivity of his? Or had she managed what she intended, and given him just enough blood to keep him alive?

After a quarter of an hour, she felt that she understood most of what she had read. She found the back of an envelope, made notes. Reduced to the practicalities, the process read almost like a recipe – *first, catch your fiend*. Don't cry now, she told herself.

She made some tea. Because it seemed best to eat, even though the thought repelled her, she buttered some stale bread and put it onto a plate. She ate alone in the dining room, and when she was finished she went upstairs to James's bedroom, watched him sleep for a little while.

When an hour or so had passed, she went downstairs again and began her preparations.

• • •

When she went to fetch him, James was sitting on the bed, waiting for her.

'Let's go and see the library,' she said.

He had lost his gloves and hat in London – he let her find new ones for him, and sat, unmoving, as she put them on for him. He did not ask her why she carried the carpetbag with her.

They went to the house the old way, through the grounds. The house was hidden until they crossed the yew walk, the arbour now quite overgrown.

She had the key to the French windows of the library; there was no need to struggle through the darkened house. Dust every-where – she could see her footprints, left from her earlier visits. She was the only person who had been in this room for some time.

James followed her inside obediently. He did not look about him but went where she led. He did not seem to recognise the place at all.

'Do you remember?' she asked. The door to the priest hole opened smoothly, though no one had used it for a long time. Inside, there were still dusters, left there long ago.

She took one of them, wiped away at the floor. Now he could sit down. She knelt beside him and explained what she was about to do. She did not know how much he heard or understood, but she could not do it without telling him first. She did not want him to think her needlessly cruel.

There was the holy water and a hypodermic, and with these it was not too difficult to subdue him. He was still weak. Beyond this, perhaps he was doing his best not to resist.

She took the knife to his wrist and cut him. At first she could not bear to press down hard enough. *The blood must fall onto the floor*, the book said, *the way must be sealed shut with blood.* There was little enough blood left in him to lose. He stirred as the blade touched his skin but did not move or cry out. *You will be obliged to make the incision a number of times*, the book said, *due to the accelerated healing which is characteristic of the un-dead*.

He did heal, the skin paling over before her eyes, and she cut him again, and once more, and let him bleed until there was no blood left in him. She had no hand free to wipe her eyes, and her tears fell on the floor between their feet, splashing onto his shoes.

Then she took the hammer and the two long iron nails and drove one through each of his feet.

The old hiding place was a good one – she had thought about this; she had wanted him to be as safe as possible. He would be warm and dry, and hidden from anyone who might come searching. She told him that he would be safe, he would be able to sleep until she returned to make him better, and she would come back soon, this was a promise.

'The next thing you know, I'll be here again,' she said. She had always tried not to lie to him. She hoped he would believe her now. She told him to wait where he would be safe.

He was too weak to move away from her or to show any repugnance as she touched his hands, put his gloves and hat back on, and rolled down his sleeves to hide the marks she had made. She kissed his forehead, and closed his eyes, and scattered salt at his feet as the book dictated. Then she closed him in.

Chapter Thirty-Eight

The leg arrived in August – sent up from London, from a specialist who made such things. It was willow wood and steel, fastened with a leather harness, the best that could be had at such short notice.

'Better than the chair, anyway,' Arthur said. They had both hated the chair, its creaking heaviness, the way it jolted at the slightest provocation.

Charlotte waited outside Arthur's room – the drawing-room, where a bed had been set up – whilst the doctor showed him how the leg was managed, helped him dress again. She had offered to help, but he had told her he would rather she did not watch.

When the doctor was gone, she went in. Arthur was sitting on the bed – bright-eyed, trying to smile.

'Feels like I'm wearing armour,' he said.

'I suppose it must,' Charlotte replied.

'Please don't cry.'

'I'm not crying.'

'Shall I stand up? Give it a try?'

She was about to move to help him – but he had leaned forwards already, begun to push himself upright.

'There.' He stood, cautiously balanced, supporting himself against the chest of drawers. 'How's that?'

'Good,' she said.

He tried another step. 'I had an uncle lost a leg in the Civil War. More proud of it than anything. He'd tell us children all about it. Kept the cannonball that did it – it was big as a grapefruit. They had no chloroform left, he always said, so—'

'Don't.'

'I'm sorry.'

'How does it feel? Does it hurt to move?'

He stretched gingerly. 'Well, this is all right for the time being. Not as heavy as I thought. But, you know, I think I'll get a new one made when I'm home.'

It was only natural for him to talk about home like that, she thought. There was no reason for him to remain in Aiskew now that he was well again.

'You think you'll get a better one back there?' she asked.

'Most likely. My uncle always said, when it comes to legs, buy American.'

She smiled in spite of herself.

'That's better,' he said.

It was an inexpressible relief to see him stand again. In spite of the doctor from York, in spite of the surgeon who had cut Arthur up – there being no help for it, the blood poisoning having progressed too far – she had been afraid for a while that he would die. And it would have been her fault if he had: she ought to have realised sooner that his condition had become serious. The doctor said that he had been remarkably unlucky to have been infected – and asked a number of difficult questions about where, precisely, he had sustained the injury.

Guilty and anxious, she had nursed him, washed his wound, brought him food and made him eat. She had seen him numb, confused with fever, hardly understanding what had happened to him. He had been angry later – the injustice, the dreadful bad luck of it. She had watched him suffer and had done what she could.

At Arthur's worst point, Charlotte had spoken desperately, anxious to make him understand. Exhausted and upset, she was not sure what she had said to him, perhaps that he was still himself, still important, still *necessary* – that she could not bear this place without him.

He was in pain a great deal of the time. He felt as if the lost leg were still there, he told her – sometimes it hurt. Other times it was only an itch, a sensation of hot or cold or of being wrapped up in cotton.

When he could go outside again, she brought him into the garden of East Lodge and let him sit in the sunlight. And when he was confident with the new limb, she made him walk about, counting each step. He was still tentative with it, not putting all his faith in the strength of the wood. He walked with a struggle, left shoulder higher than the right. When he was tired they sat down on the garden bench.

He looked around at the trees, the roses she loved and worried over. She thought he might be in pain but refusing to tell her, and to distract him she recited the names of the different apple trees – Golden Pippin, Court of Wick, Northern Spy. When he asked her about the roses, she told him their names, too – Gloire de Dijon, Common Moss, Félicité-Perpétue.

'It's nice out here,' he said.

'A bit overgrown,' she replied. 'I've been neglecting it.'

'Do you look after it all?'

'I do most of it. Spudding, weeding, that sort of thing. Or I used to.'

It was untidy, true, but not half as bad as the hall grounds proper, Charlotte told him, which were as wild as you could wish for, wilder than anyone could wish for, in fact. Some of the paths through the woods that she had walked with James were now entirely grown over.

'What'll happen to it now?' Arthur asked.

'I don't know.' What could happen to it now? 'You could see the rest of it, if you like. You can't even see the hall from here. We could take a walk, when you're better.'

'I think I'm as *better* as I'll ever get.'

She did not know what to say. He was lucid now, not drugged or confused with pain, and she did not have the right words.

'Don't worry,' he said, 'I'm all right.'

'It was a cruel thing to happen. But I hope you don't feel . . . I don't know . . . less than you were.'

'Well, strictly speaking, I *am* less.'

'You'll be strong again. You'll feel like yourself soon.' She hated to see him making that sad attempt at a smile.

'Shame about my good looks, that's all.'

If he did not know that he was still a man to be looked at with pleasure, the kind of man that women would glance at before turning to one another with smiles that said, *My dear, I know* – well, if he did not know that, then she could hardly enlighten him.

'Shall I read to you?' she said. 'You could sit on the bench and rest.'

'All right. Have you got anything light?'

'Lots of things.' She had carried out a stack of newspapers and magazines – some she had bought herself, others had been left behind by one of Mrs Chickering's nurses. She had got into the habit of reading to him when he was in pain or could not sleep.

Now she read pieces here and there, through the first few magazines that came to hand – announcements of engagements and divorces and deaths, the doings of the aristocracy, fashion notes (neither of them much cared for the new styles of sleeves that were coming in), a long interview with a celebrated actress. Howland let her talk and did not interrupt; she was not even sure if he was listening.

'. . . Mr and Mrs Kendal share the same opinion of America – it is the land of today, the land of the future,' she read. She laid down the magazine. 'What do you think of that?'

'You're going away soon, aren't you?' he said. 'To look for a cure.'

She was not startled. She had got used to him asking things abruptly.

'Eventually I will. But not until you're better.'

'I want to go with you.'

'Well, you can't.'

'Why not? You don't think I'll be any use?'

'Of course it isn't that. But you must go home. Your family will be worried.' And she picked up another paper. 'It says here that Lady Colin Campbell is the only woman in London who has her feet manicured. How do you think they found *that* out?'

'Let me come with you. I can help you, even now.' He was fighting bitterness off, she saw. She had seen him make this struggle daily, for weeks. 'We could be brother and sister again,' he suggested.

'Absolutely not.'

'Or married.'

She said nothing.

'We could be, you know.'

'You mean another pretence?'

'No.'

She was sitting close to him – out of necessity, for the bench was not large (though picturesque, everyone always said) – and now he seemed everywhere she looked. Even if she gazed straight ahead he was there, a warm solid presence in the periphery.

'We could be good friends,' he said. 'We could take care of each other.'

He took her hand, and somehow as he did so the papers piled

between were knocked over, caught in the breeze and scattered over the garden.

'Oh. Sorry,' he said 'Sorry—'

And now she was apologising, too, and telling him to stay sitting down. He would not listen, and together they chased magazines over the neat garden, and when most of the papers had been collected again, they both sat down on the bench, breathless.

'That was my fault,' Howland said. He looked better for the exercise, she thought – his colour had come back.

A newspaper had been caught by the breeze and snagged in the branches of one of the horse chestnut trees beyond the garden. It flapped about cheerfully, like a flag.

'I'm serious, you know.'

Charlotte could see the changes in his face when he stopped smiling. He was still pale, still ill.

'It's not a good idea.'

'Why not?'

'In a few months you'll see why. You can go home and get better. This will seem a long time ago.' He could marry a million-aire's daughter – born in New York and dressed in Paris – and he would be happy. 'I'm grateful, but there's no need for you to do this. I will manage.'

'I know you'll manage. But let me help. We don't have to make big promises, we don't have to make claims on each other. I don't feel as if I have any romance left in me right now, and I guess you feel the same. I won't ask you for anything but to carry on as we are. To be friends. You understand?'

'Yes.'

'I just think we should stay together. It's safer, for one thing.'

Following their escape, she had privately searched each fresh newspaper for some mention of the club, but there had been hardly any notice taken of the fire beyond a few terse announce-ments. Most of the street had been saved, but the club building itself was quite demolished. It seemed unnatural to Charlotte that such a great disaster should attract so little remark. She could only suppose that the club's influence still held. Corvish had escaped: there might be others. But thus far they had seen no sign of them. Perhaps their luck would continue.

'There are other things, too,' Howland went on. 'Shadwell said they go mad, some of the people who've seen what we've seen. We've only got each other to talk to.'

'But—'

'Look, would you *like* me with you?'

'Of course,' Charlotte said. This was hardly the question. He refused – or was really not able – to understand what it meant, his undeserved kindness, how heavy this obligation would be, if she accepted.

'Well, then.' He seemed pleased. 'That's the main thing. I don't want to – what I mean is, if you want me to promise to set you free if it goes badly, whatever you like, I'll swear to it. I'll sign anything you like – you'd always be able to do as you pleased. I don't want to make things more difficult for you. I just think it's a good idea.'

He was considering how things might go wrong, she thought. The disposing of bodies and worldly possessions. He wanted to look after her, to have a right to protect her, and for her not to lie unclaimed and uncared for if her quest should miscarry.

It was a kind plan, but the objections were so manifold that it was difficult to know which one to voice first. Finally Charlotte asked, 'What would your mother say?'

'She'll say a thing or two, mostly likely. She'd like you in the end, though.' He shrugged. 'Just think about it, won't you?'

'Very well,' she said. 'Yes.'

'You'll consider it? Really? Well, good. Take as long as you need to decide, of course.'

Then he evidently saw from her face that she had not meant that at all, and that *yes* was her final answer. 'Oh, I see. Good.'

He sounded gratified, surprised – and beneath she heard relief.

Perhaps he feared the loneliness of secrecy as much as she did. It would be a heavy thing, after all, to carry the memories of the past few months alone.

· · ·

A little while afterwards, Arthur suggested a last visit to Aiskew Hall. She had agreed. But now, as they drew closer to the house, she became more reluctant. She almost asked him to turn back.

'It was prettier when we lived here,' she told him, endeavouring to sound calm. 'Everything's gone so wild . . .'

'It's pretty now,' said Arthur. 'In its way.'

'We don't have to do this now, you know. It doesn't have to be today. And it isn't as if he would hear us.'

'But could you go away without going back? One last time?'

'No.'

They were to leave in three days. Their passage to France was booked; they had successfully completed the lengthy and complex business of arranging a secret wedding. They had travelled as far as the coast to escape any possibility of gossip. The ceremony took place in a hurry, and later Charlotte remembered only a few clear details of the day – the gulls calling from outside the church, the dark-blue clouds massing over the harbour. They walked on the beach and collected shells, and went back to Aiskew with their pockets lined with sand. Afterwards Arthur was exactly the same with her – or perhaps only slightly kinder.

Now everything else was done. This final visit to the hall was the very last task to be completed.

They took a leisurely pace through the grounds, as if to savour the day, the freshness of the October morning, Arthur leaning on Charlotte's arm. It was the furthest he had walked since his recovery; he had taken more than a thousand steps now, each one a triumph.

The rabbits were still there, bolder than ever. As Charlotte and

Arthur left the path, they passed a great rook, which hopped a little way from them and then took to the air with a forlorn caw. Apart from this it was very quiet; there seemed to be no other creatures but themselves left in the world.

'Leg's getting easier,' Arthur said when they started down the yew walk. They were only a few yards now from the house.

'Good. I thought it would – with practice, you know.'

They got into the library through the French windows, the way Charlotte had left the last time. They had to push aside the dusty curtains to get in; the room beyond was quiet and cold and dark. Charlotte walked up and down, drawing back the heavy red-and-gold curtains, letting in the autumn sun.

Arthur coughed. 'Weren't you about to rent this place?'

'It never got so far. James was always going to . . .'

A pause. Then Arthur asked: 'Where is he?'

It was a comfort to see that, to a stranger, the priest hole was quite undetectable. James would be perfectly safe.

'Here,' she said to Arthur. 'He's here.'

'Behind the bookcase?'

'Yes. The spring's there.' She showed him. *Fungi of the British Isles, Vol II.* 'If you push hard at the top, the door opens.'

'Should we check to see if he's still inside?'

'No. The door's strong – you'd have to smash it to get out from the inside. Besides' – she gestured to the dusty floor – 'there aren't any footprints.'

She was also reluctant for him to see the evidence of what she had done, necessary though it had been. In her haste, she had dropped her knife. It would still be there at his feet – he would look like the victim of a murder.

'You didn't hear the old tale about the owls, then?' Howland asked.

'Owls?'

'Yes. Shadwell told me about it.' He looked as if he regretted mentioning it. 'It's written in some places that they can turn

into owls. Shadwell didn't set much store by the notion, I don't
think.'

'Do you believe it?'

'No. I've seen some unlikely things recently, but there are limits.'

'Yes.' She laid a hand on the books. James was still there,
trapped behind paper and wood.

'He can't feel anything, can he?'

'No. It's like being asleep, the book said. Only deeper. He can't
hear us.'

Howland nodded, but he drew nearer the bookcase, too, put
one hand against the book spines, a little higher than Charlotte's.
He laid the other hand gently on Charlotte's shoulder – with a
caution that had already begun to irritate her a little. She did not
need so much care; she would not startle at such a slight touch.
'I'll wait by the door,' he told her.

She nodded. It was kind, because if he had remained she might
have felt some constraint. There was nothing now to stop her
from leaning her forehead against the books, pressing both hands
against the peeling leather spines, promising that she would
return.

• • •

During the Channel crossing, she left Arthur to sleep and took a
walk on deck. The journey from York to Folkestone had been an
arduous one – they had decided it was safest not to pass through
London but to take a longer way.

They had travelled under different names and had done what
they could to disguise their appearance. Charlotte was not certain
how necessary the precaution was. But they had acquired habits
of secrecy and fear. The winding route was expensive – but Arthur
had settled all that, smiled at her misgivings, managed things with
an extravagance that almost alarmed her.

To travel to Folkestone, Charlotte had put on Adeline's hat

with the veil, and now when she breathed in she could smell tobacco and perfume beneath the salt of the sea.

She had scrutinised the faces of their fellow passengers as they came aboard. As far as she could determine, there was no present danger.

It would be at least an hour more before they reached Boulogne, and though she was too restless to sit or sleep, she felt herself refreshed by this brief respite from anxiety. She enjoyed the space and peace, the feeling of the sea air on her face.

England was long lost in fog. She had not noticed when it finally disappeared, and she was glad of that: it would have been dreadful to look back and think, This is it, this is the very last glimpse.

Now the clouds had given way, and she could see a little further ahead to the horizon where France would soon appear. She had never been on a ship before; she found she enjoyed the sensation. A short time ago she would have been apprehensive – of sea-sickness or shipwreck or a dozen other misfortunes – but now there seemed no fear left in her for such things.

She was leaning over the railing, watching the water, when she heard someone speak – a man's voice, low and pleasant, with an accent she did not recognise, perhaps several accents mixed together:

'Good evening, Miss Norbury.'

Startled, she turned to find herself confronted by a stranger, a sallow sliver of a man dressed in a long brown velveteen coat. He had with him a little girl, somewhat better attired than himself, her hair done in bouncing ringlets.

'Good evening,' Charlotte replied, looking about her. This part of the steamer was not busy. It might be that she could scream here and not be heard.

He took something from his pocket: an onion. He held it up, like a quaint talisman. She thought of the shop at Wych Street, the sign above the door.

'You don't know me.'

'No.'

'You've heard of my business, though, I think.' He sounded Cockney and yet not, she thought. He spoke like a native of a thousand cities. 'I'm in the library trade.'

'The Rag and Bottle.'

He nodded. 'That's me. Us. There are quite a few of us.' He nodded to the girl. 'Her, as well, when she's older.' The girl said nothing but stared at Charlotte, neither shy nor impudent. 'Some of our people went to Wych Street. Shadwell always told me what to do if anything happened. I did what he asked, and I saw him and Miss Swift buried.'

'Thank you,' she said.

'Cremated, really. I know a lot don't hold with it, but Shadwell always insisted. Only safe, considering.'

'Only safe? Why?'

'Well, they'd both been bit, you see. Goes with the job.'

'What does that mean?'

'Means there's a chance of them coming back. Not like one of the creatures, you understand, but just . . . coming back. A little bit. Like a half-sleep, you understand? Doesn't last long, but it's a nasty business, when it does happen.'

'Does it always happen?'

'No. Shadwell wasn't the sort to take chances, though.' He looked then at the girl, who had put her thumb in her mouth. 'Neither am I, come to that. Got to have a plan, if you're one of our sort.'

Her hand strayed to her wrist. She wondered if he knew about the mark which had once been there. There was no sense in upsetting herself now. The thoughts would keep.

'The books,' she said. 'Is that what you're here for?'

'Yes.'

She had studied each one of the books she had saved, found a quaint symbol pencilled into the cover of each – a flower in a bottle. She had decided that it must be the mark of the library.

'We have the books safe in England,' she told him. 'If you give me an address, I can have them sent to you.'

'Good. Thank you.' He gave her a piece of paper, a much-folded card. 'You can send them there.'

She nodded, put the card away. 'I'll make sure it's done. We have some notes of theirs, other things – do you want those?'

He shook his head. 'Just the books. Thank you. We owe you a debt, the Rag and Bottle. The shop was broke into, not long after the club burned. If you hadn't saved the books, they'd be gone.'

'There's something else. I've got another book – Adeline and Shadwell's, the one they wrote. I've got it on the boat. Do you want that one, too?'

Perhaps this would be the best thing, the most secure home for the manuscript. But the Rag and Bottle man shook his head. 'Already got one. From Miss Swift's mother.'

She had thought of Adeline's mother in the months since they left London. She hoped Rafferty had been to see her, to tell her the news. Somehow she had been sure that he would.

'How is she?'

'She bears up 'bout as well as anyone could,' the Rag and Bottle man said. 'Under the circumstances. As far as the book goes, you keep your copy. They must have thought a lot of you to let you have it.'

'But what should I do with it?'

'You'll think of something.'

'Where will you go next?' Charlotte asked.

He shook his head. 'Doesn't work like that, Miss Norbury. You only know when the library's coming to your part of the world, not where it's going next. Here' – he took out a pencil and another morsel of paper, drew rapidly – 'have this. When you see it, you'll know it's us.'

A five-pointed flower, imprisoned in what looked like a wine bottle. He had drawn it without once taking his pencil from the paper.

'Thank you,' she said, and put it carefully away.

• • •

She did not see the Rag and Bottle man again. He and his daughter must have slipped ashore as soon as the ship docked in Boulogne. When she told Arthur of the encounter, she did not mention what she had learned about the bite of the un-dead. He had quite enough to trouble him at present.

The first weeks were as bad as she had feared. They arrived in Paris, seeking a name from Shadwell and Adeline's book, a man who might be able to help them. But the man was difficult to find; they were not even sure if he was still in the city.

Arthur suffered – his back ached when he stood for too long, and the leg hurt him, irritated his skin; he could not always stand to wear it for many hours at a time. In France he dreamed every night, as he had not before – often waking with a scream of pain or rage. Other guests complained of the noise; they had to change hotels twice.

Charlotte had her own nightmares, as she had since Yorkshire, but these did not wake her. Nothing would wake her, sometimes, until Howland shook her by the shoulder at nine or ten in the morning, calling to her as if she were far away. She would wake up to find she had been crying, remembering nothing from her dreams but a deep, inescapable sadness.

The first night in their third hotel, she heard Arthur again shouting in his sleep and went to him. When he let her in (they had their own code of four knocks, the same they had used at the Langham), he was shaking. Without a word she led him back to bed and wrapped the blankets around him.

He did not need to ask her to remain: it would have been cruel to leave him. There was space enough for them both. She thought, not for the first time, that as his wife she ought to have been able to offer more comfort than this. He lay against her, his head on her shoulder, and seemed to sleep again.

Perhaps, after all, he did not miss those other things he would have had a right to expect. He did not take his pleasures elsewhere, but perhaps he would, when he was recovered. She would raise no objection; she was sure he would be considerate and tactful, for he was always solicitous of her comfort.

By this time it was almost winter. Though the months had passed, she thought that at present he must feel as she did: that it was difficult to be touched. All desires were muted. There were times when every appetite seemed drained out of her, when she could not make herself eat or drink or bathe, when she only wished to lie in peace in the dark.

They did their best to maintain a sense of purpose. They examined maps, discussed names and possibilities. At last they located the man they sought – a German professor living in Paris. They found him in a dreadful little room in one of the worst parts of the city, a room which was crammed full of books and nothing else. Charlotte was reminded of Wych Street, though the air was colder here. The professor did not have a fire. He wore his overcoat indoors. Charlotte suspected that beneath it he was not wearing a shirt. His beard was straggling, his breath was foul, and he took twenty francs from them before he would even let them sit down. When they tried to speak to him in German, he answered curtly in English.

She had read everything Shadwell wrote about the professor, the intellectual curiosity which had led him into many peculiar studies and unsavoury practices, at last banishing him from his own country for ever. Even now he pursued his curious studies, it was said. He had the look of a man who knows he is condemned.

When Charlotte explained why they had come to see him, he told them to go home.

'A nice young couple,' he said. 'Too young to think of such

things.' Then he looked at Charlotte's wrist, as if he could see the vanished wounds there, under her glove. 'Or is it too late?'

She did not answer, and he nodded as if he understood.

'Well, then,' he went on. 'I know little about this particular area. But I can give you names. There may be others who can help.'

'D'you think we have much of a chance?' Arthur asked.

He shook his head. 'I would leave it alone, if I were you. Though I suppose you cannot.' He shrugged and chuckled. 'And who am I, anyway, to tell you to leave it alone?'

He scribbled a name on a scrap of paper. 'This is the best that I can do for you.' Then he stood up – awkwardly. He was old, and his body had already begun to turn against him. 'One more thing. How much do you know about these creatures?' He took a book from the shelf. 'Practical knowledge, that much is clear. But the theory . . . ?'

'Not much,' Charlotte answered. 'Though we learned a little from Mr Shadwell.'

'Well, you could do worse. He's an interesting fellow. Wrong in many things. I should like to meet him.' He peered closer at her. 'Ah. Too late for that? I am sorry. It is the usual fate of men in our profession.' He added, with a touch of avarice, 'What became of his books?'

'They're in safe hands,' Charlotte said.

'I hope so.' He handed her the paper. 'Well, this name is the best hope for you, I think. I am afraid you will have to travel further; most of the experts – forgive me a little national pride – are German. Or very occasionally Dutch.' He looked at Arthur. 'I tell you again it were better for you to go home. Take this nice young man back home, and give him a child to play with – many children – and forget this.'

'We can't give this up,' she replied

'It is someone you love, then,' said the professor. 'I'm sorry.'

• • •

Afterwards, they did not go back to the hotel. They were too glad to be outside, away from the professor's disagreeable apartment. They went instead to the Champs-Élysées and took a slow walk, stopping from time to time for Arthur to rest. After ten minutes' wandering, they discovered a performance in progress: a miniature theatre, a small crowd of children, a man with an accordion, a notice proclaiming *Théâtre Guignol*.

They looked at each other, and Howland shrugged. There seemed no harm in stopping to watch. They had no other engagement and were both too tired to contemplate any other exertion today.

She was glad to see him interested in something new. Until now she had not seen much of that old easy inquisitiveness he had shown when they first met, when he had told them how he had travelled around Europe.

Now he followed the capering of the puppets and laughed when the children laughed. She was finding it hard to concentrate and could barely follow the action of the play. But she liked to watch his face.

It was quite by chance that she happened to see the man watching them from beyond the trees. Her gaze had been caught by a branch stirring in the breeze – then she saw a still presence beyond the green, a figure in black.

'Arthur,' she said in a low voice. 'Can you see? There.'

Some absurdity from the puppets – the crowd laughed.

'Yes,' Arthur replied. 'I see him.'

A man, slight and middle-aged, neatly dressed, with a tidy grey moustache. He saw them looking and turned away. He held his right arm close to his chest, like a man shielding an injury. He stepped out from the trees, onto the path, and calmly walked in the opposite direction. Though the day was not rainy, he carried an ivory-handled umbrella – held tightly, as if he feared it might be snatched away from him.

'Do you think . . .' she began.

Arthur's expression was confirmation enough. They slipped

away, back the way they had come. Arthur struggled, muttered that she must leave him if their pursuer came too close. She could run faster. She told him sharply not to be so stupid, helped him along. They did not look back, did not speak again until they had caught a cab and were safely moving away through the traffic.

'I could have imagined it,' she said.

Arthur shook his head but did not make any reply.

• • •

After the first dreadful months, it was as if her mourning for James had been parcelled out, coming to her at odd and unexpected times. She imagined little black boxes laid out for her like gifts from an admirer. She might be quite herself, eating breakfast, only to look down and find it waiting for her, a little black box, a portion of sadness to be got through. She realised that however long she might live, she would never reach the end of this. She would be old, she thought, and forgetting everything, and look around suddenly to find some of that familiar grief waiting for her.

The professor had been right: most of the experts were German. The other people they spoke to in France told them as much. (They were a strange mixture, these contacts: a weathered old marquess, a fêted circus clown, an English family living in Orleans, all of them eager to help at the mention of Adeline and Shadwell's names.)

A journey into Germany appeared inevitable. Charlotte had told Arthur plainly that he was under no obligation to accompany her – it was likely to be dangerous and tiring, and he would find it a strain. He insisted that it was quite all right; of course he would accompany her. Was that not the whole point of their marriage, that they should stick together?

She could never repay what he had done for her. She would brood, sometimes, on how she could make things better for him – did her best, always, to be a pleasant companion. He did not seem to find her absolutely tedious. But he deserved more.

Some weeks after seeing the man in the park, they were alarmed by a second pursuer – a big man, obscenely large, impeccably dressed, with a curious silvery scar close to his eye. They had seen him three days ago at the Louvre – in the Long Gallery, pretending to admire the work of a lady copyist. He looked up at them and smiled when they came in, as if he had been waiting.

There was no recourse but flight. And so they eluded him amongst the pictures and crowds – escaped by good luck only. Arthur had known him from his time in the club. He said that the man was to be feared. He would not tell her anything else.

After this they became even more careful. It seemed best to depart for Germany immediately. They made their way to the Gare du Nord with every precaution, ready at any moment for an attack. They were gradually accumulating a small stock of weapons to supplement those taken from Wych Street. The holy water was the most difficult to obtain.

Leaving Paris, they took a first-class sleeper carriage – a *coupé-lits-toilette* so luxurious that Charlotte could not quite take it seriously. There was a private bathroom, gilded decorations, and the three seats all pulled forward into beds. During their travels, she had observed that Arthur accepted such luxuries as a matter of course, though he was able to forgo them without complaint when necessary.

They had taken to working through Adeline and Shadwell's manuscript together. In the evening they unfolded all three beds and spread out the papers on the middle one, debating over future routes, the nature of the un-dead.

When the night came and neither of them could sleep and he heard her crying, he shifted over onto the middle bed and reached for her hand – so sure in the darkness. He gave her his handkerchief, keeping tight hold of her hand all the while, as if this was important.

They took a very slow and roundabout way to Germany – as much for their own recovery as to evade their pursuers. When they at last deemed it safe, they made their way to Berlin, began enquiries again. As in Paris, it took several months to find anyone willing to talk to them – longer to find anyone who could help. At last they found the man they were seeking. They met in a café, which did not look open from the outside, where the few patrons carefully avoided looking at one another. The man would not stay long, would not let them tell him their names. He was sweating, nervous as a hare. He told them that, in Italy, miraculous cures had sometimes been accomplished. The creatures had been known in Italy for many years, almost as long as in England. They should go to Rome, he said; they knew how to deal with the creatures there.

That evening they ate at the hotel, shared a plate of *pfannkuchen* – soft balls of fried dough with raspberry jam inside, powdered with white sugar that stuck to one's fingers. A local dish, their waiter said. Arthur had been pleased – he was, she had discovered, immediately eager to purchase anything held up as a speciality of the region. She would not have dampened his enthusiasm for worlds – he seemed, to her close and watchful attention, to be mending inside, which was good. The leg did not trouble him as much as she had feared – in some circumstances it even proved to be an advantage. Ladies, especially, were often sympathetic to the handsome man with the war wound.

As they ate, Charlotte realised that it was almost a year since they had left England.

Arthur said, apropos of nothing, 'Do you speak Italian, at all?'

'No,' Charlotte replied.

'I don't, either. Still, I guess we could learn enough between us.'

'We don't have to go. I mean, you don't have to go.'

'You said that in Paris,' Arthur said. 'And you were wrong there, too.'

'I was right. I just let myself be persuaded.'

'Well, let me persuade you this time, too. We'll go to Rome. Mother wanted me to go, anyway – she told me to send her some glass beads and things back.'

'Isn't that Florence,' Charlotte asked, 'for beads?'

'You know, I'm not sure. Where's the Baedeker?'

'Upstairs, of course.'

She was struck suddenly by how glad she was that he was here. She wanted very much to make him happy.

'We might go upstairs now,' she said. 'We could – we might retire early.'

To her great relief, he understood her. But he shook his head.

'I told you. I'm not going to ask you for that.'

They sat for a few minutes in silence. She had been foolish. She had imagined that, in their circumstances, he would be less particular. As other liaisons would be difficult – perhaps dangerous, too – she had thought that she might have proved better than nothing.

'You've no need to spare my feelings,' she said.

'What do you mean?'

She shook her head. Her brief, silly rage had flared up like burning paper and was now gone. She ought not to have been irritated at his kindness.

He was gazing at her still – not quite angry but with that clear steady look. 'You know what you've done for me, what we've been through,' he said. 'We're family now, really. Aren't we?'

'Well, yes.'

'Exactly. And I'm not letting you martyr yourself out of some ridiculous idea of gratitude.'

'No, but—'

'But that's *all*, do you understand?' They were both speaking very low. 'That's my objection. Otherwise, I'd say yes. At once.'

'At once?'

He stood up. 'Yes indeed. If you must know, I think you're magnificent. Even if you will insist on being so damned grateful.'

For a second, she thought he might kiss her – they had, in the past, exchanged kisses for the sake of appearances – but he did not. He hardly even looked at her as he turned away and went upstairs. She let him go – it would have been an effort at that moment to stand. To her disquiet, he had contrived to leave her feeling not unpleasantly weak: behind her knees. Higher.

· · ·

In Rome they found more dangers awaiting them. They did not see the men from the club again, but their enemies had not abandoned the chase – rather, they had entrusted it to others, to strangers who knew the city well.

This time their escape was pure luck. They got away through the merest chance and stayed hidden for several weeks with two ancient nuns, who would not listen to their explanations and pretended doggedly that they did not understand any English. When it was safe again, they left the city in a hurry, barely stopping to gather their luggage. It was after this point that Arthur insisted that Charlotte carry a revolver with her – had a small handbag made for her, especially designed to house the thing.

They went north. Their situation was worse, in some ways, than it had been a year ago. Then there had been a number of leads to be pursued, now there was nothing left. They had been lied to by mountebanks and sneered at by distinguished professors of science. Europe was nearly exhausted. Sooner or later they would have nowhere else to try. They would have to decide whether to leave James to sleep for ever or return and take measures to end his life.

Arthur took a house for them some miles from Perugia, a quiet place to stop and recover. Both of them needed this. For a week Charlotte did little.

She lay in her room, and Arthur could not make her take an interest in anything, until he brought her James's papers, which she had carried across Europe for so long.

She busied herself sorting them – they had been mixed up deplorably. There were other papers, too: a notebook with writing in Adeline's hand, which looked like a diary; Shadwell's notes for *The Modern English Vampire*. She occupied herself for a little while in wondering if, laid together, these scraps and pages might yield something coherent, a story fashioned like a mosaic. It did not work, she found. There were gaps and inconsistencies; the pages would not fit together harmoniously.

Arthur – happy to see her alert again – said, 'We should publish these, I suppose. Your brother's poems, I mean. Might have to be at our expense. But it would make him happy, wouldn't it?'

'It would have done, yes.'

She would never tell Arthur or anyone else that she had not enjoyed the poems. She did not trust her own judgement in these matters; it was possible that there was more to them than she realised. The longest was entitled *Demeter* and had been rather hard going. She had got as far as –

> They wandered on the shore amidst the gloom,
> The lady and the monster, and they spoke
> Like friends of long acquaintance. She leaned close
> To hear his speech, not troubling to keep

– before abandoning the attempt altogether. It was all so heavy and dreary, no trace of his humour, his playful cleverness. He had told her he was writing a play, but she had found no sign of a manuscript.

For two weeks neither Charlotte nor Arthur mentioned the eventual necessity of leaving Italy. Their little house was a pleasant place in which to recover. When Charlotte could bring herself to venture outside again, she found oranges growing, a kindly breeze. They had no immediate neighbours, but the man who owned the estate half a mile off kept peacocks; their cries were audible from across the fields. Sometimes the birds would stray into Charlotte and Arthur's garden, and they would watch them. She had forgotten the pleasure in walking barefoot across warm stone.

She stayed out in the sun as much as possible, drinking tea and wrapped up in blankets. They both had this yearning to be as warm as possible, she thought. She made a note of it – it might well be some side effect of proximity to the creatures. In fact, she had begun to think that perhaps her notes might have some use in the future. By now they had travelled more widely than Shadwell and Adeline had; they had heard stories which their friends might not have done. They had both been reading as much as possible, from necessity. But the details were blurred in Charlotte's mind – at night she wondered whether it was the *pontianak* or the *vrykolakas* which was buried in unconsecrated ground, whether it was cats or dogs which fled before them. She could not sleep on those nights, could only remember the one direction upon which every authority agreed: beware solitude, beware the dark and lonely places.

It was in those warm weeks that she first went to him, one night after the maid they had engaged to cook and clean had left for her home in the village, after they had both retired for the evening.

He was reading in bed and looked up enquiringly when she came in.

'Is everything all right?'

'Yes.'

'Ah.' And bless him or curse him for being able to see her thoughts so easily. 'I told you,' he said. 'No gratitude.'

'This isn't,' Charlotte said, blushing and rather irritated.

'Really?'

'Of course it isn't. Don't be ridiculous.'

'Right.' He sat up and looked at her very carefully.

'Move over. Let me sit down.'

'You've really thought about this?'

'Yes.'

'For how long?'

'Long enough.'

He closed his book. As he reached for her, her thoughts went all to pieces – *oh my America* – and the book slid onto the floor with the softest possible thud.

To begin with, as she had feared, wanting him did not seem to be enough.

But Arthur sat close beside her, and bent to look into her face, his expression as comically dismal as her own must be, and she found that they were both laughing, in spite of themselves. 'I'm sorry. I'm quite hopeless, I'm afraid,' she said.

'No' Arthur replied, serious again. It did not occur to her until long afterwards that he, too, might have cause to be uncertain. He must have thought of his injury, though he made no mention of it.

After a while, they got things right – so right that he hushed her, alarmed, as she cried out. Then they both recalled in the same instant that they were alone in the house; they might make as much noise as they chose. She felt his mouth against hers, smiling in the dark.

Afterwards he was so pleased with himself, so cheerful. In the morning, they took their breakfast coffee outside to the terrace. He brought her an orange from the kitchen; they sat in the sunlight, and he peeled it for her with his penknife and watched her lick orange juice from her palms when she was finished.

Sometimes she wondered at everything he had been to her. So many changes in such a short time. And not at all in the right order. She did not quite understand how it could possibly work. (But it does work, Arthur would probably say. Isn't that enough?)

• • •

They allowed themselves another week in their house outside Perugia before acknowledging that they were both recovering, in mind and in body, which meant that it was time to consider their next direction.

'We might try further afield,' Arthur said one night at dinner.

'Beyond Europe?' She had wanted to suggest it but had not been able to bring herself to do so.

'Well, you do find the creatures everywhere, from what I've read.'

She had seen a photograph of his family. He said that they did not resemble it at all and were in reality a most cheerful set, as she would see for herself one day. They had heard of the wedding, and Charlotte wondered if they must hate her very much for keeping him away.

'Or we could stay here,' he went on. 'Think of it. We could raise children here, feed them on oranges. You could teach them, I could dig in the garden.'

She sighed.

'No?'

'Maybe soon we can stop,' she said. 'But there's that man they told us about at Buda-Pesth University . . .'

'Well, let's go to Buda-Pesth, then.' She loved the way he could say this, as if he were suggesting a half-hour drive in a dogcart. He had a knack of making things possible.

'All right,' she agreed.

But they stayed another week, during which neither of them mentioned their departure, during which the weather was so beautiful that they spent most of their time upstairs or in the garden, and during which both of them set aside their reading and let the books and papers alone.

The peculiar congeniality of the English climate to the un-dead has, for a very long time, been acknowledged only by the creatures themselves. Apart from William of Newbury, few of our historians have given them much attention. So well has the English vampire concealed himself, in fact, that the very word 'vampire' is practically a novelty to these shores – not yet two centuries old. The etymology has never been satisfactorily accounted for – it may be Greek or Hebrew, Hungarian or Turkish. Perhaps no people care to claim it for their own tongue. It may be that this is wise, for when dealing with the un-dead, the word becomes a weapon. The creature takes refuge in silence. He is a lord of utterance and can dominate his victim so that, even if he lives, he will not be able to name the creature who attacked him or speak clearly of his ordeal. Like the blinded Cyclops, he can describe his assailant only as 'Nobody'.

Yet, in spite of this, the vampire has been named. More than this, we know him well – at least, in some garbled fashion. Alas, he has thus far successfully eluded the brilliant searching beam of science: no educated man, who had not seen the creature, would own to believing in him. Yet in avoiding this threat, the creature has underestimated another peril. Stories have been told about him. He has been captured in novels, poetry, opera. Slowly, like an encroaching dream, he has crept from half-recollected folk tales into common knowledge. He has been named merely as a fictional being, but he has been named. I believe he may begin to suspect the danger of this (c.f.: A. Mould's pamphlet, 'The Vampire in the Nineteenth Century'), but it is now too late.

Let this victory be remembered by those oppressed by the attacker who strikes in silence and robs his victims of their blood, their selves, their speech – the victory of a simple word. To speak of these things is dangerous; it is also of the utmost importance. Those who do not believe – and how hard to believe without seeing – may at least read more about what they take for myth. Should the time ever come when the reader finds himself face-to-face with one of these creatures (and let every man and woman pray to be spared such an encounter), there will be at least a warning – vague, swathed in myth, and yet persistent. Perhaps the reader, though half-despising his own folly, will beware those persons who cause him that creeping unease for which he cannot quite account. It is in this hope that this book is written.

G. P. Shadwell and A. Swift, *The Modern English Vampire*

Chapter Thirty-Nine

He is methodical, when he considers the situation. His name is Arthur Howland. He is seventy-seven years old, he has loved one woman for the last half century, and now, as he once promised, he is taking her home to die.

They have enough money to travel first-class, New York to Liverpool. Charlotte, if she had known, would have hated this: extravagance of any kind always worried her. But now it is not extravagance but a necessity, as is the hired nurse who travels with them. She is discreet and well trained and is good with Charlotte. It is unfair to resent her for being good with Charlotte, for the necessity that someone should be good with her. It is unfair to resent her tact and common sense. Charlotte would have said that the woman was merely doing her job. Arthur pays her well and speaks to her as little as possible.

When most of the passengers are at dinner, they sometimes take a stroll around the upper deck. He has a cane now and is on a new leg – his last leg, he jokes. It is a light, ingenious piece of engineering. *Duralumin,* he told Charlotte when it arrived, making a comic pretence of showing it off. She smiled a little, perhaps because he smiled. Or perhaps she did understand the joke.

Now she leans on his arm, her expression disapproving. Three times today she has called him James.

'Where is he?' she asks one evening.

'Who, love?' Arthur says, but she won't answer.

Sometimes she is suspicious of him; sometimes she talks for hours at a time, indistinctly. He does not know if even she understands herself. He does not know how much of her is left. He nods and adjusts her shawl.

He buys her beautiful shawls. Indeed, she is dressed more expensively now than she ever was when she was able to purchase her own wardrobe. She always said that it was a waste for her to spend money on smart gowns, that she was not pretty enough to justify the extravagance. He was never able to convince her otherwise. Now he cannot help but choose the most luxurious, the warmest for her. Perhaps the feel of silk and cashmere may bring her a kind of pleasure. He chooses rich colours, simple, dignified lines.

Sometimes she weeps when the nurse comes at night to bathe and undress her. If she has strength and is in her worst humour, she will fling insults at her, try to scratch with fingernails that have been cut short.

'I killed a demon, once, Miss,' she says to the nurse one evening. 'I nailed his feet to the floor.'

'Well, fancy that. Shall we brush your hair now?'

'I killed a demon, you stupid *sow*, and I swear I'll make short work of you.'

'Just as you say, Mrs Howland,' the nurse answers. Charlotte throws a jar of cold cream at her head. It hits the wall and smashes.

The nurse clears away the glass and the worst of the mess. Arthur goes to Charlotte and leads her away from the broken shards. 'Darling, come and sit with me.'

Charlotte goes with him meekly. 'This is a terrible place,' she says.

'I know, love.'

Sometimes they walk out on the deck and look at the sea. They are sailing through cloud; there are rarely any sunsets to admire, only grey water and a steady breeze.

They are going back to Aiskew. What they will do when they get there, Arthur is not sure.

He only distantly remembers the man who saved him. It has been so long since then. You imagine a lot when you are afraid. There are days and weeks when Arthur does not believe that he saw humanity in those eyes at all.

It is most likely safe to return, after so long. They are not entirely sure. Years ago they would get intermittent news – from the Rag and Bottle, from other people, too. It was never safe to go back in those days. Then for a while there was silence, and Arthur had feared the worst. But last month he received a terse message bearing the sign: the five-petalled flower trapped in its bottle. The note was in answer to an enquiry he had written nearly twenty years before. It read, ok – *come back if you want*, and nothing more. He does not think it is a trap.

Charlotte says, 'I should like to die in England.' She says it distinctly, as if expressing a wish for a cup of tea. They are passing a genteel family and a promenading couple, and the nice people stare. The young girl from the genteel family looks horrified, as if the future were unfolding itself suddenly before her.

'Whatever you want, love,' he says.

There are days when she will smile at him, and nights when he is not troubled by dreams. He has found that one's expect-ations are lowered as one ages; one is thankful for a good night's sleep, an untroubled digestion. He has trouble with his new leg. He has been through a few. When the time came to discard his first, the one he had bought in England, they had talked about burying it in the garden. In the end he kept it in the study, though neither his mother nor Charlotte thought it was in good taste.

As the journey progresses, Charlotte's bad times are more and more frequent. On the evenings when Charlotte fights them, Arthur tells the nurse to leave and sits with her until she falls asleep. The woman (knows which side her bread's buttered, Charlotte would have said) does not tell him – as the doctors did – that he must be firm with Charlotte but merely nods and leaves. He feels that she despises him.

Charlotte is frightened and angry; she does not understand what has happened, where she has gone to. And she is in pain. It is a cancer, the doctor said. Her body and mind have each failed her in turn. Soon, Arthur thinks, she will lay both of these aside.

She never put faith in such things, but he has an idea of her continuing elsewhere, all the same. If he considers the vision too closely, he sees relics of the lessons taught to him in Sunday school – clouds, sunlight, music. The heaven he makes for her is rudely sketched, far too indistinct for Charlotte to be truly happy. In his thoughts she shakes her head, a little amused at the state of the place, and then busies herself, sets to work – a garden, perhaps. He imagines cornflowers growing.

When Charlotte is calm, or tired, or weary from the drugs the nurse administers, he reads to her. It does not much matter what book he chooses; when she is in the right mood, she will smile at the sound of his voice.

Things grow worse; he brings out a battered copy of *Sherlock Holmes* – a thick omnibus that has travelled far with him. It was one of the few books they both enjoyed. Apart from their work, they rarely read the same things: he never much cared for fiction, though he would read the occasional adventure tale to pass the time. She read slowly, choosing books carefully, considering them with an anxious look. Sometimes she would close one, put it away from her, and say, 'Give this away, Art, I won't read any more.' He understood gradually that it was not that she did not under-stand these books but that she understood too well, and sometimes the books frightened her. When she found one to suit her, she read intently, easing into each one as into a deep pool. If he interrupted her at those times, he would see her look up dazedly, as if her ears were still full of water, her eyes strange as a mermaid's.

A year ago, when her condition had already taken much of her away, she had a fit of rage, and the books were one of the things that suffered. Inside dozens of covers she tried to write her own name. He could not bear to look at them.

Now he reads *Sherlock Holmes,* and sometimes it will make her calm.

One evening he reads aloud – with a touch of grim humour – expecting that she will not understand:

'Rubbish, Watson, rubbish! What have we to do with walking corpses who can only be held in their grave by stakes driven through their hearts? It's pure lunacy.'

She looks up at him sternly and says, 'Nonsense, Arthur.'

She has not spoken intelligibly in a number of days. He turns the page and says, 'Quite right, my love. Shall I try another one?'

He began at the back of the book: they move backwards in time, towards the earlier tales.

On the second-to-last day of the voyage, they reach 'The Final Problem'. He reads steadily. At one point he pauses, wondering if she is asleep. She looks at him – not angry or weeping today, only lost. And there is nothing to say, so he carries on, he ends the story: *'. . . him whom I shall ever regard as the best and the wisest man whom I have ever known.'*

Surely she is asleep now. But, no – she looks up at him; her eyes are clear. 'Arthur,' she says, as if answering a question. Her head sinks forwards.

The nurse is elsewhere. He covers Charlotte with a shawl and lays another on top so that she will not feel the cold. She is draped in luxury, like an empress. Her mouth turns downwards.

He will walk a little way on the deck. He often takes the opportunity to get his exercise whilst she is asleep. She misses him when she wakes; if he is not there she will lose her temper. The nurse will be brutally patient with both of them.

His thoughts dance ahead of him, past the bow of the ship. He lets them run, enjoys the clean salt air.

When he gets back to the cabin, the nurse is there, waiting. She folds her hands, grave and professional, and says (as if it were necessary to say anything, if Charlotte's still look was not enough), Mr Howland . . .

• • •

If she could not die in England, she will at least be buried here. He arranges everything – this is one thing he has not lost, his ability to make men and circumstances cooperate, to get things done quickly. It is money and charm; these have not deserted him, though the money has been in danger more than once. It's been a terrible century so far.

There was something he read when they were making their researches, which neither Adeline nor Shadwell had told them: how those bitten by the creatures in life might experience a sort of rudimentary reanimation after death. To his surprise, Charlotte had shown no astonishment; she had heard a rumour of the possibility a long while ago, from the Rag and Bottle man. Of course she hadn't told him before; she hadn't wanted to worry him about a distant possibility. But she insisted – she made him swear – that her body should be burned. He does not fail her in this. He thinks it is better to get this done as soon as possible. He finds a crematorium in Liverpool.

The room where the service is held smells of nothing but flowers – not lilies but something equally heavy, which makes the back of his throat prickle. Everything has a glossy finish – grief would just slide off, he thinks. No danger of any ghosts lingering here.

No one else is there to mourn; the funeral is a quiet one. For this reason there is no one he can turn to when he seems to hear a hand striking wood, a palm flat against the coffin lid, as the box finally disappears from sight. There is no one to ask if the sound is real; he decides that it could not have been.

Outside, afterwards, he thinks he catches sight of a face he recognises, looks again and sees nobody. Empty fears, he tells himself. But he is not sure – the life Charlotte and he shared has made him sensitive to small warning signs. He makes his way to York in a circuitous way, wandering with apparent aimlessness until he is sure that he is not followed.

He makes his way to York because that is the other part of the promise he made. He must go to Aiskew Hall.

They never settled what they would do when they returned. After all they had been through, she could never quite bear to discuss what she had done. Sometimes he would tell her that it had been the kindest thing; James would not have suffered. She would agree with him.

Now he must go and put an end to this. The house will be sold after his death; Charlotte and he have no children to inherit, and his brother's family do not deserve such a burden left for them.

He hires a driver, careless of expense, has the man drive him by a roundabout route to Aiskew. They talk cars, war. The driver is a pleasant young man, understands his business well.

Arthur misses driving. The car he had at home – so cleverly modified, such a stalwart friend to Charlotte and him in years past – is now in storage; he does not have the strength to drive it any more. But he has left the car an annuity in his will (his lawyer is beyond surprise by now); it will be looked after. He cannot bear the thought of it being neglected after his death.

He will be staying in Aiskew – there is a village inn, comfortable enough. It will take a number of days to conclude all his business. He intends to be thorough; he does not plan to return.

He reaches the village at night. It feels much bigger than it was fifty years ago – he cannot convince himself that he has ever been here before. He does not sleep well. The room smells of cooking, and in the middle of the night he wakes to feel the ghost of his left foot itching. In the morning, he walks up to Aiskew Hall.

There are high black gates, spikes and winding metal spirals, and he feels like a trespasser. But it all belongs to him now. In fact, it has been his for some time, for Charlotte insisted that this be arranged when she first began to fail.

He takes the long way, the road that leads through fields. There are black sheep grazing, beyond them the ha-ha. He can see the copper beech, leaves shifting in the breeze, and knows the direction where East Lodge lies. He will go there last of all, see what has become of Charlotte's garden.

He had expected silence, the same hush that he remembers from when he walked the grounds with Charlotte, when he was still weak and suffering, struggling not to show how difficult he found each step.

Instead, he finds bustle, men's voices – instructions, chatter, the occasional laugh. It is the workmen engaged to put the place in order. He was not expecting them until tomorrow.

As he reaches the front of the house, two of the men pass him, struggling with a statue. He stops them, explains who he is.

The statue is one of those Charlotte told him about, the ones she loved as a child – an ancient Roman soldier, stern mouth, high helmet. Dry yellow moss growing over his eyes. He tells the men to put it back exactly where it was.

They nod – exchanging looks that say, Daft old fool, meddling Yank – but as they move to go, the statue is dropped (each workman immediately blames the other), and the soldier smashes against stone. The damage is immediate and irreparable.

'Not so bad,' one of the workmen says, in a conciliating tone. 'Jus' the head smashed, an' one of the arms . . .'

He tells them to leave it. No, just leave it alone. Leave it where it is. He turns away, ignores the man's apologies, makes his way round the edge of the house towards the French windows which open into the library. The bag he carries is making his arm ache. He saw the men look at it strangely. He is not sure that he will be strong enough for what may come next.

Someone has been smashing the library windows – boys from the village, probably. He lets himself in. There are stones and broken glass scattered over the rug. Whoever it was has been very deliberate about it: almost all the panes are shattered. There are torn pages drifting across the floor. Of course the rain will have got in, some of the books will have been destroyed. The wallpaper has been spoiled in places, too. The breeze makes the dust sheets stir.

He is hurrying now – anxious to know the worst, eager for this to be over, whatever the outcome. He crosses the library, finds *Fungi of the British Isles, Vol II,* presses the hidden lever. The door opens slowly, with a grate of metal.

Arthur cannot, for a moment, bring himself to go closer, to make sure of what he sees. His heart – not as steady now as it once was – pounds suddenly, making him struggle for breath.

Two nails are driven into the floorboards. A knife lies nearby, its blade stained and dull – but the prison is empty, the vampire is gone.

Acknowledgements

For my description of Oscar Wilde's speech at the premiere of *Lady Windemere's Fan*, I've drawn on a contemporary account by George Alexander, as related by Richard Ellmann in his biography of Wilde.

Thank you to my agent, Jenny Hewson, for her kindness, her tireless assistance, and her wise advice whilst this book was being written. Her support over this journey has been absolutely invaluable.

I would also like to thank Peter Straus, Stephen Edwards, Laurence Laluyaux, Eleanor Simpson and Zoe Nelson at Rogers, Coleridge and White. I am also extremely grateful to my editors, Alex Bowler and Noah Eaker, for their dedication and for their astute guidance through the rewriting process – thank you for making redrafting so enjoyable.

Thank you to everyone at Random House in the UK, US and Canada, particularly Ruth Waldram, Tom Drake-Lee, Lara

The Quick

Hinchberger and Maria Braeckel. It's a privilege to work alongside a team of such gifted and enthusiastic people.

I started this book while studying creative writing at the University of East Anglia – thank you to fellow workshoppers for your intelligent and helpful feedback. Thank you also to my teachers, Giles Foden, Trezza Azzopardi, Lavinia Greenlaw, and Rachel Hore. And thank you to Anjali Joseph, for a good turn.

Thank you to Rod, Gran, Rachel and Jack, and to the rest of my family, who have patiently followed this book on its long road to publication.

Thank you Amie and Grace, for being brilliant.

Thank you Mum and Dad, for your love and encouragement, for bringing me hundreds of books and thousands of cups of tea, for making this possible.

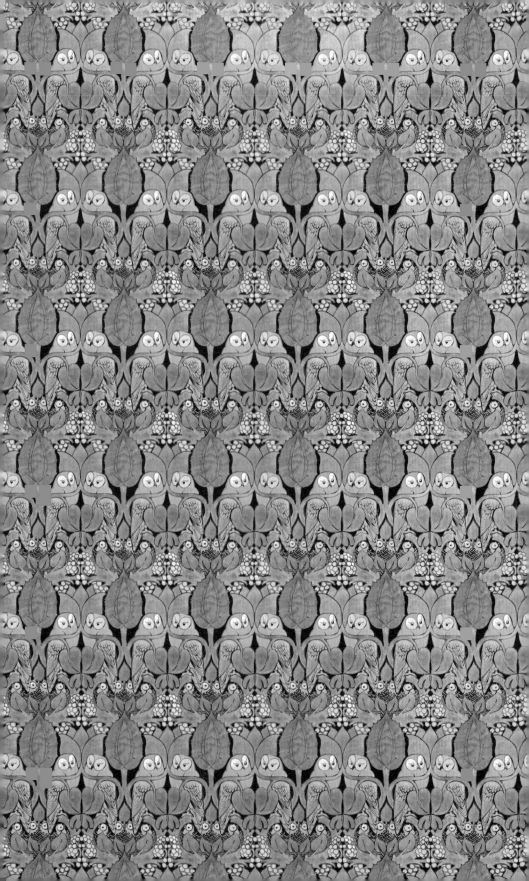